CASTING SHADOWS
BOOK ONE

CASTING SHADOWS

BOOK ONE

by

Dziyana Taylor

Dedication

For my beloved husband Rich, my fairytale grandmother, Galina, and the Town and the People of Harpers Ferry, WV.

You carried me away beyond all existent horizons into the pages of this book. I am still in awe of you.

"Keep your face always towards the sun, and the shadows will fall behind you."
— Walt Whitman

Table of Contents

ONE

JULY 2, 1863

A flock of ravens raced across the emerald sky like an artist's brushstroke. Freedom was what made them exceptional. It made them eager to dip their ebony beaks into the clouds and feel the elevation burst within their hearts. Undeniable awe caused their wings to cut through the air with ardent power. They knew, when they fell again towards the sun-lit battlefield, that their land would still be there: an eternal hill ridden witness to the upcoming disastrous collision.

As Derek Cromwell lost sight of the ravens in the disappearing sun, that same promise of freedom transformed before his eyes into a sea of tombstones, and he sighed deeply and sullenly. He would have followed the ravens in a heartbeat, but the sun had already vanished behind purple hills, and the birds had gone with it. Warm wind brought the scent of wood. Somewhere far away, spring water rippled. Thoughts of his home, beautiful Virginia, washed away the sadness that clawed at his ribcage.

The fire in the Confederate camp sizzled and popped. The night floated above the tents, causing them to step out of the darkness like shadows.

"Lieutenant Cromwell," said a young cadet perched on the fallen oak beside Derek, his forage cap resting on his lap. Flames danced above the burning logs in the firepit, and autumn leaves cruised on the wind. "The Yankees are barely holding their position.

We might have this. If Meade blinks, then… the war… it might finally be over. We would be just in time for a warm pie."

Derek stared into the distant glow of the enemy campfires, the collar of his gray jacket slightly unbuttoned, revealing his pale chest. His hands caught the warm wind of the burning logs. He continually turned his hands, palms up and down, to spread the smell of the campfire on his skin.

"Never underestimate your enemy, soldier. Especially during battle when your heads are turned towards the inevitable. Destiny is either with us or against us. Despite all, death is reigning over these fields," Derek said, a little leather-bound book peeking out from a pocket of his uniform.

The cadet ran his eyes across the battlefield grounds, his heart aching. On the other side of the hill, the Yankee cannons glistened in the firelight. He imagined that there was a cannonball resting in the hands of the enemy, and tomorrow, on the day of the battle, there would be blood splattered on it— or worse, a soldier's soul.

"What hasn't the war taken?" he asked. "Sometimes, I do not recognize faces that appear before my very own eyes. The lives my bayonet has ended. We aren't fighting the war, Lieutenant; we are fighting the demons that live among us." He pressed his hands to his temples, thinking. His boyish, freckled face was white as a sheet of paper.

"Demons or not, we are past the point of no return. You left your mom at the foot of your bed, Jackson. The tears she left on your cheek— they have dried. There is a field out there, possibly the one I am looking at now, where we will lay our heads. For freedom. For bravery. For God. Now that, my friend, is what will make your momma proud." There was only so much Derek could say to console him.

They heard the snap of branches followed by swift footsteps. An officer in gray uniform with a saddlebag over one shoulder sprung up out of the amber shadows of the fire. His strawberry blond hair fell in waves, hiding away a scar that lay above his left eyebrow, a wound from a fight early in the war. The sight of a fellow classmate from VMI brought Derek Cromwell hope that if they went down fighting, they would go down together.

"Come on, Cromwell!" Lieutenant Shawn Grimwood cried out. He patted Derek on the shoulder. "Sullen thoughts bring sullen actions. We are at war, for God's sake."

Derek turned his head towards Shawn and smiled an open, inviting smile.

"Don't you agree that a fight for a sullen truth is the best motivation? When the bayonet rests still in my hand, it does not make a Yankee happy— it doesn't make anyone happy. They want causalities. They desire a fight, so we better give it to them," Derek said, fire fiercely reflecting in his eyes. It was easy to fall into believing the worst, but seeing Shawn Grimwood caused a wave of cheerful encouragement to build in his chest.

"Now that's the spirit!" Shawn exclaimed and then quickly addressed the cadet. "Jackson, why don't you go fetch us the field map. The Lieutenant and I need some privacy." He stood close to the fire now, watching the smoke rise and fall in the shape of flowers.

Jackson nodded, standing to leave. Derek held the silhouette of Jackson with his eyes for just a moment until he disappeared into one of the tents. He was a young cadet, fresh out of the academy. His heart was pure, but his eyes had been darkened by death. It was as if Derek was looking into a mirror at his own reflection when he'd first graduated VMI. He wanted nothing more than to protect Jackson's soul from all the atrocities of the war.

Shawn exhaled deeply, his head down, gaze lost in the tips of the grass swaying in the wind. "Before I tell you what I really came here for, I need to know if you have seen any dreams that might give us a sign? I am only asking because I need to prepare myself before we step foot onto these grounds."

"I didn't, but…" Derek had almost forgotten, but not because his memory deceived him. No. Her face: it became too real in his mind. So real, he felt that he could almost touch her.

"I saw her again," Derek suddenly blurted, breaking the silence.

Shawn glanced at him in surprise and took a seat beside the Lieutenant. In the hissing of the burning fire, they could almost hear the echo of the Yankees marching across the fields. "Are you sure she is not just a part of your imagination?" he wondered, but the answer lay in his comrade's softened features and a spark that played in his irises.

Derek shook his head. The contours of her face, the blush on her cheeks, and that smile. When he closed his eyes, he saw her clearly. "I lost my Father's Bible last September in Antietam. By now, it might be resting there with the bones of soldiers and the blood that we shed. I think it was an omen. She came to me last night, holding the Bible and handing it over to me. Like it had never been lost. Her face— a thousand roses. Her eyes— oceans of blue.

A guardian angel for the battle ahead," he said and paused. The wind was bending over the treetops. "I might as well lay breathless on those fields if she is a ghost, Shawn."

Lieutenant Shawn Grimwood knew how Derek felt. The line between dream and reality was a blurry image. When his wife kissed the dimple on his chin and whispered the words of love into his ear, everything turned to sweet fog that veiled them both.

"If I had even the slightest chance to see my wife Catherine, I'd kill a couple dozen Yankees for it. You are lucky you can see her, even if it is a dream," Shawn said in a slow drawl, then sliced an apple and handed half of it to Derek. "Besides, if you believe she is real, I say there is no doubt in my mind that she is. Perhaps she is waiting for you in a town over, but you have to believe that this is not the last battle we are fighting, or she will stay a mirage forever."

Derek's eyes became wide, and he looked away from the fire. There was nothing he could hide from Shawn. It must have been the years they spent together.

"I do believe… but like you said, I want to be prepared for the outcome, whatever it might be. We both have heard Lincoln speak. I have pulled officers off the fields with less than what they were born with. I have seen great military minds walk off the battlefields white as snow. I love my country, but I want this last fight to be in honor of a woman. I want my death to matter, at least to her… Love is all I want to feel when I close my eyes, and the world goes over the abyss. I don't want to dig any more graves for my comrades," Derek said. He couldn't shake the image of the tombstones. The feeling of drowning, the grief. The responsibility for the lives taken.

"I understand. We want the same things. Though I have some news for you that might make you feel different. Your brother George joined the regiment," Shawn whispered into Derek's ear.

Derek's eyes became cold as ice. His brother was the one thing that made his hair prick on end. "That's why you were looking for me." Derek's muscles tensed up, and he bit his lower lip.

Lieutenant Grimwood nodded in response. He was focused and serious. "After what happened at Antietam, they didn't have enough medics. Longstreet brought them in, and I have heard this from the prisoners in camp."

"Is it safe?" Derek asked, his eyes glistening. The thought of his brother laying his hands on the diary was unbearable. He could unleash evil on this world far worse than the war. Derek wouldn't be able to rest until George was denied all the power he so desired.

"Let's just say it's out of his reach," Shawn confirmed as he glanced at his saddlebag.

"Keep an eye on the diary. George is intelligent; it's not a coincidence he joined the regiment. If he doesn't catch a bullet, I pray some Yankee pierces his heart for all the evil he has done and continues to pour into the world," Derek said, looking around as more officers were approaching the campfire. Hatred towards George burned a hole inside his chest.

"Gentlemen," Jackson addressed both lieutenants, coming up behind them. "Sorry to interrupt, but I have oiled your muskets. When the sun rises over the trees, the Yankees will fall like wheat before the scythe!" He tried to cheer up the others, but they all knew in their hearts that death would come searching for them. Maybe look them in their faces and make its judgments as they slept that night. In the end, that same death would make them equal.

"Amen to that!" Officers raised their coffee cups into the air, and the clinking of cups at once merged with a subtle melody of the wind.

Suddenly, a rebel yell from a distant hill penetrated the surrounding scenery like an echo, dying off above the moonlit forest. It was a wave of high-pitched Confederate voices that made the Yankee troops freeze in their camps and lower their coffee cups. The grounds had already begun to tremble, long before the battle started. It was a bad sign, and all the Yankees recognized it.

While Confederate tents stood undisturbed in the night and Shawn and Jackson had gone to look over the battlefield maps, Derek studied the moon for the very last time. It came up behind the trees, flat and glossy, the color of a silver cannon. He wondered if the woman in his dream observed this same moon. Catching its glow on his frock coat, he headed into his tent to catch the sleep he knew he wouldn't get, throwing the apple stub to one of the horses.

* * *

On a hot summer day of July 1863, the Union and Confederate armies at Gettysburg had seen the fight of a century through field glasses. The grounds were the color of gray and blue as jackets mingled among tall grass. There were thousands of men marching across the golden terrain, the barrels of their weapons gleaming in the sun.

Lieutenant Shawn Grimwood galloped along the lines of the Confederate regiment on his chestnut horse while Lieutenant Derek Cromwell, a sword in his hand, led the men into the battle. The hills were silent until the first shell burst into the air, leaving a thick line of smoke. What happened then was left only for God's eyes. The earth was trembling.

"Charge! Fire!"

Orders were floating on the wind. In a split second, the thunder of cannons raced through the fields like a wave of death. Soldiers fell to the ground, some dead, others hardly breathing. Smoke from the blasts swiftly covered the fields, creating a white curtain of fog between Confederate and Union armies. American flags flopped on the ground. In the pandemonium of fire and the echo of soldiers' voices, the trees stood like witnesses, catching the bullets that were aimed at soldiers.

After the first wave came the second. There was a shower of bullets brighter than the blaze of the Northern Lights. Against the deep blue of the sky, the shadows of the enemy charged the cannons one after the other, refusing to give up. Somewhere in the distance, a horse fell, a caisson landing on top of her, its wheels still turning. Underneath the horse, a soldier lay on his side, holding his ribcage while blood like a ruby river soaked the grass beneath them. Within seconds his eyes reflected only sky, and his hands laid limply on the caisson and the dead horse.

Lieutenant Grimwood fought the Yankees on the left flank. When the sun pierced the clouds and its light shot through the treetops, Derek could see the gold handle of Shawn's sword glowing in a fight. Behind the mask of a military man, he glimpsed a husband longing for the touch of his wife. A man who wished this war was over. He was wearing his best jacket, a present from a fellow officer. It was bright and fresh, though now blood was seeping through the fabric. Derek kept his eyes on Shawn for a few moments, thinking how far they'd come from the days at the VMI Academy and what an honor it was to fight alongside someone he so deeply admired.

While observing the troops moving up the hills, Derek came upon two Yankees and stabbed them in the chest and kidneys with his bayonet. Wherever he went, the bodies scattered, like fallen autumn leaves. In a voice he no longer recognized, he yelled commands to his officers and kept moving, kept advancing his position. Yet projectiles flew above his head in a sputter, and on the fields, the number of moving Confederate jackets diminished. They were knowingly running upon the spikes of the enemy, and it was almost too late to do anything.

When his best cannoneer was shot in the chest, Derek held him in his arms. Then, with adrenaline feeding his blood, he charged the artillery alone with a still-warm body lying next to him. For the death of one will come the death of many, he thought, watching a shell land in the crowd of Union soldiers and tear them apart. He had to defend his land, his glory, and for the first time, he knew he was destined to be here. If he killed more Yankees, he would save more of his own men.

A sudden blast from the enemy cannon threw Derek into the line of trees. He thought it must have carried him a thousand feet, though it was hard to tell. He felt weightless for a moment before his body hit the hard surface of the ground. He was lucky he wasn't killed by one of the trees.

The surroundings spun within his head, dragging the people and the horses into a carousel. He brushed his fingers over his neck. Blood was warmly trickling out of his left ear, diminishing his hearing.

"You've been hit. It's all right. I'll get you off the field as soon as the Yankees move further away from our position," someone whispered into his injured ear. It made Derek flinch and pull away in pain.

"I'm not leaving this battle," he said, groaning. "I am needed here." A shell went off over the hill and sent a rain of rocks and grass towards them.

"Fine." The soldier studied Derek's injuries and tied a piece of fabric over his arm. "But you have to stay here at least until your head stops spinning," he said, pulling Derek behind a tree to barricade themselves. Then, grabbing his musket, he ran across the field to get to the cannons that the lieutenant had charged before the blast.

Derek sat with his back against the tree, feeling pain in his head, back, and legs. He desperately needed water, his mouth dry. Derek couldn't wait; he knew there must be a canteen of water somewhere, and he had to get it.

Yankees were still crawling in the fields. It was as if they were invincible, and wading through the fields felt like being lost in a dense fog. Clouds of white swallowed everything. The sky fell into the ground, wiping away the sight of the horizon. Taking a step felt like walking into the valley of death. Things appeared out of the fog unexpectedly and brought bullets along with them. To Derek's relief, he tripped over a soldier's body before a Yankee came out of the fog.

The gray uniform of the dead soldier was a dusty rose color. His hands lay on his chest, forming a cross. He looked beautifully peaceful. Derek pulled the canteen off the soldier's belt and brought it to his lips. Cold water nurtured his body and washed the droplets of blood off his chin. He knelt beside the body to take the gun off the soldier's shoulder when his eyes swayed at his face. The canteen fell out of Derek's hands to the ground, spilling what was left of the water.

A freckled face was staring at him through the blood. He recognized the round cheeks full of youth and the blackness of his eyebrows. Jackson. His young protégé.

Derek froze. His stomach turned, and he vomited close to the body. He remembered the first time they met. The joy in Jackson's eyes when he held his first musket. The time he got chased by a horse for a bushel of carrots that looked brighter in color than the sun. He remembered his infectious laugh and his stories of his mother. Oh God. He imagined his mother's face when...

It looked like the bullet had struck Jackson's head. He hadn't suffered, though Derek couldn't look him in the face. Not again. Jackson was another tombstone he refused to see. Derek's heart ached in places he didn't know existed, and he forgot all about the soreness of his own body. This war had taken the purest and most innocent of them in just a flash. He prayed for a moment for Jackson's soul, and for the dreams that went with him into the grave, but Derek had to keep moving. Otherwise, he risked being killed.

When he finally looked away from his fallen friend and rose to try to find Shawn Grimwood and the rest of his regiment, he thought he caught a glimpse of George wandering through the fog, picking up the injured officers. As the fog finally cleared, the reality spoke for itself: George, in his medic gown, knife in hand, was stabbing the fallen soldiers just a couple of feet away. Hatred and anger raced through Derek's heart. He knew there was only one way to deal with his brother— he had to kill him. There was a mid-size dark gray rock formation to his right, and it looked like Derek could seek shelter behind it. He crawled into the bushes and then ran towards the rock. Peering from under it, Derek swiftly pulled out Jackson's gun, aiming it at George's heart.

"May the flames of the fire take you in," Derek whispered.

But before he could fire, he was distracted by a loud bang mixed with the hum of cannons. Derek glanced towards the sight and his heart dropped. The tall silhouette of a rider in the field went down.

"No!" His voice echoed in the distant landscape.

George Cromwell heard the same bang and turned his head towards it. Derek watched in horror as Shawn fell off his horse, wounded in his left shoulder. The diary fell out of the horse's saddlebag as it raced away and landed open on the field by Shawn's side. George brushed his eyes upon Derek's face, giving him a smirk. He dropped the knife onto someone's chest and headed towards the place where Shawn lay. Derek fired at once, hitting his brother in the foot. George howled and fell to the ground in a crouch. He quickly stood up. With blood spraying from his ankle, he ran forward.

Derek lowered his gun, still watching the bloodied medic, and then smashed it against the rock in anger. He couldn't believe he had missed George's heart. It was as if the universe always worked with George rather than against him, and until his very death, Derek would never know why.

At once, Derek pulled himself up, using the rock for balance, and gasped from pain, realizing his side was deeply bruised and he was probably bleeding. He knew Yankee horses weren't that far away—he just had to get over the hill.

Holding his side, he quietly advanced from the rock formation towards the line of trees, lowering his body to the ground away from the Yankee bullets. All this time, he had to turn his head to keep an eye on George, who mingled in and out of the dense gray smoke. Before Derek could reach the hill, a lost horse meandered out of the fog, stopping him halfway. He swiftly pulled her by the reins and hopped on, galloping towards Shawn.

From the saddle, Derek had a full view of the battle of Gettysburg. Bodies were terribly transformed into parts, and the field smelled of vomit, death, and blood. Derek thought he had never seen anything so frightening.

The copse of trees looked like titans. Derek knew it was the place where Shawn had fallen, and soon the bright color of Shawn's jacket caught Derek's eye. He jumped off the horse and, covering his ears from the sound of all the firing, ran to the jacket. There was no sign of Shawn Grimwood or the diary.

Then a subtle groan pierced his ears. A tree was casting a dark shadow. In that shadow, Derek saw George leaning with his back against the oak trunk, Shawn awake in his arms, and the glistening blade of a knife aimed at his friend's throat.

Shawn opened his mouth. "Derek, don't." Blood was coming out of his shoulder, where he had been shot. "It's a done deal for me."

George smiled, revealing his white teeth. "I told you, brother, that your end was near, and now you finally see things for what they are. Admit it. You have lost. There is no stopping me. I have the diary, and you... You have always been a pawn."

Derek's pulse raced with the adrenaline pumping blood in his veins. Resentment clouded his mind, and he was no longer thinking reasonably.

"You are wrong, and I will put a bullet in between your eyes to prove it," Derek said and brought his hands behind his back to get ahold of his musket.

Shawn always kept a charged revolver hidden in his uniform. When a horse sprang by, distracting George, Shawn pushed him off with all the strength he could gather, pressed the gun against George's heart, and pulled the trigger. Nobody expected it. The sound of a fired gun spooked the ravens out of the treetops. They flew out in the shape of a dark cloud, crying out. George fell back with the knife in his hand, managing to stab Shawn in his kidney. Derek darted towards his friend. He couldn't bear the thought of losing him. He knelt beside Shawn, pulling him into his arms, when a projectile landed right in between them. The ground exploded, sending dirt and stones upward in a fountain.

All three of them had thought that it was peaceful to die. Easy. None of them were prepared for what came with it.

14

As they lay on the battlefield, dying under the trees, time stopped. The sun turned into a shadow hovering over the fields. Light drifted away and let the dusk fall upon the grounds as if preparing for someone's arrival. All the colors were dull, almost marble, like death itself was paying a visit. There was a gong in the sky, and it became louder and louder, distinguishing the place where the cannon had shattered. George bled from his mouth, catching his breath; Derek shivered, his head resting on uneven ground, a piece of a cannonball tracing his stomach; and Shawn, clutching his heart, gasped as the blood from his shoulder and kidney reached the grass.

The sky became a swirled hurricane. Heavy rain streamed from the middle, reminding them of a cylinder made of water. The droplets felt ice-cold against their skin. A being crawled out of the hurricane, the sleeves of its black cloak ripped to shreds. Its head was a skull, its skin that of a rotting corpse. There were no eyes on its face—just shiny yellow spaces. The skeleton floated above George's dying body, and the medic didn't scream or struggle. He just let the being suck the soul out of him until the very last drop. There was a mist in the air, and tiny white particles scattered in a ball and left George's pale lips when he and the skeleton parted. His eyes belonged to eternity. Then the being moved on to Derek.

Lieutenant Cromwell didn't fear death. His eyes were still open to the blurry fields. The sun-kissed his face, and behind the clouds, he saw her: the woman from his dream. Her olive skin and rosy cheeks. She was smiling at him. At once, he felt the cold fingers of the being reach for his throat, its nails digging into his skin, and his blood drifted away. His heart began to turn into stone as if the being had taken the love he had for the woman. The sky shut its doors, and her face vanished behind the clouds.

Now the world was drowned in blackness, but the diary shone bright gold. It trembled as its pages were rustled by the growing wind. The skeleton squealed beneath the cloak as if the diary's light blinded it. Releasing the screams of a thousand dying men, it disappeared back into the hurricane, forever blinded.

Shawn's bloodied hand found Derek's, and they were both sucked inside the diary.

TWO

THE PREMONITION

I know what people think about dreams. They are an illusion, fragments of memory that come crawling to the surface of the mind. They linger in some mysterious cosmos which we go to when our hearts are broken or when we miss someone. They have the power to lie.

Dreams used to make me flutter, like butterflies rubbing their wings on my skin. Nightmares used to make me cringe, causing me to wake up with a black hole below my bellybutton. Never in a million years did I think a dream would come true; or worse, a nightmare.

Since I was sixteen, I have had a recurring dream. I am eighteen now, and I still somehow suffer its endless invasion. I lie awake at night, staring at the illuminated ceiling made of cheap plastic stars, and fight what seems like an eternal battle with sleep. None of my struggles matter as, sooner or later, my body gives in— maybe because I simply cannot withstand the exhaustion or maybe my subconscious wishes the dream to find its conclusion. Nevertheless, the fear haunts me even when the plastic stars above my bed begin to swiftly fade.

In my dream, I drive along a curvy road into a dark forest, the majority of which is cloaked in foggy pines. The bickering of animals, hooting of owls, and squeaks of mice are all intensified in my mind as if the creatures of the night all wander around my bedroom, and I am the only one allowed to observe them. The forest looks like the Garden of Evanescence from one of the books my parents used to scare me with when they couldn't find a more suitable punishment. The scariest part about that forest was the translucent shadow-people peering from under the trees' trunks, their eyes glowing the brightest yellow imaginable. Surprisingly, this time it isn't the shadow-people but the sinister forbidden landscape that unfolds in front of my slowly accelerating vehicle.

From the glow of the harvest moon, I realize that my car drives straight into autumn. I open the window and an overwhelming dampness envelops my entire being. The Garden of Evanescence has luminous purple flowers of algae-like cressets shedding their light onto everything around them. Strangely, in my dream, the giant streetlamps stand by the side of the road just like those flowers. What they shed their light on is something one can see only in a nightmare.

At the foot of the mountain, I spot an ambulance lying on its side in a pool of glass. Emergency lights are still circling among the pines as if lost. The piercing resonance of a honk fills the air, surrounding the accident site with despair. From the corner of my eye, I notice an overturned motorcycle on the yellow center line just a couple of feet from the ambulance, its rear fender creaking under force. Its headlight is vigorously blinking. Occasionally, the light reflects off a broken mirror, casting a lonely shadow onto the road. Each time I have this dream, my first thought is that no one is alive on this God-forsaken road.

As soon as I step out of the car, rain drizzles in my face, not like warm tears but a white curtain of hostility. The fear starts to overcome me, but my legs continue to move. The glass breaks under my feet and releases a good crack over and over again as I pull the medical equipment aside to access the vehicle's rear. It is empty. Something lies crushed on the road— some sort of ritualistic bauble. I find pieces thrown to the grass, but it appears to be too damaged to even begin guessing as to what it was before. Studying wooden beads by the curb, I suddenly hear a groan, almost unnoticeable at first, but it exists. I quickly figure out the direction the noise is coming from. In the light of purple algae, I see a dark-colored jacket, and I run towards it.

A person is lying face down on the grass, dirty and forgotten. I am afraid to look at him, but I have no choice. With my heart pounding heavily against my ribcage, I hold on to his muddy jacket and turn him over. Before I can relive the horror of looking him in the face, I awake, with rain still pelting on the roof of my bedroom.

* * *

I didn't know who he was. And even if my dream was a premonition, there was no way of knowing who needed to be saved, much less when they would meet their fate. If there even was fate. Maybe everything I dreamed was just a chemical reaction in my brain, and the chances of the dream actually coming true were minuscule. What made matters worse was the fact that the dream wouldn't leave me alone. It was like it had some sort of distant-but-locked-within power over me, and I couldn't shake it. I tried putting amethysts under my pillow, hanging dream catchers in the most peculiar places of the house, wearing weird necklaces made of crystals, but not once did any of those methods bring me a good night's sleep.

Surprisingly, when I relayed my troubles to my dad, he just wrapped his arms around me before going about his weekday routine. "Beccs, dreams have no meaning until you put one in them. If you want the dream to stop, you have to stop thinking about it. You have nothing to worry about," he said and pressed his lips to my forehead. Pulling his blazer off the coat rack in the dimmed hallway, he vanished behind the door, his scarlet tie moving like the clock's pendulum.

He always told me that dreams were just dreams and fortune-tellers were trying to make a living on believers like me. I couldn't wait to prove him wrong. For the first time, I felt like the dream had a mind of its own, and I was about to conquer it. So I found a fortune teller in the heart of Washington DC— and finding a fortune teller in this city of Oz (or what I imagined to be Oz) was harder than one might think.

Washington looked marvelous this windy day. Cars rolled through puddles of rain and mud. Crowds of people, forming a heavy mist of faces, spread over the streets in endless directions. Shiny colorful umbrellas emerged one by one under the roofs of the buildings like mushrooms after the rain. And here I was: lost in between them, moving with the same electric pace as the crowd, head under the abundant blue skies, legs moving in the direction of the countless glistening cafes.

As I turned the corner of 14th and 16th Street NW, I saw a sign in front of one of the windows shaded by the trees. *"Madame Rose, the Fortune Teller: Tells past, present and the future."* I entered quietly, holding the door with both hands and expecting the loudest creak from the rusted hinge, but nothing came except for the sweet tinkling of the wind chimes as the door shut close behind me.

No one was inside. I set foot in some sort of ritualistic worship room, which made me feel unsteady and doubtful I was in the right place. The dark walls were fringed with paintings of half-dragons, half-zebras, an apocalyptic third eye, and scenes of paranormal battles. I carefully studied each one, brushing my fingers over the paintings' frames, until my attention was caught by a collection of stones on a pedestal under a cloth painting. It depicted an elephant with two heads. The stones glimmered, projecting their own natural colors and forming a stream of light that resembled a rainbow. Against the back wall, I spotted two china cabinets. The numbers *12* and *14* glowed on the jars behind their stained glass. They reminded me of tiny pumpkins. The main attraction—the fortune teller's table—was round at the edges and located in the middle of the room. I slowly approached it like a warrior in heavy armor and put my hand onto the giant pyramid of scarves on the chair. To my shock, the scarves moved and the silver head of a woman appeared from under the table. I jumped.

"Welcome, welcome, child," she greeted me. Slowly, the head rose until the upper half of her body was in my view. With skinny skeleton fingers, she gestured me to have a seat at the table. "You are my first visitor of the day."

"I have not been in a place like this before. Ever," I admitted.

"Well, child, it's all right. People who come to see fortune tellers are usually here for the first and last time," Madam Rose said, watching the silhouettes of people pass by her windows.

I felt droplets of sweat appearing on my forehead. "The truth is, looking into the future scares the living hell out of me, but my intuition tells me that without taking a glimpse, I will never figure it out. Do you get that a lot from people? This *need* to know more than life gives you?" I asked. This could change my life once and for all.

The fortune-teller shuffled her chair a few inches closer to mine as I lowered into the seat. It was a soft velvet armchair that was two sizes bigger than my body.

"People from all walks of life find themselves doubting the future. They need assurance. They desire prosperity. They'd like to take the right path when they get to the crossroads. But their intentions are what blurs out the readings. The cards don't lie, Ms. Grimwood, nor do the dreams. Your heart is pure. You didn't come here to gain something. You came here to seek the truth," she said and reached over to seal my hands inside of hers. I wondered how she knew my name and why she referenced the dreams. Her skin felt cool to the touch, and soon I found myself staring into a globe that changed colors as if I were hypnotized by it.

She was asking questions and I was responding. It was as if I drifted into a trance. Throughout the session, she didn't look me in the eyes. Not once. It was almost as if there was an invisible bird in the room with us and she watched it building a nest, flying by, speaking "bird"— all while I sat in front of her, oblivious and invisible. She hovered over the globe and soon, I observed a purple mist creep closer to the surface, forming a face. My face. The chandelier lights on the walls dimmed as she chanted something in Latin with her eyes half-closed. The wind, uniting with her voice, howled and whistled. She pulled a stack of tarot cards out of her sleeve and began laying them in front of me on the table.

"You were a very happy child…"

I heard a rustle behind us. A door to what looked like a tiny perfumery squeaked open. A parrot flew into the room and landed on Madam Rose's shoulder. It was blue and had a gray stripe going down its back. The parrot squawked and rubbed his beak on her neck.

"You have such a beautiful parrot," I complimented her.

"Don't mind him," Madam Rose said. "He is just here to witness."

"I was happy." My eyes ran across the fortune teller's face, which was focused on the dark purple globe between us. I wondered why she needed to know about my childhood. As she moved her hands away from the globe, I briefly noticed a swirl of alabaster incense that floated freely on its surface.

"When she left you, you knew… Something wasn't right about her. She drifted away, and you feared that it would happen to him too. But he stayed," Madam Rose whispered as if she were trying to listen to someone's voice conveying the message, but there was only the hum of the wind.

"Are you talking about my mom?" I asked, searching for answers in her facial expressions, but I wasn't finding any.

Madam Rose's flower bandana lowered, hiding away her eyebrows. "It's possible. Women in your family tree are like roses with thorns. One can burn from their touch. They are also good at keeping secrets," she said and fell silent for a moment. "The voices," the fortune teller continued, "she heard them too. She wanted to save you from them, but they were too many. And the dreams... They will never stop until you destroy it. Until there is an eclipse of both forces." Madam Rose knocked her long, spike-shaped nails on the table. A crescent moon was painted on them.

"I don't understand," I pleaded. "What eclipse? What forces?"

"They will find you, and then everything will fall into place," she said and smiled at me, startlingly genuine, her colorful scarves wrapped around her like a thousand garments.

I wasn't getting answers. I felt more confused than before I stepped foot into this place. I wanted to leave. I was afraid of what I might hear next, but my intuition was telling me to stay. As I watched her, she pulled out a new card from the tarot stack.

"Reversed Wheel of Fortune," Madame Rose said assertively. I swayed my eyes at the card. The arrows on the wheel fell upon the angels with flutes, who flew out of the sky. It was a shimmering gold card that turned black and silver when you angled it, and the other side depicted those same angels trapped in demon claws. "I don't get many of those. People and change don't usually go together. Though luck can play both sides, like a coin flip. Remember that you have to stay true to yourself, even if luck decides to go the opposite way."

Luck and I lived in two separate universes. Madame Rose had just read the story of my life.

The burning incense swirled in circles like smoke above our heads. I nodded in confirmation of her words, and she revealed the image of a dark stone tower being struck by lightning and going down in flames. *This can't possibly be good*, I thought to myself, waiting for the fortune teller's final verdict.

"This is the Tower." She laid the card in front of me. "You have a special talent, and you have come to use it. But this gift isn't something to perceive lightly. It has dark power, much darker than you may think. You have to be cautious with it, for it will be the cause of your destruction, as well as your salvation."

"The dream that haunts me since I was sixteen, where a man lies on the road... I have a talent for seeing the future through my dreams? Do I see *his* future?" I asked.

Madam Rose shook her head. "The dreams have meaning beyond my understanding. The dream is talking to you. It might be the future, it might be the past; it could be a sign, a warning. You won't find an answer on the surface. It lies deep within you," she explained.

I watched her put away the cards inside of her sleeve. They disappeared like a magician's trick. She was telling me that the reading had come to an end when one of them fell out of her sleeve and landed on the table.

Her hand swiftly picked it up and revealed a card with a man dressed in medieval clothes hanging upside down from the trunk of a tree.

"The Hanged Man says you are the ultimate sacrifice." And as her words splashed me like iced water, she looked me in the eye. Madam Rose was blind. I froze, afraid to disrupt the silence.

The cards weren't listening anymore, as if they had their own power. The rest of them fell out of Madam Rose's sleeve and scattered on the table like magnets. One card stood out to her the most, it seemed, as she grabbed it and pressed it against the globe. I saw her hand suddenly shake and her lower lip tremble. The chandeliers were going off one by one, knocking out the lights.

"This isn't working. You shouldn't have come," she said finally, lifting her head and collecting the blankets from underneath her. A strong gust of wind entered with the door, scattering eggplant-colored leaves and triggering the hum of her wind chimes. The candles threw hard dark shadows on Madame Rose's face. My heart stalled with worry, but my curiosity was taking the best of me.

"What does that mean? What did you see?" I asked her in disbelief. "Does the dream have anything to do with it? Please tell me." I reached forward and clung to her scarf.

"It's darker than coal, timeless as the tides, scarlet, scarlet, scarlet…" Madame Rose mumbled in a deep voice that didn't belong to her.

"What was the card that you saw?"

Her only response was more mumblings. "Death… darker… than the coal, timeless… as the tides… scarletttt…" She laughed, and that laugh reminded me of something demonic, making my hairs stand on end. The alarmed parrot flew off Madam Rose's shoulder and landed on the fortune teller's globe. I saw the shadow of a large hawk reflect on the wall behind him. Horrified, I picked up my duffel bag from the floor and ran outside, hearing only the wind chimes fading into the sound of the city as the cool air filled my lungs.

I walked with the wind behind me, pushing me forward. The fear was curdling in my stomach, and I eventually stopped to catch my erratic breath. I thought I was seeing shadows, but they were just people brushing past me. I anxiously slid my eyes across the street. Before me and behind me were faces that I didn't recognize, but I was certain they were human. People leaned against bus stops, crossed the street in pairs, and came up from the corners like someone had sent them a mass message with a time and place for a retreat. And the worst part was that I felt like they were all looking at me, a silly little girl who decided she needed to know what the future held for her. But apparently, I amended, she might not have any future to speak of.

I felt a hysterical giggle bubble up in my throat at this thought. That ball of nervousness kept bouncing inside of my stomach.

I stopped when a familiar brown building appeared on my left, like a phoenix rising out of the ashes. I realized I had just walked up to the steps of Georgetown Waterfront Park, which had a beautiful view of the Potomac River and its many ferries. I had wandered here before, long ago, after dropping off my college application at Georgetown University. I had always found this place peaceful and magical. Sitting on the bench under the rustling leaves, sun shining through the branches, casting shadows on my face— it all was therapeutic. I used to escape here when things veered out of control. When Dad met Alice, and my mom vanished from my life. I guessed my feet had just dragged me here. They knew the way.

The sun radiated in the azure sky, turning the water to a golden color. Laughter flowed from the top of the steps, causing me to turn around. A little girl and her mother were drawing something on the concrete. I stepped closer to have a look.

At first, I spotted a crown, like perhaps one belonging to a princess hiding away in a castle, but by the time they had finished the picture, it was clear that their drawing was of a ferry and a giant mountain or iceberg. It reminded me of one of my paintings that Dad had hung on the fridge when I was in kindergarten. I pulled out my cell phone to take a picture of the chalk painting when suddenly a flock of birds raced in the reflection of my cell phone screen. Startled, I lifted my head towards the sky, but there were no birds in sight except for one lonely airplane leaving a dead wake of smoke behind it.

Almost simultaneously, I heard someone humming. I peeked behind me but only noticed a couple eating ice cream on the bench at the park entrance. They were so in love that they didn't care about the world.

In the corner of my eye, I watched a shadow race across the concrete. It was long and human-shaped, and it popped out of nowhere. I gasped and jerked away, causing my cell phone to fall out of my hand. I heard the piece of technology land by my feet, breaking into parts.

"Come home," the shadow whispered, or I thought it did.

I was so preoccupied with the shadow that I didn't notice how a little girl had approached me. I didn't know where she came from. She pulled at the sleeve of my shirt and pointed at something drawn on the concrete— the numbers *12* and *14* in pink and dark gray chalk. The girl peered at me with her bright blue eyes. I had seen those numbers before, I thought. At Madam Rose's...

"My grandma lives at 1214 Potomac," I said to the girl, surprised at my own discovery. I had always believed in synchronicities but this one had snuck up on me.

When I turned, the girl was no longer there. Nor was the painting. The park was completely empty; only passing cars were here, honking at a drunk man walking on the bridge.

I tried to reason with myself, but I was terrified. It wasn't every day you saw strange fortune tellers, shadows, and unexplained visions. My heart was beating out of my chest. My hands trembled, and I felt like I was running a fever. But the dream... it was not something I had imagined. It had tormented me for years.

I lifted my bag off the ground, shoving my shattered phone inside, and got ready to head out back to Dad's. That was when I saw a beautiful snow-white ferry float by. It looked crowded. Forte piano music was playing and people were dancing, their feet carrying them away. I shuffled closer to the overlook and observed a groom pick up his bride and give her a swirl, her dress twinkling like the stars, while the guests clapped and drizzled champagne over them. I would have given anything to be this happy, I thought.

There was only one place on earth I felt safe and *happy* and where I had someone to talk to, or at least someone who could help me forget about almost anything— my grandmother's house in Harpers Ferry, West Virginia. I had to get there. If the monsters really haunted me, there was no way they would get past my grandma.

The sky turned purple, darkening the park, and the droplets of cool water reached my cheek. A witch was brewing a storm in her cauldron, and it would only be a matter of time until she pulled me into it. I watched a monster made of water reach its hands into the trees. A spark of lighting hit and, shielding my head with a duffel bag, I scurried out of the park.

THREE

HOME SWEET HOME

After the night at Georgetown Waterfront Park and the visions, I reckoned that Harpers Ferry was a part of the premonition I received from Madam Rose. It followed me everywhere like a ghastly shadow. A few days later, I was browsing the Washington Library catalog for another volume of *War and Peace* when a woman walked out of the secluded history section wearing a shirt with *Harpers Ferry* written against her chest in cursive. Two days later, I received a card in the mail with the Potomac River on its glossy cover. Dad bought tickets for a ferry ride, and on it was a boy with the numbers *1, 2, 1, 4* tattooed on his arm, looking over the railing next to me. All of a sudden, my world was full of synchronicities and signs that I had never noticed before. I felt like I was at the right place at the right time. The future was glancing at me through the darkness. It was as if I had a third eye into the magical, mystical world of foretelling. The more I wondered about it, the stronger it dragged me in. The moment our stars aligned with the unknown, the signs just poured out of it, leaving me clues as to where to go next. And that next clue transformed into visiting Grandma.

Dad felt like it was a great idea for me to get away from Washington. Grandma always looked for ways to lure me back into the house, so when she heard, she pledged to tell every stranger and townie that her granddaughter was coming back home. I couldn't wait to be smothered with Grandma's hugs and stuffed full of cookies that looked like the Russian cartoon character *Kolobok*. Besides, Harpers Ferry was my favorite town. It was a ghost town where rain droplets drew silhouettes on wet glass. And I missed it dearly.

When I arrived at the train station, the wind chilled me to the bones like an invisible scarf. A heavenly breath of autumn spread over the pyramids of colorful luggage and set itself on neatly tucked uniforms of train conductors. I could even see it dissolve beyond the lights of departing trains in a thick mist, as if it had a human face.

I hated goodbyes. I was glad Dad and Alice stayed home. I was still adjusting to how much they had started hovering after Mom left. If Alice hadn't become my father's girlfriend so soon, I might have looked at her differently, but I chose to keep my distance for now. No faces to look at when the train departed meant no tears. It was easier to leave alone, jump onto the first platform of the train, lift the duffel bag over my head, and push it until it fit into its designated spot.

Despite the chilled air, the train cabin preserved its warmth. I set my legs on the freshly installed carpet, perched on a seat with a comfortable head cushion, and unfolded the mini table in front of me. As we started to move, I noticed the clouds looking puffy and gloomy. Soon I heard a series of knocks, as if someone had dropped a giant bag of M&Ms and they had scattered onto the metallic surface of the train. The scenery turned a little darker than usual as the rain continued to fall. It didn't bother me; it looked magical— like I was staring at a painting in a gallery.

I moved closer to the cold wall of the train and pulled the curtains out of their ribbons. My face reflected in the window for a moment, and I discovered that a couple of years had gone by unnoticed. My long walnut hair had become a shade darker, and my blue eyes had some stillness or sadness in them, just like seawater on a stormless night. The pink rouge on my cheeks had drifted away, and I looked colorless— almost ghostly.

I pressed my head against the head cushion and closed my eyes. I realized just how tired I was. Someone was shuffling in between the rows of seats. Newspaper pages rustled and water glasses chimed. The echo of clattering train tracks and children's voices bounced inside the train cabin. All the sounds soon died off. Tree branches brushed by the window, causing me to turn in my seat.

Through the veil of a dream, I saw my grandmother's house. Flowy lavender curtains with strings of fairy lights that shone behind them. Shelves filled with books my great-grandfather had bound together, and boxes and boxes of my childhood memories. It smelled of happiness inside— a feeling that I now longed for more than ever.

I ran up to the landing, my footsteps echoing on the hardwood floors. The door to my childhood bedroom upstairs had not been replaced since I was three years old and it creaked, unlike the door of Madam Rose's.

There was a poster of a Japanese cat with a waving paw by the wardrobe in my bedroom. Maneki Neko, the lucky cat. I put it on the wall in the seventh grade. Back then, I chose to believe in fortune, but the more time I spent thinking about the cat, the less luck I had; and suddenly it was luck's fault and Meneki Neko became the Unlucky Stray. I wasn't alone in my observation. There was someone out there from the same town as me who shared that same belief in luck— my best friend Nicholas. Our grandmothers had immigrated together from Russia and built houses in Harpers Ferry only a couple feet from each other's welcome mats. And unbeknownst to them, Nick and I started borrowing each other's pacifiers, climbing into abandoned houses after curfew, and borrowing too many books from the library between our two card numbers.

One of my favorite memories of Nick was from when we were five. He had handed me a white dandelion, and told me to blow on it and make a wish. I knew back then he would be a loyal, trustworthy, and proud keeper of my wishes. We were connected from the first time we cut a Maneki Neko poster in half with a pair of scissors, making a promise to each other to never think about luck again; to never tell of the time we broke Grandma's favorite vase and replaced it with a store-bought one, swearing on our lives that the vase was green and not blue when she asked.

Of course, life threw us around a bit. My dad moved to Washington; Nick's father became a prominent architect in New York. We wrote letters, exchanged gifts, and on days like today, we found our way back home, no matter how far we lived from each other. In a couple of days, my best friend would be back in town, and it all would be okay.

Suddenly, I felt a kick, jerking me awake. It resembled a slight shake or a miniature earthquake. The train met a bump, or the bump met the train; it was hard to tell. My thoughts of Nick and Grandma scattered. The conductors circled through the rows, blaming the bump on the old myth of a ghost caught on fire during the Civil

War— a woman who jumped onto the tracks and, by freak misfortune, was hit by the train. Luck, I tell you, is a real thing. It happened each season exactly between Harpers Ferry and Washington DC, as if the tracks were cursed. I had believed it to be a myth or folklore— simply a legend of an old town— but not anymore.

After a few more stops, an orange sunrise with morning fog coming up over the forest caught my eye. The train was passing through the familiar landscapes of Harpers Ferry. The lights of the station shone through the fog, bright yellow eyes glowing in the distance.

Harpers Ferry remained just like I remembered.

Potomac River rocks, like dwarf icebergs, pierced the flowing water. The fog moved fast, dragging the mountain with it into a merry-go-round; all the while, the bells of Saint Peter's church chimed in the distance. Harpers Ferry always welcomed me so fondly: its narrow-bricked streets, misty pinecone-shaped lights, mossy ruins of railroads and armories. My heart surrendered to its beauty, perfectly blending in with all the existing ghosts of an old town.

I knew that I could search the map, rotate the globe, but I would never belong anywhere else. One little town on a cliff, just below the misty mountain, a resident of Ghost County with a timeless echo of the trains lingering in the air— my Harpers Ferry, forever holding my heart.

A warm smile ran across my face and a sweet wave of joy burst inside of my heart when the train came to a stop.

* * *

Grandma stood on the platform, waving vigorously. I saw her through the window and stuck my head out as far as I could, trying to catch her attention. Her face began to glow as she spotted my silhouette moving among the passengers. She hadn't aged a day. Strawberry blonde hair fell in waves on her forehead. A purple over-the-shoulder bag sat on her hip and an oversized teal shirt that matched her eyes fluttered in the wind. The only difference about her was the smell of her flowery perfume, which was a tiny hint stronger now. She looked like the same fairy godmother who cared for Cinderella and every time she smiled, I knew anything was possible and that everything was right in the world. If the world had her, it didn't have cause for concern.

"How was your trip, dear?" she asked, pulling me into her embrace. "You look tired, maybe hungry."

Here we go again, I thought affectionately. I haven't even had a chance to unpack yet, and she's already trying to feed me.

"I ate a croissant with cheese on the train. Time went by fast."

"Just a croissant? That's not enough for a growing girl like you." Grandma squeezed me tighter. "Your father already called. He wondered why the train was late and was going to call the station. A man's mind is a powerful instrument, and I think he forgets it at times," she said, warming me with her eyes. I remembered the ghost on the train tracks.

"It sounds like him. Leave the man for a day and he starts to lose it," I said, hiding my face in my grandma's arms.

"You know why, honey? Because you are a jewel. Fathers do adore their little girls. I can't blame him," she said and lightly bumped me on my nose. "Are you ready to go? Do you have any checked-in luggage? We need to get back. I have your favorite soup on the stove."

I showed her my duffel bag, which was heavier than any suitcase. "This is all I got, Grams. Let's go home!"

She put her hand on my shoulder, and I hugged her around the waist. Gossiping about my father, we walked away, leaving the lights of the station fading behind us.

FOUR

HOUSE WITH LAVENDER CURTAINS

Over the emerald bridge, across the Potomac and Shenandoah rivers, hidden from the eye, stands a house with lavender curtains and candlelight shining from the attic. My childhood home, a place where, on Sundays, I would wake up to the flowing melody of church bells, the echo of women's voices singing "John Brown's Body," and the occasional ghostly cannon firing from the Bolivar Heights.

When I think of that house, I think of spring. Warm wind rattling the window, dusk and dawn over the train tracks. Civil War kepis shining in the storefronts, barrels of gunpowder, and the ruins of the armory where Nick and I used to play snowballs. Grandma with a Pekingese dog curled up by her feet in her favorite velvety armchair. She always stepped on that poor dog by accident, sunflower seeds in a bowl, a pattern on her apron, and the scent of the laundry detergent floating in the air. I think of Nick and the yellow Civil War photographs we found in the attic, along with an old creepy doll which we had to get rid of. We had some of the deepest, most curious, and even life-changing talks of my entire life there. All of these memories were etched into the four walls of the house.

Because our house was built during the Civil War era, Nick wondered whether it had any ghosts. Grandma told me that they heard the doorknob rattle early October mornings near Halloween as if someone was trying to enter the house. Whether it was true or not, I couldn't open the bathroom door on the second floor without turning on the light switch. I would always look away from the mirrors so the red eyes of before wouldn't find me again. Their reflection had left me feeling unsteady for many years to come.

I also knew of a ghost of a woman who haunted one of the houses across the street. She and her baby were killed during the Civil War by a cannon blast. Visitors said they occasionally saw her wander by the window with a candle in her hand. Apart from her, there was a spirit of a Confederate spy lurking around town. He was shot while searching for shelter in one of the homes. The house he selected was full of Union officers who had gathered for a meeting inside, and when he attempted to enter, they shot him point-blank in the chest. Our town had stories, just like most old towns did. Whether or not they were true, I wouldn't know, but they sure made the history of Harpers Ferry interesting.

Grandma had soup boiling on the stove. A young man wearing a jacket that said "Harpers Ferry Plumbing" was kneeling on the tile floor, hands and head under the sink, screwing and unscrewing pipe fittings. When he heard the door open, he stood up in alarm but relaxed and smiled once he saw Grandma. He then leaned back down to continue fixing the sink, stopping only to take a bite of pastry that Grandma left out for him.

"I see you don't waste any time, Grams. Young plumbers in your kitchen," I teased while we were coming up the landing.

"Oh, stop it, Becca. He was the only one on call." Grandma chuckled as she went by. "You should talk to your Aunt Lida. She is an expert in breaking and fixing stuff. There is usually nothing wrong with anything in her house," she said, her eyes playful and kind.

"Oh, you guys are having all the fun in the world, aren't you?" I grinned.

"That's what you do, dear, when you're are in your seventies: you bake and make life more interesting. You'll see soon enough." She smiled, pulling on my ear. "You should rest. I'll be back with the soup."

I placed my duffel bag on the shelf of the Victorian coat rack next to the door and climbed onto the bed. Lying with my back on the quilt, hair spread on the covers, I stared at the stars Nick and I had placed on the ceiling when we were kids. They still glowed but only faintly. I sat back up and walked across the room to open the closet door, checking for the bedroom monsters. A bunch of old dusty books fell out, so I shoved them back onto the top shelf. The closet needed some serious reorganizing— maybe a whole day of it. Not to mention that I had promised Nick to search for my grandfather's camera, and I was pretty sure it was tucked away inside of one of those boxes. He always reminded me how rare the apparatus of the camera was and how much he would have loved to restore it to its original beauty. Now that he was going to New York for photography courses, it seemed like the perfect timing. After all, it would be incredibly selfish to keep it away from the world.

I heard a gentle knock on the door. Grandma floated into the room with a bowl in her hand, which she carefully set on the side table.

"Thank you, Grams," I said and smiled.

She gazed at me for a moment, as if she knew of the place where I hid all my secrets and worries— a place I didn't invite her into. Scanning me with her eyes, she sat beside me and put her hand on my knee.

"Are you all right, child?" she asked with the same warmth radiating from her face.

"Oh yes, I couldn't be better. I'm just so glad to be home."

"Well, in that case, I have a little homecoming present for you," she said with delight and pulled a box out of her apron. It had a lovely teal ribbon on it and was packaged with all the love the world could give. Inside revealed a charm bracelet with a miniature house on it, and my face lit up.

"It's an exact replica. Grandpa and I wanted you to have this close to your heart, even if one day Harpers Ferry decided to change. This way, you can always find your way home, Becca."

Her words made my heart ache. I wished Grandpa was sitting beside her, and I wanted to believe that he was. I hugged her as tight as I could against my chest.

"Oh, are those tears? No crying in Grandma's house!" she commanded.

I let out an awkward chuckle and reached for the tissue at the nightstand. We both heard scratching at the doorway, and within seconds a little dog appeared. Like Napoleon on the battlefield, he held his head high and proud. Charlie barked at us once, brilliantly and intensely. Then, acting like his work here was done, he headed downstairs to terrorize the plumber.

After talking to Grandma, I finally let *happy* thoughts of being home push the premonition out of my mind. Fear and shock all

41

drifted away but with that came emotional and physical tiredness. Despite the fact that the day had just begun, I shut the curtains and crawled into bed with a book. *Scarlet Sails* by Alexander Green seemed like a fitting companion, and I delved into the pages of my most beloved fairytale. I didn't notice how the book fell out of my hands and I, leaning on the cushioned bed frame, slipped into a dream.

I was running through a forest, as if something was chasing me. The sun changed into a bloody moon, and I stumbled into an open field. Raindrops sat in beads on the fresh grass, and the whole field glistened in the streaks of light. Fog hung thick, so thick that I couldn't see the other part of the forest. And as I stepped into it, I saw movement— a silhouette of a young man in a leather jacket appeared out of the fog and headed towards me. I screamed, but the sound wouldn't come out. I awoke, squeezing one of my loveseat pillows so hard that my fingers went numb. Something was happening to me. Cold sweat ran down my forehead as I pulled the blanket over my head and hid my head between the pillows.

When I looked up, I recognized the stars on the ceiling. I grabbed one of my old dreamcatchers out of the closet, put it on the bedpost, and hoped that no other nightmares would get inside of my head. As soon as I pulled the handle of the door to head downstairs, I heard a loud bang at the window. With my heart pumping blood at an impossible rate, I froze, letting a shiver make its way down my spine.

FIVE

OLD FRIENDS

If I imagined a perfect evening, it would look like this: I would pop my head out of my bedroom window and watch the town ignite with lights, welcoming the night. I would pour hot water into the old Japanese cup with a missing lid and listen to the soft sounds of frogs and crickets against the silence of the train tracks. I would pick up the round apple-like clock on my nightstand, set the alarm to 5:45 a.m., and wake up to the smell of lilies just in time to see the sun rise above the mountains. I would repeat this routine every night with no exception. That was the level of obsession the old town had over me.

That night it got quieter. There was no clock ticking, and Grandma had already gone to bed, as I couldn't hear the dishwasher running downstairs. My heart was trying to gallop out from my chest. It sent blood to all the tissues of my body with the flow of a swift river. I was about to pull the window blinds down when a head appeared through the curtains, and I reared backward, collapsing onto the satin bed sheets.

"A little help here, please. I haven't climbed ladders to your window since I was twelve, I think."

The voice started to take a physical shape. Except for a salt lamp, there was no other light in the room, and the figure looked like the man from my crazy dream coming out of the fog to haunt me. A guy with wheat-colored hair and a bright smile was looking down at me.

"Nicholas! You scared me to death. How did you know I was home? You weren't supposed to arrive until tomorrow!" I exclaimed, scanning him with my eyes.

"Your dad called me." He grinned, getting his legs out of the twisted curtain.

"I don't know why that surprises me. His life is all about mine," I said, helping him out and guiding him towards the salt lamp's light.

"Just as it should be! I love your old man," he said, his eyes wandering around the bedroom. His figure rose in front of me. He was clean-shaven and tall with long brown eyelashes outlining his prominent blue eyes. With his two legs on the hardwood floors, he pulled me tight into his arms.

"God, I have missed you so much! I don't think I could have waited another day." He beamed. His cologne and the smell of forest campfire filled my nostrils.

Something was different about Nick. He looked so grown-up, so incredibly handsome. A tint of mischief raced across his face. I held my hands inside of his, and I noticed how tiny I felt locked in his broad palms.

He tried to grab the ladder, which was hanging for dear life on the maple tree outside.

"Would you be quiet? Grandma just went to bed," I warned.

She slept so lightly that sometimes a cat drinking milk on our porch forced her to wander outside. Life had never been easy on her; each wrinkle was the solemn proof. If I could give her at least

44

some peace at night, I would. She deserved to be loved— to be cared for. I imagined myself as a dreamcatcher veering in the wind, collecting her nightly adventures, protecting her like I would a drop of rain on the palm of my hand.

"I'm sorry, what would you like me to do? Leave it? Your grandma would think we had a thief climbing up the ladder. Do you want to see her throw a rolling pin directly at my eye?" Nick joked, still breathing heavily. Climbing took all the living strength out of him.

"Oh, come on. I didn't think you were so easily scared," I replied. I could feel the butterflies in my stomach playing volleyball.

"Your grandma is the strictest person I know when it comes to you," he whispered, his tone serious. Then he added: "I am scared of her."

"She's known you since you were a kid," I assured him.

"That was a long time ago and right now, I'm in your bedroom."

"I think she can make an exception to the rules this time. You're forgetting that I'm an adult now."

"So am I. I think you don't know your own grandmother. She will kill me. I better head out now." The next thing I knew, he was playfully headed towards the door.

"Hey, no, no, no. That would be too easy," I protested, still smiling.

There was no distance between us. His skin looked so silky, so mesmerizing. I couldn't get enough of him. The long separation we had endured started to consume me. We weren't just two kids with a plan to get out of the house on a Friday night and drive to the end of town to look at the stars. We had grown up. He reminded me of someone Assol from *Scarlet Sails* was waiting for, staring at the horizon. A prince with a fairytale ending. A man who just came out from a page in a book. He was so dear and familiar to me, yet so foreign. His mysteriousness drew me in.

* * *

The flower chair patterns were not as distracting as Nick's eyes going up and down my silhouette. He brushed his hands over the kitchen counter as if checking for dust that would not be there. Grandma's kitchen was small, but somehow with Nick standing so close to me, it became a lot smaller. And the air stuffier. I tried to divert my attention towards the rooster bowls inside of the china cabinet by the window— anything but swaying my eyes to where Nick was standing.

"You couldn't wait to get away from your father?" Nick asked as I tried to silence the boiling kettle. His words felt like cold air that made me jolt awake from my thoughts.

Charlie was the only one who came out to check on us. He stumbled into the kitchen, half-sleepy, half-hungry. I knelt to rub his ear. He stopped by my feet and immediately lay down.

"It's not him. But it's more complicated than that."

I remembered Madam Rose and her chanting about "scarlet" and death. Someone lying on the curb of the road. I pushed the thoughts aside. I hated hiding things from Nick.

"You know me. I can't stay in one place for too long. The trees seem to look sullen; the emptiness of a place gets to me." I

46

paused, looking through the kitchen cabinet. "Oh, there's only Rooibos tea. No bergamot. Grandma also made *shangi* with puree in the middle, if you're hungry, and soup." I pushed the plate with food towards him.

"Rooibos is great, thank you. I can help you make tea."

He attempted to take the kettle off the stove. The warmth he projected was consuming me whole.

"You know the rules of this house. Guests aren't allowed to touch anything. So sit your butt down. Tell me, how is Lida these days? Grandma told me they have a new game of tormenting Harpers Ferry plumbers," I said and chuckled.

"She's good. When I left the house, she was watching *The Shining*, snapping her fingers as Jack Torrance chopped through the door," he said and stopped, thinking. "You know what? Hell yeah, plumbers *are* their obsession. I blame your grandmother. She's the troublemaker," he said, taking another bite of the *shanga*. "You inherited the gene."

I laughed so hard I almost spilled the tea from my cup onto the floor.

"How are things with that photography course?" I asked, wrapping my hands around the cup once again.

Nick placed his teaspoon on the saucer, and it made a pleasant ringing sound.

"I registered for next summer. Dad asked his friend from New York to let me stay with him for the duration of the course. Looks like he has some connections there, so I'm hoping for the best."

He sighed, putting two cubes of sugar into the mug, and began twirling the spoon to create a wave inside, a mixture of sugar and water. For a moment, his face darkened, as if he had entered some strange cosmos. A state so deep in his thoughts that he caught himself staring at the table without blinking.

"Oh, Nick, you're so talented. I'm sure a door will open for you. Believe in yourself and your dreams." He heard my voice and blinked awake.

I sipped the tea slowly. The steam from the hot water was touching my face.

"So, what are you planning to do until then?" I asked.

"Work for the Historical Society of Harpers Ferry. Maybe visit some battlegrounds. By the way, did you have a chance to look for your grandfather's camera?"

I gave him a guilty smile. "I thought about it. The closet is so cluttered that I'll have to get an excavator to dig through all the stuff. But I promise I will do it soon."

"I'm glad you are back, Becca," Nick said after a moment of silence between us. "Talking to you over the phone and having you here with me is night and day. Sometimes I fall into this dark hole with photography that nothing is working out, and I stop believing in myself. I lose focus and forget what is important. Thank you for being there to remind me," he said with gratitude shining in his eyes.

"Always," I promised. I felt his sadness; the wave of it overcame us both.

Nick's gaze lingered on me, like light diffused through mosaic glass. It was a soft, delicate peering, but I sensed the difference in him. There was no way of knowing what bothered him. He was a man of few words, but his eyes were two oceans that reflected his soul so vividly. I saw pureness, divinity, desire, calmness before the storm— the whole unfolded truth about him. He needed to stay; his eyes practically begged me to let him.

"I can't stay," he whispered, looking into the night from the kitchen window.

I squeezed his shoulders in my arms and after nestling my head on his heart, I said, "Please stay. I want you to. We can talk. You can photograph the sunrise from the roof. You know how beautiful Harpers Ferry is immersed in morning light."

Oh, it was so easy to convince him; he had a soft spot for me. We unrolled two flannel blankets out from the closet, and Nick pushed the pillow down with a broom from the third "unreachable" shelf. We stayed up late with a house of cards, a domino, and memories like jam bursting out of the jar of life.

I woke up once throughout the whole night. I headed to the bathroom. Nick was lying on his side, pillow in his arms, mouth slightly open, forming a smile. He was dreaming about something; he was making subtle noises like he was agreeing with whatever was going on. I stepped closer to him, slid a pillow under his head, and covered him with a blanket. He mumbled in his dream language and turned to another side. I was about to perch beside him when I noticed that the scarf I had hung on the old vanity mirror lay crumpled on the floor. I worried Charlie would rip it to shreds, so I went to pick it up.

I held the scarf in my arms, feeling the silk slide between my fingers, when I glanced inside the mirror. What I saw only lasted an instant, but even then, it was enough to send me running for the hills. The creature resembled a gargoyle, eyes flashing yellow like bright headlights of a car. I quickly threw the scarf back where it belonged and nestled inside Nick's sleeping bag, hiding my head under the covers. I pretended that it was just a part of my crazy imagination.

* * *

Nick must have been awake before me. He had covered me with flannel blankets and sat in one of the armchairs until I drifted out of sleep. From where I was laying, I could spot his ruffled hair and marble skin revealed at his torso. He made my heart yank. I rustled out of the blankets, and he gave me a smile. That smile made me never want to let him go again.

When the sun peeked from under the mountain and its light raced through the open window, we were up on the roof with a thermos filled with toasted pecan coffee. Nick put his arm around me and brought his camera forward, photographing two friends, an old town, and the sunrise over the amber crowns of the trees. I somehow felt that there were not two but three of us on that roof.

SIX

THE TREE HOUSE

"Rebecca!" I heard footsteps disappearing down the stairwell. "If you sleep any longer, you are going to miss all the morning's beauty."

Grandma's voice scattered like particles to all four corners of the house.

"I'm coming," I replied, pushing the blanket away from my face. Streaks of light splayed on my quilt in hues of tangerine.

The fresh scent of the morning entered the room as if nature spilled its perfume into the air. Under the roof of the house, I could see the leaves sailing like colorful confetti. Traffic was non-existent this time of the day but for one reason or another, I missed the school buses passing by, dragging their shadows onto the busy streets. Nick was gone. He had carefully folded the flannel blanket and put it onto the chair, placing the pillow on top. I already missed him; the night seemed to be a day in a fairytale land and his eyes, full of secrets, were stuck in my memory like two oceans with no bottom.

The wonderful scents from the kitchen dragged me out of bed. There had not been a day Grandma appeared in the kitchen without her apple apron. She buttered the toast, brewed the coffee, rolled airy dough for pies, filled glasses with milk, and wrote something in her blue recipe book, all while holding four measuring cups on her finger. I admired her elegant posture, the soft melody of her vocal cords, and her caring nature. She and I— we shared a secret.

She was the mom I never had. I cried on her shoulder, knitted wool socks with her while sipping coffee, watched Argentinean soap operas with her, and devoured pastry with raisins, walnuts and cinnamon while Charlie was sneaking bologna out of the fridge, which he usually threw up the next morning.

Apart from singing lullabies to me and cooking, she recited the prose of Akhmatova, Pushkin, Esenin, to name a few great poets of Russian classics. I was so in love with the words back then that I pretended to be that clever cat from Pushkin's poems that walked around the tree on a chain and told fairy tales. I climbed on the highest shelf of the cupboard and held a book, walking from right to left, and read to the world, even if no one was watching. I was endlessly thankful to her for showing me the world of books.

Today, in a satin dress falling weightlessly to the floor, my grandma was mixing the batter with a big wooden spoon while peering outside, searching for the line that separated the sky and the green fields. She had lived most of her life in Europe in the birthplace of Father Frost, the town of Veliky Ustyug. I always wondered what it took to live in Russia during those days. A bird building the nest and one day leaving it without ever looking back. By the way she was looking outside, I knew that her heart was split in two.

"How is Nick? I heard his voice coming from the kitchen yesterday," she asked, pouring batter into one of the ceramic tins. It filled the tin like lava, spreading to all corners and taking its entire form.

I was surprised she had heard him. "He asked me to say hello to you but only after worrying that you might use a Russian punishment on him. You know, like quartering. Which is medieval, but who cares. I'm sure that's what he pictured."

"Good," Grandma responded mischievously. "I like the power I have over him. At least he knows his boundaries." She smiled and added: "I remember he was such a sweet child, carrying grocery bags for me, asking me if he could bring you a box of candies. I think he always had a special place in his heart for you."

I blushed. "Oh, stop it! We have been friends for such a long time! We never looked at each other that way." I grabbed a piece of candy off the counter, unwrapping it nervously.

"Love always starts as friendship. You can't build love on anything else but trust. Friends make pretty strong couples," she assured me, washing her hands under swiftly running water. Her eyelashes were lowered.

"That's your fairytale, Grams, but I can't argue. You are right. We'll just have to wait and see," I mumbled. I decided to change the subject. "What are you making that smells so delicious?"

"Oh, Lida and I are preparing for a baking fundraiser in Winchester. She was supposed to be here an hour ago."

"She's probably busy with Nick. You know, he needs all the time he can get," I said, thinking that Lida was probably giving him a lecture on driving more carefully or eating something other than the chips he so loved.

Grandma offered me a croissant, then handed me a cup of coffee. It instantly filled my veins with hot liquid and energy. We sat across from each other at the breakfast table. Her glasses were pushed so low on the bridge of her nose that I wondered how long it would take for them to fall, hit the tablecloth, and take the shape of over-easy eggs under the table. It never happened.

We watched the news for a moment, "ooh-ing" and "ah-ing" about the weather girl's outfit and the shades the oak tree by our window had turned this fall, when I remembered I had forgotten to grab my cellphone from the vanity. I knew Dad would not leave me alone until I texted him back, so I ran up the landing and peeked inside of the room, which now was bathed in sunlight. There was no cellphone on my vanity. In fact, I couldn't find it at all. I searched the bed covers, sleeping bag, bathroom toiletries, and inside of the chest of drawers. I considered blaming Charlie for having my cellphone for breakfast. I even thought that Nick might have snuck it from under the bed when I wasn't paying attention. Both of those assumptions were unlikely, though. I must have misplaced it.

Flustered, I ran down the stairs, avoiding a barking Charlie. He was pulling a toy tied around one of the posts.

"Is there a fire?" Grandma asked, throwing me a concerned gaze while I stomped around the living room opening drawers.

"I can't find my phone. I have looked everywhere," I said quickly, tearing apart a bag by the door.

"Well, you are not going to find it throwing stuff around. Do you know where you last had it?" Grandma asked, standing up from her chair.

"I have already checked that place," I said, then threw my arms in the air. "Nick is going to meet me at our treehouse, and I don't have time to search for it now."

"He has a phone with him. I can call you. That's all that matters. It will find itself, don't worry," she said, and I felt the anxiety subside.

"All right," I agreed, sighing deeply. "Love you, Grams. I will see you later, okay?" I said cheerfully.

In the doorway, I stopped for a moment, as I had forgotten something more important than a piece of technology. I ran up to Grandma, wrapped my hands around her waist, and hugged her, going back in my memories to the days when she would rock me softly in the crib, singing. When I became older, she would sit beside me on the bed, hands turning the pages of *The Wizard of Oz*, her angelic voice going through chapters like she knew every word written inside by heart. I felt like I was an amber locket on her chest. She treasured me, kept me under her heart— her precious cargo. I was submerged in her affection, floating merry and carefree.

"Love you too. Get home safe," Grandma responded.

She continued watching the weather girl, and I, dressed in my burnt orange coat, headed to the treehouse.

* * *

Oh, how much I wished for the rain! For its mischievous play on the leaves and its resemblance to Chopin's nocturnes. For sabotaging someone's day and being a simple inconvenience. What I loved most was its spontaneous droplets on umbrellas, bubbles popping, sliding on the flow of water into the drains, the feeling of unanimity with everything rain-affected. Helmets of motorcyclists, roofs of old houses, windshields of cars. It all came together so easily into an outdoor play, an unforgettable orchestra of nature. I couldn't be a prouder spectator. My heart loved the rain, even more so a thunderstorm. The weather girl had promised me just that.

The treehouse rested on the branches of three oak sisters. It used to look like a fairy tale home for the gnomes of the Snow White. We build it with our dads, panel after panel, on the grounds of an old church in Harpers Ferry. As the seasons faded through the pages of a calendar, Nick and I preserved it, repairing what needed to be fixed and praying no wild animal would find it appealing to live inside.

From the treehouse, far beyond our line of vision, the landscape opened up into a river and a majestic mountain. It was a place to open a jewelry box full of dreams. A place to come back to in a state of reverie while looking at the glistening, star-scarred sky. The silky mountain and the forest seemed bathed in blue smoke, and the emerald hills looked like waves over the sky. The first time Nick climbed a hanging ladder into the treehouse, he was breathless. He told me afterward that a house located so high made the mountain look tiny. The strings of his very heart were pulled, which he tried to hide. I didn't dare to expose him; after all, he had confided in me.

Apart from the natural conveniences of a house in the woods, we possessed a twin bed, two lanterns, a couple of patio chairs and a marble table, a pair of teal curtains, and one headlamp. From a Ferry fundraiser sophomore year, we had gotten a collection of plates, a kettle, and some antique silver spoons, which were all stored in a messy compartment underneath the bed. When night, like a raven, spread its wings over the town, I hung the lights from the railing. I welcomed the levitating spirit of the wilderness into my heart. It soothed me, calming the darkness that sometimes overshadowed my life. I would watch the candles in the windows of the Ferry light up and then go off one last time before the sun raided the hills. The light in Mr. Wolf's window, the town's last living era historian, always shone through the night. The old man was simply afraid of the dark or so we assumed.

I followed a curvy trail into the woods. The grass looked as if someone had put a hand on it and gently brushed it to the ground. I had mapped out the roads that led to the treehouse, studied the turns, and calculated the mileage. I learned to identify the trees by the bark and their growing fungus, hollow inside the oaks. I knew where bucks rubbed their antlers and rabbits left their pawprints. The forest was my lurid beauty untainted by blood and gunshots, and I wanted to keep it that way.

I approached the treehouse, absorbing the chirping of birds, the rustle of leaves under my feet, and one steady drumming of a woodpecker beak. The light streamed through the tree branches, playing with the shadows on my face. First it was dark, and then bright again, continuously changing as the moving carnival of leaves shook and swirled. The forest breathed with freshness. I could hear it inhaling. Ink melted off of the sun, dipping the treetops in gold.

"Hey, Beccs!" I heard a familiar voice. Nick was leaning over the railing, waving at me. "Wait a second; I'll throw you the rope."

"Okay," I said, trying to look up to where he was standing. The sun was blinding me.

I heard Nick shuffle across the wood floor. I rubbed my hands on my coat to make myself warm, walking in circles, and waited until he lowered the rope ladder. I began climbing, looking back at the ground as the ladder swayed, but soon I felt Nick's fingers find mine.

Nick held my hand tight as he helped me off the rope ladder. We dragged it up and let it sit there, twisted like an old pair of headphones. Staring at my dearly-missed landscape, my mind wandered to Nick's face. His smile held countless stars on a dark winter morning.

"Haven't you missed this place?" he asked, handing me his flannel scarf and a silver thermos.

Hills in festivity. And clouds, like cotton puffs, gathered together in the shape of the *Pegasus* constellation. I sighed. "I sure did."

"Becca, what is going on inside of your mind?" Nick asked suddenly with the softest tone of voice. "You seem… I don't know. Bothered. I let it go yesterday because I thought that you were tired. Do you really expect me to drag it out of you?"

"You wouldn't believe me, even if I tried to tell you," I said, feeling a wave of blood rushing to my face.

"Why don't you just tell me instead of hiding whatever it is that's worrying you, and maybe I can help you.." Nick leaned over the railing. He was magnetizing with his openness, his sincerity. No one ever looked out for me the way he did.

I turned my head away in the direction where the crowns of the trees formed a circle. I remembered colorful scarves and tarot cards, and a cold feeling ran down my spine.

"I went to see a fortune teller," I said finally. "Before you say that it sounds stupid, believe me, I know." My hands began to tremble.

Nick didn't judge. Not as I expected. "Did she say something to you or do something that made you feel this way?"

"Well, she said…" It was hard to sum it all up. Once I laid the words on the wind, it would become very real, and I was afraid of real. "She told me that I was some sort of sacrifice. Like I would die." There, I said it.

Nick shivered. "That's pretty harsh." He sat down in one of the lounge chairs. "I think you just have to let it go. It may be hard, but if you don't focus on it, you won't have this omen follow you."

"Nick, it's all I can think about."

"That's why people don't see fortune tellers— because of things like that. You make yourself believe in it. And then find yourself fulfilling the premonition. You will drive yourself crazy thinking about it."

Nick's hair was brushed by a gentle breeze. His bangs fell on the left side of his forehead. I wondered if he knew how gorgeous it looked on that side. He usually wore it the opposite way.

"I think I already do. I'm starting to hallucinate."

"What? Did you see the Grim Reaper moving on you from the shadows?" Nick asked, borrowing my thermos.

"Something like that," I said and laughed from the silliness of it.

The wind blew through the branches, sweeping the leaves off the treehouse's boards, sending them cruising onto the ground. I shivered and pulled my beanie back over my ears.

Suddenly we heard a rumble of the leaves beneath us, a loud hissing and swaying of grass. We rushed to look at what caused the commotion and saw the end of an orange tail disappearing into the fog past the roots of the trees. A nest, torn apart, was floating on the wind. Branches like spikes were sticking from every corner. I saw one little bird lifting its beak into the air. It hid its head into the nest, spread its wings— as if it were ready to fly— and leaned on the branches in search of shelter. Vulnerable and all alone. One bird facing the darkness, the fear, this harrowing turn of events. Its mom was lying in the leaves, only feathers wafting on the wind. The picture tore my heart to pieces.

"You know what I'm about to say…" Nick whispered as I wiped the brown mud from my jeans, standing up from the broken nest site.

"It is not fair, Nick. You wasted all this time telling me the fortune teller didn't know what she was talking about, like her warnings don't mean a thing."

"Oh, I don't believe they mean anything but you do. That's where your mind just went. Isn't that right?" He smiled and patted me on the shoulder.

I didn't respond. Instead, I stared at the bird that was facing the unknown. Alone. Nothing ever happened to me that didn't have an underlying meaning. And whatever that feeling was had just become darker.

* * *

I was watching a tangerine sunset slide under the roofs of the houses while rocking on the swing set on Grandma's wraparound porch. The train in the distance had just picked up its pace, and the air smelled of waffle cones and cinnamon. As I retreated inside, Lida came out of the living room holding a golden cupcake trophy. She sat it on the floor and hurried towards me, locking me in her arms like a child with her favorite teddy bear.

"Let me look at you!" she said with excitement. I felt like I was a museum exposition. "What a beautiful lady you raised, Galia. Sure, she would be a lovely bride," Lida said and peered at Grandma in the living room, who was knitting a sweater.

"She is still too young to be a bride. Have to get a broomstick out of the closet to shoo all the boys away," I heard Grandma's faint voice say.

I felt my cheeks burning. "How was your fundraiser? Raised enough money for the Historical Society?" I asked.

"No, not even half," Lida explained. "They don't need that money. They have so many rich people donating, but it's worth this golden cupcake." She picked it up again and carried it to its proud spot on the shelving, mumbling in Russian.

"Are you guys going to polish that thing now?"

"No, we are saving it for you to polish," Lida replied.

"And the whole drawer of silverware for Nick," Grandma added.

I let out a groan. They were being silly, but I didn't want to take my chances.

"Did Nick leave?" I asked, setting my shoes close to the stairwell, fixing the family photo on the wall that was lopsided.

"Yes, honey. He said he needed to develop the photographs for tomorrow's exhibition."

"All right, then. Would be nice if he said goodbye. I'm going upstairs. It's been a long day, and I need to get some sleep."

"Sleep tight," Grandma said and continued knitting.

When I entered the room, I felt that same cold feeling. The window had been forced open, and the curtains bounced up and down on the breeze. I turned the lights on, and my gaze fell upon the quilt. My phone buzzed under the darkness, screen glowing all shades of blue. Only the wind chimes were warbling in the night as if they held a secret of their own.

SEVEN
GETTYSBURG

The Historical Society building stood on a narrow street surrounded by maple trees. Broad rectangular windows acted as a prism for the light that fell onto the dusty desks, in between the maps rolled into tubes and velvety book holders. The building had one of the nicest mahogany staircases in the county, its animal-shaped form swirling to the second floor, opening up into a gallery of countless boxes and Civil War relics.

Night after night, the light shone inside of the building's windows. Shadows of Historical Society workers playing on concrete diffused from above. They wheeled the carts full of boxes, carried them carefully to the shelves, and stacked them on each other like dominos. And when the workers were gone, there was just one lonely figure in the window after dark, head tilted towards the desk, digging through the town's archives. Most times, before we grew up and moved away, it was Nick's figure up there. At first, he was just a spectator, but slowly he became a catalog prodigy who taught and assisted Harpers Ferry newcomers.

Mr. Ira Wolf, a Historical Society curator, watched over the visitors for years like a hawk, making sure their sticky fingers were nowhere near his precious boxes. When one evening he spotted Nick sitting at one of the desks, looking through the letters of Civil War soldiers, fingers gently caressing the yellow pages, he didn't find it in himself to just pass by. Instead, he brought the light back up, took out his magnifying glass from the leather cover, and slid into one of the adjacent chairs. He knew exactly what line to point out with his long-wrinkled fingers. There they were: both old and young minds mingled together with strings of history. They soon became a mentor and a mentee.

When the maple tree outside of Mr. Wolf's window lost its last leaf and rotted to the ground, he knew the same was happening to his body. Cold winter mornings brought tenderness to his muscles, his wrists ached with the rain, and he could no longer recognize the phases of the moon. Was it because of his blurry vision? Or, perhaps, forgetfulness? The maple tree still kept its secret. Mr. Ira Wolf retired, and, being the lonely poet of golden autumn, he began to write. That was the only thing that kept him going—recording history, dipping his feather into the ink under the dimmed light of a burning candle. He almost never left the house, and so grocery bags promptly delivered to his doorstep lay on the porch, plastic rustling in the wind.

Mr. Wolf recognized Nick's gift for photography a while back when he showed him the Gettysburg battlefield and discovered that each picture Nick took of the grounds revealed something he had never noticed before. There would be orbs in the trees; the moon, instead of silver, would drip crimson; water would gleam gray instead of bright blue; and there would be fog, dense even under the myriads of shining stars. Mr. Wolf donated a quiet room in the left-wing of the Historical Society for Nick's art and hoped that his gift would subside. Through the years, he was right. The photographs remained locked inside a little room with no sunlight, exactly like the lifelessness that they depicted. Oddly enough, in New York, Nick's photographs thrived. Somehow that eeriness was no longer present. It was only in Harpers Ferry that a photograph of a green forest turned to one of lifeless branches with no leaves on them.

I, on the other hand, believed that he had a talent, and the lifelessness of his photos was just another way he stood out from the crowd. Yes, the photographs made me cringe, but I also admired them in some twisted way. I couldn't see why Mr. Ira Wolf would try to lock them away in a tiny room. They should be allowed to cruise the world just like any other art out there. They should be allowed to live.

I was drying the dishes in the kitchen when the phone rang. Grams was upstairs taking a shower, and I shoved the last dinner plate onto the shelf, hurrying to answer the call. Lida's merry voice boomed through the speaker, and that was how I found out that Nick had already gone to his photo laboratory, like some crazy scientist who woke with the rise of the sun. Gulping the coffee down with one hand and brushing my hair with the other, I grabbed a pair of shoes out of the closet and headed to the Historical Society, hoping to run into Nick— either by coincidence or a pleasant, well-planned surprise.

The last time I visited this place, I had had to write a history paper on John Brown's Raid and had spent all afternoon on the second floor researching the archives. Back then, while glancing out of the window during my coffee breaks, I had gazed at the fountain. It now glistened in the middle of the empty square. I was certain it had been under renovation for a few years.

Now the plastic was pulled off, the giant construction ladders were moved, and the statues were no longer pale and washed out. It had finally become an antique accessory to this old Civil War town, thanks to the generous donations of the people who lived here.

The fountain's centerpiece was a statue of a girl. She was giggling, catching birds with her hands. Her form overlooked vast blocks of marble that came together in a circle, creating steps. The sun peaked in the sky, and the water glowed white, making it easy to see the faces of the coins resting at the bottom. They were all different in shape and color as if someone had drowned their entire coin collection in its waters. *I should make a wish*, I thought.

I dropped a coin into the fountain and watched it join the others until it chimed against the limestone. I lifted my head and saw the angels scattered at the fountain's sides, tiny stone hands directing the flowing water down into a cradle. Feeling upbeat, I stretched my hand to the hand of the girl statue to say "hello" and lay my head down onto the steps, studying the clouds. *Nick will be here any second.*

I must have laid there for about twenty minutes daydreaming, because I soon heard the church bells ringing in the distance. There was also another ringing in my ear, and it didn't belong to the bells. I rose from the steps, my elbow keeping me steady, and I saw bubbles suddenly coming out of the fountain. They were gurgling, boiling, and popping. I touched the water to see where the bubbles were coming from, but from my nearness, they subsided. On cue, I pulled my hand away and the bubbles returned. *What the hell is going on?* I thought.

People were now bursting out of the Historical Society building, but no one noticed anything. I kneeled over the marble and soaked the sleeve of my shirt. The surface of the water looked shimmery— the light penetrated it in such a way that the gold and silver of the coins made the water a tint darker. I dusted the water with my hand, creating soft waves, and gazed at my own reflection as the ripples appeared. The warmth of the water made me feel at ease. I was about to make it splash, but the water shaped into what appeared to be a hand. In an instant, it clutched onto me, yanking me forward and trying to drag me in. I screamed and pushed my legs as hard as I could against the ground. I lurched away from the fountain, still catching my breath. *That's enough. I am losing my mind.* I stared at the fountain from behind the bench, my face hiding in between the wooden cracks, but the bubbles never returned. The fountain functioned just like any other time before.

I heard familiar footsteps break through the hum of people's voices. Maple trees whispered their lullaby to the wind while squirrels ran in circles, climbing up trees. Nick walked swiftly, leather duffel bag swinging on his shoulder, disheveled hair the color of a barley field. He must have spent the entire morning and early afternoon developing his photographs. He hadn't noticed me at first, and only when the wave of his cologne hit me with the scent of pine needles and hazelnuts did I retreat from the shadows, leaving my cardigan ruffling on the wind. I pulled at his jacket.

"Hey there, stranger," I said, my voice cheerful and steady as it slashed through the air.

He peered down at me for a moment without making sense of who I was. Once he recognized my silhouette, he brought his art pad behind his back. He was lost in the state of reverie or exhaustion from his sleep-deprived nights, but his face glowed with delight.

"Becca! Where did you come from?" he asked.

"From your dreams, silly," I said and smiled brightly while he wrapped his arms around my waist.

"Then I better start dreaming again. You look so beautiful today," he said, playing with the yellow bandana on my head, which perfectly matched the lilac dress and navy ballerina shoes I had brought home with me from DC.

"Thank you, friend. I appreciate your kindness."

As the words reached his heart, he looked away, fallen into the world of thought.

"I tell you what, since you're here anyway, would you be willing to ride with me to Gettysburg? They're in the process of designing this Civil War collage for the Harpers paper, and I happen to have gained enough of their trust to add my personal touch. I need those photographs. And I need them today," he said and sighed, hope glistening in his eyes. "I also promised Mr. Wolf," he added. "I'm exhausted, so we won't be long. We'll be back in time for dinner."

"Oh my gosh, yes! I'd love to watch you work. You know as well as I do that it's such a big deal for you! We should celebrate when we are back. But first, we need to get you a cup of coffee and do something with that hair of yours."

"What's wrong with my hair?" he wondered with sincerity. I reached over and brushed Nick's hair with my fingers, and he giggled, pulling away.

"Nothing. You look like a bird. A cute tropical bird with messed up feathers."

We walked towards downtown Ferry, and as the sun fringed the sky with its apricot light, I noticed our shadows gliding on the pavement. They were like nothing I had ever seen before.

* * *

If you ever stood on top of the highest mountain, your legs would go numb— not from the height but from the view itself. From the feeling of pure awe. A place where summer fell at your feet and winter grazed from the mountain peaks. Then you could imagine what Gettysburg felt like when you looked at it from a hill. You waved summer goodbye as you stared into the wide, wild, and fiery eyes of autumn, drifting by with a mist made of leaves. Both had always left me breathless.

While Nick adjusted his raven-colored camera stand, zooming in and out on the golden fields of sorrow with his Canon lenses, I wrapped my hands around the trunk of a witness tree at Picket's Charge. It was a centuries-old swamp oak with cannonballs and shells so deeply merged into the grain of the wood that I felt like I was putting my hands on the Civil War's last standing descendant. Nevertheless, it was the most magnificent feeling ever.

The rain had almost stopped, and only once in a while did the sun shift the clouds apart and pour light onto the monument alley, the brass cannons, and a myriad of scattered wildflowers. It seemed that my hearing was deceiving me because in the distance, I could hear the echoing of hooves growing stronger and louder.

"Nick, do you hear the horses?" I asked, carefully stepping down from the giant roots of the oak.

He lifted his head towards the wind, listening, then glanced back at me and said, "No, I don't." He turned to catch the shadows on the monuments. "There were about a million horses and mules that died in the Battle of Gettysburg on these grounds, so you may hear them running free, just like people hear the bursting cannons as residual energy."

"And you believe that's true?"

"No, but I'm not going to ignore the fact that people reflect on those things."

"Right," I mumbled in response.

He shook his head. "Why are you asking? Do you believe in ghosts?"

"Yes and no. But you know what? It's silly. My imagination is stronger than my beliefs these days." I tapped the grass down with my hands, waiting for it to tell me a story. It felt cool and fresh, like the morning dew.

The sky turned gray and lifeless, and the wind decided the battlefield grounds were to be its rendezvous. My inner voice of reason told me that ghosts didn't exist, but my intuition was portraying quite a different picture. Maybe the feeling of being watched didn't constitute paranormal occurrence, but there still was an undeniable chill in the air, the candlelight that suddenly faded in a farmhouse window, and the curtains that shifted in a room with no wind. Such occurrences didn't have an explanation, nor did they need one. Those things just existed.

I ran my eyes across the fields. In places like this, sorrow for lives lost settled in my heart. The statues of Civil War regiments drowned in that sorrow as if we had entered a forbidden forest of unfulfilled dreams. I tried not to be drawn inside of it; I knew that magic would happen when the sun reappeared again, bringing back all the colors from the gray. That sullenness would drift into eternity just like the gloominess that was left after the rain.

Nick's back was the color of amber as his hunched form surrendered to the wet leaves to take a perfect photograph of the 71st Pennsylvania Infantry monument. His face— so familiar, yet so unknown— drew me in, natural rouge from the wind slightly covering his cheeks. Grandma's words appeared in my memory, even though I tried to push them away. He was standing in front of me, so exposed, so concentrated, and I was at an advantage. I could admire him all day without being noticed. Even if he were in love with me, would that be such a bad thing?

As if Nick had heard my thoughts, he looked up at me and smiled.

"You want to go for a walk? I think I'm done for today. The sun is setting. The hills will be purple, if you can believe it. We don't want to miss it," he said, putting a plastic cover on the camera lens.

I nodded. "Sure."

"Here, can you hold on to this for me while I pack up the rest of the equipment?" He handed me a sketch pad and his camera stand.

I placed the stand carefully onto the ground by my feet and, holding onto the pad, began turning the pages. At first, it looked like a collage of paintings, but then there were photographs corresponding to the markings. Headings and encryptions in bold. Shadows walking through the fields with undeniable frames of uniforms, boots, and forages. Suddenly the sketch pad shut in front of my very eyes.

"I gave it to you to hold, not to peek through," Nick said. His voice was steady and cold as he retrieved the pad out of my hands.

"Those look like ghosts," I said, confused.

Nick scoffed nervously. "Yeah, right."

"Then, what are they?" I insisted, staring him down.

Nick ignored my question but shifted in my direction, trying to place a hand over my shoulder. "C'mon," he said brightly, almost too upbeat to be genuine. "Let's go on that walk."

I moved away from him, hooking my eyes on the pad, then his face. "Nick, can you photograph ghosts?"

Nick let out a laugh that seemed unnatural, even to me. "Becca, do you hear yourself? Ghosts? That's insane."

I inched closer to him until there was no distance between us. "Nick," I said softly.

He raised his eyebrows as if he were going to say something but stopped. I shook my head.

He sighed deeply, closed his eyes for a moment, and then let out a breath. "Yeah," he said quietly. "They are ghosts."

"Did you take those? Why didn't you tell me you can capture the ghosts?" I asked.

"Because I wasn't aware myself until recently. Turns out that Matt Brady, a photographer from the Civil War, was my direct ancestor. They say he saw such horrific things at the battles that they left a burn on his soul. He wasn't aware of spirits, but he passed down through his descendants a gift that I seem to possess. In

Antietam, the ghosts are prominent and easier to spot. Same with Gettysburg, which is why I brought you here. I thought I was crazy until you told me about that fortune teller. But then I read about paranormal activity here. And things became different," Nick explained, shoving the sketch pad into his duffel bag.

"You knew the entire time and didn't tell me?" I realized he was entitled to his secrets, but I felt like I deserved to know. It didn't seem fair.

"I hoped that you would forget all about it if I didn't bring it up. I didn't want to overcomplicate things. I can only see the ghosts in the photographs. It's not like they're wandering around trying to engage in a conversation with me," he explained.

"Maybe they are. Maybe you just don't know how to communicate with them. But for the record, it won't make the ghosts go away if you decide to ignore them. Next time, please don't lie to me." I shrugged and picked up the stand. "Is there anything else you're keeping from me? Now would be the time and place to tell me."

I saw his face burn ruby, but no response came off his lips. He was ashamed and that was something I didn't remember from childhood.

The sky was crisscrossed with the cries of birds, just like my mind was with its disarray of thoughts. We passed the statue of Union General John Gibbon. I followed his bronze eyes to the fields of glory and froze for a moment, thinking of the occasions he had spent looking into the eyes of the enemy from this same place, fearless. What an astounding example of bravery and honor so beautifully joined together in one general.

Nick walked behind me, pacing steps as if he was forgetting something. I reached over for his hand, but he pressed it against his thigh. He got lost again inside his own thoughts.

No matter where you looked in Gettysburg, even the bushes had their undeniable history; every stone, every bend in the road, carried a piece of remembrance of the days spent in battle. Nick spent that time looking at his feet when the scenery was all he had to admire.

When a stairwell opened into a view from the Pennsylvania Memorial right into the skies and the grounds, I could no longer contain myself.

"What in the world is going on with you? I promise I won't get mad again. I'm over it," I said, putting my hand on his shoulder.

"I didn't come back to Harpers Ferry for photography, Becca," he stated. "I came to be with you. All this distance and time we spent apart made me realize how much I missed being around you."

I slowly put my hand down. His warm breath on my cheek lingered down my neckline. Grandma was right.

"I don't understand," I mumbled in response, even though I knew what he was about to say. I just had to hear it.

"I want to see if we can be more than just friends," he said.

A surprised "huh" solidified on the wind. His eyes shone with excitement and only the irises betrayed him. Worry circled through them like an arc. He pulled me closer and his lips were slowly moving to mine. Because of the light piercing through the tree branches, his lips looked coral. I closed my eyes in anticipation. Then the melody of my cellphone cut through the air. Quickly glancing down at it, I saw that there was no caller ID on the screen—just a polka-dot colorful mirage of collected images all merged in one, like a phone that had been overheated or submerged underwater and then sat in rice for an hour. Nevertheless, it continued ringing.

I backed away from Nick, still staring at his lips. I felt my heart racing and my cheeks blushing. I closed my eyes for a moment, feeling the moment slip away. "Nick, I'm sorry. I need to get this," I said very gently. I put the phone just under my ear and heard nothing but soft breaths on the other line. Then the phone released a continuous monotone sound and went dead.

"Becca," Nick was calling my name. He had a look of concern on his face. He moved to hurry after me. It was so awkward; I wanted to be the wind. I wanted to be invisible.

"It's my dad calling. God only knows how many messages he has already sent," I retaliated, hoping Nick wouldn't follow me. "Do you mind if I just take a walk to that hill over there? I want to see if there is a signal…" I said, hiding my face away from him.

Nick's eyes followed my shape towards the fields. His eyes accumulated a storm inside of them. "Sure, go ahead. I'll go pack the car. It's a mess." Short, cold speech and a withdrawn gaze. It was inevitable.

I saw him headed towards his Mini Cooper, shoving the dust from the road with his sneakers. The pebbles scattered on the road in front of him supported by a cloud of dirt, but he didn't turn to look at me. He continued walking.

I dragged my feet along a broken road. Insects chirped in the tall grass, their tiny bodies hiding on the sharp points of the velvet stems. The bushes and trees in the distance became sinister without sunlight and as I walked, their shadows danced like monsters on the narrowing road.

Saved by the bell, I thought. How convenient. I was drenched in cold sweat. Why now? What was he thinking? I wasn't ready for this. I just wanted to get away— not get involved in another relationship. Damn it. Damn it. Damn it! I would just pretend to play by his rules and be nice... very nice. And try not to hurt his feelings or I'd lose him forever. I couldn't let that happen.

I didn't notice how I had waded into the field beyond the hill that was visible to Nick. There were two tiny baby raccoons staring at me from the opposite side of the road, one sitting on top of the other, two furry balls digging for food. They acknowledged my presence for a moment and went back to salvaging worms. I, on the other hand, waded further into the field and stopped by a rock formation that rose out of the ground.

I took off the phone's cover to have a better look at it when I noticed I was standing on something soft. It was a piece of fabric that stuck out from under the rock and was covered in sand and grass stains. I kneeled towards it and examined the spot: it was a gray wool garment. I needed to dig it out of the ground, so I took a line of rocks apart, one by one. What appeared to be a Confederate uniform at first wasn't a uniform but a faded cloth, and as I was pulling it out, a book came out with it. It had a leather belt wrapped around it and a rough, shabby cover. I pulled at the belt and the book blew open. The pages, with golden ink lines on the edges, glowed the color of Eastern European church domes. The paper was gossamer and yellowed with spots of garnet splatted in the lower corners. It reminded me of a soldier's old diary. I flipped the pages, and they rustled like an eighteen-century dress dragged on the floor. As if the book sensed me, a shadow raced through the fields like a dark sheet, drowning the entire scenery in its deathly breath. An echo vanished behind the hills. My heart beat fast in my chest. There was one word carved into a front cover: *Grimwood*.

"Rebecca!" I heard Nick's voice cut through the air behind me suddenly. "It's getting dark."

"I'm coming!" I yelled back, catching my breath.

I knew I couldn't leave the book on the field. I had to take it with me, so I wrapped it back in fabric and shoved it into my leather bag.

* * *

When we drove home through the forested roads, the fog settled heavily in the air. The birds sat in pairs on cable wires, tweeting. Nick switched the radio channel to country and kept his eyes on the road that swirled more than a dozen times, taking the car with it from one hill to another. This whole "in love" thing triggered paranoia inside of my brain. I expected awkward glances, holding of hands, words that, like tongue twisters, crossed the air and came out all wrong. But there was nothing, just the same old us and a bunch of boring highways, and I was fine with it. Tonight, I had been taken by surprise and needed time to figure things out.

Nick didn't come inside. He paced his steps into the night after waving "good night" in a haze of the fallen stars. I watched him drag his shape away from the house, the light of the moon shining brighter than my illuminated bedroom. If I offended him by keeping silent, it was not because I was trying to hurt him. I hoped he knew that. How was I supposed to let my heart decide if I didn't know what my heart desired?

Holding that thought, I crept into the bathroom when I noticed that the closet door had been left ajar and books were scattered on the floor—some wedged under the door, some lying around with broken spines and folded edges. I collected them into my arms, but gravity worked against me, and I soon found them lying loose at my feet once again. I wondered what had caused them to fall out of the closet. It looked like they were forced to bind together, and it was hard to separate them.

With a loud sigh, I shoved all the books back, leaving my duffel bag on the top of the vanity. I moved the boxes around, searching for my great-grandfather's camera that I had promised to Nick. These boxes— full of photo albums, antique candle holders, baseball cards, Russian dolls, a chess set, and other memorabilia— reminded me of times that I hadn't gotten to experience. Tucked away in a velvet purple cloth, which I unfolded corner by corner, lay a vintage camera with a little wobbly wooden stand, dusty on the leather surface but still in perfect shape.

When I took the lens cover off the camera and looked through the glass onto the vanity to get an angle for a photograph, I noticed that the diary was out of the bag and glowing. I slowly shifted my face away from the camera for a second, looking closer. This time, the diary was gone. I ran around barefoot, lifting the cushions from the carpet, searching behind the vanity, looking inside of quilts, bookshelves, closets, wardrobes and boxes, and came to only one reasonable conclusion. The damn book with the golden edges had just vanished.

EIGHT

STRANGER IN THE NIGHT

The day before Halloween, I woke up to the whisper of leaves being dragged by the wind. It was a cold autumn day in Harpers Ferry. B&B's café was full of guests, and the tables outside were pushed together, like a pile of tree branches. Steam from the hot brewed coffee and morning talk fogged up the windows of the B&B's. Suddenly people were wrapped in colorful scarves. They had unpacked their boots from the storage boxes and strolled the streets with pumpkins under their arms. The scent of cinnamon and apples circled the air, and all I wanted was to sit by the fireplace in the living room with a fleece blanket covering my feet.

The dream that had haunted me the night before wasn't like any other I had seen. I had traveled in time. I had found myself standing on the porch of a Civil War-era plantation home, maybe in South Carolina. There were three carved ivory lounges outside, shaded by the trees. An African-American man in a ripped linen shirt was folded in one of the chairs. Five children were at his feet, all carefully wrapped into white sheets, motionless. With his hands deformed by the hard work, he sobbed. Another man was coming his way. He had a gun on his shoulder. I longed to be a wall between them, protect him from the harm heading his way. Before I could do anything, I had opened my eyes.

The dream was so real, yet it was locked inside my mind. The vivid images left me feeling so emotionally deprived. I cried in the shower while the scent of the lavender spread all over my bedroom. The pain the man felt was curled up inside of me, and I started to think that I might be slightly psychic if I could hear, see, and feel an echo of the past.

Nick stopped by in the morning to give me a kiss on the cheek that smelled like peppermint shaving oil, and after placing my grandfather's camera inside of his duffel bag, he headed to the Historical Society. I couldn't tell him about the dream— not unless I was sure what I had been experiencing was real. After all, he had lied to me before.

Before Grandma headed to the farmer's market to get her secret ingredients for her world-famous pumpkin pies, she poked her head through the slit in the door and invited me to come along. I couldn't refuse.

The market we went to was located between Harpers Ferry and Gettysburg in a little Civil War history town outside of Frederick, Maryland. It was crowded with visitors and vendors. Tents extended to the streets of the town. Hay bales formed pyramids with ghost pumpkins and gourds on top with decorative Indian corn swinging from the tent poles. Scarecrows stuck out from the ground with brush-painted faces. A kid would stop by the scarecrows from time to time, pull on his father's sleeve, and hide behind his mother. It had always been a scene I loved to watch.

I lost sight of Grandma as soon as we came in. When that woman was on a shopping spree, you had better stay away or she would sweep you off your feet in an instant and run you over with a cart full of groceries afterward. I had to entertain myself. I walked in between the tents, picking up little heads of Brussel sprouts, weighing pumpkins on the scale, sorting through organic eggs. I had stumbled upon a line of people for the roasted corn when I heard a popping sound. Taken aback by the noise, I quickly dropped to the ground. Then I heard wild laughter, and two kids with locks of gold and fake pistols sprinted beside me like two maniacs. I wanted to chase them, but my attention was suddenly locked on the place by the jam and honey tents; Confederate soldiers were gathered next to a horse wagon, and all I could see were rows and rows of heads and the sun glistening off of their muskets— a re-enactment display. I stepped closer to the commotion, and that was when I saw him as clear as the bright blue sky: the man from my dream.

He appeared to be young and boyish, with freckles scattered on his nose. He stood with the soldiers in a gray jacket with brass buttons and a Virginia belt buckle. His dark buckeye hair played in the wind. He caught my gaze and tilted his head, motioning for me to follow him. He held something in his hand, and when I realized what it was, I couldn't believe it. The golden edges, the dark cover... it was the diary! It seemed that nobody else saw him except for me. I wanted to follow him, but everything inside of me told me not to.

As soon as the re-enactment began, the young man vanished, and I was left with an army of soldiers doing the rebel yell. I searched for a place where there were less people. Someone had arranged step-seating around the old oak by the corn and pumpkin carriages, and it appeared to be empty. I bolted there for a better observance spot when Grandma came out of the crowds with her arms full of bags.

"Thank God! I have been looking everywhere for you since they started the gun show! I was going to see if you waited by the car…" she said and suddenly stopped, noticing my pale face. "Are you okay, child? Have you eaten too much of that buttered corn?" Grandma asked, pushing her lips towards my forehead to check for temperature. "If you don't eat that in DC, you can easily get a little sick. Not to mention the flu going around."

I held on to my stomach, pretending to have cramps. "You're right, Grams. Just not feeling it today. We got to get back home before I decide to leave the insides of my stomach here."

"Of course, dear, let's just throw those pumpkins in, and we will be all done. Would you please hold on to your insides?" she teased me. Before we drove away from Frederick, I looked behind us at a stone bridge to make sure we weren't being followed. In the distance, I could only see the leaves waving at us with the wind. It was quiet, and the air coming through the open window was crisp and sweet. Leaning back onto the soft leather cushions, I allowed myself to let go of all my worries.

* * *

I forgot about the young man until I was reading Grandma's favorite book of poetry out loud. My body was submerged in the coverlet, legs forming the shape of a crossroads. The grandfather clock released three continuous chimes, and I saw the lights outside go off one by one, receding from view into the night like the tail of a comet. I slid one of the bathroom drawers open, looking for a wooden comb. Among the empty prescription bottles, nail polish, and hair ties, there was a butterfly pin that Dad claimed he had found in one of the gift shops in Harpers Ferry. I untangled it from the ribbons and carefully folded my bangs under it. Years had passed, but I still remembered the day he had brought it home. He had no idea what to do with a pin, but he said that I would look beautiful wearing it. Its iridescent glow hadn't faded nor had the childhood memory. Oh, how I missed him.

I combed my hair slowly, trying not to catch the pin with the comb's sharp teeth. On the opposite wall from the window, there was an antique silver mirror. I could see my reflection linger in the glass as if I was a stranger to myself. I watched the waves of my hair fall down my back in bouncy curls. I had to admit there was something therapeutic about combing long hair, making it as smooth as the surface of water, without a single tangle.

Suddenly, a face appeared in the reflection of the mirror. It was almost like a spark, hardly distinguishable, and yet I knew it was a face— a human face with thick black eyebrows, emerald eyes, high cheeks, and an aquiline nose. I only saw him for an instant, but his features burned clearly into my mind. My hair comb fell to the floor. I jolted to the side and closed my eyes. I could feel my heart beating hard out of my chest. As I brought my hands away from my face, I realized that the room was empty. The curtains were floating in the wind. The ticking of the clock seemed to correspond with the beating of my petrified heart.

I shifted towards the window, and the doorbell rang. On cue, I peered at the oak tree right by the front porch to see who was playing a prank on me, but there was no sign that anyone had ever approached the house. In a few seconds, the entire street was dazzling with lights. The cars were buzzing, their windshield wipers moving like the hands of my grandfather clock, humming. *What the hell is going on?* I wondered, panicking.

I squinted into the hallway and, seeing chandeliers on above the stairwell, I headed down. "Grams, is everything okay? Is there someone by the door?" I asked, holding on to the twisting handrail.

I saw her silhouette glide up the stairs in a white robe. She looked a bit feverish and ghostly. "Child, it's the middle of the night. What are you doing wandering around? Did you have a nightmare? There is chamomile tea in the pantry. It can help you sleep."

"Yes, Grams. I must have had a dream. I'm so sorry to wake you," I said and kissed her on the forehead. Charlie was twisted around her slippers like a snake.

"Wake me up if you need anything, all right? No more horror movie nights with Nick. I'll have to confiscate Lida's movie collection," Grams said and continued chattering, going down the landing: "What is that woman thinking? Giving kids *Nightmare on Elm Street*? I've got to have a talk with her…"

I watched her wade back into the darkness for a moment and then tiptoed back into my bedroom. As I shut the door, it released a whooshing sound. *Damn doors*, I thought.

Yet the doorbell rang over and over again as if someone was playing a melody. It must be trick-or-treaters. For them, Halloween started a day early. *I'll shove that candy down their pants!*

I bounced towards the door and, grabbing an entire bucket full of candy, stepped out onto the welcome mat. The book with golden pages was lying on the front step, each letter of the cover glowing. *Grimwood.* My heart sank.

"Grams?" I called into the house but no one came out. Not even the dog.

I approached the steps. "Hello? Is anyone out there?" My voice echoed, lost in the multitude of lampposts.

The lights were still igniting the roads and trees like an electrified veil, as if they were supernatural. As soon as I picked up the book, it trembled in my hands and unlocked. I watched it glow, petrified. In the corner of my eye, I noticed a figure emerging out of the dark. I let out a scream and ran inside, holding the book against my chest. Then I shut the door and pressed my back against the doorframe, listening to the footsteps following mine and coming closer. I breathed heavily for a moment, checking in the gaps and crevices of the windows if the figure outside was gone. Suddenly it became quiet— so quiet, in fact, I could hear myself gulping.

The footsteps faded. Then I waited and waited.

There was no movement behind the locked door. The porch light buzzed as if the bulb inside the glass lantern had malfunctioned. From the kitchen window, I noticed a black cat sitting on the cement next to a flower bush, staring at me. Her eyes shone a dark lemon color. I left the chandelier lights on and quickly headed upstairs. I had to barricade the door with pillows, close the shutters on the window, drink three cups of tea, and place pepper spray next to the bed to finally fall into a deep sleep.

It was strange to run through a field of wet grass; my legs drowned in the golden carpet of flowers. There was nothing else around. The sun had just shown its face from behind a hill, and I saw a thick line of fog that lay on top of the grass. Someone was watching me. I felt their gaze crawling up my spine. I turned around to find a woman in a white dress and long black hair standing behind me, breathing down my neck. Startled, I gasped and fell, and she instantly vanished.

The air was fresh, like an ocean breeze, and I walked slowly through the field towards a tree that seemed to shine in the distance. It was a majestic oak tree with a thick brown trunk. I felt sweat accumulating on my forehead when I saw what looked like a lion peering at me from within the fog. My heart stopped beating while I observed the monster. It had long streaks of fur and cold scarlet eyes that glinted. I noticed its claws, and its tail reminded me of a flame. Its eyes were wide and dangerous and seemed to be hunting me through the field. I only saw its shape rising in and out of the fog. I was trapped prey without a place to hide. I knew I had to run. My feet were soaking wet with water, mud, and grass. I fell to my knees only once, stumbling on a rock. The monster was a ghoul. When it chased me, I knew it would take me. I had no choice but to climb a tree if I wanted to live. I didn't know how, but I managed to pull myself up and hold tightly to an oak branch. The monster soon found me. He began making his way up the tree. He was covered in blood; his angry eyes were aimed at me, his teeth sinking into the trunk.

And then the unexpected happened— the branch snapped underneath me, and I fell into the darkness. The last thing I remembered was the monster's eyes forever imprinted on mine.

I woke up staring at a face. His face— the man from my dream. He looked startled, like I had surprised him. His gaze was soft, but at the same time, so serious. Green eyes reminded me of frosted sea glass. His arms were wrapped around my waist as if we were dancing together, their warmth spreading through me like electricity. It seemed he couldn't believe he was holding me. Was I captivating? Was I a girl from his past? Why was his gaze lingering on me? Why didn't I fear him? Why didn't I scream? Was I still dreaming?

I felt a raindrop on my skin. Then a thunderous roll poured out of the sky. I wasn't dreaming. I was levitating. I was falling from the roof of the house with lavender curtains, and there was no lion hunting me, just a stranger holding us in place a couple of feet off the ground by means of... magic. The man from the Farmer's Market in the same gray jacket. He was tall, masculine, broad-shouldered, and had hair the color of espresso, which moved freely with the wind. His face shone with youthfulness, a natural blush giving Bordeaux color to his high cheekbones. The corners of his mouth formed a genuine smile and his lips, full and raspberry-tinted, complimented the emerald in his eyes. He carefully lifted me up from the air, where we drifted holding onto nothing, and placed me onto the rooftop without saying a word. All this time, I felt like there was a connection between us that I couldn't quite pinpoint. It felt strange and foreign, but it was there.

The man watched me for a moment, as if he was making sure I was okay, and then gave me a salute. He vanished into the night, leaving me alone and breathless on the roof. This man had just saved my life.

* * *

To say I didn't think about the man would be a lie. It wasn't simple curiosity; it was more of a quest for an explanation of what had happened. Each time I closed my eyes, I was afraid that a demon would chase me and kill me. The line between what was real and what was not had been erased, and it was troubling. What I felt towards him couldn't have been my imagination. I could touch him, and I could smell him. There was a possibility that I had drunk too much of Grandma's tea, but my intuition had never misled me before, and I doubted that that was the case this time.

There were mud prints on the sheets, and my pajama pants hung on the armchair soaking wet. That served as the ultimate proof of me being chased. Nothing confirmed the existence of the man with bright green eyes, however. Nonetheless, I wasn't one to give up. I spent hours on the roof trying to figure out how two people could fly without falling, hoping that maybe I would see him again or that I could spot him watching me. My attempts didn't bear any fruit. And to make matters worse, I had to keep it a secret from Nick and Grams, because they would have locked me up in an insane asylum if they found out.

The night of Halloween, I had a migraine. The kind that kept me in bed and left me feeling nauseous. I needed to rest my eyes, but I feared the monsters. I had no idea how I could make it through the night.

I happened to look out of the window, hoping to spot the stars over the train tracks, but instead, I saw the man from the Farmer's Market standing alone on the road. My heart jolted. I could see his silhouette projected from the streetlight. His hands were behind his back; his attire seemed darker than a widow's face. He was gesturing for me to come down. At once, I stepped aside from the window, and hid behind the wall and the curtain. I slowly poked my head to spy at him, but this time the road appeared empty.

My feet sank inside of the soft plush carpet. I surrendered backward in the direction of the bed. I stumbled on a chest, which caused me almost to fall over when I realized that someone was holding me in place. My eyes met his, and as I screamed, he muffled me by holding the palm of his hand to my lips.

"Shhhhh… I mean you no harm, that's a promise, but you have to believe me. I am here to warn you about the diary." His voice was firm and convincing. My hands trembled as he released his grip around my arm.

"How did you get in here?" I was taken aback for a moment, but at the same time, I knew I was protected. I immediately felt safe with him.

"I came through the window. I'm not a big fan of doors. It's that creak they make; it gets to me," he explained. There was a smile that ran swiftly across his face, but he tried hard to hide it.

I knew he wasn't lying about the diary— I read it in his eyes. How? I had no idea. It was a matter of trusting a total stranger. After all, he had saved my life. I might have been a fool, for all I knew. He was right about the doors, though. I hated that sound too.

"Leave, then, if you really mean me no harm," I whispered, not believing I was actually saying this so sternly. I didn't know anything about him. Under my bedroom chandelier, the man looked handsome; his eyes were the most distinguishable feature on his face. It was like they had changed colors— from amber to green and back.

"Please let me introduce myself first before you push me out the door," he said and offered me his hand, which now felt cold to the touch.

"I'm Derek Cromwell, the gatekeeper. The kind of man you would see guarding the gate to the old cemetery. Sentinel to the world of the dead. Would you mind if I take a seat?" he asked.

I nodded, watching him move past me with confidence. He had manners, and there was a smudge of adulthood that lay on his face despite him being so young. He took a seat on the ottoman by the four-poster bed. He was fit; his torso radiographed through the cotton fabric of his shirt.

"So, you are really a Sentinel? And it is God's honest truth? Not some Halloween prank?" I asked.

"The gatekeeper. I like it better," he corrected me. "If I wanted to make a prank of it, I would have dressed accordingly, wouldn't you agree?" A smile brushed off his lips.

"What's up with that old book? It isn't even mine," I explained, studying the curve in his eyebrows. His gaze was chained to the floor.

Once Derek was done thinking, he pulled his hair up and tilted his head.

"It belonged to one of your ancestors from the Civil War. Please accept my humble apologies. I thought you knew." There was a brief pause that followed. He studied the dreamcatcher swinging off the four-post bed and then continued: "So when was the last time you had a dream that made you jump off a roof, Rebecca?" he asked carefully, running his eyes over my frame. There was no sarcasm in his voice. He was genuinely concerned.

He knew my name! My eyes became wide. "Since when do you care about what dreams I'm having? You show up here unannounced, scaring me half to death, and now you delve into my life?" I felt my cheeks burning ruby.

Derek's face barely changed. It was as if a fog came over him. I must have stirred something inside of him.

"I wouldn't have asked if I didn't think it was of high importance. Please accept my apologies again. With all due respect, you have been *this* close to dying," he said, tracing an inch with his fingers. "I was worried about the outcome of your nightly adventures. If, in the future, you prefer no interference from my part, I would gladly honor your wishes," he said gallantly, but I felt like he was lying; there was no way he would have let me die. I saw the way he studied my face.

"I will forever be grateful you saved my life," I stated. "It's just… it's a lot to take in."

"Well… sure it is. You don't need to thank me, it's my duty," he said, following my eyes across the room.

"How did you manage to save us from falling?" I asked, but I heard no response.

Instead, he grimaced at my concerned expression. Then he stood up and walked around the room, admiring the artwork on the walls of my bedroom.

"Harpers Ferry viaducts are powerful structures. Elegant and yet so powerful," he commented, admiring Nick's photography.

I picked up the diary from the nightstand where Derek had laid it before. I turned around to find him standing beside me, looking over my shoulder at the inscription on the book.

"Some call it the path to salvation, others a journey through the depths of hell. This Civil War diary belonged to your ancestor, Shawn Grimwood. You happen to be its next Keeper, Rebecca. The way you handle this task will affect generations of lives," he said with pride. Our hands joined on the book's spine, which began to glow gold like the color of the sunrise.

"I don't know what it means," I stated, breathing in the aroma of times past.

"It means you have to protect it at all costs, just like your ancestors," he explained, still standing beside me, the scent of the pines floating around us.

"From what?" I asked, the echo of my voice ricocheting against the walls of my bedroom. He removed his hand from the golden cover, and it stopped glowing.

"A dark demonic energy that will try to take possession of the diary," he explained, and my heart skipped a beat. Demons? *I don't think I can handle this.*

"It's no easy task for a human, but if you let me, I can guide you." I felt his breath on my skin. He smelt of cherries and campfire.

"I didn't ask for any of this," I protested, still listening to his soft voice in my ear.

"I am afraid you don't have any choice. The diary chose your family line long before you were born."

"Let's assume I survive this demon attack— which sounds unrealistic, by the way— how in the world do I keep the diary safe from the demons?"

"Keeping it in the closet among other relics is the safest place for it yet. If you happen to leave the house, I would plan on taking it, because you can't leave it unattended. There is one problem, though. You don't know when a demon will try to take it out of your hands. Make sure you always bring it back home." He paused, his shining eyes amber. "You must never leave it lying around without an attendee unless it's locked up in that closet," he said, and he pointed at the dusty room.

I glanced at Derek in disbelief. He looked nineteen, maybe, if I could guess.

"How do you fit into all of this? Is stalking people part of your job description, Derek?" I asked, opening the closet and placing the diary inside.

"I am here to protect the diary and make sure it finds its designated Keeper. I am here to establish the balance among the ghosts and demons. I had to find you once you threatened the relic's safety. That's all there is to it."

"Wait... you followed me to Harpers Ferry all the way from DC?" There was a note of bewilderment in my voice as I shut the closet door.

"Like I said, you made me run around like a mouse in its wheel. But there is nothing I wouldn't do to protect the relic," he said, staring at the distant landscape through the window.

"Did you plant those dreams in my head?" I asked, watching him hide his eyes. There was something he wasn't telling me.

"No." There was a pause again. "It's part of being the Keeper of the diary." It seemed like something came to his mind, because I saw his eyes light up. "Well, well... are you asking because I had the honor of being in one of those dreams?" Derek looked amused and very pleased with himself.

"No," I lied. Of course he looked familiar. His silhouette had come out of the fog in one of my dreams. Like a premonition. I only hoped that he didn't see my cheeks burn; that always happened when I lied. Just ask my grandmother.

"The gate is the only one who can control your dreams. I have nothing to do with it. I can assure you," he said and looked out the window onto the road.

"Now there's a gate?"

"Every gatekeeper needs a gate, don't you think? It's a metaphysical separator between the demons and the ghosts. As long as the diary is safe, so is the gate," Derek said softly, and I rolled my eyes. Then he continued: "If you don't want to see vivid dreams, don't think of them as real, and you will be fine. Belief is one of the strongest attributes in your subconsciousness."

"Thanks for the advice, Mr. Cromwell, but you're a little late," I said.

"Let's talk about the demons… Have you had the pleasure of encountering one?" Derek asked.

"No. I see shadows; they make themselves known. Nobody else seems to notice these things except for me, which I have found strange, to say the least." If it wasn't a demon haunting me, I had dreams, figures, ghosts, and premonitions.

"The diary brings ghosts to life. It has always been that way. Don't worry about the demons. I'll teach you what I know of them. It's an eternal battle, and we have to fight for protection," he said, running his fingers through his hair.

"Ummm… I don't know if I'm ready for an 'eternal battle,'" I said and felt goosebumps run down my legs.

"Sure you are. It's part of your job description now," he said. "Besides, I'll be there the entire time. You don't need to be afraid."

"You aren't a serial killer, are you, Derek?"

Derek rolled his eyes. "Most certainly not. You have to trust me with the diary and yourself"— his eyes glittered— "or this relationship will never work out."

"I trust you," I vowed.

"You don't mind if we take a ride, then?" Derek jumped onto the cushion by my window and looked me in the face.

"Where to?" I asked, holding on to the curtain while he climbed down.

"If I told you everything beforehand, what fun would that be? People this century are so wicked. Don't you love surprises? Where is the passion? The excitement?"

"Our century's people have trust issues."

"I can see that," he said, and his eyes met mine in a dimly lit bedroom. "You are safe in my hands, Rebecca Grimwood."

"Derek, just to let you know, it's not the best night for secret trips. Let me remind you that it's Halloween—All Saints' Eve. It has bad connotations," I said, climbing out of the window after him.

Derek smiled in response. "Oh, you have no idea how wrong you are. It's just the opposite." He held me by the waist tightly as he lowered me out of my bedroom window. The feeling of him touching me vibrated through my body like a warm wave.

I was afraid, of course, but I felt like I knew who he was, and somehow that was enough for me.

NINE

CARNIVAL OF HORRORS

The concrete was wet from the rain. The wind shook the branches of the trees surrounding the house, occasionally even picking up the hem of my dress. There was a motorcycle parked by the streetlight where I had last seen Derek. It looked almost gothic, jet-black and shiny like a new penny. A helmet was carefully strapped to its back.

I glanced at Derek, puzzled. "Is this your ride?"

He looked back at me, confused. "Yes. I apologize. I should have warned you about the bike. You could have brought a change of clothing," he said, directing his eyes at my dress.

"Oh, please stop apologizing," I said. "The dress is not the problem."

"What is it, then?"

"You're the gatekeeper. I didn't think a motorcycle would be your way of transportation," I said and smiled, picking up the helmet.

"Did you think it would be a broomstick?" Mirth played in the dimples of his cheeks. "Every century has something to delight me. Your century has trust issues and bikes. It is what it is. And I have affection towards speed and beautiful landscapes. Who would have thought one could combine the two?"

"Then you might as well get yourself a helicopter," I remarked.

His eyes followed mine. I couldn't help but think that he looked at me as if it wasn't the first time we had met.

"I appreciate the suggestion, but I do not like heights. You better buckle up, Rebecca. We are about to hunt some demons," he said, and the motorcycle raced into the night.

* * *

After an hour of cruising over the countless freeways, we finally came to a stop.

"What is this place, Derek?" I asked while the motorcycle slowed.

In front of me stood a house, shaken by loud music and people's voices. Darkness was scattered over the brass fence; trees were the only witnesses to the still silence of our surroundings.

"It's a haunted house. I'm sure you have been to one of those places before," he said and helped me take off the helmet. He carefully placed it on the seat.

I tried to clarify my confusion. "But it's a fake house. All the people inside are actors."

When we slowed our steps, an illuminated head appeared out of the forest. Monster's eyes mingled, and their tongues slid back and forth. Lines and lines of people stood by the entrance, and only one VIP lane was empty. Standing outside, we could smell fear racing out the door.

"You're so tense. You have to let it go. You will be surprised what you can find under the shiny wrapper. It's all about perception," he said, smiling his mysterious smile while we continued following people in line. He was so determined and fearless. I wished to be like him.

"Umm, Derek, I'm not sure I want to do this."

The longer we waited, surrounded by the stuffy air and people's voices and the warmth radiating from their bodies, the more claustrophobic I became.

"It's a piece of cake, Rebecca. I thought you were tougher than that," he said and let me go in the line first.

Oh, that hurt. I *was* tough! How dare he? I had survived the hauntings, high school, and calculus with Mr. Shaw.

"I am not helpless, Derek," I said haughtily. He shrugged.

I couldn't say more, as we were forced to enter the long hallway of the haunted house. The lights flashed gold, alabaster fog enveloped the rooms, and the faint background music camouflaged any and all sudden movements we were able to hear. I felt even more claustrophobic after passing through a long tunnel that squeezed us in. My chest started to hurt. I was gasping for air and my stomach grumbled, but I still tried to hide my nervousness. Derek knew what I was going through, yet he didn't bring it up, which I felt thankful for. He came up behind me and put his hands around my waist at first; then he carefully placed his hands onto my eyes in a blindfold. I felt my muscles relax, and my breathing was finally slowing down.

"Now, Rebecca, keep your eyes closed and wander," he whispered. The warmth from his arms consumed me. And I knew he felt it too.

Despite the fact that my eyes remained closed, I could see clearly that the rooms were changing shapes. From oval to rectangular, from pyramid to diamond contours. I saw distorted faces materializing out of the walls of the haunted house. Most of them had animal parts, not the human features I was used to seeing. Sometimes a visitor would pass by, dragging a demon with him like a ghastly shadow. That shadow would crawl behind him, drawing happiness, kindness, and love away from him in the form of a dark mist. With Derek standing next to me, I wasn't afraid. I stared at the demons with curiosity.

"Demons do exist, and they are closer than you think," he said, still holding his warm hands over my eyes. He smelt like a campfire in the middle of the wilderness, and my heart trembled from his touch.

"What are they doing here? Are we going to let them just devour peoples' goodness like that?" I asked, observing a pig-faced girl cut through a gentleman's pocket with scissors, revealing a pack of Marlboro. Then he pulled one cigarette out and locked himself into a blue-ridden deathly kiss.

"It's where they live. Beside people with addictions and immorality," he explained. "I can destroy them when they run loose. But in this case, when a person chooses to keep his bad habits, bad behavior, or cheat on his wife, his demon will always follow. Until the person lets the demon go, there is no work for me there."

"Why can I see them?" I wondered. He lowered his hands away from my face. The lights still played on the walls, and in between us, people dressed as Halloween creatures still terrorized children jumping out of corners.

"Because I let you. And I want you to know what a real demon looks like for when you encounter one." His skin radiated all colors of the rainbow because of the projectors. His amber eyes reflected the shifting walls of the haunted house.

"*When* I do?" I asked horrified.

"You are the last living descendant of your line, Rebecca. They are going to do anything to destroy the diary and find you." Derek's voice shattered like glass onto the floor.

I should rethink that tough thing.

We began walking through the haunted house, but nobody could see us. The surroundings turned to blurred shadowy shapes that walked inside. A man ran past Derek, the echo of his voice disintegrating into a time tunnel, his silhouette evaporating into thin air and a cloud of ivory confetti setting behind him like snow. It was as if we drifted in a parallel world, roaming through the hallways, where people weren't actual people but crystalized shadows, fast and furious and at times dimensional. I loved being separated from them. I finally felt like I was in solidarity with the world. I could travel any path. I could watch the world without interruption. And for that alone, I would have gladly given my life.

I also knew that I was in danger, and the demons were watching me as if they had eyes cut out in wallpaper. I was the haunted girl. That strange girl that somehow was in the wrong place at the wrong time. That eeriness made me special— incredibly stupid, in my opinion, but still special.

After the first room, we entered a forbidden territory of fog with nothing but brass tarnished doorknobs all around. There was a current of air hissing on the ground and a gate that shook slightly. Tiny, muddy footprints were scattered on the floor as if they were left by an animal with claws.

I leaned closer to examine the ribbon of mire when a shape appeared in front of me. It was a jet-black, bear-sized raven with three rows of sharp teeth. It aimed them at my throat. At once, Derek covered the monster bird with a cloak. When it was disoriented enough, he slammed its head against the haunted house until its body became lifeless, and it spilled away in a form of ebony lava. I, short of breath and unnerved to the core, was crunched up in a corner. I didn't leave it until Derek perched beside me.

"I know how terrifying it must be," he said.

"You have no idea." I broke down and hid my face in the palms of my hands. His face was so close to mine that I could feel his breath lingering on me.

He pulled my hands away, and all I saw were his determined green eyes. "I want you to remember that this isn't some sort of game— that people don't come back from the dead, that demons can and will try to possess you and inflict hell on you. You have to be prepared. Don't be afraid, Rebecca. We will push through."

He said "we" and it made it feel much better. I wasn't alone in this. But...

Easy for you to say, I thought. *I'm not strong; I'm just a girl in a world of shadows. I'm not supernatural.*

"Derek, I can't kill a fly. How do you expect me to battle with a demon?" I kept staring into the fog. My gut was telling me the fog was crawling with them— demons.

"I don't. But I have something that might be of help to you," he said, placing a golden kaleidoscope in my hand.

I stared into the diamond-shaped, multicolored instrument. Its tender form was written on with cursive letters, and it couldn't have been bigger than a teacup. As soon as I twisted it to the side, the kaleidoscope lit up bright azure and a swarm of metallic butterflies burst from their confinement. Their wings blazed in the night with the sharpness of a thousand steel knives, and their color was that of titanium with specks of stardust. They swirled in pairs above our heads, sublime and, at the same time, intimidating.

"I've never seen anything so beautiful, except for the rainbow over the train tracks in Harpers Ferry," I breathed, admiring the kaleidoscope, rolling it in my hand.

"The butterflies are now yours. You are free to command them." As Derek stopped talking, a metal creature landed on my fingertip, shaking silver dust off its wings. It wasn't anything like a monarch butterfly, and it felt as heavy as the world's tiniest cannonball.

"How are they going to defend me?" I asked.

Derek swiftly rose and walked over to the line of fog. He shone with such a warmth that it was hard to keep my eyes off him. The features of his face invited, captured, and allured me. Long eyelashes, unusually long for a man, reminded me of guitar strings wonderfully crossed together.

While I was admiring Derek, I hadn't noticed that a bull-headed demon had come into view, growling loudly at both of us. Shaken and panicked, I twisted the kaleidoscope. A wave of titanium color raced to the demon, wings like razor blades, shattering him in a matter of minutes, but I saw nothing but a dust storm. When they were done, there was no trace of evil.

"And that," Derek said, grinning wryly, "is how they work."

"Very nice. They didn't waste any time. That's what you meant by preparation." I silently watched the butterflies fill the core of the kaleidoscope. I paused and looked up at Derek. "Is it a gift or a punishment to live in a world as compelling as this one?"

"There is a place and time for this world, Rebecca. You got here faster than you were supposed to, and this world won't always seem as great to you as you may find it now," he stated, bowing his head down. "Use the kaleidoscope, keep it close, and cherish it."

"I will. I promise," I replied, and my voice echoed as if it was trapped inside of the mountain. A raincloud of moroseness suddenly draped above Derek.

Who was I to understand what it took to be around demons for centuries? I was just a girl in the world of shadows.

* * *

Warm autumn night broke into the early morning in Harpers Ferry like the tide onto the shore: when you least expected it. I ran up the front steps of the house with lavender curtains, filled with excitement and fear and, above all else, worry— worry that I had dreamed the entire night up. Regardless, the kaleidoscope's weight rested in my pocket, and in the shade of a maple tree, there was a motorcycle. Derek stood on the road surrounding the house, his hair flaming brown and reflecting the light of the moon along with the chains on his leather jacket. He looked calm and unbothered. Somehow relieved and thankful. He kept pushing his hair to the side away from his face. I stopped before unlocking the door to wish him a good night.

"You know… I had a very strange but interesting night. And I might have enjoyed it a little bit more if not for the monsters," I said, my heart beating in my neck. I felt nervous. The wind was warm, and the air was cool and fresh. The sun was rising behind us. Derek glanced at the streaks of the sun bursting into the dark canvas of the sky and then back at me. His skin looked velvet soft.

"You're home safe, and that's all that matters. I am glad I could have been of service to you," he said, strangely cold in tone, and put his hands into the pockets of his jeans.

What? We had shared a bond, and now he was treating me like I was his project— a charity case.

"It's the only reason why you came here, isn't it? To keep me safe?" I asked.

Derek shrugged. "It's my duty, Rebecca. What did you think it was all about?" The words flowed so easily off his rose-hued lips that I forgot for a moment that he was talking. I knew he wasn't trying to be mean; he just couldn't bring himself to care.

A bird was crying inconsolably at the crowns of the trees.

"The way you look at me… it's like you know me. And I understand that you saved my life. But what was the reason? There has to be something you aren't telling me…" My voice died off as I watched his eyes change from amber to iridescent green.

"I wouldn't imagine things that aren't there. I saved you because you had to live a supernatural fate; it's the only way things would fall into place. I didn't mean to give you a false impression, and for that, I am sorry."

I bit my tongue. I was offended, and I didn't understand why it was so hard for him to admit the truth, whatever it might be.

"Oh no, it's all my fault. What was I thinking?" I said and smiled. "How silly of me, huh? I have to go now. Thanks again for... the kaleidoscope. Have a good night." I felt the tears coming. I couldn't let him see me cry.

"I'll pick you up tomorrow," he said sternly, watching me open the door. "There is a place I'd like to take you."

"What if I don't want to go with you?" I asked, jingling the keys in my hands, my back towards him. The lights on the porch started to flicker.

"I am not going to beg you, Rebecca, if you don't want to. I am giving you a choice, but it's to your benefit that you do allow me to show you the world of the dead." He was now leaning on the column of the house, staring at me.

"I'll think about it, Mr. Cromwell," I told him haltingly, returning the coldness.

I turned the key in the door once and the lights went out. I glanced into the street. The maple leaves were moving at the top of the trees, and there were tire marks on the road, but they were already fading away.

TEN

OLD CEMETERY

A dusty photo album on the second shelf. I had always pushed it back in the corner when Nick and I were growing up. I had hated his braces and perky ears, and my balayage caramel-blond hair that hung to the shoulder. Now, it was like opening the door to the past and sliding into a booth to enjoy the slideshow. Pictures of who we were and where we came from. I laughed as I turned the pages of the photo album, of the little notes we left to each other, of the letters we exchanged in summers. Not one of them was a love letter... and look where we had ended up. I thought our friendship would beat all the odds. I truly believed it.

Nick stopped by to pick up some history books and disappeared for the rest of the day. He had certain days that he wished to spend in solitude and the absence of intrusion. I respected his decision.

I organized the closet and called Dad. He said he was traveling to London for work this weekend, but he and Alice would be visiting for Christmas. I waited until Grams went to pick up her dry cleaning before I brought the diary out of the closet. Each time I had seen it unlatch, its pages had rustled, shoving the air with them. They all remained empty, like a store-bought, freshly printed notebook.

This time that wasn't the case; this time, I saw pencil sketches and inscriptions resembling instructions or a guide— drawings of demons and fire, rivers, and battlefields. I couldn't take a good look at them because as soon as a car entered a driveway, or a bird sat on the roof, or a mailman came into view, the book shut itself, hiding away the story.

When night came to the small town of Harpers Ferry, I heard the motorcycle engine hum outside. I looked at myself in the mirror. My hair was so wavy I had to pin it to the side. I wore jeans and a colorful tunic, a more comfortable clothing choice than on the last motorcycle ride with Derek.

I popped my head out of the window; the night was quiet, and the roads were empty. There was a single star shimmering like a gem over the house. *I could have sworn I heard a motorcycle running.* Then there came a loud bang from the rooftop as if someone were hammering it.

I looked towards the chimney and spotted a metal machine parked on top of the roof. Derek had gotten off the bike. His helmet was swinging in his hand. He climbed into my bedroom window.

"Derek... I'm glad you came to pay a visit. Guests usually park in the driveway," I said numbly. It didn't take him much to look polished: his hair fell in waves on his forehead, and his cheeks had an autumn color tint to them. The five o'clock beard was shaved neatly. I was set on behaving as coldly as he had been to me the night before.

"I thought the ride would be more scenic if I used an alternative route," he explained, running his eyes across my entire attire. Then there was a smile. "You look... refreshed."

"More like taken aback. I didn't know you had a motorcycle that could fly."

108

"It can't," Derek whispered. "It converts the moonlight into energy waves. They carry the bike like a surfboard."

"Do phases of the moon affect the way the motorcycle operates, then?" I asked, picking up my fish-scale purse from the vanity. It was surreal to hear that nature played such an element in the bike's mobility.

"When the moon is full, the waves are at their peak, strong and colorful. It's the only time it's possible for me to travel. And it happens about fourteen days a year," he said and glanced at the beautiful silver moon hidden by the clouds.

"And traveling on rooftops trumps your dislike of heights?" I asked, catching his green-eyed gaze.

"I associate the heights with the position of the enemy. No place to hide, no place to run, like a target in a field that has no escape but every chance to catch a bullet," he said.

"Position of the enemy?" I asked and paused, remembering my own dream with a lion. "Darkness chases Sentinels in the underworld? I thought you were invincible," I teased.

His eye suddenly got a darker shade to them. He really meant what he said. Derek raised his thick eyebrows at me. For his young age, he seemed too mature, and that scared me a bit.

"I am not afraid of heights," I stated.

"You should be." I saw a speck of light in his eyes as if he was mocking me. The darkness which was in him had just let go.

"Well. I'm not. And you shouldn't let it reign over your heart either," I said.

There was a stillness in his eyes. "It doesn't. It's a memory, Rebecca. I am afraid those stay with you forever."

"I dare you to forget, then."

"I dare you to get on the bike."

I didn't like speed; I liked feeling safe, but how would he know that?

"All right," I said as I climbed back onto the roof. "If I get on that motorcycle, you have to promise to be more carefree and not so serious all the time."

Derek nodded and watched me with interest. I perched into the backseat of the motorcycle when he came and gestured me to take the front seat. I looked at him, surprised.

"No. It's time you take the lead, Rebecca Grimwood."

"I've never ridden a bike, Derek. I'll wreck it." I noticed the fear crawling into my heart.

"Then the deal is off," Derek said coolly.

"All right. All right," I said and patted the leather seat.

My hands started to sweat. So did the back of my neck. I sank my hands into the handles of the motorcycle, opened the throttle slightly, and closed the choke lever. I felt Derek's hands on my waist. A stream of rainbow color suddenly moved the motorcycle. It was a forceful lift at first that magnified into a shocking burst of power. We began gliding.

My heart worked on overdrive. I squinted my eyes when the machine was going up and down on the rainbow waves. I was so afraid of how high up we were that my hands began to shake. I pictured us falling into a very dark and very black hole. Despite gravity, the slippery rooftops of neighboring houses, and the fact that the tires emitted a drumming sound all working against us, the landscape the bike revealed took my breath away. The undeniable fear and that deeply seated doubt in my heart— they both subsided.

The houses looked like specks in the night under the light of the moon. The rivers resembled blazing threads that ran into the dark frame of the forested land. The world suddenly became enchanted with silver and gold. A wave rocked the motorcycle for a moment and then let it free-fall, only to pick it up again.

We landed in a valley that resembled a labyrinth, and only then did I let go of the throttle, its shape reflected on the palms of my hands. Derek looked like he wanted to trade places. "Okay, I promise not to be so serious."

"Good, because I can't do another one of these rides," I said. Seeing him lean to the front, leather jacket carefully folded on his hips, I asked, "Where are we headed now?" I was moving backward slowly; after all, it was past my bedtime.

"Don't you want to meet real ghosts?" He smiled at me mischievously.

I had to admit, traveling around with a handsome guy from another world sounded appealing. I grabbed the helmet from the back of the motorcycle and squeezed my head into it, instantly fogging up the glass.

"So, Derek, where do the ghosts hang out these days?"

Derek knew I was easily convinced. Once I tasted the forbidden fruit, I couldn't be kept away from it, and there was so much to learn.

"Where the living people don't wander at night."

"You're taking me to the burial grounds?" My heart palpitated.

"Unless you have somewhere else to be. I have some business to take care of," he said, his tone serious. "But if you wish, I could bring you back to the house."

"No. That won't be necessary. I find it quite adventurous," I said, and a rosy color spread across my cheeks.

"Good. Get on, then."

I wiped the raindrops off the back of the bike with my sleeve then put my arms around Derek. Soon enough, we were on our way.

* * *

A narrow road led the motorcycle through the forest. It cut too close to the edge of the mountain, so tree branches touched our shoulders as we moved by. Once in a while, I heard rocks clattering behind us, hitting the concrete, and disappearing into the dark. The wind howled and died off, losing its voice over the landscape. The first thing that came into view was a marble fountain that looked more like a flower vase that someone had forgotten to fill with dirt, worms, and seeds. It stood in front of the house made of leaden rocks and caught the lonely light of the moon on its cracked surface. Nothing felt right. It was as if I wasn't invited— as if demons were coming to get me. For miles, I saw mausoleums and unmarked graves, which rose out of the dark like a stack of forgotten cards, but there were no faces featuring in the dark, just the blunt silence of deathly bells.

I clenched my fists in horror and tried not to show my fear to Derek. He was looking at me with interest as we waded deeper into the cemetery, leaving the antique gate fading behind us. "How are you doing there, Rebecca?"

"Oh, I'm fine. Not a big deal. Just an old, creepy cemetery," I lied.

Nightmares that haunted me at night now slowly took the shapes of stones and creatures hiding behind them. No matter where my gaze fell, I saw movement— noise that penetrated the air— and I had no idea where it came from. Something bone-chilling breathed down my neck, and I couldn't pinpoint what it was.

Passing by the Civil War cannon, I snapped a branch and it felt like I stepped over something alive. It startled me enough to release a scream. Derek caught me in his arms.

"You can hold my hand if you are afraid. It's all right, you know. I'm not going to bite you. I promise not to judge you either."

He found it amusing to watch me. I, on the other hand, was jealous that he didn't have anything or anyone to be frightened of. Nevertheless, I took him under the arm as he led the way.

I hadn't noticed before I took Derek's hand into mine, but the mausoleums were all lit up like houses on Christmas Eve. I heard Vivaldi, Beethoven, and then notes of Daniel Armstrong. This centuries-old music flowed on the wind, but the notes never mixed; there was time for each one. Somehow, all of them became one whole, perfect melody. The shadows were moving inside the mausoleums as if it were their own ballroom from Leo Tolstoy's *War and Peace*. I saw fireworks, a lady leaning over the railing, joined in a kiss with a soldier who had just handed her his kepi. Children with wooden drums and horses lulled a baby doll to sleep. Rose petals were scattered on the marble floors. I saw a dead poets' society. Before I could pass out from wonder and astonishment of seeing the real ghosts that were these ivory shadows, adorned with all their human features that were no different than mine, my gaze fell upon her— the Russian poetess Anna Akhmatova.

She sat in a garden of irises and anemones with birds chirping over her hand. She was writing in her little gem of a notebook, where she kept all of her love poems that my grandmother and I read in an armchair in front of the fire. I couldn't take my eyes off her. I desperately wanted to ask her what it was like to live in the epoch she did— to come up with the verses that no other poet could ever replicate. As I moved towards the mausoleum, Derek intervened.

"What's wrong, Derek? I thought we were seeing ghosts," I asked, still watching the poetess.

"Do you really want to interrupt her? She is composing one of her famous poems."

And I really didn't, but it was such an honor to look, to admire her beautiful features, her hand moving up and down. She had an aristocratic nose, high cheekbones, and raven hair braided down her shoulder— and the pearls. They glistened.

"Then why did you bring me here?"

"We aren't here to disturb peaceful spirits, but to take care of the ones that are worse than a thousand children at the candy store," he said and, as his voice disintegrated, it was replaced with a bell tolling.

I didn't know how, but we migrated to an open sunlit space. A crowd of people in uniforms stood in front of an old chapel. All officers were loudly arguing, some of them rebelling, coming at each other with bayonets. They created a real pandemonium.

"Who are all those people?" I asked. I saw a face in the crowd that I might have seen in one of my nightmares before.

Derek sighed and pushed the golden doors of the chapel shut. "Those are people who were killed and are seeking justice. People who died unexpectedly. People who can't live with themselves— who either can't forgive themselves or just refuse to move on. I work with each and every one of them. And then we put them on the train to another side to see if the gate accepts them or if they need more time to come to terms with their deaths."

"I am afraid to ask who you're helping right now."

"A child. Those are the most complicated ones. A drummer boy from one of Harpers Ferry houses. He fell through the second floor and broke his neck. He was a Confederate boy in a Union camp. You can imagine the treatment."

Poor youth during the Civil War. You had to grow up fast and skip the whole phase in between cocoon and butterfly. He was probably scared, wanted to be comforted, but instead, he was forced to be a slave— to exchange his toys for a rag and a bucket full of hot water.

"What do you tell him to make him move on?" I wondered.

"That's the problem. There is not much I can say. He's pretty stubborn, and I think a male presence doesn't do him any good," he said. "Follow me to the back. There is a garden here." Derek took out a silver key to the mausoleum.

"Can I talk to him?" I asked. This boy needed me, just like I needed a mother to read me a story before bed and kiss me goodnight. I felt deep inside my heart that I could help him.

"I don't see why not. I was going to visit him anyway to see how he's doing."

When Derek unlocked the next mausoleum, my gaze fell upon a boy sitting on a bench in the middle of the garden. He was about eight years of age. He was wearing a kepi pushed to the side and tall dark boots. His face reminded me of a porcelain doll with the same ruby blush. The drum was swinging down off his tiny figure, almost forcing him to lean over. He welcomed me with a smile.

"Hello there," I said, walking over to the drummer boy. "What's your name?"

"Philip," the boy whispered.

"My name is Rebecca." I offered him my hand. "You are one brave little boy, Philip. It's very important that you understand that. Your mom would be so happy to know who you grew up to be," I said, moving his strawberry blond hair to the side of his face.

"My mother is not here. I am afraid I might never see her again," he said and tears began to gather inside of his eyes.

"Philip, listen to me. Your mom is waiting for you on the other side. She has so much love for you stored in her heart; you don't want to miss out on it."

Philip shook his head. "But the soldiers— they will try to hurt me, hurt my momma, and I can't let it happen." The drumsticks trembled in his hands.

"The soldiers are gone, little fella. They have moved on. They won't cause you any more harm. They have paid a steep price for the evil they did. You don't have to be afraid anymore."

"Do you promise?" Tiny eyes the color of espresso looked up at me.

"Of course I promise. You want to know a little secret?"

The little drummer boy nodded.

"My grandpa passed away when I was a little girl. And now that I've grown up, all I want to do is tell him how much he means to me. Tell him that I love him. You should always tell people you love how much they mean to you. Even if it's just a thought, it won't hurt them to know. Time is so precious."

"I understand. I will always try to tell them, Rebecca," the boy said and ran towards me, burying his face inside of my sweater. His hands felt cold against my skin.

"Thank you..." Philip mumbled.

Suddenly, through the glass doors of the mausoleum, I saw a translucent shape far greater than the monument itself. It was a train— an ebony locomotive with endless wagons. Philip ran out the door, hopped onto the steps, and disappeared inside. His kepi flew out of his pocket and landed by my feet. I only heard a loud whistle and a goodbye frozen in the wind. I picked up the kepi and held it to my heart.

"I start to see why you were chosen to carry that damn diary."

Derek came up behind me and put his hand on my shoulder. There was no coldness to his touch compared to the drummer boy.

"Because I'm good at small talk?"

"Because you can handle ghosts, and you have a heart made of gold," Derek stated. "I am genuinely impressed by you. It's pleasant to watch someone do my job. Want to trade places?" Derek's voice was soft and quiet.

"No, I think I might have enough time spent with ghosts today. I would like to return to the world of real people. Crawl into bed, and as the sun rises— "

"— sit on the roof," he finished.

"Yeah, how did you know that?"

"It's a little hobby of mine too."

* * *

When Derek pulled his motorcycle by the road near the house with lavender curtains, there was a full moon shining down on us like an ice globe. We both climbed onto the roof and spread the blanket from the window to the chimney. Stars were just appearing on the sky in pairs, glistening like diamond powder. From the roof, Harpers Ferry looked like a town fringed with a curtain of stringed lights.

"You should be proud of yourself. You saved that boy today." Derek lay down on the blanket, his one hand resting under his neck. Our heads were close to each other, the shapes of them forming a heart. "You're not just a girl in the world of shadows, despite what you might think."

"It felt amazing to help someone. To drag them out of a dark place. To show them the world still has color in it," I explained, and I remembered Nick.

"So, I'm safe to assume that you will be fine once I'm gone?" Derek asked. His legs in their rocker boots were crossed over, stretched to the chimney.

I didn't know him well. Who was I kidding? I didn't know him at all, but part of me didn't want to let him go. He was like a gasp of fresh air in my life.

"Are you going to come back?" I asked, my eyes following his.

"I might. I want to make sure things go smoothly, and that there are no strange ghost occurrences, and that nobody tries to go after you while I am away. Oh, I also wanted to give you this." He handed me over a little book with trees on it.

As I browsed through the pages, I saw majestic oak trees dressed in their leafy attire— all different species with unimaginable, unreproducible colors.

"This is an antique calendar. Each month has its own tree. Once all the trees shed their leaves, I will come back, but you have to keep turning the pages."

"What if I forget to turn a page?" I asked.

"Apart from the fact that you will lose track of time... You might bring out a ghost or two. They love lurking around." My eyes widened, but Derek continued. "I have seen it happen all the time. That's why they say you have to put sage on antique furniture. It's a gateway portal for the ghosts."

"Forgive me, I don't quite understand. What do you mean by losing track of time? You sound like we operate in two different universes."

"Well, we do. The gate has its own time constraints. Its equivalent of the month appears to be the life of an oak tree," he explained, gazing into the distant landscape.

Before I met Derek, I had never realized what effect ghosts had on our world. People had unknowingly drawn a veil in between the two worlds, but the idea of the ghosts being the watchers— stalkers, if you will— in our powerless universe terrified me. Not because of their appearance but the uncertainty of their intentions. Though I did believe my family was safe on the part of diffusing sage inside the house. Grandma had done so unknowingly, just to get rid of the bad energy she claimed possessed the building at times.

"Remember that you have to turn the page at midnight before a month collapses into the other. I'll return on the third month."

"Doesn't seem that difficult to follow a simple rule," I noticed.

There was a piece of parchment paper still resting inside of Derek's hand. I forced his hand open and retrieved the note, unrolling it. It was one of the poems Anna Akhmatova had been writing when we visited the cemetery.

"Oh my God!" I exclaimed. "How did you manage to get this?"

"I knew it would make you happy to read it, so I borrowed it," Derek said.

"I don't have the words. I am so grateful for this… gift!" I wrapped my arms around Derek's neck. He flinched from my sudden closeness but nevertheless smiled warmly.

Our hands were sitting close on the plaid blanket. My hand slowly came over his for a quick touch, almost a tremble. Our eyes met. My attention was chained to his face, and I knew he felt the same way. The wind started to pick up around us, causing us to fall into the mist of stars enveloping the roof. He handed me a star, its tiny arms more fragile than a flower, yet glowing bright. The star was breathing, laying in the palm of my hand. It was alive. I couldn't believe my eyes; Derek had just pulled a star from the sky for me.

Suddenly I heard a door rattle and a voice behind the door.

"Becca, can I come in? Are you there?"

Nick was turning the doorknob, entering the room along with Charlie, who was dragging his bone with him.

* * *

I opened my eyes. Derek had already gone and only a star lay breathless on his side of the plaid blanket.

ELEVEN

THE DREAM

I thought about Derek a lot more than I expected. Sometimes it felt like I had imagined him. I couldn't tell Nick about him because he just wouldn't understand. Not after what had happened between us in Gettysburg. How was I supposed to explain to him that the Sentinel from the world of the dead had just shown up on my doorstep? Despite that, he managed to notice a change in me when I met him at the Coffee Roosters Bar about a month after Derek left.

"You seem preoccupied the last few weeks. College applications taking a toll on your well-being?" he asked me, ordering a macchiato, smiling at the blue-eyed cashier in a tiny yellow apron.

"Nah," I said.

I took a glance at the people surrounding the bar tables. They were chatting, leaning over the soft velvety cushions of the loveseats while the rays of the sun played on the refinished floors. Porcelain cups and saucers of all sizes and forms covered the knee-high tables of the coffee house.

"I am still waiting to hear from Georgetown. It's my first choice. By the way, my father and Alice got engaged. We haven't been in touch since then. It's not that big of a deal. I was just taking things slowly." My coffee was scalding. I glanced at the happy, carefree face of the cashier girl, who smiled in return.

"It's a big deal!" Nick's eyes lit up. "You'll have a stepmother! Who would've thought?"

"It's been a long time coming. I can't say that I'm surprised. He conveniently waited until I skipped town," I explained. All of that was true, but my father was the last person in the world that bothered me. I knew he could take care of himself.

"Any dreams you've been having that you conveniently forgot to mention? You tell me you aren't like your father but I'd say otherwise. Living on the other side of the moon is in the Grimwood bloodline."

I noticed how seductively the words flowed out of his mouth. No wonder cashiers in tiny skirts paid so much attention to him. I sighed. "Not since Halloween." The coffee was still too hot to drink.

"What is that book I found on your nightstand? Looks like a magical terrarium. Do they rent those out of the Harpers Ferry library? I would like to get one," Nick said, biting his lips slightly after noticing a concerned expression on my face.

"You went through my room?" My voice spiked at the news that he'd seen the calendar.

"Beccs, it's all right. Grams told me you went to the Point to get some air, so I dropped by your house to get a book. Lida donated all the books to the church library. I had to read something. I am sorry." He was gesturing with his hands, which made me think he was worried he had done something wrong.

"Listen, I'm not angry."

"Clearly," Nick cut me off.

"It was unexpected. That's all. It was the tarot cards guide— you know, the fortune teller's gift back then when I visited her in

DC. She believed in nature spirits and flowers and blooming... Long boring story," I explained. My knees were trembling.

"I'd like to read it sometime. Boring stories are my thing." It was like he was looking at me but wasn't really seeing me.

"Oh, Nick, I got rid of it yesterday. Thought it reminded me too much of the premonition. I am sorry. If only I knew you wanted it."

I hoped that I sounded guilty or at least remorseful. Hoped that he would believe me, at least for a little while, until I could no longer carry the secret that was ripping me apart.

"I think you should ask the cashier for her number. She can't keep her eyes off you," I said and pointed towards the coffee bar.

Nick shrugged and threw me an empty glare. "Really, Rebecca, that's the card you're going to play? I thought you knew better," he hissed and then burst out laughing.

Hearing him laugh made me laugh even harder. He held a napkin in his hand with the cashier's number on it. She'd scribbled it on the paper when he wasn't looking. I knew he would never call her.

* * *

I caught the first taxi back to town. The driver was a tattooed woman in her fifties with curly red hair and a bandana. She glanced at my jeans and white shirt.

"Aren't you dressed a little light, honey?" she asked, turning the heat on. "They're calling for rain."

"I miscalculated the weather this time around. I hope to be home before the storm kicks in." I slid into the back seat.

"Last time we had a storm, I found a tree resting on my shed. My husband and I thought it was time to move out. He yelled 'bad karma,' and I yelled back, 'then start packing,'" she said.

"The winds are strong in Harpers Ferry. They chill you to the bones. Other times, you just don't know," I said, looking out the window at the café signs swinging in the wind. The gloomy skies were a reflection of the colorless ground. The wind was picking up, and I knew the whole town would head into the storm in just a couple of hours.

"Be careful out there," she said, fixing her hair under the bandana as she pulled up by the house with lavender curtains.

"Will do," I said, handing her a couple of dollars through the window before running up to the front door.

Grandma had hung a couple of Chinese lanterns from the porch, and now they swayed like tall grass at the seaside. I found the key under the flowerpot and quickly got inside. Charlie greeted me with his two muddy paws sliding on my jeans, and I scratched his ear as I guided him into the first-floor bathroom where I washed and dried off his paws. He grunted and snorted as I lowered him onto the tile floor.

I had left the bedroom light on, and it was projecting onto the landing, filling in the gaps and creases in the floorboards. I threw my purse onto the bedpost and stared at the quiet room. The "terrarium book," as Nick had called it, lay amongst the rest of my home library. If it weren't for the bright cover, I wouldn't be able to tell the difference between it and Edgar Allan Poe's poetry collection. I moved all the other books aside and opened the calendar.

Its covers fell upon the dresser top, and in between them appeared to be a tree. The bark felt rough and edgy, the leaves moist and curvy. It was a miniature prototype of a real maple but from a different "gate" species. It breathed. I could see the bark rising up and down, the roots moving underneath the ground. The leaves turned into cardinals, some of which broke off the branches and raced upwards, bursting into flames once and then vanishing forever. Sparks of blue, sparks of green, sparks the color of almond milk. I had seen fourteen pages of these trees, and yet each one stood in front of me individually, like no other before it. This one was my favorite so far.

Grandma had been stuck at Lida's for almost two hours, drinking tea out of her flower-fringed mugs, watching the news, and trying new recipes for raspberry and peach jams. I, on the other hand, was stuck nowhere. I lay on my four-poster bed, eyes closed, listening to the rain outside soak the lawn. Out of the blue, I heard a melody pouring into the room. It sounded almost like Beethoven's "Für Elise."

I opened my eyes and grabbed a bedpost, pulling myself forward. The calendar had a piano underneath the maple tree, and the black and white keys were moving like the tides. The tree was all rotten now. Skin was forming on the branches, and it swung down like moss that had withstood prolonged winter. The trunk was dried out and mutilated.

I started to panic. I slid from the bed onto the floor when the lights went off, and thunder rumbled outside so hard that my heart skipped a beat. I desperately searched for the candles in one of the bedside tables, but Grandma must have cleared them out before I arrived. I grabbed the diary and ran towards the stairs, the melody of the calendar still playing inside of my head.

The bulbs kept going off as I raced downstairs, only to find the house standing in darkness. Charlie noticed me coming down the stairs and barked underneath the landing. Grandma had drawn the curtains before she left, and now the storm was raging outside, the lightning never making its way into the rooms. I found the car keys dangling off the metal hook in the foyer. Draping myself in a jacket and rain boots, I fled outside.

At once, the headlights of the car shone through the misty weather, and I started the engine. I was still trembling from the wind and moisture. The only store that I knew would be open late was Ms. Gibson's gift shop located by the old bridge. Ms. Gibson was a chubby woman with a big heart and a love for town décor. Her store had to have candles in it.

The car wobbled on the brick streets, water splashing below the tires in a foamy rush. When I reached the shop, I noticed that the lights were dimmed and the "Welcome" sign was turned to "Closed". I exited the car and approached the shop window. I rattled the doorknob a few times and pressed my face against the cold glass, trying to peek through, when I heard a voice behind my back.

"What do you think you're doing? I'm calling the police!"

A shape of a woman emerged from the shadows.

"Ms. Gibson!" I exclaimed, pulling the hoodie from my head.

"Rebecca! What are you doing here this late?"

I shrugged, letting my hands fall to the sides. "The storm started and knocked out all the electricity. There were no candles at the house, so I was thinking you would be kind enough to let me in and buy one. I apologize. I didn't know where else to go."

Ms. Gibson stared at me, her eyes full of wonder. "You could have called; I would have left you one in the shop's mailbox. Anyway, we'll get a cold standing here. Come on in," she said and unlocked the wooden doors of the gift shop. "I have cinnamon twist and paradise bird." She laid the candle boxes in front of me.

"Doesn't really matter, but I'll take the paradise bird," I said, picking up the box from the table.

"This way, you can combine work with pleasure. Isn't it always the best choice?" Ms. Gibson smiled.

"Says the saleswoman," I whispered. "Thank you very much." I knew I had to get back to the house before a demon came after me.

The car door slammed into the metal gap as I shut it. The rain was drizzling droplets onto the hood, and the wind was chasing the water into the gaps and crevices of the car. My windshield wipers worked overtime, and I felt the heat spread inside of the cabin.

"Candles? A safer, less hazardous choice would be a flashlight."

I gasped as I saw a face come out of the darkness in my rearview mirror. "What the hell, Derek!" I exclaimed, my hands still trembling. "You can't just sneak up on me like that."

His smile was shining brighter than the lightning itself.

"I suppose I could have waited in the foyer of the house, but with demons crawling around and the lights out... I don't know. I

128

hesitated. Not every day do I have the pleasure of waiting around. I must admit, it's entertaining since I am in control of the centuries at all times and simply don't have to wait for anyone."

"The calendar and the creepy melody that I heard—did you have anything to do with it?" I whispered, staring into his amber eyes in the mirror.

"I travel by means of a portal, if that's what you are referring to. When I pass the gate from another side, the calendar projects music."

"I thought there was a demon in the house," I admitted. "I was afraid."

"Demons don't do calendars or alerts of any kind. If they came, there would not be an entryway or any other obstacle that would prevent them."

"What about the lights? They kept flickering over my head," I said, mimicking the sparkles bursting.

Derek fixed his leather jacket and laughed. "It's storming outside, Rebecca. Not everything in your life is supernatural."

"You're very upbeat for a dead guy. I wasn't expecting you back for another two months," I grumbled, picking up the speed of the vehicle.

"I thought I'd stop by to check on you and your grandmother. Make sure the relic is safe," Derek said, his gaze lingering on the road ahead of us.

"It's usually back at the house. Inside the closet where it always is."

My eyes were catching the headlights of the passing cars.

"Does anyone else know about the relic?" Derek asked, putting his arms on both front seats of the car, leaning towards me, the scent of the pine forest spreading around.

"My friend Nick might. He's seen it on the nightstand," I said. "He kind of lives in my house most of the time. There is nothing I can keep from him. He snoops around."

"You spent a lot of time with that fella. Are you sure he won't interfere?"

"Is this why you came back? To ask me if my best friend would keep a secret?" I asked. The road in front of us was turning into two pathways.

"I think you might have taken the wrong exit there, Rebecca," he said. He was right. I was too distracted to think. "There is another road you can take. It will take you into the alley by the old plantation house," he said, pointing ahead. "Pull in by the gate."

"How would you know about this road, Derek?"

"Because I have been here before. It's been centuries, but the landscape is still the same. You know, the world doesn't do navigation justice. Back then, maps had accuracy that your time undervalues."

"Oh, I'm sure they did," I said.

A massive metal gate came into view suddenly. It rose over the ground a couple of inches and was fringed with angel sculptures and flowers. Behind it stood two stone pillars with dome-like decorations on top.

"What do you mean you have been here before?" I asked, bringing the car forward and pulling the keys out of the ignition.

"I should have phrased it differently. This used to be my home. It's one of the few houses in Harpers Ferry that survived the war. The bombardment, of course, destroyed the others," Derek said, his face pressed against the window, his gaze lingering in the corridors of thought.

"The diary gave you a plantation home?" I asked bewildered.

"No. I lived here before the diary came into existence, during the War Between the States, what you may know as the Civil War."

I stepped out of the car and glanced at the plantation house. The porch sat high over the stone steps. The ivory columns pierced the building's façade. Each window was encased in closed emerald shutters. The sledged roof reminded me of Roman architecture. And above all, there was an old pool that stretched along the entire perimeter of the house.

"I've never seen anything so beautiful and remarkable. But what do you mean 'before the diary came into existence?' Have you not always been the Sentinel for the dead souls?" I asked while admiring the magnificence of the old building.

"No. I used to be like you. I had a family, a home, reasons to wake up early in the morning. And then, in a blink of an eye, it all faded away as the bloodiest years claimed the entire country. Nothing was ever the same."

I wanted to ask him so many questions, but I couldn't bring myself to. The past— it was something each of us mourned, like a pony ride we'd grown out of a long time ago. I knew that his past was shaped by too many painful memories.

As the headlights of the car faded, we stepped onto the plantation territory. My hair started to curl from the moisture, and I forced it underneath the hoodie. Derek was watching me curiously. Scarlet color brushed like a wave upon my face.

"I'm embarrassed. My hair gets so curly when it rains. I can't help it."

Derek smirked at me. "I think your hair is beautiful. Curls were an elegant part of Civil War attire. Women were proud to wear them."

"I'll take your word for it," I whispered.

He raised his hand slightly above his chest, chanting. In front of my own eyes, water turned into little white flowers. I glanced at Derek, stunned.

"I am the Sentinel for the dead, but I also have a gift of channeling nature, which is more like the demon-protective mechanism. Water happens to be more responsive than wind or fire. Thus, the flowers," he said and sat down on the marble skimmer. I perched next to him. Periwinkles were streaming from the sky.

"It's incredible."

The plantation house stood still against the sky. "Which one was your room?" I asked, looking at the green shutters on the second floor. Derek followed my eyes to the house but didn't respond— just shrugged. "What?" I asked and watched him smile for a moment. "You said you lived here. I want to know where your room was," I explained. "It's only fair. You've been in mine."

"Second floor. Do you see the window that faces the field?" He pointed. I nodded. "That was my room. Also, the room that caught fire. Mom left a candle upstairs on the washstand, and a storm started. They put down the fire, but you can still see the damage on the walls. The smell of fire soaked into the wallpaper and stayed there forever," Derek explained.

"Is that the reason you're so keen on flashlights?" I asked, watching him run his eyes over the house façade.

"Fire reminds me of hell. And demons. I'd rather leave them on the other side," he stated, blowing blue circles of mist on the water.

"Fire reminds me of fireflies. They aren't that bad," I said and let out a giggle.

Derek smiled in response. After a few moments of watching the flowers float from the sky, he leaned forward until his arms rested on his knees. "I saw you in my dream the night before I died. I thought you should know." His white teeth shone between his thin lips. His tone of voice was steady and calm. Hearing his remark made my heartbeat fast and curious under my ribcage.

"How is that possible? We were born centuries apart," I said.

"I don't know. I thought if I got to know you, it would help me understand," he said, his head tilted, his buckeye hair forming a slight curve on his forehead.

"There are a lot of things I can't make sense of. Most of them are human, not supernatural. I must have been a bad omen. I'm sorry about that."

He suddenly turned his face to mine. "Rebecca, there is nothing in this world you have to feel sorry for. I have never regretted seeing you. It was a gift— a gift to hope and to find peace. You made it all possible. Not once in my life or afterlife have I ever doubted you were real. And when I finally found you in that train station in DC, I couldn't believe it. You stole a piece of me. A piece of me I have forgotten about. A piece of me I let go with the war."

"I don't want to remind you of the things that have passed. Things that tarnished you." I spoke with the wind creaking the old gate.

"But those things made me who I am. Do you believe in destiny, Rebecca? Because I do. The dream was just another premonition. It wasn't death it carried, but the future— a future in which I had a chance to find you," he said.

I didn't know what it was that drew me to him, but his posture, his tone of voice, the glow in his eyes—it was so electric and somewhat charming. I was afraid to close my eyes and find out that I was, in fact, dreaming. The water inside of the swimming pool rose and formed a constellation of a bear. It swirled inside with glitter for a moment and then broke into an endless fountain of rainbow sparks. We were sitting in a cocoon made of fading lights as if it was a real starfall. Colorful shadows played on his face. We caught green, then yellow, red, and orange.

He still managed to look striking in all those colors. Under a charming demeanor and a bright smile, he conveyed a basket of sorrow. He might not have thought about the war or death this very second, but inside him existed a flame that was put down by the past. And I wondered if anyone could help him forget... if love could beat all odds. If it could heal scars. I wondered if I would be the one to help him forget.

TWELVE

THE SKELETON IN MY CLOSET

December thirteenth, the day before my birthday, was one uncanny day. I was taking a hot shower upstairs when I suddenly heard a rumble inside of the water pipes, like a long continuous scratching sound. The water stopped its flow, leaving me standing in the shower with my hair soaked in foam. I swiftly threw a towel over my head, wrapped another dry one around my shoulders, and got back into the room, thinking it would be better for me to boil some kettle water and dilute it later with cold bottled water to finish my shower. But as I was searching in a closet for my robe, I felt a stare on my back, and with fear like a ball crawling at the bottom of my stomach, I turned around to find the diary lying on my bed. I came closer to examine it. Derek had mentioned that the diary might move if it felt threatened, but I found wet footprints on the carpet below the bed. And I knew for a fact that they didn't belong to me. Grandma was leaning over the recipe book in the kitchen when I came down for the kettle, slippers drawing a circle on the hardwood floors. She lifted her eyes off the book and stared at me in surprise.

"We have a water problem upstairs. I couldn't finish my shower. I think I might boil some water to at least rinse my hair," I explained, digging into the cupboard for the dishes.

"Everything seems fine here. The pipes must have rusted. I need to call in the handyman," she said and smiled. "You know, you have been different these last few days. Has something changed?

There is an unusual spark in your eye," Grandma added and took the meat out of the freezer.

I was sipping a glass of water, and I almost choked. I spit the water back into the sink.

"No, Grams, it's just me in a happy state, away from Dad, stress, and DC."

"Is that so? And it doesn't have anything to do with Nicholas?" She closed the recipe book, and it released a dull sound. "Stuffed peppers for dinner tonight. Great-grandma's recipe. You may want to invite him to keep us company."

I still coughed, but the water finally went down the right pipe. "I'll think about it. Sounds like a great way to spend the evening." I turned the gas on the stove and shrugged nervously. I had to pretend the whole evening that I was a normal girl in a normal family, forgetting about the creepy diary, an old calendar, and a man nobody even knew existed.

The handyman didn't find any problems with the water pipes. Moreover, he stressed the fact that they were in perfect shape. By the judging grimace of the handyman and the concerned gaze of my grandmother, I understood that even Charlie thought I was out of my mind. And he was a dog.

When I went back upstairs to change for dinner, Nick and his buddy Ryan were already sitting at the kitchen table, loudly discussing the fantasy series both had just finished.

"I don't know… I think Roy and his ghostly companion are unstoppable. Whoever comes in their way would be destroyed. The knife of honor has to be found!"

Nick shook his head in disapproval: "What about the dark lord? He possesses some magic power to command minds. It's pretty amazing. I was so impressed with the final battle and the ravens that feasted on the flesh of McGregor. It's only a shame it takes him about two years to come up with another book in the series. Now I've got to think about how to occupy my time, maybe read some Stephen King in between."

"Oh, Princess of the Seven Seas!" Ryan exclaimed, watching me come down the stairway. "Rebecca, you look like a diva." Ryan stood up and offered me a chair, which he slid towards the table.

"She does look like her, doesn't she?" Nick stared at me in disbelief. It was the most obvious conclusion, and he was evidently shocked at how he couldn't have thought about it before.

"Who is *she*?" I wondered and dipped my fork into the salad while Grandma served the stuffed peppers on the plates.

Ryan darted his eyes at me. "She's a flame goddess. Burns everything in her way, but she's also the most beautiful woman alive, and when she speaks, men are mesmerized until she sets them on fire. Revenge is her second sister, but you obviously just possess the beauty and charm."

"That's one of the best compliments I have ever received. Thank you, Ryan." I was blushing; I put my hands to my cheeks to hide them from embarrassment.

"I'm lucky I have such a beautiful girlfriend," Nick said, grinning.

Girlfriend? I thought. I must have sent out the wrong message. Maybe I gave Nick too much credit… he must have just been trying to make Ryan jealous.

137

I didn't say a word, just kept it to myself. I smiled awkwardly. The whole time, Nick couldn't take his eyes off me. We ate in silence, only once in a while commenting on how good Grandma's cooking was.

"If you kids are still hungry, I have pies in the fridge," Grandma said, peering at us from the corner.

She always ate in the living room by the fire. Charlie, with his tail up in the air, followed her submissively and, from time to time, jumped up to see if a piece of bologna was lying on the floor.

Nick caught me by surprise as I was walking out of the bathroom upstairs. Ryan found an excuse to return to reading his fantasy series as soon as we were finished with dinner.

"Is Ryan gone?" I asked. "I can't hide in this house from you, can I? You know it like the back of your hand." My expression was soft.

"He left a while ago. Do you have a minute? Can we talk?" He was standing under the chandelier in the hallway, his frame reflected on the wall of the house.

"Umm…" I began. But suddenly, water burst into the bathroom, and by "burst" I mean that it was coming out of every drain, soaking the walls like a fountain. I signaled to Nick to get the towels. We both unloaded the cupboard and started soaking the water from the floor into the towels. Despite our greatest efforts, the water found its way into the hallway; it was an uncontrollable stream of power.

"I told that idiot handyman that there was a problem in the pipes! Nobody ever listens!" I exclaimed, standing up from my knees.

"Where the hell is all this water coming from? We aren't even by the water pipes," Nick noticed, examining the site. "You better tell your grandma we need someone from Harpers sent right away before it floods downstairs."

"No, you're right. I'll go get her." The minute I raced to the landing, I heard Nick's voice piercing the air behind my back.

"Beccs... You might want to hold off on that."

The bathroom was unrecognizable. It was dry and spot cleaned. The towels were laid in the formation of a pyramid below the sink like we had pulled them out of the cupboard and set them onto the floor. The whole scenery was disturbing, not to mention Nick's was as white as a sheet.

"Did you do this?" Nick asked, examining the dry towels.

I was more than surprised. "Why in the world would you think it was me?"

"You have been behaving so strangely recently. What else am I supposed to think? Do you have any explanation for this?" His eyes looked wildly around the bathroom. "This isn't real. This simply can't be happening. Please tell me I have lost my mind."

"I wish I could tell you that." My voice was steady, but I couldn't magically turn back the time. Nick had already dipped his toes into the unknown; he would never back down now. It was just who he was.

"What do you know, Becca?" He grabbed me by the arm.

"Nothing! I swear!" I protested. "I think we might be haunted! That's all!"

"By who, or by what?" Nick didn't notice that he had knocked over the bathroom vase, causing it to shatter to pieces on

139

the floor. He knew if I was trying to hide something from him. He could see it in my eyes.

"Kids, are you all right?" Grandma was coming up the stairs. I met her by the family photograph on the wall that had turned pale yellow with age.

"We're good, Grams. I was just showing Nick the color of the tile that Lida wanted for her bathroom renovation."

"Oh…" Grandma sighed. "She always wants what I have. It isn't surprising. I'll leave you to it."

As Grandma's silhouette disappeared downstairs, Nick pulled me into the bathroom and shut the door. "Tell me right now what is going on," he whispered angrily.

"I found a diary the other day in the closet. It summons ghosts. It might have been controlling the water." I doubted that was what it was, but I had to come up with a hell of a good story for him to believe me. Anyway, it was half-lie, half-truth. I still felt like I had committed the original sin.

"Well, get that thing out of the house! Before we have demons living here," he demanded.

"I can't really do that," I protested.

"Why not?" His eyes shone emerald. He evidently reckoned it would be as easy as eating a pie.

"It chose me. I am its Keeper."

* * *

Every breathing creature, every house, every antique chest has its secret. They might not be aware that those secrets exist, but trust me, they're there, consciously constrained or not. I have never delved into someone else's secrets unless they willingly disposed of them, and I never expected someone to dig deep into my closet for the skeletons that I buried there. Life is interesting like that. Somehow, it gets tired of carrying the secrets, and through pure happenstance or perhaps an unkind childish game, it allows the secrets to slip through the cracks.

That's exactly what happened to me. Nick wasn't supposed to know. I didn't want him to. I was only grateful that I was able to stop the crack from spreading to the root. I could keep Derek and the monsters in the dark for now, and hopefully forever.

"How did you get this diary?" Nick's eyes were concentrated on the leather covers. In his hands, it didn't glow; it pretended, posing as a forgotten artifact of the past.

I sat on the coverlet with two legs underneath my buttocks in a yoga pose. "My great-grandfather. It has been in my family for years."

"Looks like a simple book someone would borrow from the library. And you think it summons ghosts— the kind of ghosts that appear in my photographs?" He said it with a note of judgment and slid into the armchair, leaning towards the bed and turning the diary in his hands.

"It summons some sort of spiritual energy that I can't really explain."

"Can't or don't want to?" Nick knew me well enough to be suspicious. I let him, because not letting Nick do something could have turned out far worse. I didn't want to sound defensive.

"Okay, you got me there. It's psychic. It makes me have a third eye, turns my dreams into reality. And on occasion, it revolts, opens up and summons ghosts…"

My heart beat fast. I pressed my back against the metal headboard. *Please don't ask any more questions. I beg you,* I thought.

'What happened in the bathroom with the towels and water looked like a manifestation and not at all a ghost." Nick stood up and began walking around the bed in circles.

"Can you please stop pacing?" I begged. "You are making me nervous."

"Shhh," he silenced me. "It helps me think. So…" He scratched his head. "You are all right with me throwing it out of the window, then?"

I attempted to stand up as I saw him heading towards the curtains: "No, you can't, Nick! It belongs with me." With a terrified look on my face, I watched him open the window. "Nicholas!" I yelled. "Put the diary down!"

"Relax. I'm just messing with you. God, you're so uptight."

Someone had already told me that once, I thought.

"I just want you to feel safe in your own house, not jump from the sound of every footstep that you hear going up the landing. Tomorrow we'll take it to the Historical Society. We will see what we can find out about it."

My heart now trembled like a buckeye leaf. "Okay," I agreed, even though I dreaded the fact. There was still a chance no Harpers Ferry resident would know where the book came from, or I just had to make sure the book disappeared tonight. That thought would keep my bed warm at night.

The grandfather clock struck midnight, and I heard the birds cry outside. Nick and I exchanged two worried glances.

"I need to go," he suddenly proclaimed. "Lida will raise hell if she finds out I didn't walk Luna."

My eyelids felt heavy, the late hour pressed against my window, and I felt that as soon as my head touched the pillow, I would be drifting into a dream. "Of course," I said gently. "I feel tired, anyway."

Nicholas's emerald irises smirked at me. "Try not to get yourself in trouble."

"I am sure it's inevitable, even when I am asleep."

His eyes shone with tenderness, and the way he looked at me—wow. I wished every man looked at me the way he did. In his eyes, I was faultless; I was the perfect girl.

"Good night, Rebecca. Don't let the demons bite you," he said.

"Nick, I'm not your girlfriend, you know."

"I know, Beccs. I don't know what's gotten into me tonight, and I'm sorry." He smiled warmly and disappeared behind the door.

* * *

I woke up at three in the morning, drenched in sweat from head to toe. If I was dreaming that night, I wouldn't know, as memories crowded in my head, forming one dark black hole. I reached for the calendar under the bed when, with terror, I realized that I had forgotten to turn the page. The curtains were pushed apart, and the windowsill was on display with my pillows thrown around the bed. I sat up at once, trying to make sense of the silhouettes that danced around the room. There was a gray cat sitting on the windowsill, wagging its tail, ears pointed up, but I never owned a cat, nor could I imagine what it would be doing in my room.

"Hey, Kisa, Kisa," I whispered, calling the cat. It glanced in my direction, acknowledging my existence, even meowed once. But then the cat changed into a lion with red glowing eyes and sharp teeth bursting out of its mouth. I heard a snarl, the one you would recognize on a Safari ride, a snarl so distinguishable and unique that it would be stuck in your head for years. It prepared for an attack; its body arched, its paws moved together for a better push from the ground, and its eyes, full of vengeance and hunger, stared down at me. I thought I was going to pass out, but adrenaline rushed through my veins and I grabbed the kaleidoscope, which I kept under my pillow with a variety of protective stones. The creature turned into a blue mist and raced out of the room, slamming the door shut and leaving me breathing hard, eyes still locked on its dead wake.

Dziyana Taylor

THIRTEEN

THE AWAKENING

Harpers Ferry hadn't yet awoken. The cold air crawled inside my ribcage and the coat which I left unbuttoned. It lay in folds underneath me, forming a blanket. I had taken care of the diary. It rested peacefully under the bed in one of the card boxes. If you wanted to find it, you would have to know where to look. *One less worry in my head*, I thought.

Blue smoke swirled in front of me in a perfect string of circles. I was a goody-goody at school: never had a bad habit, never did anything that would compromise my life or leave a shadow on it. I was careful not to fall on my face, get an unworthy grade, or disappoint people who loved me. But there was a part of me that always existed, a dark reflection of myself that was eager to enjoy that one cigarette when no one was looking. I didn't need to be told by my grandmother, or my father for that matter, that it was wicked and ill-behaved. I knew it was. I didn't even inhale it fully— just kept it in my mouth— and when half of it burned out, I threw it away. It smelled foul, I must admit, and the aftertaste lingered unpleasantly in my mouth.

Harpers Ferry lit up with lights in the windows, like the star constellations emerging out of the night sky. People started their vehicles to go work, enjoyed their first cup of coffee, but not me. I looked after the world from the roof, the one place where I felt at peace with myself and where Derek handed me the star. I turned the pages of the calendar cautiously yet impatiently, as the hole of missing him grew stronger in my heart.

"Becca," I heard a whisper behind me. Nick's head appeared in the open window. He smelled of aftershave and coffee. Charlie stood beside him with my slipper peeking out of his mouth.

"What are you doing here so early?" I asked startled. I wasn't prepared for another adventure; I was still in my pajamas, slippers, and a coat.

"I thought we would go to the Historical Society with the diary before it is busy," Nick explained, grinning, then sniffed the air around us. "What is that ungodly smell? Have you been smoking?"

"Must be the neighbors," I lied and hoped he would believe me.

In response, he only shook his head. "Why did you?" His tone was serious.

"Doesn't really matter the reason. It was my last one. I had one left in the pack, I swear. It's two years old, probably."

"Come inside. It's freezing," Nick commented. "Nobody wants to kiss an ashtray."

"So my grandfather used to say." It was a fair judgment. I crawled back into the bedroom.

"Where is the book?" Nick asked while helping me out, holding me by my waist and pulling me into the bedroom.

"I put it in the closet," I said. "You can look there, if you like." I knew he wouldn't find the diary.

Nick stared into the closet with uncertainty. "Gosh, you could fit a family inside of this thing if you clear all the unnecessary…" His voice froze. "Oh, here it is."

I was expecting a baseball bat, a calendar, old guitar strings—anything but what my eyes fell upon. The diary. It had magically created a twin, but I knew that wasn't true. The book had migrated from under the bed to the closet without a single rumble or a rustle. I became paralyzed.

"What's up, Beccs?" Nick eyes ran across my face. "Are you okay?"

"I'm fine," I admitted. How the hell did this book travel like that?

We leaned over the bed, the relic exposed, unhinged in my hands. I didn't dare to breathe as the pages turned, revealing the images of teethed gargoyles, winged monsters, and demonic entities. Some of them were stuck on the pages, and they were moving as the pages continued flipping like some sort of horror film. There were symbols that looked like Morse code, glowing letters that showed a labyrinth. Then I saw the kaleidoscope. The diary trembled and groaned. It fell out of my hands, but Nick managed to catch it in time. And as soon as he touched it, the diary emptied itself and locked.

"What had just happened?" Nick asked, trying to open the diary once again. "It's like the book is alive."

"I think it's haunted," I revealed.

"I think it's haunting you," Nick said and handed me over the relic that was set alight with only my touch. "It's somehow connected to you." His eyes widened, but he noticed my face. "You knew that the diary behaves this way around you?" Nick asked, sitting down on the coverlet. I gave him a guilty smile. "Why am I hearing about it just now?"

I perched beside him. "I didn't want to worry you. It's nothing."

"Clearly it's the opposite. And you are out of your mind if you think I'll leave it alone. Well, get something to wear. We have a long day ahead of us. Let's move."

I thought I was the keeper of the diary, and with that I had expected full control over the damn book. As it appeared, the diary had a mind of its own, and I could hardly suppress my disappointment. Nick would find out about Derek and the demon haunting, and it was the beginning of the end— maybe the end— of our friendship. Nevertheless, I kept walking.

When I finally cleared my head from the thoughts of the world ending in front of me, we were at the doors of the Historical Society. Nick knew his way around the place and took me to the catalogue room, which was guarded by a blonde receptionist and a guy with bright yellow glasses. Both greeted us like royalty. The blonde girl lay her welcoming smile on Nick's face, twisting her curl on a finger.

"Nick! How lovely to see you! Can we be of any help?" She turned to Nick, her eyes glistening. "Mr. Wolf already left, and he asked me to tell you that the photographs you took are the work of a genius."

"Yes, Jeannie, we need to look over section ten, if you don't mind. Nineteenth-century scriptures and newspapers," he said, not noticing the compliment. It seemed like it wasn't the first time

Jeannie and Nick had crossed paths, and I was sure he was aware of her liking him. "I'll have to find him later; Becca and I have some work to do. Give me some reference numbers."

Jeannie threw a withering look at me. "All right," she said, clicking the keyboard.

After about four long minutes of us breathing and staring at Jeannie while she searched the catalogue, we heard her address the guy with glasses: "Mike, get boxes 8, 15, 56 and 27, and promptly, please. Roll them like your life depends on it."

Nick was very grateful. "Thank you, Goldilocks, we'll catch up later. I'll meet Mike with boxes in the main hall. I assume I can use him to help me in the search?"

Jeannie tilted her head and put her hands on the counter as if she were looking out of the window: "Keep him as long as you like. He's new here; it will help him learn. And I'll keep you to your promise." She lightly squeezed the pencil in between her lips. Her eyes glistened as she ran them across Nick's face. She threw a smile my way to be polite but deep down I knew: she wasn't thrilled that I was his company.

The phone rang and she picked it up with a deep sigh. She watched, knocking her nails on the keyboard, as we loaded our duffel bags over our shoulders and meandered in the direction of the stairway that led to the main hall.

"Keep you to your promise?" I rolled my eyes at Nick, passing a couple of historians in white shirts with boxes of photographs. They nodded at me in acknowledgement of my presence. "Who is she? And why is she behaving like that?"

"Jealous much?" Nick asked, taking a seat at a beautiful mahogany table next to the window.

"Not at all," I said, blood rushing to my face. "I thought if you claimed to date me, you wouldn't be interested in some rosy-cheeked receptionist in pink heels."

Nick let out a laugh. "According to you, we aren't dating, so I don't see why Jeannie would bother you so much. And how would you know that she's wearing heels? Pink ones, at that?"

"Believe me, they always do," I responded, pushing my chair closer to his and watching Jeannie at the end of the hall throw a curious glance in our direction.

Michael was pushing a rickety cart of boxes stacked to the brim with files, and the wheels of the table trembled as it shambled by. My heart stopped each time Michael took a pause to breathe and pushed the table a little further. At last, the boxes were in our arms and we all sat across from each other at the round table, digging through the paperwork.

"What are we searching for?" Michael asked, getting files out of the paper folders.

I saw Nick reach into his duffel bag for the diary. I mouthed a silent "no," and he let go of the bag handle and addressed Michael: "Anything to do with a hundred-year-old antique diary of the Grimwood family tree and ancestral lineage— Civil War battlefields."

"All right, then," Michael said, and he opened the first file.

All this time, I had a pit in my stomach that pulled a number on my intestines. What were we going to find in those boxes? What would history uncover? I grabbed a handful of files and laid them out in front of me, and a photograph slid out of the cover and got jammed in between the pages. I carefully pulled it aside, placed it onto the table, and stared at it with fright. The picture depicted a Civil War tent and a couple of folded, grass-stained fabric chairs. Two men sat in those chairs. Their faces looked familiar but not quite recognizable. Both were Confederate soldiers with weapons on their hips and tall muddy boots. The Confederate flag shone behind them at the tent entrance. Then I recognized the face in the picture. I had seen him before in my grandfather's wooden valet, in a shiny gray Confederate uniform with polished brass buttons, and the glare in his eyes gave him away. With a trembling hand I turned over the picture, which was yellowed with age and shrunken at the edges: *Shawn Grimwood, July 1, 1863.*

I lost track of time after that. I was looking but not actually seeing. Half of the Historical Society left and was replaced by a handful of workers moving boxes back into their shelves. They dragged their legs across the floors, followed by the screeching of the carts' wheels, disturbing the silence. Citrus and lavender dusting agents floated in the air. Nick patted me on the shoulder twice, but I didn't move to look at him.

Suddenly I heard heels clicking over the hardwood floors, and then a perfumed plume encased us all in its sweetness. Jeannie was leaning over our heads with three cups of aromatic coffee. "I reckoned you might need it. It's been a couple hours," she cheerfully noted, swaying her blonde ponytail.

"How very thoughtful of you." Nick grinned at her. Michael just gave her a tortured nod and lowered his eyes to the manuscripts.

"I need to use the bathroom," I stated, surprised at the notes of anger that my voice projected. Was it because of Jeannie's perfume stuck in my nostrils, or because I couldn't quite understand how two hours had gone by without me noticing? I laid the picture on the chair, so Michael, whose head was practically lying on the table— bad eyesight, or wrong prescription— wouldn't find it accidentally in the files I left open. Nick threw a quick concerned glance at me and returned to turning the pages of his giant ancestry book.

The bathroom was large and tidy, and it smelled of peaches and cream. I picked the stall in the middle, not too far away from the door and the marble vanities with automatic water-release systems. I always disliked the crack of light that streamed through both sides of the bathroom stalls. I hated the feeling of being watched, and the cracks didn't help.

I zipped my jeans up and noticed my shoes were untied. Bending down to fix my Converse laces, I saw a shadow floating beneath the toilet. My heartbeat spiked. I scooped my legs onto the toilet seat, hoping whatever was in the bathroom with me would think no one was around. Instead I heard a wild bang at the door. The bang had so much force that the metal locker unhinged, and the door swung open, crashing into the wall. An enormous shadow in the shape of a person was before me, so tall it had to bend over at the ceiling. It stretched its giant hands to catch me when I released a scream and slid in between its legs towards the door.

"THE DIARY... WHERE IS IT?" I heard the demonic voice bellow.

At this point, all of my senses were working on overdrive, and adrenaline hit my bloodstream. Before the figure could make another move on me, I sprinted out of the bathroom, faster than the wind itself. Nick and Michael were still browsing through papers at the table when I flew into the chair, causing it to turn sideways.

My heart was pumping inside of my chest and it was hard for me to steady my breathing.

Nick didn't lift his head up. "Took you long enough. Did you know your ancestor had the same diary in his belongings? I found this picture of him at the battlefield. Look." He shifted the disarray of papers away from the photograph.

I ignored him. "Nick, listen to me, we have to get out of here! And do it now— forget the damn pictures!"

Michael's dark hair stood up on his arms. It appeared that panic was infectious.

Nick rose from his chair at once. "What's wrong?" he whispered.

I didn't care that Michael was listening. "There is a freaking demon in the bathroom, and it's after the diary! It should have never left the house. We need to get back!"

The silence stood in between us. Nick was looking at me, and me at him, and then in the direction of the bathroom.

Michael threw us a concerned glance. "You guys all right?"

"Never better. We'll head out now. Something came up," Nick responded, smiling at him.

He picked up his duffel bag and, holding me under his arm, we retreated through the security checkpoint, into the gate, and out of the Historical Society building. Jennie waved at us with her skinny manicured fingers and her shoes lit up from afar. They were bright pink, just as I had predicted, but I wasn't worried about her blonde ponytail anymore.

* * *

We ran like there was no tomorrow. Shadows followed us. They flew on the wings of ravens, fell from the roofs of the Civil War houses, crawled underneath the fire hydrants and sewer drains. The world had suddenly fallen into the dark, and I felt like the darkness was catching up with us. I had injured my leg in the bathroom; it felt bruised and painful to put weight on it. Meanwhile, thunder roared outside, and the rain was soaking the leaves at the doorstep of the house with lavender curtains. Grandma had gone to visit Lida, and she had left the front porch light on. Nick pulled the key out and opened the door. The house stood in still silence, like there was nothing alive inside.

"Jeez, this place feels like a funeral parlor," Nick whispered to me, unzipping his duffel bag.

"Put the diary into the closet and shut the door. We need to make sure all windows are closed so it can't get us," I insisted.

"Do you think it will follow us here?" Nick asked, walking around, shifting the curtains and closing the latches, while Charlie ran circles around him.

The kaleidoscope was lost in the covers. I was shaking the coverlet and the pillows in hopes of discovering it, but luck apparently wasn't in my favor today.

"I believe it has the ability. I'd rather be prepared," I said, and as if in slow motion, I spotted two giant, black hands crawl out of the window and grab Nick, silencing him. Charlie ran towards the window and began barking inconsolably.

With no delay, I also rushed to the window, but everything happened so swiftly. I didn't know what to think or do. As I poked my head out, I saw Nick barely holding on to the flower box outside, and the creature: it was the same tall figure that had attacked me in the bathroom of the Historical Society building.

"God, Nick, hold on to me! I'll try to pull you out!" I yelled, trying to grab his hands. They were slippery, and every time I attempted to hold him, he would slide down the flower box another inch.

"Leave him alone, you freaky demon!" My voice was louder than before.

"Becca, my hands are slipping, I can't pull myself up..." Nick was giving up. I felt it— his arms were trembling.

"Keep holding!" I then yanked Nick up as hard as I could. "Come on, just a little bit more..." I operated on an adrenaline rush, nothing else. My leg was cramping. "Let him go!" I commanded the tall shadow man.

Suddenly, I spotted something glistening by my right side. It was the kaleidoscope. "Nick, I promise you, it's not going to win; you just have to cling to my hand with both of yours for one moment, all right? Do you trust me?"

I heard a weak groan. "Yes."

"Okay, now!"

Nick found the strength to shift, and at once I felt the weight of two horses on my arm. I grabbed the kaleidoscope, and a swirl of butterflies fluttered out from under the antique glass. The creature retreated, formed a ball, and backed down, but the metal wings still cut its flesh into strips. It collapsed onto the ground in pieces, releasing Nick's legs. With my last pull, he flew into the window of my bedroom. Charlie jumped around us while we held each other, trying to catch our breath. My head was on Nick's chest, listening to the fast beats of his heart.

"I am so sorry..." My tears were rolling down my cheeks. I noticed that his shirt was ripped to shreds, probably from the siding that stuck out from the house.

"Shhh..." he whispered. "It's over now." He began to stroke my hair.

I buried my face in his arms while the kaleidoscope lay on the floor at my side. My body felt like I had run a marathon: my arms and legs trembled, and my chest felt sore from breathing so rapidly.

Nick obviously wasn't concerned for himself, not at all. He worried if I was okay, if I was hurt. The warmth of his body started to consume me. It relaxed my muscles, causing me to lean into him some more.

Part of me knew that Nick holding me wasn't entirely because of the demon threatening our lives. He wanted me close. His arms slowly let go, taking the smell of the forest with him, and I found myself staring into his aquamarine eyes, searching for comfort.

But as I looked down, I saw spots of blood on his shirt.

"Oh my God, Nick…" I said and ran my fingers over the stained fabric.

"Don't worry your little head," he said, and put the palm of his hand on my cheek. "I scraped my arm on the siding— no big deal. I think I will be okay."

"It's a big deal to me," I said and exhaled deeply, letting out all the anxiousness of him being hurt. "You have to take it off. I probably can find something from my dad's closet that can fit you," I offered.

"Yeah…" he said. He took off his shirt, wrapped it up in a ball, and handed to me. His torso was brilliantly smooth and inviting. "The butterflies… you can command them? How?"

"He gave them to me. He said they'll save me if I need them to," I confessed.

"He? Another ghost?"

"No… Actually, I have no idea what he is. He wanted to protect me because of the diary." Nick's shirt still felt warm in my arms. A look of concern appeared on his face. "You don't need to worry— he's old, and he can't harm me."

"We should throw the diary in the Potomac. That is the only way to get rid of the demons." Nick's eyes widened, and there was no fear in them— just concern for my life.

"We can't. If we do that, I'm afraid we will give the demons what they've wanted for centuries— a pathway to our world." I lowered my eyelashes. I knew that none of it was my fault. Just a strange premonition from Madam Rose's, along with bad ancestry. "I don't think we want the shadows to be alive."

"But they already are," Nick protested and pulled himself closer to me on the floor. A piece of his ripped shirt was wrapped around his wrist like a leather bracelet.

"I don't want to be responsible for destroying the world I love. It could turn to a nightmare while we are awake," I mumbled.

"How do we send the demons back?"

"We don't. We have one job, and it's to keep the diary safe and not take it out of the house. Everything else the ghosts will take care of."

He was talking back, but I wasn't listening anymore. I was staring at his sea-foam eyes and all I wanted to do was to lay my hand on his chest, find the artery that sent blood to his heart and feel the warmth of his skin.

"Becca, are you listening?" His hand slid underneath the locks of my hair, under my ear, and my gaze fell onto his coral lips whispering: "I shouldn't have taken it, but we didn't have much time." He took out a photograph from the pocket of his jeans.

I woke up from a deep haze. "Oh, if they caught you, you would have been in a lot of trouble! Stealing from the Historical Society is a federal crime."

"Good thing they didn't catch me, then."

The photograph was old, like most of the artifacts stored inside of the boxes at the Historical Society. It showed men who were clearly a part of a Civil War regiment (just like the photograph I had seen before). Shawn Grimwood was sitting down. I couldn't tell if that was because he was wounded or not. I knew he had been at some point; he had been wounded twice. The other man was a medic in a long ivory gown and stethoscope like a snake hanging down his neck.

The third one was Derek.

My hands trembled and released the photograph; it fell to the floor between us. There was a quick kiss on my cheek, and Nick's hands and his bare shoulders wrapped around me. His warmth was finally consuming me. I closed my eyes and all I saw was his smile, a face at the back of my head. *Where are you, Derek?*

FOURTEEN

HAPPY BIRTHDAY—CAKE?

Counting the candles on a birthday cake is no easy task for a mind: the older you get, the more monotonous it becomes. You gaze above the flames into the world, everyone is smiling, at times laughing, and you hear the wrapping paper rustling, the clinking of champagne glasses behind your back. You are the one they are waiting for. You have to make a wish. And you travel back inside of your mind for an answer, and when you finally find it, buried there with other thoughts, you gently blow the candles, and you hope and pray that the wish you made does come true. I decided to make a wish the opposite of what I wanted this time. And it was, I must say, a great success.

Nick was the first to congratulate me. My phone vibrated in the middle of the night, the blue screen depicting cupcakes, fireworks, and exclamation points. Dad also called and told me I would always be his little princess, which made me tear up. Grandma appeared at the entrance of my bedroom with a bowl of fresh strawberries, which were hard to get given the date on the calendar— December fourteenth. Even Charlie had a festive bow tied around his Pekingese neck. He revved like a motorboat, paws behind his ears, bobble-headed, digging into the carpet, scratching the bow off.

The scenery beyond the roof of the house with lavender curtains was breathtaking. The sun burst from the sky in waves of orange, and the snow glowed from within, like a carpet made of diamond powder. I stared at myself in the mirror to see if I really had grown up, but what was visible to me was hardly satisfying. It was what I didn't see that made a difference.

We always wish to grow up, and for the life of me, I don't understand why. My eyelashes weren't longer, but behind them was the sad truth— that when we grow older, so do our hearts.

I wished not to see him today, a reverse wish that I knew might never come true and was silly of me to even believe in. I studied the birds from the roof of the house. They poked their tiny heads at me and continued chirping, and I reckoned if they heard me whispering to them on my birthday, maybe there was a slight chance that Derek also heard me. Despite my continuous efforts, there was only silence staring back at me, as if I wasn't welcome. To make matters worse, the diary acted like the day was wiped away from the calendar. I shrugged at it, folding it with other clothes in the dresser, deeply inhaling the scent of a candle burning on the counter, which was a gift from my grandmother. In the burning fire, there was no trace of phantom creatures of the night.

I finally changed into my nightgown. Because of the dull light from the broken chandelier, I accidentally stumbled into the nightstand. It almost fell over, but I managed to push it back to its place. It was then that I saw him, standing in the open window, curtains wobbling in his way. I thought it was a shadow. I stretched out my hand to touch him, but he retreated to the wall, igniting the carpet with lights.

"Happy birthday, Rebecca," I heard a familiar voice.

I turned another lamp on to give my squinting eyes a rest. In the dimmed room, I recognized his face, and my eyes lit up with iridescent excitement.

"Derek!" I approached him closer and noticed that something was different about him. His skin, which I used to see shining with health, now had tiny scars scattered all over it, some deeper than others. I was horrified.

"Oh my God, what happened to you?" I asked, rubbing my fingers on one of his face cuts. They felt like rocky streams in the mountains.

"Don't worry. They'll go away. They are already starting to fade," Derek said with a slight smile. "I was battling a demon on the other side. It had claws, long black ones, and it came at me." As he spoke, he mimicked the scene of a fight. "I grabbed it by its tail and swirled it in the air, but it got out and pushed me against the ground, almost sinking its teeth into my throat." Derek walked to the wall, pressed the palms of his hands onto it, and then opened his mouth to parody canine fangs.

"It's not funny! You're hurt." My expression didn't change as he danced around the room. "You'll have scars. Are you sure they aren't permanent?"

"Yes, yes. You think it's the first demon I've fought?" My heart melted as he approached me. He sighed. "I'm not going to kiss you now, even though I have missed you like you wouldn't believe."

"Why not?" I asked, grinning.

"Because a kiss from a birthday girl is full of magic, and I'd like to take you someplace special for it to count."

"What do you have in mind, demon-slayer?" I teased. His footsteps were approaching me, but he stopped just in time.

"Please tell me you are here to stay." My eyes begged him. I started to worry about how I looked. My hair was like a spiderweb, and I was wearing pajamas— who would want me like that?

"I have to go back the second the sun rises. But we still have some time. I didn't come here empty-handed. I would like to take you for a ride."

A motorcycle, a train, a bus, a taxi? What would it be this time? I was thrilled regardless, but I still wondered.

"It will be nothing like you have experienced before," Derek lowered on one knee, "but first, I want to see if they fit." He unveiled a box from behind his back; inside there lay a pair of tall riding boots. They were fringed with veins of pearls through the leather, and they had a heel that resembled an arch, which curved beautifully inwards in the form of a leaf.

"These aren't just ordinary boots... They are almost like mirrors. They reflect demons away and trap them in another realm. But most importantly, you can ride shadow horses in them."

The shoes were stunning. They sat on my legs so elegantly. I felt like I was a fairy, only without a magic wand. "Thank you," I smiled. And his smile followed after mine.

* * *

Pathways like arteries on the human body stretched out in countless directions in front of us. Derek was able to navigate the grounds well, as if he had a map inside of his head and he was following it to a T. We turned at the mossy rock by the side of the road and walked about one thousand footsteps left; then at the orchard, the road waved to the right, and we finally came to a stop.

The contours of the scenery resembled a lake. The fog hung heavily over the pearly water, creating a mist. It appeared and disappeared, like a blinking mirage of the past. The clouds floated on the dark canvas of the sky, guilty and tortured. Despite how beautiful the day had been, the night reminded me of the cold winter evenings I had spent alone in Dad's house in DC, and my heart ached. I would always watch the tree lights illuminate the room in the reflection of the window and the dying traffic on the other side of the glass after rush hour. Empty bus stations and the silence of the streets, wind knocking on my door with branches and a kettle going off in the kitchen. And nobody to turn off the whistle.

Derek watched me closely as we were standing at the banks of this magnificently purple lake, which I really couldn't make out in the dark.

"This place makes me feel unsteady," I revealed to him.

"Just wait. Give it a chance," Derek said.

Suddenly, up ahead, I saw waves of lights headed towards us like swirling mist. Ultramarine in their color, they were flickering in the distance. As the mist approached, I heard hooves— the same ones that I thought I had imagined in Gettysburg. My vision didn't betray me this time, and I knew that from the smirk on Derek's face. I saw the horses— plasmatic, translucent, and utterly free. Their hair was like strong full vines fluttering on the wind. They were so beautiful; they took my breath away. There were hundreds of luminescent tails moving just over the soft spot of the land, each oddly in unison. And the closer they got, the shakier my legs became from the awaited meeting.

In a few seconds, a horse stood by me, its hair-like flames cutting the dingy skies. I was afraid to put my hand on it. As I finally decided to bring my hand forward, a loud snort came out of its nose. I got spooked and jerked my hand away, laughing.

Derek observed our interaction. "She will not hurt you. She is my most trustworthy companion."

"She's beautiful," I remarked.

"That she is," Derek said, running his fingers through the horse's mane.

The horse rubbed her head onto his shoulder and her eyes, full of kindness, laid on his face, comforting his very soul, it seemed. They both had an invisible but undeniable understanding wrapped around them.

"So, what's her story?" I asked, holding my hand on her side, feeling her great muscles move under the palm of my hand. "I guess, their story?" I corrected myself.

"Her name was Moon, and she was my battle horse. She caught a bullet and died in the field, like many others. But we have gone through fire together, right, girl?" Derek addressed the horse and pinned his head to hers. "It's the lingering spiritual energy that's left by the lake that keeps them here. There is no better place on earth for them."

I remembered the photograph— Derek in the gray uniform with my great-grandfather. His body brought to the mausoleum in a carriage and soldiers standing by the doors, forage caps off. *What is it that he is hiding, and how is it still possible for him to still be here with me?*

"Hello, Moon," I greeted the horse, who in turn licked my nose with her long purple tongue. I had so many questions for him. "Are they all battle horses?"

"All stages of ghost matter are present here. But mostly, those are the shadow horses from the Gettysburg days. You see the white horse with a swinging black tail on the other bank of the lake?"

I squinted my eyes into the dark. Shaded by the oaks, with its tiny head and muscled torso, I saw the horse Derek was talking about. He was drinking water out of the lake, and his eyes glowed gold. They contrasted dramatically with the dark.

"That's Traveler, General Robert E. Lee's horse," Derek declared.

The horse was a magnificent, delicately shaped creature with strong long legs. Its habitat was now the pages and pages of history books, the one and only companion of a general through countless battles. That horse knew him better than anyone. I couldn't believe I was staring at Traveler. Through Derek, history wasn't so far out of my reach.

The owls were hooting, reminding me. "Derek, do you promise not to be mad at me?" I felt my hands sweating, heart racing under the ribcage.

"When you have been around for a long time, you learn not to keep promises like that. But regardless of what you just said, please, ask away," he stated, and he switched his attention from Moon to me.

"This is sort of confusing. You told me before that you are the gatekeeper for the diary, and you haunt things you meet in the dark." My voice trembled, but I hoped he didn't notice.

"Aye. That is correct," he nodded.

"How old are you?" I asked, and my hand ended up meeting his in the mane of the horse. It was too direct of a question, but I had to know.

"I'm pretty old." He raised his velvet eyebrows at me.

"But you don't look old. You are roughly my age or a little older?" From the expression that appeared on his face, I knew talking about his life would anger him.

"What is this about?" His green eyes crinkled.

"Nothing," I cut him off, but I was burning inside from curiosity. Kissing him was the most incredible feeling, but I had to also know him. He had no clue those two went together, like two swirls of ice-cream. "Which battle were you referring to when you spoke of Moon?" Another direct question, but I couldn't contain myself any longer.

Derek shook his head. "Why such interest in my life? You ran out of things to do at home?" The spark in his eye diminished, and I recognized that irritated look. I had seen it before multiple times on my father's face when I refused to let him peek into my life.

"I didn't mean anything by it. I just want to know you."

"You already do. What else do you want?" Derek snapped and pulled the horse reins, moving Moon away like he was protecting her from me.

"You think I do? Then how do you explain this?" I opened my purse and showed him the photograph.

His demeanor changed at once, and he backed away from me. "Where did you get this?"

I heard a rumble above my head. Dark, ominous clouds spiraled over our heads. There was no snow on the ground anymore, just the beginning of a storm. Shortly after that, a yellow spark pierced the ground, and we were covered with the rain; not drops of water but stars literally falling from the skies.

"Is this your doing? The weather?" I asked, but Derek threw a withering look at me and then continued to ignore me.

"Answer the damn question." Four words came out of his mouth with no emotion whatsoever.

"I got the photograph from the Historical Society of Harpers Ferry. Well, Nick stole it from there."

Great, I thought, *now I'm also a rat.*

"How do you know my great-grandfather? And why are you keeping it a secret from me?" At this point, I was happy to wear my mirror-like shoes. No starfall could destroy them.

"Some things are better off buried in the past. And you have no right to dig your curious little nose in things that aren't any of your business, to be truthful. And tell your minion the same."

The storm was now so extensive that the lightning set the trees on fire. I saw the horses race away from the site, except for Moon.

"Stop it, Derek! You'll burn the whole place down!"

I came up to him and put my two hands on his back. It worked; the wind subsided, the stars magically took their places in the sky again, and I even caught a glimpse of the sun peering through the clouds. Short silence collapsed in between us.

"Don't you think I deserve to know? He was my relative. Do you realize how unfair and unkind you are?"

"What's unfair and unkind is life. The whole thing. I knew Shawn, yes, because we were at war together and died together."

Derek's words shocked me. He knew how my great-grandfather died, and I didn't think I was prepared to have that knowledge. And Derek… was he a ghost?

"I am not a ghost, if that's what you are wondering," he answered as if he heard me. "I am not alive, and I am not dead. I'm stuck in the middle. And I am not going to tell you how he died because I simply don't believe he would want you to know. And I respect his wishes."

An idea came to my mind very swiftly. "Can I please talk to him?"

"You can't. He is long gone. He is not like me, nor other ghosts. He has moved on. Now, if you don't mind, let's take a ride," he said. He jumped up onto the horse and offered me his hand.

"Who is the third man in the photograph? A buddy of yours?" I asked, sliding my legs in their mirror boots. Derek held me tight as I climbed onto the horse.

"I could hardly call him a man. He is nothing but a monster— a battle surgeon who caused the death of two people because of his undying desire to bring evil. At one time, he was our companion. We thought we knew him well." There was pure hatred in Derek's voice.

"I am so sorry," I said and pressed my cheek onto Derek's back.

He didn't respond but raised the reins and led Moon into the open fields of wheat. We retreated into the night on the cloud of sapphire mist away from the lake.

* * *

Time— what a unique element of life. It slips away so easily, and yet when missing someone you love, it seems to stop, dragging you with it into the everlasting spiral of uncertainty. It was unbearable to think Derek had to leave again. Letting him go, when his heart beat heavy in his chest with the weight of the past, appeared to be the worst departure ever. But I knew that no matter what, I had to push through. Even if it meant draining his heart from the world of shadows.

The horse galloped swiftly over the water and the mud, neighing with freedom and amusement. Willow trees, luscious bushes, the mirage lake— all of it faded behind us when Moon raced to the clouds. We floated over broad fields, and I had to keep my eyes closed. Apparently, I feared heights almost as much as I feared demons. Derek was silent the whole way, but I didn't blame him. It was pleasant for the stillness to pass between us. After all, it didn't hurt anyone.

When Moon suddenly began to lose height, we ended up standing next to a medium-sized house made of terracotta bricks. A wine barrel rested at the wooden front door, but it was empty; someone was using it for a rose garden. White-framed windows on both sides of the house opened into the wheat fields and the forest, with nothing else in their view. I stepped inside, and the aroma of flowers hit me with a wave of sweetness. Derek tied the horse to the ivory column of the house and followed the sound of my footsteps inside. The chandeliers on the walls lit up as he walked.

The ceiling was a carpet of beautifully carved tiles. The walls were royal wallpaper. I followed him down a long hallway into a living room fringed by vintage furniture and heavy auburn curtains. We stopped by two armchairs with lion heads forming their arms. I inched closer to Derek. He was right about the scars— there weren't many left. As I traced them with my fingers, he flinched.

"Why is it so hard for you to let me in?" I asked, breaking the silence.

He slid into one of the armchairs near the fireplace. "Because I am not used to someone picking my life apart. I am not some chess game. I don't need to be solved. I know my worth—I am sick of judgment. I came a long way to get to where I am. And you, of all people, should know what that feels like," Derek said and scratched his head. "This house is cold." He only looked once at the logs, and they set themselves ablaze. "There. Better."

"I'm not going to judge you! Whatever it is you did! You think you're the only one with skeletons in your closet?" I'd had enough this time. "I'm always the villain in your story. I'm sick of it— like I'm not to be trusted. I never did anything to you to form such an opinion of me."

It looked like I had frazzled him, but he somehow managed to hold his emotions in. "You're right. I am sorry if I offended you. If my behavior did." The shadows played beautifully on his face.

"Look, I don't want to know if you don't want to share. But it would be nice if you did because that way you won't forever be a stranger with incredible, magical gifts. You'd be a man I'd like to fall for."

His eyes caught mine, and we stared at each other for a few minutes.

"I don't need you to know the disappointing parts of me because, whether you want it or not, I will be stuck in your memory that way."

"I promise you, Derek, I am not going to let you go because some part of you sinned in the past. Whoever you are right now—that's who I'm fighting for. Who I wait for, who I'll always wait for. Not some dark Derek Civil War soldier. You aren't going to scare me away. Not now, not after everything," I said, taking a seat in another armchair.

His piercing, green eyes wandered the room. I only now noticed how aristocratic his nose was and how darkly shaded his cheeks were because of the beard.

"I had a brother, George. He is the man in the picture," Derek admitted quietly after a deep sigh.

"The battle surgeon you were talking about?"

"Yes. He possessed an incredible gift— an intelligent mind like no other. It was a blessing but also a curse. Every task became his fierce obsession. One desire could turn him into a vengeful chaser. A book of magic fell into his hands one day and put a dark shadow on all our lives. We soon noticed how sickness enveloped our entire residence, dragging our mother with it. Instead of blooming flowers, there were dried stems; the horses laid upon the ground breathless from no cause known to man. Eventually, George and I drifted apart. The next time I met him was at the battlegrounds, where he chopped up an unconscious soldier in the camp. Instead of just amputating his injured arm, he thought that the other one should go too. When I confronted him, he said it was for the symmetry." Derek's voice faded.

The logs crackled with enflamed wood tops. Derek wasn't looking at me anymore. I approached him slowly, putting my hand on his chin and bringing his face closer to mine.

"That was not your fault. You didn't make him that way."

"I covered for him. I didn't mention his deeds to anyone— except your great-grandfather, Shawn, but not until later. Do you know how many people he mutilated? How many lives he managed to destroy? He was worse than the fact that we were at war."

I had never had a sibling. I had no idea what it would feel like if my brother grew up to be a monster. Derek's pain lay inside of his eyes like an obelisk. It wasn't going anywhere, and that pain— it had a way of spreading. My heart started to ache for him.

"And I am as bad as him," Derek said, staring sullenly into the fire.

"You are nothing like him." I chased his fingers with mine. "Life changes us. You don't know what he had to bear— what made him the way that he was." His lips looked soft and warm.

"I know that whoever he used to be, that part of him is gone now. I will never get him back. The only way to help the ghosts now is to put a knife deep inside of his dark heart." Derek absentmindedly curled my hair with his fingers. "Your hair is so luscious, just like silk," he murmured, but there was no smile on this face. I realized that I was his distraction.

I studied the ovals of Derek's face when I thought I saw a shadow cross the room. It was quick, like a gust of wind. The shadow, it seemed, was made out of lights, and it was soon swallowed by the jet-blackness of the house.

"Did you see that?" I turned to Derek, who was still entangled in the curls of my hair.

"Was it a spark?"

"Something like that," I explained and continued watching the room as it evolved around us like a field of fireflies. The sparks became fast and spontaneous; they collided into each other as they traveled the same route. They bounced off the walls crazily, and when I stood up, letting go of Derek's hand, they froze in mid-air.

Suddenly I felt as light as a feather and hands, his warm hands, lifted me off the armchair. Derek's glowing eyes were locked on mine and the ocean of lights surrounding us. For a moment, I forgot all about the darkness. My hands were wrapped around his back tightly, and I felt his skin touching mine.

"Are those ghosts? The sparks?" I asked in wonder.

Derek smiled, exposing his straight white teeth. "No, it is you. This is how I feel about you."

I didn't know if I wanted to laugh or to cry. My heart burst with joy so abruptly. He pressed his lips against mine, and his force absorbed me whole. We were lost among the lights, but what mattered was that we were lost together. I heard clapping of hands on the wind, and when Derek released me, the house was filled with ghosts of Civil War soldiers; they were all applauding us. Translucent, all in uniforms, groomed and happy, like the war never happened. I couldn't have asked for a better birthday kiss.

As the night drifted away in the smear of the upcoming morning, I was ready for anything but that one thing. The windows were fading in the first light of the sun. We sat on the porch, wind in our hair, when his hand let go of mine. I closed my eyes. Derek was no longer beside me. A tear rolled down my face, salty and foreign on my skin. A stream of light pierced the sky, pushing back the clouds. I stood up slowly and untied Moon from the column of the house. She slid her head behind my hand and snorted, promising me she would take me home safely.

FIFTEEN

AT THE FROZEN RIVER

Winter glided into Harpers Ferry like a bride in her ivory gown, her weightless satin train spreading over the sleepy houses, the Potomac and Shenandoah rivers, and perky mountain tops. Snow crunched under Mr. Wolf's heavy foot like a bag of cheesy crackers while he hurried to Sally's *Tis the Season* store on a Saturday morning. In winter, darkness hardly had a chance to bother him; the streets stayed bright with lights, and the snow glowed from within even after hours.

Hiding behind the window of the town's taxicab, I noticed how fast my breath had fogged up the window. I could still see the square through the rough, sharp circles. The Swanskin family, who lived two houses over, made a snowman and twisted a lovely scarf around its neck.

"Becca, it's for the cold!" their voices muttered.

Even though autumn still breathed down winter's back, Christmas trees emerged from the ground, resembling mushrooms popping out after the rain. Soon after that, poinsettias appeared in the café's windows and, with them, elves stormed the streets in their long olive shoes. Children's voices faded behind my back while I stared into the water, which had turned to a heavy natural glass of dazzling beauty. It was strange to think how the world resembled a garland with frosted golden balls, joyful and full of holiday spirit, while my heart longed for the one thing I couldn't have. That alone took over my holiday spirit.

At home, things seemed great. Grandma kept adding logs into the fire, singing under her breath and bragging about decorating the house to the best of her ability. The stairs to the upper floor now sparkled with azure lights. A bronze coat hanger had a *Deduska Moroz* (Russian Santa, as I knew of it) lying underneath it, half-sticking its head out from the wooden legs. This time around, the Christmas tree smelled of pinecones and cinnamon. I couldn't tell whether the scent was coming out of the oven from Grandma's cupcakes, if it was from the tree itself, or if it was simply a figment of my imagination.

We spent most nights sitting by the fireplace— Charlie in his Christmas sweater and a beanie, me in my long wool socks, and Grandma in her red gown. We pulled out toys and wrapping paper from boxes. Grandma had a real talent for placing ornaments on the tree. It would take a trained eye to find them. I, on the other hand, did not have this talent.

All the toys were original circa 1955 and looked like antique masterpieces, glossy and hand-painted. Silver teapots, old Russian samovars (which operated on coal), colorful cups with saucers, stars made of beads, dolls, tiny squirrels, and small glass balls all found their designated places. Some of the balls were white but had red stars pressed inside, making them look like an optical illusion. Grandma still dropped cotton balls onto the tree along with long shiny beads— a tradition she and her six brothers and sisters used to abide by. I guessed I knew now what the bragging was about. The house stood festive thanks to her sacred family traditions and years of ornament preservation.

I kept looking at the tree, mesmerized. Its green needles scratched the ceiling, and Grandma continued walking around the tree in circles in an attempt to decorate it from all angles. For a moment, I was lost, drifting in the memories of her past. Children picking the nicest, tallest pine tree in the woods; men cutting it down, and the sound of the horse-sled cruising the ruffled snow, its blades cutting straight lines on the road. The world had changed since then, and I wasn't sure if it was for the better. Grandma swore on those stories. The more she told them, the more I wanted to travel in time.

Suddenly, the sound of a ringing doorbell filled the living room. Grandma and I gave each other a smile, as if we both knew who was standing behind the door. In a floppy red hat with fur, oversized gloves, and two pairs of skates over his shoulder, there stood Nick, grinning.

"Took you long enough." I hurried upstairs for my rose-colored parka. You see, I had a tradition of my own.

I had held to the rim of the skating rink since my grandparents bought me my first pair of skates. It took a couple of awful landings on the ice to bruise my ankles, followed by a sprained wrist from a fall. But I still tried. Turns out, bumps and scars are the roses of striving, and if they hurt, they are a reminder of what it took to get them.

When we reached the skating rink, the sun was sitting high in the sky, as if it were an astronaut waving at us from the moon. Bright and unusually hot, it blinded us along with the children scavenging the ring-like wild animals.

"Becca, where did you take me?" Nick asked, looking around. Faces of red-cheeked children came at him from every corner.

"I thought you took me here," I contradicted him, not believing the commotion.

A couple of feet away, a boy in an ugly sweater was kneeling on the ice, searching for his lost glasses, when another boy crashed into him. Both went flying like two hockey pucks aimed at a steel goal. On the benches by the entrance, things didn't look any better. A girl with two ponytails was wailing and suffocating a teddy bear in a hug while her mom tried to fit her into a pair of skates. Winter hats and gloves were flying around in the air, unclaimed.

"Busy day— winter break and all. I doubt we'll be able to skate undisturbed," Nick said, putting the skates over his shoulder.

"You'd be surprised. There's another rink just behind those trees. We've been here before, remember? Fifth grade? It's not as crowded," I explained.

"No, I don't remember." He rubbed his hair into a triangle.

"You followed Sally here. Where you wrote 'I love you' on the ice with the skate blades. She was so ecstatic!"

Nick let out a groan. "Thanks, Becca. That's an embarrassment any eleven-year-old boy would try to forget. I'm a man now."

"Big scary man! I know, I know. Didn't mean to hurt your ego," I teased him.

I was right about the skating rink. Behind the tall pines just over the hill lay a mirror-like surface, frosty and glossy. From afar, it looked like seafoam cradled by the wind. There were a few people on the rink, but none that were skating. The ice itself was riddled with skate lines in countless directions, and the cuts formed a road.

I put my blades on at once and began walking. Nick held me tight, leading us onto the rink. All I could think about was his hand resting on my waist, his warm fingers touching the edge of my back. I knew he wouldn't let me fall, even if I longed to accidentally slip on the ice, just for the sake of it.

"You know, I've done this since I was a little girl. You don't have to hold me," I told him.

"It's just a habit of mine…" he said, and a smile floated onto his mouth. "Any strange occurrences since we locked away the diary?"

"Not that I know of. Way to change the topic," I said, thinking about Derek and our shadowy horse ride.

"I apologize. It's just that it's not every day that you find an old relic that summons monsters," he said amusedly, his figure moving away from me and then coming back forward to bring crisp winter air with him.

"You mean demons," I corrected Nick, skating in circles around him.

"Of course. Do you think it's the end of it? I mean… Do we have to take any more precautions? Drive the diary to the end of town? I know it's been a couple of weeks, but its presence in your home concerns me."

"Well, I guess it concerns me too. But what can I do? It's not like I can suddenly erase it with a magic marker. It's destiny. We just have to learn to live with it," I said playfully.

"Endangering yourself isn't what destiny is, by definition. And by the way, the files in the Historical Society we looked at … There is some pretty dark history over there. I went through them the other day."

My eyes widened in surprise. I slowly slid next to him, my heart skipping a beat. "What do you mean by dark history?"

Why would he be roaming through the files? Why couldn't he just leave it alone? *He must have found out about Derek,* I thought. *This will not end well.*

Nick's eyelashes flickered at me. "The diary once belonged to a man known as 'the butcher' during the Civil War. Rumor has it he chopped up healthy men and then claimed that they were a sacrifice to the ultimate gods, which he referred to as the Devil. Some sort of soul-sacrifice. The photograph of the diary he used looked like the twin sister of our diary, minus the black cover."

Air escaped from my lungs rapidly, followed by a sigh of relief. *Thank God, he doesn't know.* "Really?" I asked, feigning disbelief. "I've never heard of the other book. I think we need to stop digging now. If someone finds out— if the other book has any power whatsoever, and I bet it does— and we drift off track, we'll be in a lot of trouble."

"If our diary summons demons, what in the world does 'the butcher's' diary do?" Glancing down, Nick noticed his skates were untied, and he carefully lowered himself to his knee to fix them.

"We better never find out. Evil has no boundaries; it lives through time and history and gets carried through people. When you really give it some thought, evil is indestructible."

"Just like love," he said, and our eyes met. Despite the cold, I felt a wave of scarlet burn my face. "At least we have that."

"You don't say," I mumbled. Nick was sweet and kind, and we could understand each other so well. But the word "love" escaped his mouth, and all I could think about were Derek's emerald eyes hooked on mine.

It felt wrong to look at Nick this way. To feel a yank under the ribcage when I was waiting for Derek. Yet the answer, like a skeleton key with no door to fit into, eluded me.

We drew pirouettes on the ice with our skate blades: pretty pictures of tomorrow, blooming faces of spring, and autumn nights by the fire. With every turn, it seemed like we explored the underground. We raced to catch the falling stars. At the bottom of the lake, the sun burst through the mossy water, strikes of light penetrating the surface like pillars. It was magical to feel free from the world for once, wind blowing in my face and Nick chuckling in the background from a silly joke I made.

His eyes stared at the bottom of my soul, at the parts that I didn't want to share. Nick somehow understood me, and that didn't scare him. With dreams from hell, paranormal occurrences, and demons, he didn't find me insane. It might have been a decade of friendship lingering between us, but there was something else too. Something I didn't allow myself to feel.

As I was slowly drifting into a dream about my best friend, I suddenly saw *him*, drifting in between the figures of children and parents who were joyfully chatting in the background. Everything around me, and everyone on the skating rink, just simply froze by a swing of a magic feather. A soldier walked towards me, carefully placing his boots on the ice, a gun swinging off his shoulder. He had big black bushy eyebrows, eyes as dark as the ashiest caves, and hair as curly as a thousand intertwined telephone cords. His eyes jammed on mine as he lowered on one knee, lining up a shot.

And then he fired.

I fell onto the ice, bruising my ankles, but there was no sign of a penetrating wound. It seemed the soldier had fired into the air and missed. I stood up and looked over to where I had last seen him, but he was long gone. Not a trace of his existence. Beneath me, under a thick layer of ice, I suddenly saw a face. It almost looked like a person made of ice—a frozen doll. I let out a scream and quickly scooted to the side. The skating rink turned to still water; I was soaked in it. I tried to stand up, lifting the hem of my parka, when I noticed that the water had a rosewood tint to it. I was actually standing in a pool of blood. I was so terrified by the sight that I felt dizzy. I buried my face inside of my hands, and as soon as I did, my vision disappeared. The next thing I knew, a plump-looking boy from the other side of the rink swept me off my feet. Literally.

* * *

When I opened my eyes, Nick was standing over me with a cup of mocha. He looked curious and concerned.

"I don't know how to tell you this, but, oh boy, you won't be able to go outside for a week— not to mention look at yourself in the mirror— with a bruise like that," he said, pointing under my left eye.

Hardly breathing, I flew off the bed, compulsively feeling the sore spot above my cheek. I realized there was no bruise. I grabbed one of the pillows and, with all the strength I could gather, threw it at Nick. He bent to the ground, laughing hysterically, holding on to his stomach as if we were in the middle of a circus, and I was the main source of his entertainment.

"You are such a liar, Nicholas! You know how to say just the right thing to get me out of bed!" I took a sip of mocha. The hot liquid spread to all parts of my body like the light of the rising sun setting its rays on the prairie.

Nick lowered onto the velvety duvet. He put his hand on my cheek, right under the ear. Pushing my hair to the side, gazing inside of my soul, he asked in all seriousness: "What happened to you out there?"

"What do you mean?" I asked, confused. "I collided with a kid twice my weight."

"No, that's not it. You looked like you saw a ghost," Nick explained, holding my bed pillow in his arms. He didn't take his eyes off my face.

The memory of the soldier still lingered inside of my mind.

"All right, Holmes, you want to know the truth? I saw a ghost of a Civil War Soldier, who I think tried to kill me. But the bullets were ghost bullets, so he didn't actually kill me. Can you help with that?"

Nick's eyes got wide and dark. "Are you serious?"

"Couldn't be more serious," I confirmed.

"I thought your specialty was demons, not ghosts." Nick chuckled, popping his head into the closet to make sure the diary was in its place.

"The other side is an unexplored world of shadows; both of the creatures exist there. For one reason or another, I think the shadow world opens its gates for me whenever it feels like it. I'm not sure why," I said and sighed deeply.

"I think I know why. It wants you to be a part of it," Nick said and lay on the bed next to me, our heads directed at the ceiling made of stars.

"But why would I be of such importance?" I couldn't wrap my mind around his thinking.

"Because being vulnerable is what the other side despises most. It only makes sense."

"So, you think that the other side wants me dead? That's the reason I see soldiers running around trying to shoot me?" I said and lit up a candle at my nightstand.

"I think it's more complicated than anything we had ever imagined."

"Maybe the ghosts are trying to help me? Did you consider that?"

"By gunning you down?" He pulled out a bag of Skittles, threw one into his mouth, and offered the next one to me.

"No, thanks. I like the red ones," I said. "Well, maybe it's his death site we invaded. Harpers Ferry was a battle zone, after all. It could be a simple coincidence."

"I don't know enough dead people to give you advice on this. Do you?"

185

I remembered the drummer boy. "No."

"You know, when I was researching your grandfather and the crazy surgeon, I also found an account of a soldier who lived here in the town…" But he didn't have a chance to finish.

We heard a commotion downstairs. The sound of the doorbell seemed to travel into a new dimension, like a UFO, and we didn't have a good grasp on it. The voices became louder, their echoes ricocheting off the corners, growing stronger. Nick went silent, and I peered from the corner of the bedroom down the hall and saw my father standing by the staircase with a woman I barely remembered.

When I was gravely sick (or I thought I was), with a 102°F temperature, wrapped in apple vinegar at about fifteen years of age, I had seen her—her buckeye hair in soft curls, touching my forehead to make sure I wasn't burning up, a scent of honey and ginger absorbed in her hair, and her name… Alice.

"Rebecca, come here, honey," my father called.

He must have seen me from the stairs. What is he doing here? I will always remember that walk down and the seriousness of his voice. I thought the walls were crashing down on me. My father's face, a colorful mosaic of shapes, and the fog… It caught me, threw me off guard, its hands dragging me by my feet into a hole.

The words were coming from above, like thunder, loud and clear: "I am sorry, Rebecca, but your mother has passed away."

The faces— they all became distorted. And as much as I tried to find familiar shapes, contours— as much as I wished for the ground to split apart and devour me— I couldn't make out the faces of people. One minute they gazed back at me; the next, they were gone. I remember hands, hugs, whispers, but no tears. Grandma, my father, Alice. I was bigger than the room, which kept shifting around me. I was tiny. People with demon-faces stared down at me, and I, confused and somehow relieved, just sat there, breathing weakly through the beats of my racing heart. At that moment, silence became loud. Too loud to bear.

The next thing I knew, the cold air took my breath away and the lights in the Potomac street blinded me, as if I was chained to the sun and couldn't shift away. Falling snow covered downtown in the form of sifted flour.

I ran, faster than my shadow, lost in the pinecone light of the disappearing town, snowflakes burning into my skin, soaked up by the wool of my beanie. With each breath, I watched a white cloud of warmth rise above me, freeze like a crystal ball for a moment, and then diminish into the coldness. The town was already empty, the streets bold and frigid. The stars shone brightly upon the white mountain, and I knew they were as lonely as I was, as lost. I felt sadness forming a bubble around my heart.

Then I suddenly stopped. Not because I was tired or directionless, but because I was standing in front of an incredibly large frozen space. There was an antique bench in the middle of that space with a bump of snow resting on top of it. You would find such stone benches at the town's fair or by an old ice-cream shop, and they would usually look gray. But not this one. Under the moon's reign, that bench radiated blue. I could see butterflies bursting into the air like fireworks, filling it with a train of rainbow color and sparkling dust. The night was beautifully reflected on their wings like in a mirror.

I approached the bench with no hesitation. As soon as I did, the butterflies shattered away, and instead, floating above, there was a white ball of energy made up of lights. The sky was covered with millions of them, hanging in the frozen air. I sat beside the ball, eyes focusing on the lights, and for a moment, my sadness, the pain that I attempted to bury inside, ceased. My hands, two icicles under the mittens, became warm as if I were sitting by a burning fireplace. I reached to touch it— and the lights went out. Then I saw nothing but enveloping darkness.

When I came to my senses, one familiar feeling still remained— my cheeks burned with warmth. The room was drowned in sunset colors from the burning wooden logs. A wool throw blanket swirled in wide folds by my feet, and the pillow I laid on kept releasing feathers onto the air. They reminded me of snow. I was still trembling, and not from the cold I had exposed myself to, but from the feeling that the world had faded in front of me. I had lost someone. Someone who could never return.

Nick followed my eyes across the room and shook his head. We were in his bedroom in Lida's house. He was tossing the logs onto the fire, igniting them by poking them with an iron. The blizzard hissed by the windowsills, falling in between the cracks of the house. I could hear the wind wailing outside, as if it were drawing circles with air.

The dim light of the fireplace played shadows on our faces. Nick looked shaken up. Catching my eyes with his, he spoke. "If I hadn't found you, you could have died out there," he said solemnly, hanging the fire iron in its designated place on the wall.

I didn't know what to tell him. There was nothing I remembered.

"I know," I whispered, holding on to the corners of the throw.

"You know? Don't give me that. What the hell were you thinking? Your Grams, your father, even that woman of his have never been so worried." This time he crawled onto the floor with me and took my hands into his while laying my hurting head back on the pillow.

Tears began pouring down my face. *Another droplet and I won't be able to talk,* I thought.

"She died." I let go of those words like they weren't mine, like they didn't belong with me.

"You didn't know her," Nick said.

I knew it was stupid of me to have run. There must have been a wave of rage building up inside of his chest, and I knew it took everything inside of him to send it away.

"She was still my mother." It was a fact.

"And you are still my best friend. The thought of losing you... You don't want to know what I feel right now— how mad I am at you. We have demons crawling around this town— real demons, not some fairytale villains— and you decide to wander into the night. What were you thinking? How selfish of you! You have people who care about you. Your well-being. People who love you, who are terrified that something may happen to you."

A wave of anger crossed my face. "Are you talking about my family or yourself? Because it's pretty evident that you're too involved with me. And nobody asked you to be."

Nick flinched and backed away from me. "If you want to be cruel to me, please, be my guest. I can take it. I know you're hurting, and I can understand that. But you could have talked to me. I was right here!"

"Sometimes, people simply want to be left alone. I am not your charity case. Not your damsel in distress."

I couldn't believe I was talking to Nick in this tone after everything he had done for me. Yet my pain suddenly turned to anger, and I had to find relief for it before it swallowed me. His eyes became sullen.

"Nick, I'm sorry," I said, sitting up from the pillow. "I didn't know what I was doing. I didn't think. I can't tell you what happened between the moment I left the house and ended up here," I confessed.

Then there was silence between us, followed by the crackling of the fire logs.

"It's okay, Becca. We just have to get through this together." His voice was soft and calming.

I wanted to be held, to be cherished, to fall into his arms and forget that— out there in the world— there was pain, there was death. Nothing was immortal.

Nick suddenly pulled me closer, and my heart gave out. Anger drifted away, and all I felt was the overwhelming pain of not having a mother. I nestled in Nick's arms, face just underneath his chin, his warmth coming over me like a mist. I felt his heart, its quivering correspondence with mine. The connection we so desperately tried to veil from ourselves was obvious. Now, more than ever, I didn't want to let go. Derek's face mingled with the wind outside, and I longed to be with him.

"How did you find me?" I asked while we watched the fire consume the wood.

"I followed your footsteps into the forest. This time of year, they're pretty easy to see. And then I saw you lying on the ice of the Potomac River. I lifted you up from the ice and carried you back here."

"What do you mean, the Potomac River? I was sitting on the bench. Under the light," I said, confused.

"There was no bench, Rebecca, and definitely no light. It's a miracle the ice didn't break," Nick assured me.

"But I remember the lights, like snowflakes falling from the sky… Someone took me under their wing. There was warmth and kindness like I've never experienced before," I tried to explain.

Nick lightly shook his head. "I think you're still in shock, and that's okay. Everyone reacts to trauma differently. You just need to sleep. Tomorrow will be better, I promise you. It's all in your mind. For all we know, you might have seen another ghost."

But I knew there was no ghost.

SIXTEEN

IN THE END OF THE RAINBOW

I woke up when the grandfather clock chimed three a.m. The winter storm had already ascended as if someone had picked up an invisible pencil and formed snow into the shapes of ponies, snowman, and gingerbread cookies. Like a creature with its own mind, the wind was growling at me, slipping into the wilderness through a crack in my bedroom window. It had raked the snow onto the roofs of houses, resembling diamond powder waves. Once in a while, with the roofs at the back of its mind, the wind hissed, forcing me to peer out through the blinds into the street to watch uninvited guests crawling out of the night.

Chronic insomnia was getting the best of me, caused by my undying fear of demons stumbling into the house. The thought of ghosts wasn't comforting either, and after running into the Civil War soldier at the skating ring, I was convinced that they were going to follow me, just like the demons did. The diary possessed power that was beyond anything I'd ever experienced, and I knew nothing about its limits.

I needed to find Philip. It was essential that I knew the truth. The easiest way to talk to the dead was to call for them in the place they departed. I figured if they could see me, then there must be a way for us to communicate. I decided to abandon my bed and head to the townhouse where the little drummer boy had died.

The streets were so empty and motionless that I had to watch my back in case monsters of the human world wandered the streets at this hour. My feet were cold, and it felt like needles were poking at the tips of my toes.

The house stood in the heart of the Historic District, silver moss hanging lifeless from the roof. There were still footprints in the snow from the Harpers Ferry tour guides that occasionally stopped by the house to recall its story, but they had begun to fade away— just like the day when the little drummer boy was last seen alive.

I jerked the door handle, and the door swung open. Coldness brushed by me, and peering into the room was like looking into a black mirror that didn't have a reflection. It was the same feeling I had when I'd seen the spirit tunnel— when I had held my dad's wedding ring on Christmas Eve in front of the mirror. They said if you saw something traveling through the tunnel, and the ring spun, you would be lucky to marry. I never believed in magic, but on spiritual nights like that, I was willing to give it a try. The tunnel, though, had its secrets. Once you peered inside, you never knew what would crawl out.

The house was a two-story building with high ceilings and unique shutters. If restored, it would have been a lovely place to live because of its old architecture and grandiose vestibule. I took a step, and the floorboards creaked underneath my feet as if they were made of glass. I heard a whisper, and then the door behind me closed shut. I slowly lifted my foot off the floor and peered into the blackness. My heart lurched.

"Philip? I know you returned here. Derek told me. Do you remember me? I'm Rebecca. Derek and I— well, mostly Derek— were taking care of you. I have a favor to ask. It's very important that you talk to me," I said.

There were footsteps and childish laughter flowing down the staircase. Then a figure of a boy in a uniform appeared next to the doorway. It raced towards me and grabbed me by the hand with all the strength he could gather.

"What are you doing here, Rebecca? You have to get out of this house. There is energy here you don't want to mess with. Demonic energy."

I whispered into his ear, "I need to know why I see the ghosts and why they're after me."

"All I know is that things are out-of-balance among the dead. After I left you and Derek at the cemetery, I crossed over and found my mom. She has been educating me since on the ghost movements. She told me that the gate is unsteady, and the ghosts are confused because evil has escaped to the other side. I learned that the gate enlightens the ghosts about the demons, serving as some sort of protection mechanism. So, when they heard that the butcher found the book, they became concerned that our world will cease to exist. The ghosts are seeking help. And I think it's your help that they are seeking," Philip explained. He breathed heavily and kept turning his head towards the staircase, in case someone was coming.

"By the book, you mean the diary. It's safe. I can assure you. There is nothing to be afraid of," I vowed.

"No. You don't understand. They're talking about the relic that has been lost for centuries and is now found. The book that rules the underworld and turns spirits into the slaves of the dark. They say when it is open, there will be raven shadows in the sky, which will steal our souls and summon them to hell. That's what my mom told me." Philip nodded. "Rebecca, the two books— they can never know of each other's existence," he said, and I suddenly heard a growl coming from the roof, the sound of one hundred trucks revving in the distance. My hands trembled. Philip's concerned eyes lay upon mine.

"What does that mean? What will happen if they do?" I insisted, feeling paralyzed.

"There would be such an explosion of power that it would wipe away both worlds. Not just the dead, but the living also. Please don't let that happen," the drummer boy begged. He then lowered his voice to that of the wind. "Now, get out of here, before the monster awakens," Philip said, shoving me into the street.

"What about you? Why are you still here?" I asked.

"I spy on them for the gate. In life and in death," he explained.

He vanished. I found myself standing by the door with snow falling heavily from the sky. The porch of the house had already been covered with a white carpet.

I descended into the night, snow crumbling under my feet. I felt exhausted, like the energy I carried had been sucked out of me. Ghosts did drain people, they said. The thought of them crowded my mind. I thought about my mother— of her luxurious hair spread onto the covers and my fingers playing with it like it was silky thread. How did one live without a mother? A mother that left still counted as a mother that lived out there, somewhere. Maybe not inside of a heart, but in a fragment of memory as another ghost. At least she had been alive. Not that I had ever wanted to find her.

I climbed back into the open window of my bedroom. Once inside, I observed the street through the misty glass. Snowflakes separated from the ground and ruffled the street. November's forgotten fiery mum pots and pumpkin patches lay on their side, snow covering their dried-up flowers. Tree branches hung low, holding the white path of snow on their bodies like upside-down arcs. In the distance, the hills darkened as if giant shadow figures had surrounded the town to perform a ritual. The lights— they shone amber, guiding one's eyes in the dark. Even with the silence pressing against my eardrums, it seemed I could hear my heartbeat. Winter did indeed pretend to be a beautiful woman, but her heart was cold and sullen.

At once, my doorknob rattled, breaking the silence. My heart trembled. A white head peered through the slit of mahogany wood, eyes wandering around the room. Charlie was at Grandma's side, clinging to her skirt, and stared at me with his wild eyes.

"You're awake! I thought I'd check on you while you were sleeping, but you are up. How are you feeling, darling?"

"I'm fine, Grams, don't worry about me," I thanked her. "I didn't expect you to be up. It's quite early."

"Couldn't miss an episode of Magnolia finally telling Luke that she fancied him. And then I thought of you." She smiled. "Wait, have you been outside in this ungodly weather?" She grimaced, noticing my dripping wet parka hanging on the armchair.

I wobbled to my feet. "Went out to get some air. It feels stuffy inside. Crisp winter air is all I needed."

"Child"— she turned to me— "there is a winter advisory until midafternoon. You, little miss, need to stay indoors. I don't know how those people are planning to attend a fair tonight. I've clearly forgotten what a troublemaker you are. You didn't use to be this way when you were younger. Time flies so fast. It's hard to believe." She waded back into memories. "So precious."

"I grew up, Grams. Life became a little boring. Needed to spice it up. I'm still precious, I hope," I said.

My grandmother, like a swan, glided towards the window where I stood holding on to the curtain as if I found comfort in it. She didn't have to say a lot; we understood each other from one gaze, one simple embrace. She silently put her arm on my shoulder, pulling me closer. I almost broke down in tears from the meek touch, but I held them in tight. I didn't want a tint of worry or concern showing on her face.

"You know, there are leftover pancakes with apples if you are hungry. Your dad couldn't keep his hands away from my second batch with strawberries, so those are gone. You know, I miss the times when he was a little boy. He was almost as much trouble as you are," Grandma said and shrugged her shoulders. "But if you don't feel like pancakes, there are *Mishka Na Poliane* candies. Chocolate and sadness are like two sides of one apple, inseparable parts of one whole. One treats the other," she said and wrapped her shawl around me, bringing us together.

"Thank you for making me feel like everything is right in the world," I mumbled. I couldn't bring her down. She meant everything to me.

"How else can it be, child? That's what grandmas are for!" she said and hummed a melody; then she picked up Grandpa's photograph from the vanity.

"You remember when your grandfather died?" she asked suddenly, her voice serious. I knew she was referring to my mother's passing.

I did remember. It hurt where it had never hurt before. "I do."

"I knew I would never be the same. It was hard to find direction in life because there was suddenly no compass. Not anymore. Death does that to people. Leaves them lost, leaves them broken, reminds them that they are mortal after all. Death can and will take everything you have, squeeze you like a sour lemon, but there is something it cannot take: the love that lives deep within you. Whatever it is you feel— no matter how lonely, how desperate death makes you— hold onto that love. It's your only solace. It will always show you the way to go. Even in a place where light doesn't always shine," Grandma concluded. Tears sat still in her eyes, ready to burst out.

"It's okay, Grams. I have already let her go." I comforted her with a hug around the neck. "But I will always remember what you said. I promise."

I decided on the pancakes, after all. We stepped into the hallway, and I felt like the walls were closing in on me, the same way a block of cement could crush my chest. The worry of seeing Dad nestled upon my heart like a snake. Each time I shifted, it wrapped around and squeezed tighter, locking me in an ever-lasting embrace of power. When I walked into the living room, I noticed two olive socks on the alabaster ottoman, one over the other, peeking through the clatter of books, wrapping paper, and scarves. Alice, drowning in an armchair that was bigger than her by ten sizes, was snoring sweetly under a fleece throw. Her magazine lay crumpled on the floor, open to Christmas pastry recipes.

Dad, in his raven-colored sweater, was curled up by the fire. I could hear the pages rustling like the hem of an eighteenth-century dress. His finger was tracing the lines, stopping at the end of each sentence. In the shadow of the blazing fire, the book spine shone gold with the name I remembered from childhood: *Crime and Punishment* by Fyodor Dostoevsky, a Russian classic. Funny— Dad had read the first half of the book at least twelve times. He probably knew the beginning of it by heart, but he could never finish it. To his credit, at least he tried, but I also knew why he never succeeded: the soul-tearing suffering of a murderer wasn't his cup of tea.

Doing my best not to disturb the sleeping Alice, I approached the fireplace. I touched Dad's arm lightly, afraid of breaking it—breaking him. He jumped, but after seeing that it was just me, his eyes softened, and he pulled me into his arms without a word. He smelled of cinnamon elephant ears and sweet date pudding, but he was all I needed. I was his little girl, and no matter how many years went by, I still felt like one.

"I am so sorry, Daddy. I never meant to scare you," I said, still holding him in my arms and still searching for his forgiveness.

"Honey, I should have never let you out of my sight." Then he gazed in the direction of the armchair. "Bringing Alice wasn't my brightest idea, given the circumstances. I apologize for that."

I was so stricken by the fact he said it that I didn't know what to think.

"Alice has nothing to do with this. It's Mom. I can't help but feel like I've lost someone. The anger that I trapped inside for years after she left us— well, it's roaming now. I'm hurt," I confessed.

"I understand," he said and paused. "You know that I've lost someone too. How can I not love her? She gave me you."

Tears rolled down my cheeks, their saltiness burning my eyes.

"Oh baby, don't feel bad crying," he said and wiped my tears with the sleeve of his sweater. "You're allowed to miss her. She was a bad mother, but she was your mother, and she loved you in her own way, which I found hard to understand."

The flames from the blazing logs danced on the walls of the living room, dragging our silhouettes in a constantly moving carousel.

"All I know about her is what you told me."

"There is not much else to tell." With sadness clawing his heart, he closed his book, releasing a soft clap.

The wind whistled on the windowsills one more time. I remembered her scarlet lipstick and white teeth shining in between, her velvety hair that dropped down her shoulders in curls, and the soap operas she watched in the morning while getting ready for work.

I interrupted the silence between us. "I only have one photograph of her. She's like a book I began reading and never finished, and I will never know the ending to it." I sighed and, with that movement, the snake in my chest released its deathly grip.

"You don't need a picture to look at. She's in the contours of your upper lip, the curve of your collarbone, and the thickness of your eyelashes. She also taught you to love fog, the one and only place you can get lost and find your way back," he said and traced his fingers along my chin.

"What if I turn out to be just like her? You know, not only in appearance," I wondered.

"You mean become a selfish witch on a broom? God bless her heart. Of course, I haven't seen her for years, so maybe she changed," he remarked. "I raised you, sunshine, and something tells me you're far greater than anyone I know." He smiled. "Shh, don't tell Alice— she might be a little jealous." Dad's voice echoed around the room, maybe a little loud.

"Rebecca," a woman's voice joined ours. "I am so glad you're all right. I was worried..." Alice stared at me from the armchair with her little face glowing. "I must have dozed off. What did I miss?"

"Dad was just telling me about your famous gingerbread cookies," I responded slyly, catching a glimpse of my father's smile.

* * *

Just like everyone expected, the snowstorm cleared, leaving the town shining like a myriad of stars. The Christmas fair illuminated the mountain as if there was a giant light projector shining upon it from the middle of the Harpers Ferry square. The weathergirl reminded viewers about a new winter advisory. Nevertheless, people crawled out of their houses for the winter festivities. Tents and people, all mixed up together, danced in the commotion of falling snow on the town's square. Christmas carols hung in the wind along with the ringing of the Salvation Army bells. I could hear their echo down by the Point. There was undeniable magic in the air, hearts full of laughter, kindness, and joy. The whole town came alive, despite the prolonged winter and its lack of orange sun. I was caught up in their joy, one tiny heart among the others, beating fast and curious.

Right above my head, the lights of the fair were a sparkling carnival net made of yellow crystals. I stood in the epicenter of the square. I had no idea how I ended up here, nor how I had dragged myself out of the house. A miniature skating rink to my left had seen the first round of skating blades. The houses across the street flickered with candle flames in the windows once in a while, like a blinking stop sign. I thought I saw a shooting star, its long white tail diving into blackness, disappearing without a trace, and its tiny reflection glistening in one of my eyes. A tear ran down my cheek, stinging from the cold air. I was lost in the ocean of people's faces, just like Mom. I still thought of her. I still grieved.

Half of the ugly sweaters on the hangers from Mrs. Petty's tent were covered in snow, but hers remained the most popular stopping place. I slowly went through the rows of Christmas toys, trees, and stockings. I picked out vanilla candles and cinnamon soaps to inhale the spirit of the holidays when I finally realized I was longing for someone— a friend.

The feeling fell upon me, not giving me a chance to catch up. I needed Nick. Pictures of him suddenly changed to pictures of my mother, and I started to ache to the point of breaking down. Sadness was now mixed with my warm, salty tears.

Dziyana Taylor

I put the soap down onto the shelf and closed my eyes, but someone came up behind me, putting his hands on my eyelids.

"Guess who?" I heard a familiar voice.

We always greeted each other this way. Since we were kids. It added to the surprise.

"Look what I got for you," Nick said.

He was wearing his navy coat, and he looked as handsome as the day I first met him. He was freshly shaved, his walnut hair laid in one curl on the side, and his face and coat were covered in white specks of sugar. The smile on Nick's face shone bright, but what shone even brighter was the kindness he so proudly carried in his eyes.

"I thought you were out photographing the fair in Gettysburg!"

"They canceled last minute. I was thrilled. I thought I'd find you here, among the lights. I know how much you love them." His cheeks were burning scarlet from the cold.

"I do love them very much," I said, and my gaze traveled to the crowds of people. I was searching for Derek's face. "I see someone had some pastry. Didn't care to bring me any? I thought you were my friend," I asked, grinning while running my fingers through the wrapping paper. I was so happy to see his face.

"Croissants with almonds. Got them at the second tent over there. The lady told me you didn't get any," he mumbled and pointed out his finger into the crowd.

"I bet she did. Did she also tell you I gained weight and have a bad attitude?" I asked, but I lost my words in surprise when I took out a red ball. It had a hand-painted bird on it. "It looks like Felix!"

I added, thinking about a bird Nick and I used to have. "This is beautiful. Where did you get it?"

"Oh, Marvin, Keller's son, sells them. He's a true artist. Harpers Ferry has its own talents," Nick pointed out.

"Oh, yes!" I finally remembered. "Marvin, who used to pull my hair in the third grade! How could I forget? Well, I guess he should be forgiven. I didn't know his hands were meant for creating beautiful things— I only knew them as wonderful creators of pain."

Nick laughed. "It's just brilliant. I forgot all about that. But thanks for reminding me! Now I have something to tease you with, just like you did with me and Sally."

"Oh, don't be that way. It was a joke." I poked him. "By the way, thank you for the gift," I said, catching his eyes with mine.

"You're so welcome. You owe me a favor now." He smirked and took my hand in his. "I want to show you something. I'll lead the way, like a true Roman emperor."

"Great. First presents, then favors. You're so predictable," I said as he dragged me through the crowd of people.

"Oh, you thought I would make it easy for you. I can't believe you, of all people, would think that."

"Nope. Can't expect that! Not from you!" I said, letting the cold winter air absorb both of us. Our lips were chapped, but we were happy and spontaneous heading into our next adventure.

* * *

We reached the doors of one of the most treasured places in Harpers Ferry— the town's library. I always imagined this place as a castle from a fairy tale. It was hard to get to, but my prince in shining armor had a key— a patinated key to a diverse world of thousands and thousands of book collections.

When Nick turned the key and forced the door open, I was hit with a wave of perfume. The library smelled of lavender and peppermint oils. The scent was so fresh and so familiar that it put a sharp thorn into my heart, one tiny spike for every missed day of summer. Light bulbs hummed and buzzed in an electric melody. The walnut railing to the second floor loomed out of the darkness, tiny lights flickering through pine needles. The giant bookshelves gave out dark shadows on the oily walls. I thought I could touch the crystal icicles emerging from its center if only I stood on a taller ladder. I was inside of a bubble full of unread treasures of the universe. I was allowed to observe and wander the hidden corners. It was hard to believe.

"Nick," I whispered, watching him climb the steps to the second floor. "How do you have a key to this place?"

"I have a lot of friends, and one of them lets me borrow the key," he responded.

I bet it's a girl, I thought to myself. *Another blonde ponytail.*

"Aren't we going to be in trouble for browsing through the town's relics after hours?"

"No, we have permission, and to tell you the truth, we'll do more than just browse," Nick said while I climbed the twisted staircase behind him.

I almost ran into one of the marble end-tables near the golden-colored sofa.

"I don't get myself in any trouble. Not like you do. Keep going." He led me through the long open aisle to row "T" through "V".

Then, out of nowhere, he picked up a book from the lower shelf and handed it over to me. It had a black binding, and I felt a shiver run down my spine. It was a first edition of *War and Peace* by Leo Tolstoy.

I couldn't find words; my throat went dry, as if I had swallowed a pill without water. I had never in my wildest dreams imagined peeking through the pages of a book that appeared at auctions only once in a hundred years. The rarity of its appearance made me shed a tear.

"I can't believe this!" I exclaimed after the lights finally got bright again. "How did you... wait. Don't tell me; I don't want to know. This is... incredible."

"I thought you would like it. I haven't seen a smile on your face for so long."

"And you managed to pull it off! I'm ecstatic! To hold it, to cherish it in my hands... means so much... thanks..." The words floated out like a song.

Nick's shadow hovered over me as I studied the relic and talked. If the dust in this place were hail, we would hear it clatter. He suddenly kissed me.

It brought our warmth together, joined the beats of our hearts into one symphony. We both breathed heavily, confused and scared, while the lights flickered erratically over our heads. I didn't have a chance to process what was happening. I tasted the hint of pomegranate on Nick's lips and thought that that sweetness would haunt me forever. There was a weak tingling in my legs. I pushed Nick away from me.

"What do you think you're doing?" I asked, keeping my hand on his chest to distance myself from him.

"Proving to you I'm worth a kiss."

"You can't kiss me."

"Why not?"

"Because I said so," I told him angrily. "If Derek finds out… Do you have any idea what you've done?" I felt like I had betrayed Derek's trust.

"Derek? The ghost Derek? Rebecca. Enough is enough. I'm starting to worry about you. If you don't want me to kiss you, just say so. No need to bring the ghosts into this. They're like your protective veil, and I am sick of it." Nick leaned on the bookshelf.

"I am not lying," I said and stared him in the eyes until he released a sigh.

"I believe you. I saw the demons. I'm not heartless. I hate that you make me feel like I am, though. Nobody can see Derek. C'mon. Be real. Plus, you told me he was old."

I rolled my eyes at him in response.

"So, he isn't old? How old is this ghost? And why are you so protective of him?"

"Why does it matter to you?"

"Because you're losing it."

I knew he believed me; I saw it in his face. Why he wasn't admitting it— that was another story.

"I'm certain he carried me off the river," I revealed to Nick.

He stared at me, his eyes wide as quarters. "I carried you off the river with these two hands. There was nobody there, except for both of us."

"I know. You're the hero; I'm not trying to take that away from you. I just have this feeling that something else was there," I said, then squeezed my tongue between my teeth.

"Like what?"

As soon as he spoke, there was a loud puff in the air, and the smell of rusted metal spread amidst us in the form of smoke. Nick pulled me into his arms, and we ran for shelter underneath a librarian's desk, leaving the tablecloth still moving, providing us with a tiny crevice to observe the occurrence.

What we were staring at wasn't a demon— far from it. It was a person, as strange as that seemed. He had a slim figure and a pair of spectacles on a jet-black chain. The torchlight he held veered among the bookshelves, light going off the floor erratically. From time to time, he would study the device in his hand, searching for a signal. When his figure passed under the chandelier, I could finally take a better look at him. He was wearing tight, straight pants, freshly waxed shoes, and a vest that was made of the insides of a clock. His heart was ticking. We could hear the beats loud and clear.

It was dusty underneath the desk. The cleaning lady must not have vacuumed here in years, and Nick was allergic to dust mites. As the man headed towards the open portal with the device, Nick sneezed. He covered his mouth with a shirt and inched backward. The man turned around fast, his hands and legs shifting like rubber bands, and he arched his body our way. When I met his eyes, they changed colors, from white to olive green. He was searching for us;

the light bouncing off his device mingled on the floor in polka-dots and then froze again right by my legs. I couldn't breathe, and neither could Nick.

The man walked around us in circles until he stumbled upon a footprint. I tried to distinguish who it belonged to, in case it was ours, but it didn't look human. It was a paw with fangs on it. He lifted his head, and that was when the monster's head manifested itself right above him. The monster looked like a giant dog, drooling onto the floor, hungry as ever, strong muscles bursting out of its skin. The skin was so thin you could see its organs. The device gave out a blaring alarm, and the field around the demon electrified. The dog fell onto the floor, unconscious. More than anything, it looked like it was heavily asleep. It was dead, though— we both knew it. After fixing the spectacles on his face, the man dragged the dog by the tail, leaving ruby ribbons in his wake, and vanished into the portal.

"This town is cursed," Nick whispered. "I should never have returned. What in the world was that thing?" Both of us were breathing hard. We exchanged concerned looks. "We should get the hell out of here," he said, and I saw specks covering his forehead.

Without saying a word, I followed him. His head popped up first, just above the curtain, to make sure no one was around. Except for the hissing of the foyer lamps and people's voices ricocheting from Harpers Ferry square, the library stood still. Heavy wooden doors slammed behind us, whooshing out warm air. The night had already seeped through the town's streets.

"I don't know who he was, but I wouldn't mess around with him," I said, pulling the scarf on my neck and shoulders as I opened the door of Nick's Mini Cooper.

"Have you seen him in your dreams before? Is he a ghost?" Nick asked.

"No, nothing like that. Strange place to pass through— a library. It's almost like…"

"He traveled through time," Nick interrupted. "Books are elements that carry energy. I wonder if they have anything to do with his ability to travel."

"He had a device. He knew what he was doing. It can't be a simple coincidence. And the demon. How did he know where to find it?" I said and set the heat in the car on high. The windshield showed a negative thirty. Frost shaded the glass in a thick layer of crystal white. "He must have tracked it with the device. It is the only explanation to this nonsense."

Nick saw me rubbing my hands together in an attempt to warm them up. He extended his hand to me with a pair of mittens. "You can keep those. I have a pair just like that at the house."

I broke into a wide grin and accepted the mittens. Nick opened the glove box and pulled out the Kings of Leon album I had bought him for his last birthday. I turned the speakers on and stared at the melting windshield while Nick searched for a bottle of water underneath the back seat. Suddenly the disk got jammed and started skipping songs, rattling like a broken record. I attempted to release it, but it only made it worse.

"What the hell?" I whispered.

On the windshield, in a place where the ice had just melted, there was a face. It was staring right at me. There were no eyes, just empty sockets. Long nails were gashing into the glass with force. I screamed. Nick jerked, and the car lurched forward.

"It's a demon! Demon!" I yelled.

It clenched both of its arms to the car. It had teeth, like the ones on a shark, and a brown body, the same species we had seen in the library.

"Jesus Christ! Give it some speed!" Nick begged the car.

Snow prevented us from gaining traction. Nick swirled the car from side to side, veering through the lanes.

"Nick, watch out! There is a pedestrian crossing!" I screamed in a voice that didn't belong to me. "Try slamming the brakes and knock the damn thing off!"

He did as I said, but the demon remained on the hood of the car. Moreover, we heard it sinking its paws into the Cooper, bending the metal like it was a rubber band. I clenched my hands into the dashboard, horrified.

"Get off my car, you bastard!" Nick exclaimed and brought the vehicle forward.

The tires smelled of burning rubber. The engine revved. Suddenly we felt a forceful push, like a wave of ice or snow accelerating the car, and the Cooper shot out through the street at about eighty miles an hour. It knocked all the snow off the hood, along with the demon. I turned around, still holding on to my seatbelt. I watched the demon roll into the ditch. Harpers Ferry, the Fair, and the mountain were all turning miniature in the distance.

"I'm starting to really hate this town," Nick commented while the Mini Cooper rolled up the hill away from the site. He gripped the wheel hard and didn't release it until we got to the house with lavender curtains.

* * *

Grandmother had a spacious vestibule with a mahogany coat rack and a grandiose ottoman for the guests' shoes. I recall her telling me that her furniture was inherited from one of her ancestors during the Russian Revolution. Oddly enough, she didn't remember how they ended up being transported to America. She just knew they were old— older than at least two generations of women in her lineage. Someday, I would be the one to inherit them to continue the tradition.

Today, both the coat rack and the ottoman were filled with ponchos, vests, khaki parkas, high boots, and shoes. Restless voices came from the living room in a wave, along with a dozen heels knocking on the oak floors as if scattered beads were being chased by the wind. Nick and I stepped inside the house. At once, Grandma appeared in the vestibule; she wore a long olive dress with shoulder fabric. Its oval shape beautifully outlined her cleavage and intensified the paleness of her skin.

"Oh, good! I was worried you weren't going to be on time. Family," she addressed the rest of the guests, "the kids are home, at last!" She extended her hand in warm greeting.

"In time for what, Grams?" I asked and signaled Nick to take off the boots, which were dripping with salt and water.

"Silly kids," she said, thinking we had had way too much fresh air. "It's New Year's Eve. I am preparing the table. Please come along."

She shut the front door, causing the door knocker on the other side to tremble. Nick and I dragged our bodies beside her as she glided into the room.

"What's going on?" Nick whispered. "New Year's Eve is two days from today."

I chuckled nervously, staring back at him. "Don't you think I know that? She might have forgotten. Just play your part, smile, and let's get through this. I've had enough 'strange' for one day."

But strange didn't stop there.

Just about everyone I knew was gathered in the house tonight. Uncle Tim— with his head pointing towards the ceiling— snored loudly while Charlie walked around him, waiting for the right moment to jump on his lap. My cousins, Jesse and Lindsey, couldn't decide who had the privilege of having the remote. They kept tossing and turning, tangling in each other's arms and legs, their backs swimming in a pool of candy and wrapping paper. Dad and Alice stood under the mistletoe with two glasses of Bordeaux in their hands. Golden dust from the wreaths fell on top of their heads. Lida sat in the sister-armchair across from Uncle Tim, solving a crossword.

It indeed was New Year's Eve: the kind flame of the fire burned bright, and *Ironia Sudby* (Irony of Life) had its first advertisement break. *Olivier* salad rested in a bowl on the dinner table with a silver spoon shining from its core. *Is this some kind of twisted rehearsal? Or have we traveled through time? Time…* Then I had an epiphany. *It's the man from the library—it must be. He turned the time forward when he appeared.*

"Nick," I mouthed his name.

Nick glanced at me, his expression asking me silently, *What is it, Becca?*, but I didn't have a chance to respond. We all heard the door knocker chime. My heart was pounding inside my chest. It really hurt this time.

Uncle Tim woke up, startled, and by the look on his face, hungry as ever. The kids finally calmed down and froze like the sea figures from the game *More Volnuetsia,* and Alice almost got a piece of chicken stuck in her throat.

Dad hurried towards the door while Grandma peeked through the curtains in the kitchen to identify our guest, but there was no one outside, except for the wind hissing, shifting the doormat. Nick swayed into the vestibule with his camera to see what was happening.

Dad shrugged at the strange occurrence and shut the door close, rattling the golden keychain. After a few moments, Nick returned with a photograph, which had just made its way through the apparatus of the camera. Behind the emerging yellowish lines, I recognized Derek. I lifted my eyes away from the print for a second, surprised, when I saw him taking a seat at the dinner table. Neither Nick nor my family was able to see him.

I sat at the head of the table, watching Grandma show another picture of the clouds, explaining that it was an image of Dracula, as if nothing strange had just happened. Derek had his bright, wide-eyed gaze aimed at me from the other side of the table. The straw in my glass of cranberry juice was stuck in ice, and I kept slamming the ice against the bottom of the glass to get it out. Nick was telling me that the man in the photograph was the same man from the Historical Society memorabilia, but I wasn't listening. Not anymore.

"Nick, he's sitting right in front of me," I said, interrupting his speech. Derek heard me address Nick and shook his head.

* * *

I lit a sparkler and watched it glow. Its tiny stars, like pinecone needles, burst into the air. I could hear them crackle, leaving a trace of alabaster smoke. I lit another one, and another one, until I ran out of matches. I waited for the snow truck to roll its tires and come down from the top of the hill, but I heard nothing aside from a cry of a raven bathing in the cold winter night.

Nick was searching for comfort in my uncaring expression. "Say something, Becca."

"What do you want me to tell you?" I said, throwing away the faded sparklers. "I am not some mediator between you and Derek. I've had enough of paranormal encounters, and I'd like to celebrate New Year's in peace. By the way, why is it December 31st? What have I missed?" I asked and directed my eyes at Derek, who sat in the armchair with the diary in his lap. "Is this because of that scientist who slays demons?"

"What scientist are you talking about?" Derek asked, surprised. He'd been observing Nick pace around me.

I brought my arms to my face. I was getting bored. "What scientist are we talking about?" I said to Nick.

215

"We met a time-traveler in the library. Someone with a device that tracks demons. I managed to save us. It took a miracle," Nick explained. "He hears me, right?"

"He does," I confirmed.

Derek rolled his eyes. "'I saved us! I saved us!'" Derek made a parody of Nick, squawking like a parrot. "I don't like this guy's ego. If he lived during the Civil War, he wouldn't have done well. He needs to be disciplined. Hold a gun in his hand or charge a cannon for a change."

"It's beside the point. We live in a different time."

"What's beside the point?" Nick interrupted.

"Nothing. Derek is just being obnoxious. And unkind. What do you know about the man, Derek?" I asked.

"From your description, I believe you met someone from the Coterie. I am not sure who exactly. There is not much known about them. They like to remain out of sight. If he disappeared back into the portal, I don't see a reason why he would bother you again. He is not after the diary; I can guarantee that. The Coterie has its own role to play. And about the whole New Year's confusion… They are able to speed time. And push it back whenever they feel like it."

"So, they are basically paranormal gods of the universe?" I asked astonished.

"Who are *they*?" I heard Nick chime in. "Can someone tell me?"

"They belong to the Coterie," I explained to Nick, watching Charlie push the bedroom door ajar from the other side. I hurried to shut it, but the dog ran in and began jumping on my slippers. "They are not paranormal gods of the universe. They are servants of the Gate," I repeated the words after Derek. Then I threw him a withering look.

Nick sat down on the bed and raised his hands in the air, perplexed.

Derek caught the look with a slight smile. "I told him because he asked. It's not the time to lie to the guy. Is it, Rebecca? When will you tell him? Do you really think it's fair to him?" Derek asked, holding his chin with the palm of his hand.

I felt a slight fever burning my cheeks. "I can't breathe."

"What did he tell you?" Nick asked, worried. He helped me onto the bed covers. The diary lay undisturbed in the folds of the sheets. I scooped it into my arms.

"The truth," Derek said, tone serious. "God, I wish he could hear me. Would save us all the trouble."

"I wish I could see you," Nick addressed Derek. "You deserve someone to put you in your place."

"Wait, did you just hear him?" I asked, looking at both of them, confused.

"I heard him, Becca! I think it's because you're holding the diary," Nick said ecstatically. "I can hear you, ghost from another time!" He then whispered into my ear, "If you told me a week ago that I would hear a ghost talking, I would have never believed you!"

I rolled my eyes and glanced back at the glowing diary.

"And you would have made a rookie mistake," Derek confirmed. "There is a whole world of ghosts out there."

"What are you, exactly?" Nick asked.

"I'm the gatekeeper, but back when I lived, you would have known me as Lieutenant Derek Cromwell. Pleasure." Derek stood up and offered his pale-skinned hand to Nick.

"He doesn't see you," I mumbled, twisting a curl of my hair in my hands.

"Who cares if I don't see him, I want to be polite," Nick said and stretched his hand to the place where Derek was standing. "Pleasure is mine. Which war are we talking about?" Nick asked.

"The war between the North and the South. Also known as the Civil War," Derek said.

"Get out of here! And you know how to charge a cannon?" His eyes got wide and glistened. Nick's shelves were filled with history books, and he always traveled with them. It wasn't surprising to me that his first question was about the cannons.

"Absolutely. Charging a cannon is more than one man striving for success. It is a matter of efficient teamwork. The ones that really do some damage are the twelve-pound Napoleons."

"Those cannons are the centerpieces of the Antietam battlefield," Nick muttered to himself.

"That they are. I am sure you are well aware that the battle of Antietam was a strategic victory of the Union, but if you count my opinion, it was a draw. Confederates lost thousands of men, and the grounds at Antietam will forever be stained with the blood of the bravest souls I have ever met."

Nick's eyes were glowing. He had already thought of the next question to ask.

"Okay, that's enough," I said and let go of the diary.

"Becca, I hadn't even gotten to the most interesting part. We were just talking," Nick protested.

"You've got to love the role you play," Derek teased me, referencing the diary.

I must admit, I had panicked. What if the truth slipped off Derek's lips that we kissed? What if Nick figured it all out? What was I to say? Where would I be? Stuck in between two men? And they had just started admiring each other. I'd lose them both, and I couldn't let that happen. Though, to be honest, for the very first time, I felt safe. They were both my stone castle.

"I know ghosts don't eat, but I am human, and I'm going to the Tavern. What do you both say?" I raised the question loud and clear.

The two men in my bedroom nodded.

SEVENTEEN

THERE WAS MAGIC

Like a widow in her silky black dress, the night fell onto old Harpers Ferry houses, dragging their front steps with her into the gloom. Ravens rattled on hanging phone lines. I could distinguish the sound of their wings raising up on the wind from the silence of the town. Despite the night making me feel unsettled, I kept my head low and continued moving forward with Derek and Nick strolling behind me.

The tavern was not more than six houses away. We walked slowly through the serene streets, side by side, and I could see the warmth of our breath drawing circles on the fresh winter air. That and the rustle of our boots on the snow were the only distractions from the doors of a ghost universe closing in on us.

Nick wore his lightest jacket, or so it seemed. He went on trembling like Osinovyj List, catching a gust of wind on his shoulder. Grandma used to call people "aspen leaves" if she believed they let the cold get to them. That was how I learned that word. Don't let anyone fool you.

Derek, walking on my right side, wore an emerald-colored scarf. It sat tightly around his neck, covering his perky nose, beautifully shaped mouth, and a leather jacket. Cold didn't get to him. I did, though. He kept glancing at me as I passed under the light of the streetlamps, their shades making my hair look golden-brown.

When we reached Hog Alley, the road became icy. The bricks glistened gray, and because the road came to a slope in between the two-house walls and my shoes didn't have winter soles, I slipped. It was as if someone had forced the ground from underneath me.

"Would you watch yourself?" Derek caught me in his arms. I could feel the freshness of his breath on my face. "Let me help you up. You are in so much trouble, Rebecca." His voice was subtle and soft.

I was indeed in trouble— caught in the love triangle of hell, I thought.

Nick lifted me, fixing my tulle skirt and sloped shawl, and then carried me into the tavern while Derek watched like a hawk.

As soon as the tavern door opened, the three of us entered an incandescent forbidden realm: there was a great commotion combined with the subtle voices of people and merging with the tinkling of the beer glasses. A tall man in a wide-brimmed hat sat far back in a dark corner and smirked at us, raising his eyebrows. Then he proceeded to play darts with his short but handsome companion, who was holding a frosted beer bottle in his hand. Two women were in the middle of a wild and feisty discussion at the bar. Occasionally, they threw the bartender glances full of bewilderment, seemingly to ask why their wine glasses were sitting empty.

All the tables against the tavern wall were occupied; two exhausted waitresses kept bouncing from one barrel to another like a pair of tennis balls running from their captor. We managed to find a seat under the curvy ladder on the second floor. Blended with the hum of the voices, the footsteps going up and down the landing were almost unnoticeable.

"It's been years since I have been in an establishment of this type," Derek said. "I expected the ladies to look a bit different."

"Not a fan of the beer-whiskey club?" I wondered, looking at Nick, who didn't know what was going on. I had to open the duffel bag and lay the diary on the table for them to hear each other.

"I've always wanted a cup of freshly brewed coffee. Union soldiers after the battle would leave it behind, and we would raid the fields in search of it," Derek explained.

"Coffee? It would be difficult to find a place now that doesn't offer it." Nick picked up the conversation with a snap of sarcasm.

"Coffee was like gold. If the Union soldiers hadn't had coffee, the Confederates might have won the war."

"That's cutthroat," Nick said. He then ran his eyes across the tavern, stopping at a picture of Robert E. Lee in the very corner behind dusty whiskey barrels. They overshadowed half of the general's uniform. "I hope I don't offend you by asking you this, but I can't help but wonder— why the Confederacy?"

Derek curled his arm around the chair then swayed his eyes over at the picture, ashamed. "No, it doesn't offend me. I am glad you asked. I thought I was fighting for independence, but how does one become independent by taking someone else's freedom? I used to be different back then... during the war. There was so much death, it shattered my soul. I became so sullen... so serious. Nothing used to make me *happy* because everywhere I looked, everyone I met reminded me of the crippled futures of the people I loved. Since I became a gatekeeper, my eternal existence healed those wounds. I do not look at the world the same way I used to. I became fully unburdened by the ideals of the Confederates, and I resent them," Derek said and sighed deeply.

Nick nodded at him, accepting his response, but didn't say a word. Derek had lived with the pain of choosing the wrong side for centuries. I could see it in his green eyes, warming my face.

When the silence became too unbearable to handle, I decided to revert our conversation to something a little less depressing. "Does anyone care to know what I miss this century?" I asked, dipping the bag of green tea inside of my cup and swirling it against the ceramic.

"Please tell us. There is not much that I really miss except for the beauty of the land. To the regret of many, it has changed," Derek said.

"Civil War dresses," I said with excitement and paused. "Hoop skirts and bodices. Brooches and dangling earrings. Hair pulled up in a neat bun and a fan to skillfully hide half the face from the gaze of an officer."

Outside, the ravens landed in pairs on the widest part of the road. I watched them fill the street with their dark presence.

"I am sure you would think differently once you tried one of them on. It's a suffocating piece of wardrobe. In the Southern weather, the dresses were the cause of ladies collapsing from lack of air. Not to mention the cruel hand of the hot Carolina sun. But they surely looked beautiful," Derek said and took a sip of his coffee. His dark, walnut hair matched the color of espresso.

"I miss the architecture. The splendor— the nobility— of an old, Victorian home. The magnificence. Wraparound porches and matching shutters. For a photographer, it's a treat for the mind," Nick said, digging his teeth into the salad.

I watched the tavern doors open and close. Chairs slid against the wooden floor. People's faces blended with the interior of the tavern. The birds kept landing on the street. There were hundreds of them outside now.

"What's wrong with the birds?" I said suddenly, ignoring Nick and Derek's conversation.

"What birds?" Nick asked. Derek pushed the chair closer to the window, observing the street through the frosted glass.

"Yes, what birds?" Derek asked.

"Are you kidding me?" I exclaimed and pointed outside at the black pool of ravens. "How can you not see them? They fill the entire street! You can't miss them! Look!"

Derek sighed, watching me blush. "Relax, Rebecca, it's fine. They are just birds. There is nothing wrong with them."

"Well, do you see them?"

"I do," Derek confirmed, setting his coffee cup back on the table. "Just like I see any other bird out there, dead or alive. Alive, preferably."

"Tell us about the battles," Nick cut in, forgetting about the birds. "Are the history books accurate in their descriptions of the encounters between the Yankees and the Rebels?"

The shadows on Derek's face darkened. "There are accounts of officers and soldiers out there in the world. Letters from the war preserved in Historical Societies. I'd say you can't get more accurate than that. The memory of the soldiers who survived the war will remain untarnished. For them, the bloodshed will always be 'yesterday,' and 'tomorrow' will be nothing but a reminder of what it took to live it. Will there be a pitch-perfect account of war? No. But those accounts will come pretty damn close."

"Wow. That answers my question," Nick commented solemnly, looking at the empty seat by me.

I was the only one lucky enough to see Derek.

"You fool!" We suddenly heard a groan coming from the bar. The man in the hat was crouched over by the pool table. "Hasn't your mom taught you to play fair?" he muttered under his breath, holding his companion in a tight grip.

They were both drunk. The other gentleman pushed the hat-man away, who laughed hysterically and scooped the cheese out of the taco bowl with both of his hands.

"Go figure." Nick broke into a smile.

I couldn't concentrate on the commotion. The birds... Something about them haunted me. I clenched my fists tight, leaving bloody marks on the inside of my palms. I grimaced at Derek and Nick, who were discussing the "happy faces" of people at the bar, not paying any attention to anything or anyone else. I stared at the street. Tavern lights reflected off the snow, creating an upside-down rainbow.

There was a shadow wandering among the ravens outside. I watched it over Nick's shoulder, moving in the reflection of the glass. It passed the closed Harpers Ferry pharmacy and stopped at the red light to cross the street. I saw the silhouette of a woman wearing a white gown, carrying a parasol umbrella in her hand. She wore a flower tiara that glistened on her head like a halo. My eyes followed her to the middle of the street, and I heard a sudden cannon blast, its rumble piercing the air. I saw the concrete shatter. Dust and pebbles burst into the air. At once, the ravens reached for the sky in a train of black color. It seemed that the woman was devoured by the smoke, which stood like a veil between us.

"No!" I shot up, causing my chair to fall behind me. I raced towards the door of the tavern, knocking a tray off one of the waitress's arms.

"What's the matter with you? Where are you going?" Nick asked, his face a gray sheet of faded fabric.

Derek, concerned, got off his stool and glided into the street through the window. His coffee cup lay on the table on its side, droplets of liquid covering the floor. When the smoke dissolved, I finally spotted the woman. She was lying on the road, white garment stained with ruby color. She was suffocating on her own blood. With horror, I approached her fading body.

"Don't, Rebecca," I heard Derek's voice behind me.

"She's dying, Derek," I insisted.

"Beccs, I think you have to listen to him," Nick said, catching his breath from rushing outside after me. "I do trust him with this, you know."

"I am not just going to leave her here! Are you both insane?" I muttered.

"You can't interfere. It's ghost business, residual energy that's left behind," Derek tried to explain.

"I don't care! Please, help her! Someone! Help!" I yelled, picking the woman's head up off of the shattered road. She was as cold as ice.

"You're making a scene. You can't help her. You have to let her go. It's not real; it's just a mirage." Derek's voice echoed against the Harpers Ferry houses.

The tears were rolling down my cheeks. "I hate death. I hate it," I mumbled. For one reason or another, Mom's face appeared in front of me.

As I said that, the ghost lady vanished. I leaned over the empty place where the woman had been, parasol umbrella broken at her feet. Nick offered me his hand, breaking the circle of ghost presence with his soft voice.

"It's all right. I am right here with you. You will be fine."

Derek hadn't moved from where he was standing. I studied his face, picking up the train of my skirt from the ground. There was no more Officer Cromwell in his expression— just a man who was watching a woman he liked suffer from something she couldn't make sense of. He felt for me. I knew he did. He caressed me with his eyes full of tenderness. All I wanted was to run towards him, wrap my arms around his neck, lay my head at his heart, and tug on his leather jacket until the world faded around us.

There was a moment that resembled silence falling on top of our heads. It was like a slow-motion film was about to begin. I saw Derek's eyes go wide and eerie, horror settling on his lips. That was when I heard the horse's hooves knocking on the pavement. A general riding a horse was headed to the cannon blast site, demolishing everything in his way. Nick's figure was the only thing that blocked him from reaching his goal. My heart lurched.

Derek shot across the street in no time, dulling the nature around him. He knocked Nick off his feet, causing him to land in the snowdrift. The horse rider slowed down, and the lights on the buildings in Harpers Ferry started to flicker. Nobody moved. Nobody.

I knew the general was searching for her, for the woman. Derek chanted something in Latin, his voice merging with the voice of the town. The horse neighed, catching a glimpse of me, and the rider raced away from the site as if they were both spooked.

"One hell of a mirage, isn't it?" I said, pushing Derek aside and checking Nick's pulse, who lay unconscious in the snowdrift.

"That one was real, if it changes things." He sighed. "I can take him home."

"No. Take him to Grandma's house. I need to make sure he'll be fine. No one is dying on me tonight. That includes you."

"Oh, I died a long time ago," Derek smirked, running his hand through his hair.

* * *

The house with lavender curtains stood motionless against the gray sky. The ravens, as it turned out, followed us home. They occupied the fallen-in parts of the roof, filling them in with their feathered bodies. Nick laid under a quilt on the four-poster bed with Charlie nestling in the form of a pillow on his back. His head was bruised from the fall. A purple hematoma was shining on his forehead.

"I have a remedy for the pain," Derek suggested, carrying a Mason jar with him towards the bed.

"Please don't hurt him. Don't you think he's had enough for one day?" I begged.

Derek sent me a withering glance. "Just be quiet and watch," he whispered while taking off the lid of the jar.

First, he chanted in tongues and then blew inside of the jar, which at once lit up with fireflies pulsating against the glass. I looked up at him, surprised.

"At night on the battlefields, the soldiers would see single lights mingling amongst the fields. They knew it was a medic coming to find them and heal them from their wounds. And most of the time, soldiers died still waiting for this light. These fireflies are medics' souls, and in death, they are more powerful than ever before."

It was astounding to watch them work. The fireflies accumulated on the hematoma, and soon there was nothing but an iridescent glow. Within seconds, Nick's skin returned to its original tone. The medics, done with their work, returned to the jar, and when Derek tightened the lid, they were gone.

"Who was the man on the horse?" I asked, sitting down next to Nick on the bed. He was quietly snoring.

"A ghost."

"I got that part."

Derek broke into a smile. "Civil War officers on the other side are a little bit different than other ghosts. Because of the way they crossed over and the violent nature of their death during the war, they are more prone to interact with people who are alive. It was the other side's reward for their death, and without realizing it, sometimes they abuse their gift."

"He could have killed Nick. That's what you're trying to tell me?" I whispered. Derek nodded. I took his hands into mine and stared into his eyes. "Thank you for saving his life."

"I didn't do it on his account," he said. "I saved him because you would have."

"If you didn't save him, I don't think we could have been a thing."

"So, we are a 'thing' now?" he asked and locked me in his arms.

"There's a masquerade ball at the church tomorrow. It's a Remembrance Day Ball to commemorate the Civil War's fallen comrades. I'd like very much for you to come with me."

"What about Nick? Is he staying?"

"Yes, he stays here until he gets a full night's sleep."

"I don't trust him." Derek rolled his eyes.

"He doesn't trust you, either."

"Rebecca…" Derek said, playing with my hair. "All this time, I have been stuck on the other side, and the hope of seeing your face, the longing for your touch— it's what kept me going. I don't think I can let you go another time."

"You won't. I promise," I said.

"It's like going to war and never returning." He was right about that; that was exactly what it felt like.

We were still holding each other's hands when Nick awoke, and Charlie began barking at the invisible spot Derek was standing. The diary was still in the duffel bag hanging on my shoulder. Horrified at what Nick might have seen, I dropped the duffel bag on the floor.

EIGHTEEN

THE NIGHT OF THE MASQUERADE

The rain's pleasant moisture followed the wind into the room. Harpers Ferry hadn't seen a glimpse of the sun for quite a while, and I had started to believe that our own Misty Mountain had been drowned in woe. In front of the house with lavender curtains, the oaks stood in silence, and only rusty leaves tumbled down from their mourning branches.

It was a perfect night for the Harpers Ferry Remembrance Day Ball. Dark and slightly stormy, with fog nestling in the streets. It was the night for mischievous deeds, sudden appearances, and new acquaintances (though the latter instigated fear, as meeting spirits lately was troubling enough). Historically, the Remembrance Day Ball was an elegant gathering of the town's elite to honor the souls who fought for the freedom of our country. Centuries had passed, and now the Ball had turned into a celebration of winter's departure and ceremonial praise for the dead officers, soldiers, nurses, townies, and heroes of war. This was the only night of the year the locals could be anyone they wanted to be.

I stood in front of a tall antique dresser in my bedroom. Its mirror captured my entire figure. I wore a black tulle dress with silver stars scattered along the hem of its skirt. When the sun shone through, reflecting onto the dress, the tiny stars radiated like fish scales. I was convinced I wore the entire night sky.

I just needed the right pair of shoes. I had shoved my heels into the closet last summer, and despite knowing they would be the perfect addition to the metallic color of the dress, I was afraid that as soon as I opened the closet door, something horrible was going to happen. I felt it. I had to settle for the silver ballerina slippers that my dad had sent from DC after Alice bought the last pair from the store window display. God knows she had an eye for those things.

I picked up the mask I had bought from the antique store in Gettysburg with Nick. Its velvet was raven-colored with crocheted edges. Putting it on caused memories of him, the snowdrift, and the fireflies to come over me like a wave. As I glanced in the mirror one more time, fixing the curls with spray, my heart galloped. I saw a shadow lingering in the reflection of the mirror. I gasped and put the palms of my hands to my face, but as soon as I opened my eyes again, I realized it was just the dreamcatcher moving on the wind. I held the dreamcatcher in my hand for a moment and then let it go, causing it to bounce and send shadowy feathers toward the ceiling.

Downstairs, Grandma was sipping coffee in one of the armchairs. When she noticed me coming down the stairs, she stood up with a look of delight on her face.

"Rebecca…" she said gently, "you look marvelous. Like a black swan wading on the moonlit water. The dress fits you beautifully."

She came closer, embraced me in her arms, and all I could think about was that light, tender warmth she brought with her. When my grandmother thought I was beautiful, I started to feel that I really was.

"Thank you, Grandma," I mumbled.

"Don't forget your coat and your clutch," she reminded me. I thought I noticed tears rolling in her eyes. "Go have fun."

After kissing her on the cheek and giving Charlie a quick pat on the head, I headed to the church for the Remembrance Day Ball.

* * *

Shadows danced on the walls of the church in the shapes of tall animals and winged creatures. I could have stood there for hours guessing what they were, but nothing would have changed my perception about them. It was what I imagined demons to be like.

A man by the door smiled at me as I walked in, his black glasses shading half of his face. His white, feathery wings rose above his back like an arc. All I could think about was the scent of menthol lingering in the air around him. It reminded me of Girl Scout cookies and peppermint gum wrappers. Two jesters with scepters danced in the middle of the floor, their bell hats trembling with confetti. There were shining, brass cages coming down from the ceiling with women dressed in short Snow White attire trapped inside, their masks glowing neon blue. They floated on ribbons, which gave their bodies freedom of motion, holding them tight at their waistlines. A guy with a beak and skeleton head passed by me in his hooded robe. With each beat of the music, the stage released a cloud of smoke, resembling fog. Trays of marmalade, mini apple strudels, and caramel cakes circled the dance floor.

There were bubbles drifting above everyone's heads. A man ran into me, his face all smudged, the mess transforming into different shapes like the inside of a kaleidoscope. It reminded me of a mirage of spontaneous images.

I ran my eyes across the church interior, looking for Derek. I thought I recognized him in a Confederate VMI Cadet uniform by the bar. He wore a blue jacket with a crystal white collar and red tassels over a set of shining brass buttons. When I approached him, though, a stranger's face appeared in front of me instead of Derek's. I gave the stranger a guilty smile, and I retreated into the crowds of people.

The lights from the projectors were blinding, and dancing people were bumping, brushing past me. The church broke into an aquamarine ocean of tile medallions. The room was transformed. The dance floor was infested with marionettes, Roman emperors with porcelain faces, jokers in gold hats with chiming bells, and clothed women with flowery compositions on their heads, dragging their heavy dresses behind them across the floor.

Though everyone looked as if they had wandered in from another dimension, the atmosphere of the church was light and extravagant. I addressed the bartender to order *A Fountain of Hope* (a silver liquid drink) but decided against it when I felt someone watching me. At once, I recognized Derek. He was standing by the stairs among the ballerinas fixing their pointe shoes. He looked like he'd walked straight out of eighteenth-century France—a gracious prince with a crystal white frill and flared sleeves. His tailcoat hung low, and the buttons dazzled silver along with his pointy shoes. I started to slowly walk towards him, hoping that he would turn around and notice me, but instead, a mask was staring at me, blocking the view of Derek.

"May I have this dance?" I felt a cold hand wrapped around my waist like a belt. The voice sounded so familiar, but I couldn't quite catch it. "Becca..." I heard him repeat my name.

I searched for the voice at the back of my mind as if I were running down a long dark corridor. Then I had an epiphany.

"Nick! I thought you would miss the Ball with everything that happened yesterday! I didn't expect you to be on your feet so soon."

"Believe me, bed rest is not how I wanted to spend the Remembrance Day Ball," he said, bowing to me. "Strange thing, though. I remember hitting my head, but I have no headache or even a bruise for that matter. I think I got lucky."

"Well, that horseshoe you keep underneath the bed must work magic. Nice costume, by the way. Let me guess, you're a poet?" I put my hand on his chest and slid my fingers onto his shoulders, locking him in an embrace while the ballerinas moved around us in a carefully planned routine. His long raven scarf was tucked inside a broad collar while a bottle of ink and a feather poked out of the coat pocket.

Nick's turquoise eyes glistened. "Alexander Sergeyevich Pushkin. My pleasure, lady."

"Even with the curly hair and the beard," I said, running my fingers on his fake sideburns.

"It would be a disgrace not to try and mimic Pushkin's attire to the T. He would have rolled over in his grave. And with the ghost world looking upon us, let's just say, I'm a little intimidated," he whispered in my ear and pressed my gloved hand to his lips. I continued looking towards the stage, behind Nick's shoulder, where just a few moments ago I had seen Derek. He had vanished.

"Did you bring Derek?" Nick asked suddenly. "I must say, I appreciate the fact that we have a one-hundred-year-old antique as our companion. Makes life a little more interesting."

"He said he would be here," I explained. "It must still be early. I'm sure he will show."

"Who are you searching for in there?" Nick asked, catching my hands into his, pulling me in.

I could feel his heart beating against my ribcage. His eyes absorbed mine like he was looking through me, not at me. If he knew, why wouldn't he say something? Maybe he didn't want to spoil the evening?

"Oh, no one," I said, creating distance between our bodies. Now I was the one who felt intimidated. "I feel thirsty and lightheaded all of a sudden. And there's a tiresome line at the bar. Do you mind getting me something to drink?"

"Of course. I would be honored. I'll get you a glass of lemonade," he said and paused. "Or a water. Are you sure you are going to be all right here, waiting for me?"

"Yes. I'll just sit over there, on the benches." I pointed at the row of metal furniture along the west wall of the church.

"I'll be at the bar if you need anything," he said and quickly disappeared into the crowd.

I headed towards the benches when I felt my locket tossing and turning in different directions. I caught it in my hand and pressed it against the skin. The chains felt hot, almost burning.

"Derek," I whispered his name. "I looked for you everywhere. You promised me a dance."

His shape rose out of the smoke from dance floor projectors.

"Don't you love this? It's like we're stuck in some secret universe, where no one is allowed to see us." His face was close to mine. He was staring at my lips, almost touching them. "You look beautiful, Rebecca. You don't need a Civil War dress for all eyes to be on you. They already are."

I looked around. The entire church was suddenly filled with Union and Confederate officers and women with ruffled lace dresses resembling colorful umbrellas. They were ghosts; there was no doubt about it. Piano music flowed from under the hands of a timeless musician, and the ladies, under the leadership of their escorts, flowed graciously across the dance floor in pearl corsets and bell-shaped skirts, the curls in their hair shifting to the melody of the music.

It was a real Remembrance Day Ball hidden within a Masquerade Ball, two centuries intertwined in one continuous timeline.

"Shall we?" he said and offered me his hand. This time his frock changed to a pristine Confederate uniform. He carried me in his arms across the aquamarine tiles like I was weightless. The color of his uniform intensified the sparks of emerald in his eyes. Holding him, I forgot about the world, the diary, demons, everything—including my best friend.

* * *

The line at the bar was out of a horror movie— long and noisy. When Nick finally managed to break through the crowds of angry, hungry patrons, he came over to the benches with a cup of lemonade in each hand. Apparently, the bartender had run out of glasses, so they started using teacups as replacements. He didn't find me on the dance floor or sitting on the benches. Instead, he ran into a man by the fountain. The man had familiar features.

"Derek?" Nick said, and the two glasses fell from his hands.

"What's so troubling, my friend? I tried to clean up nice. I didn't expect that sort of reaction out of you," Derek explained, studying his costume. "You're a poet? Something tells me you aren't Walt Whitman."

"I can see you. Holy moly," Nick said, his eyes wide and confused. "You look better than the man in the old photograph. Why...What...How is it that I can see you?"

Derek fixed his frock and glanced at Nick. "I have no idea. Do you mind telling me where Rebecca is?"

"Hell if I know," Nick said, watching a server come by with a broom, pushing the broken teacup pieces into the dustpan. "I was getting her something to drink and told her to wait here, and then she disappeared. Maybe she left. She told me she felt lightheaded."

"So you lost sight of her," Derek said angrily.

"I'm not her bodyguard, Lieutenant. I thought that was your job," Nick said sarcastically.

"You *are* when the damn church is crawling with demons!" Derek growled. "Why are you still standing here, soldier? Let's go find her!" he said, and both advanced into the crowds of angels.

* * *

"Derek," I addressed him while the music changed between songs. "I was thinking. Would you take me to see the Virginia and Pennsylvania battlefields? I want to know what you know, see what you have seen, be where you have been." I gazed into his eyes and at once realized there was something very odd about them.

One minute he looked at me; the next, his eyes were still and almost soulless. I hadn't noticed a change in them until now. Derek offered me a fan with roses blooming on it while pouring whiskey from a glass decanter with his other hand.

"I don't know, Rebecca. Isn't being in Harpers Ferry with me enough? Why hurry to see the rest? There's not much out there," he said.

His answer kind of took me by surprise. I opened the fan; the smell of roses was hanging in the air.

"Forgive me. I don't understand... I thought that's what we both wanted. You told me that when the diary business is done, we could be free. You said we would take Moon and get away, camp in a tent under the stars in the old battlefields."

"Tell me, Rebecca, do you want to get out of here? We could stand at the Point under the moon. Nick won't be a bother, that's a promise," he suddenly said, his eyes changing. Green to blue to black to white.

"Derek." I grabbed him by his arm. "Are you all right? You are scaring me."

As soon as I touched his skin, I flinched away. It burned.

"Ouch. What the hell?" I exclaimed. "Do you have a fever? You are burning up."

"We must get out of here, Rebecca. Nick will be here any minute now."

"Are you jealous? That's what it is?" I asked, confused. "You have nothing to worry about. I still have to talk to him about us. But he'll understand. I know he will. That's how he's wired."

His eyes were telling it all. Impatience set in. His gaze was frantically circling the floor.

"Fine. I'll go," I said, catching his eyes. "I have to tell him that I'm leaving. A friend's promise is a promise you can't get out of," I mumbled.

Then the realization came to me: he couldn't have known about Nick and the drinks. He hadn't been there. My heart lurched. Derek seemed strangely agitated now. His eyes twitched. I saw drops of sweat on his forehead.

"We have to leave," he kept insisting. "Now! Give me your hand."

Without giving me a chance to find Nick, he locked my hand into his and pushed me towards the door.

"No!" I yelled. "Let go of me, Derek! Why are you doing this?"

I resisted. I called Nick's name, but nobody heard me; it seemed nobody even saw me.

I held on to a woman by her hoop dress, pulling her in, but as I saw her face, I realized that before me stood a demon. Her mouth opened wide, and I had to pull my hand back, afraid that she would take off my entire arm. I screamed bloody murder. Derek kept dragging me through the crowds of people in the direction of the glowing "Exit" sign, and I barely held on to the wooden railing with my two hands. As soon as the strength drifted away from my body, my hands slipped off, and I hit the floor. After that, the only thing I remembered was ripping off the bottom of my dress by the church gate, but even then, Derek didn't lessen his grip. If anything, he held me tighter. He stopped only when we reached the point of the two rivers.

Then, something very strange happened. The hand that was so forcefully, even coldly, holding me turned a lifeless gray. I noticed the fingers had become skinny and long. Its nails resembled those belonging to a skeleton who had just dug itself out from its own grave, making its way towards me. Derek's whole form changed, and in front of me stood a blue shadow rising like smoke over the mountain. Faceless. A horrifying shadow. It spoke in Derek's voice. Shivers ran down my legs and spine, and I froze. I couldn't believe what I was seeing or hearing.

"What do you want from me?" I shouted, horror veiling my sight.

The shadow turned to me as if on command, swift and sudden. Eyes appeared in an oval face— big, cold, angry eyes. Its mouth opened to show razor-blade teeth, and it let out a growl from Hell. I lay motionless on the ground by the Point while the shadow hovered above me. I pretended that I wasn't alive— that I wasn't breathing. Maybe it would leave me alone, I thought. *Just maybe, I have a slight chance to escape.* But I was wrong.

Failing to find the diary, the shadow grabbed me. It was about to jump off the Point into the blue abyss when it suddenly released its grip.

"Rebecca!" Nick shouted my name, noticing me lying breathless on the ground. "Jesus Christ!"

He spotted the demon floating above me. He picked up the rocks from the pile of dirt next to John Brown's Fort and threw them at the shadow. It lessened its size to that of a mid-sized stone, curled into a ball, and rolled back over the bridge with the help of furry legs and arms sticking out of its sides.

But it was far from being over. The demon crawled out of the water and hung upside down on the ruins of the bridge in the middle of the Potomac. It stared at us with its yellow stone eyes glowing in the dark like a bat's. Wings, two silver parachutes, were growing out of its back with the speed of a blooming flower on steroids. Its strong legs thrust into the structure, collapsing it, and within seconds it was up in the air, two wings carrying it to the place where I was lying. I could sense death, the cool breath of the end swiftly approaching.

Then I felt warmth just below my shoulder blades, and a hand lifted me off the ground. I heard whispers, the echo of human voices, a train whooshing, and suddenly Derek's face found mine in the darkness. He had some kind of tree branch in his hand, and he was drawing neon circles with it in the air. When the demon ambushed us, we were sitting inside of a glowing bubble of Potomac water. It was like the head of a mushroom but perfectly translucent. No matter how hard the demon banged its head on the bubble, it couldn't get to us. Nick was covered by the same water bubble but a couple of feet away from Derek and me. The demon was flying above us, growling and hissing.

A figure glided out of the church in dark attire. She had remarkably high cheekbones and carried a tray of tools in her hand. Down by the hill, lights came on, and a train of those lights followed the figure from the tents down to the Point. She wanted the demon, and so did the soldiers she had nurtured back to health, marching in behind her. She was their guiding light, turning into a white storm and bashing the demon.

There was a struggle. The demon screamed in agony. Amputation scissors injured one of its wings, and a probe plunged into its chest, just missing its heart. The demon backed down and fell into the confluence while thousands of soldiers— adorned in head and arm bandages— stood by the railing, their rifles and bayonets aimed downward. The Potomac river rose like a wall and fell, carrying off the demon. One of its wings floated like driftwood on the water, rushing away from the site.

I knew the demon was alive. I saw it in Derek's eyes, in the turmoil on Nick's face, and the silence of lowered rifles. I knew that, without a doubt, the demon would come looking for me.

NINETEEN

TAKE A BREAK

"Would you tell me what is going on?" I heard Grandma's voice cutting through my dreamless nap.

The screen of my phone glowed blue inside of my duffel bag, messages from Nick popping up with the same question over and over again: *Can we talk?*

"No, I can't. At least not yet. We have to get as far away as possible," I mumbled. The words were coming out of my mouth, but they felt like they didn't belong to me. Memories of last night mingled inside of my mind in pieces. The diary lay still in the bag by my feet, not one page faded or damaged.

"Child," she suddenly said, breaking the silence, dragging me by my feet from the clouds where my mind had drifted. "I will have to stop the car if you don't tell me this second."

One by one, the hills drowned in the scarlet color of the emerging sun. Tiny houses peeked through the road dust and quickly disappeared in the distance. Apart from the first streaks of light, only a murder of crows hung high in the sky. I glanced at Grandma. Her eyes were emptily focused on the road. Suddenly, she lost control of the car, causing it to swerve into the opposite lane.

My heart jumped inside of my chest. "Watch out!"

I saw her jerk the wheel. Within a few seconds, she somehow regained control of the car and put it back in our lane. We both stared at each other, breathless. Luckily, this road wasn't widely traveled this early in the morning.

"Grams, are you trying to kill us?! Please pull the car over!" My life had flashed before my eyes. I could hardly catch my breath.

"Rebecca, pull yourself together. We are in the middle of a highway— I can't stop here. What in the world is going on with you?"

I felt frustration and fear growing through my skin like copper wires.

"Damn it!" I exclaimed as my mint tea spilled onto the mat of the car.

"Watch your language, young lady! You're the one who dragged me out of the house."

She was right. I said nothing.

"There is a sign here. Let's see…" Grandma muttered to herself.

A distant, rusty metal sign peeked through the forest, shining like a diamond, slowly emerging out of the dark. We slowly passed the gates to the closed farmers' market to our right and traveled underneath a viaduct that stretched over a river.

Shepherdsville was a place made of narrow roads and red bricks. The streets were coated with the scent of blooming flowers, which hovered over a gallery of colorful houses and hidden alleys. The balconies on the houses were somehow always occupied. There was also a gathering of people in the cul-de-sac in front of a giant tent, which looked like an outdoor theater. The town was dressed for festivities, and I felt like it was the best place to be.

We parked by the yellow fire escape— or what used to be a fire escape. It was now a gardenia garden that had a penchant for attracting northern cardinals. We walked a couple of feet to *The Falls B&B*. A café sign popped up behind one of the giant glass panels that surrounded it from all four sides. There, we managed to find a table close to the fireplace. Curtains drooped casually to the floor, and their sea-green color matched perfectly with the rose-embroidered tablecloths, ceramic tea sets, and vases filled with white peonies. Among the lingering shadows of people, I stood in disbelief inside one of the most beautiful places in town. A fountain in the shape of a bird feeder reached to the sky in the cul-de-sac, and a bronze statue of a Civil War soldier with a proud flag waving behind him on the wind caught my eye. At that moment, I felt at peace. I felt that I could overcome anything— that fear was only a feeling, and it wasn't able to conquer me; it couldn't, and I was the only one who controlled it. I felt like I had seen hope shining through the clatter.

Grandma and I had a tête-à-tête by the wall filled with flowers that flowed to the floor, settling under our feet. Hot lavender teas with honey sent steam into the air, and my hands started to sweat. From the steam or nervousness, I didn't know.

"All right," Grandma said. "Out with it. I can't take this silence any longer."

She meant business. Her pupils were wide, her tone steady— she would have shaken me senseless if I didn't start speaking. Nonetheless, I was paralyzed. Instead, I took out the centuries-old diary and put it on the tablecloth between us. With a heavy heart, I pushed it closer to her. If I imagined my paranoia to be water, it grew from a couple of drops to a full-blown storm. In my mind, all the people at the café would soon turn their fake human faces towards me and begin laughing ruefully. But, of course, I was just imagining it.

"Oh, God! Becca, where did you get this?" Grandma cried, standing up.

"Have you seen this before?" I asked horrified.

"It belonged to your ancestor, Lieutenant Shawn Grimwood, during the Civil War."

My quarter-sized eyes locked onto my grandmother. Apart from my beating heart, I could hear music and the whispers of the crowd coming from the cul-de-sac.

"I pulled it from the battlefield in Gettysburg," I explained. "It was wrapped in a Civil War uniform, pressed under a rock, as if I was destined to find it."

"It's not possible," she stated. "He destroyed it. I watched him do it."

If the chair didn't have some weight to it, I would have flipped over backward.

"Do you see the ghosts?" she asked abruptly.

There was no reason for me to keep the truth from her any longer. I just nodded. Grandma pulled her shawl on her shoulders as if a chill had run down her back.

"Why didn't you tell me sooner?" she asked sadly.

"I was afraid that you wouldn't believe me," I said, looking down at a cube of sugar dissolving in my cup of tea.

I knew this conversation would deeply upset her, but I was just as scared as she was, if not more.

"Who else knows about this?"

"Only Nick and I. Nobody else," I confirmed.

"God, you two are quite the secret keepers," she said and put her tiny hand on mine.

I gathered the courage to look her in the eyes again. "I beg you, Grandma. Tell me what you know."

The wind picked up a napkin from the table, but I managed to stop it before it went cruising around Shepherdsville. Traveling down memory lane wasn't easy for my grandmother, but it was necessary. We ordered porridge with honey, bananas, and raspberries as the morning progressed into afternoon.

"Your grandfather showed me this diary long after his visions developed. He told me it was a family heirloom he had found in the closet upstairs," she whispered nervously. "One day, we were walking down the riverbank when he told me he had had a vision of a woman drowning. He said her whole house collapsed into the stream and she was searching for her son, who went down with the house. And I didn't believe him at first, but as the time went by, I started to hear them: unidentified whispers, dishes falling to the floor in the middle of the night, footsteps, loud banging on the walls. His experiences worsened after that, and before he died, he threw the diary into the canal far away from Harpers Ferry. But... I never imagined it making its way back to the house." She froze as if she remembered something.

"What is it, Grams?" I had watched her closely the whole time without breathing. After all, she had just confirmed that my craziness wasn't a symptom of an underlying condition.

"He told me that... it must go where it belongs."

I didn't know what that meant, and I wasn't sure if she did either.

"Did Grandpa mention anyone by the name of Derek?" My thoughts were scattered inside of my head like broken glass, and his name was the only reflection I could pick out in the fragments.

"Not that I know of. He knew of a Derek, but that was back during the war and had to do with his family heritage," she said and brought the cup to her lips, the saucer drenched by a leaking tea bag.

"What did he say about him?" I asked. One way or the other, I was going to find out the truth about him.

"He said that Shawn and Derek used to be comrades. They would give their lives for one another. But the war was hard on people, and they came out of it almost unrecognizable. Dying was a gift in comparison to what the soldiers were left with. Their broken minds and hearts," she said, glancing outside where a boy was standing with a basket of roses in his hand.

"What do you mean by that, Grams? Did Derek betray Shawn's trust?" I watched the boy hand over flowers to the women passing him in the street. It was almost like I hadn't seen him there; I was so absorbed with my thoughts.

"Far worse than you think. Your grandfather used to believe that Derek was the reason why Shawn died," Grandma whispered, her eyes following mine.

I blinked. Another secret in Derek's box of things labeled "don't open". It was upsetting to me that all this time, he kept so much of the past hidden inside of him. It must have taken a toll on his soul, and yet he decided not to say a word. It was as if he didn't trust me enough. And Shawn Grimwood... Even though I didn't know much about him, he was my ancestor, and I felt like I had to know the truth about his death. I owed it to my family. What if the truth would hurt me? What if Derek did cause his death? What was I to do? How was I to live with such a truth?

I reached for Grandma's warm hands, pushing the thoughts aside. "I am so sorry. I don't feel well; we should get some rest before we head back." I really meant those first four words.

* * *

When we got back to the B&B, I told Grandma I had forgotten my toothbrush in the car, giving me an excuse to be alone. I grabbed a key from the TV stand and slipped into the hallway, running into an old lady and a pug. The dog grunted and snorted, brushing past me, and I started to miss Charlie. He was probably chewing on something he wasn't supposed to.

With a toothbrush in my hand, I took a sip of cold fountain water by the bathrooms and headed into the lobby, which was surprisingly empty. From here, the world seemed normal. People hurried into their rooms. Delivery drivers showed up with warm pizza boxes in their hands. Cars left and new ones arrived. And yet, I knew there was nothing normal about this world. Not for me. I knew of the ghosts, and I cursed them as much as I cursed the fact that, sooner or later, I had to talk to Derek about Shawn Grimwood.

My phone released a subtle chime, breaking the soundlessness.

I slid the phone out of the pocket of my jeans. The last message from Nick said: *Where are you, Rebecca? Please talk to me. I am worried about you.*

I dialed the number, and soon a familiar voice appeared on the other side of the line. "Thank God. Do you know what I've been through? What the hell happened?"

"I wanted to get away," I explained.

"I understand that. You should have at least let me know you are okay." He sounded irritated.

"I'm sorry. I lost track of time. I just had this horrible headache. But now you know what's going on."

"Listen, I know things have been weird between us. I just wanted to let you know that I am here for you. I will always be there for you. I love you, Becca. If there is anything— *anything*— you want to tell me, I am ready to listen," he said, and my heart dropped. I had heard him say those words before, but today they seemed different.

"I love you too," I whispered. It felt like the words came out all wrong.

"Please come back to me. I miss you. I will do anything to keep you safe. Anything. I promise. We can hide at our treehouse."

"I'll have to spend my night here, but I'll be on my way tomorrow." I felt my eyes getting heavy. Lack of sleep was getting to me.

"Is there anything going on between you and Derek?" he asked, and I hesitated. I wanted to tell him— I did. I was fighting a battle I couldn't win.

"What makes you think that?" I asked.

"I don't know. You have been so distant. You skipped town. I've seen him, Becca. In the flesh. And he looks like he walked out of another century. He's a Civil War lieutenant— a handsome one at that," he grumbled.

"You saw him?" Now things had gotten interesting.

"At the Remembrance Day Ball. It was odd. I just ran into him. I feel like I hit my head too hard that last time."

No. No. No. When Derek healed the bruise on his head, he must have given Nick the ability to see.

"Did you see anyone else, except for Derek?" I asked.

"Yes, the demons. That thing that dragged you out of the church."

"Beetlez," I corrected him. "That's the name of the demon Derek once told me about— head of the butcher's filth."

"That thing, yes. Did I do something that made you run away?" Nick continued, still worried.

"I... I had a lot going on," I admitted. I knew my voice was wavering. I hoped he didn't catch it on the other line.

"You wouldn't lie to me, would you?"

"No, I wouldn't," I confirmed.

"Hey, I got to go. Lida just walked in. I'll see you tomorrow. Sweet dreams, Beccs. Don't pull any more surprises."

"Good night, Nick," I said. He got off the phone so fast that I thought I must have hurt him.

I promised myself I would try, but I knew the surprises wouldn't end here. The time had come for me to deal with Derek.

* * *

252

One by one, stars appeared in the night sky, like the lights in the windows of Harpers Ferry cafés. I was standing on the B&B's balcony. Two lounge chairs, wet from the rain, faced the blooming rose garden in front of me. The night felt warm, and the wind gently caressed my face, occasionally chiming the bells of the entrance door. A boy, maybe six years of age, climbed out of a car parked by the willows. When he noticed me, he waved his hand. I returned the gesture, smiling. I wished to be a kid again— to live my life like ghosts didn't exist in my world. That was just a wish, though.

Grandma was sleeping underneath her two blankets; her face turned in the direction of the wallpaper. I left a couple of cinnamon candles burning on the windowsill so that I could find my way back inside the B&B. I waited until the lights faded and the town's residents locked the doors of their houses and retreated upstairs into their tiny beds.

Grandma and I shared the same room, but it was divided. The water in the shower wasn't hot, but it was warm enough for me to take a bath. Lavender oil spread like rings onto the water, and I slid into the tub, putting my head onto ceramic tiles. The condensation from the bath quickly fogged up the bathroom mirrors. I noticed that the screen of my phone was illuminated. I stared at it for a moment and then shoved it back into my purse, pretending Nick wasn't trying to talk to me.

The water dripped softly from the bathroom sink faucet, tiny droplets hitting the ceramic and disappearing into the drain. I felt at ease with myself for the first time. The sound of the water calmed me down, and the warmth of it released my muscle tension. If the water hadn't been getting cold, I would have laid there all day, meditating.

I soon wrapped a towel around my head and curled inside of a white hotel robe. The bathtub water was still draining when I came out of the bathroom.

A wave of thunder followed after a flash of lightning, startling me. I quickly pulled all the blinds down and closed all the shutters. The rainstorms in the area were known to be wild, and with strong winds like that, I was afraid a tree would come down, breaking a window or two. It had happened once before at Grandma's house.

As I blew out the candles and finally lay down, I heard a slight rattling sound just outside the room. I thought it was a cat. I pushed the blanket up, covering my head, and turned my face towards the wall. Dancing lights drifted into the room from a slit between the carpet and the door. *There is no way I'll be able to sleep.* The rattling sound continued. I quietly crawled out of bed. I wandered towards the door and put my ear on the wooden surface, trying to listen, but this time there was no noise.

I was about to return to bed when I heard the rattling so clearly behind me that I froze. I pushed the door handle down, and I stuck my head out into the hallway.

A man in a flawless concierge jacket had just exited one of the guest rooms with a woman hanging on his left arm, feather duster sticking out of her apron. They were both laughing. They probably had just finished their long shift. At least someone knew how to have fun, I thought. A smile crossed my face, and I creaked the door closed, burying my hand into my wavy wet hair.

What happened next was a blur. The windows that I had shut began opening and closing as if on command. I glanced over at my grandmother. She was peacefully sleeping, nothing disturbing her. The room fell into still cold silence, as if death itself had stormed inside like an uninvited guest. The slit between the door and the floor barely shed light onto the beds. I could feel my heart beating in my throat with agonizing pain. My first thought was to use the kaleidoscope, but I realized I had forgotten it in Harpers Ferry. Now I had no way of defending myself.

I lowered myself to the carpet and pressed my back against the corner. At least there I was safe from being bombarded by whatever was in the room. I never understood why, in movies, characters would go and investigate what caused the disturbance. I couldn't move a muscle, never mind stand up and wander around. This time I didn't need to. I heard the rattling sound like a hiss into my ear. Whatever was in the room was standing right next to me. I couldn't make out its face, but it resembled a shadow, with a black head and a dark velvety cloak hiding its ugliness. The rattling was coming from its teeth. It was hunched over and standing with its spiked back aimed at me. If I had let the air out of my lungs, it would have been over for me.

"We need to talk."

I heard a whisper coming from another side of the door.

"Rebecca, open the door, I beg you."

The candle started burning again. The creature had vanished.

"Nick? Is that you?" I asked through the tears.

I unhinged the door, and it blew wide open because of the wind. Instead of Nick, there stood Derek with his eyes locked on mine. All at once, he grabbed me and pulled me out into the hallway.

"Derek!" I tossed like a fish in his arms, wrapping my arms around his torso, leaving traces of mascara and tears on his snow-white shirt. "I thought it was going to get me. I thought it would kill me, and I didn't have the kaleidoscope…" I mumbled. Tears were rolling down my cheeks.

Derek held me close to his chest, and we both were breathing into the night.

"Wait, how did you know where I was?" My voice echoed against the walls of the B&B.

"I followed you," Derek responded, his forehead leaning onto my wet hair. "Beetlez feeds on fear and likes to spy on people, and after you left, I knew it was a matter of time before he found you. It's not safe for you here."

"Is he going to return?" I asked, terrified.

Derek's voice pierced the human voices coming from outside. "I isolated us for a short time. We are in a veil. Demons can't see us, but he is not done. Demons never stop coming after us. It's in their nature."

I ran my eyes across the long hallway. He was right. We were in another dimension, with lights around us hanging in the air. Derek was stretched out on the floor, holding me tight in his arms. There was not a soul around.

"Derek, I need to ask you about Shawn…" I said, biting my lip so hard it hurt.

"What about him?" Derek asked, confused. "You were almost attacked, and all you can think about is Shawn Grimwood?"

I filled my lungs with air, held my breath for a second, and then let go. "I know you told me you were his friend..."

"Rebecca... What are you saying?" He pushed his dark brown eyebrows together.

"Did you have anything to do with Shawn Grimwood's death?" I finally asked, watching his face for any change that would give away his secret.

He sighed and pulled away from me. "That's what you think of me?" I saw his lips move.

I felt like he had scolded me, even though he hadn't. "I didn't mean to offend you, Derek..." I addressed him softly.

He was silent for the first time.

I dragged Derek by his shirt. "The demons are after me. They're trying to kill me. What if the solution lies deep inside your past? Don't you think I deserve to know?"

He gently moved my hands away and placed them on my lap. His eyes were hooked on mine.

"I did not kill Shawn, Rebecca. He died at Pickett's Charge from the cannon blast. George sure played a part in all of that." He paused. "Shawn Grimwood saved my life, and I saved his." Derek's amber-green eyes had sadness in them that I would have given anything to take away.

His tone of voice changed, and I spotted the notes of worry in his words, which made me panic even more. I somehow sensed that he was telling me the truth.

"I am sorry, I didn't know," I mumbled in response, catching his eyes.

"There is a lot you don't know. But one thing you have to sure of— I would never lie to you. So why are you hiding at a B&B? I assume you don't believe I am capable of protecting you, either."

"It's not that," I said and touched his hand, which was cold as ice.

"Then help me understand," Derek insisted.

I heard footsteps heading our way, but there was no one in sight.

"At the masquerade, the demon pretended to be you. He spoke like you; he knew things that I shared with you. He was you. And I believed his act… I feel like I've lost touch with reality. I'm fine with seeing dead people because it's my gift for me to bear— but being dead myself? I wasn't planning on that. And he almost killed me."

Derek's face darkened. "If they are imitating the appearance of others, we have a far greater problem on our hands than I imagined. You should have told me this before you went on your little trip. Do you have any idea how long I searched for you? It's time lost that we both don't have."

"What does it change?"

Derek's eyes widened. "It changes everything, Rebecca. It means they are gaining power. The butcher knows where the book is. We have to kill the demons because now they'll be haunting you regardless of where you are. I have to get you back to Harpers Ferry."

"I can't leave. Not without my grandmother," I protested.

"We can write her a letter. She will wake up in the morning, find it on the dresser pressed against the mirror, and know you are all right. Please, Rebecca... Don't make me throw you against my shoulder and carry you out of here, because I have certainly thought about that."

Derek smirked at me. A smile played so warmly on his face that I wanted to kiss him and then run my finger across the dimples on his cheeks.

"Fine," I said, standing up.

"Don't ever run away from me because I'll always find you. In any century," he said and pulled me into his arms. I felt the warmth of his lips on my forehead and the beating of his heart against my chest. My phone was vibrating in my purse, and I wasn't sure if I could keep Nick in the dark anymore. I was truly starting to fall for Derek.

We did write a letter. It was short but to the point. And just like Derek promised, we left it on the dresser by the bathroom. He held my hand in his as we exited the room under the flickering lights. When we passed the other rooms in the hallway, the stairway doors to the landing opened. They bounced off the walls. There was a moan coming from the floor below, and then hotel maids streamed into the hallway, their faces melting off, dripping onto the carpets. I squeezed Derek's hand and hid behind him, trying to forget what I had just seen. The monsters were moving fast. It was only a matter of time before they would surround us.

One of the demons managed to sneak behind me and rip the purse off my shoulder. I saw my makeup bag, notebook, and my cellphone plunge onto the carpet. All I needed was a key to get back into the room and, thankfully, I had slid that inside of my pocket. Derek cast a spell that made the maids wander around without seeing us. We ran down the hallway, back into the room, sparing time only to shift the curtains as we jumped off the balcony into the street. This whole time I was thinking about what kind of mess I had gotten myself into.

"Don't worry. She can't see them. They won't harm her," Derek whispered, watching me throw a glance at my sleeping grandmother.

"Thank you," I mumbled.

"For what?" He acted surprised.

"Caring for her the way I would."

Derek smiled with his shiny teeth. "Rebecca, you forget that I had a grandmother once. She was one of the best things that ever happened to me."

I had forgotten. He didn't belong only to me; he had a family that loved him. Just like I did. If only he knew what I was thinking, then he would have been the ultimate gatekeeper— a supreme being.

The engine of a motorcycle revved. Derek hopped on the leather seat, and I perched behind him, mellow wind wrapping around us. With no time for doubt, we began moving, the oak leaves landing on the road as we raced out of the parking lot.

* * *

As the miles disappeared behind us, I watched the side mirrors. In their reflection, I noticed a dark storm rising, enveloping the B&B and all the gardens around it. It bubbled and blew into a mass that treated the sky like its playground. The more I watched it, the more it swelled and expanded, and soon it resembled a face. The same face that had dragged me off the Point.

There were a few seconds before the demon-faced storm caught up with the real thunderous rainstorm. It burst into thousands of blackbirds, all chirping in a creepy wave of tortured human voices.

"Derek," I said firmly. He caught my eyes in the side mirror. "That engine better be good because there is a flock of demons chasing us. Give this baby all you've got!"

Derek laughed and slowed down the motorcycle.

"What the hell are you doing? Did you hear what I just told you?" I yelled.

"Oh, I heard you well."

He set the motorcycle on its kickstand, his leather jacket freely moving off his torso. He chuckled and pulled his hair up, the scent of the forest drifting after him like cologne.

"Then why aren't you moving? What are you waiting for?"

He smiled and said: "The storm. I am waiting for the storm."

At first, I couldn't understand what exactly he was talking about. We were in the middle of an abandoned road that curved into an alley and a street with just one lonely house on it. The birds rushed after us. I had never seen such a pandemonium of feathered bodies, except maybe on my walks at the cemetery with Nick when the crows were sitting on tops of the trees, calling to each other—calling for death.

"Please, Derek. Let's go, let's get out of here. They're coming!" I begged, realizing how close the chirping was.

"Have patience, Rebecca. Have faith. That will get you far in life," he said, his tone serious.

I heard him, I did, but the reality of things was a bit terrifying. I hid my head into the anorak, foolishly thinking it could save me.

The storm he was referring to was not a demonic one. He was waiting for the rain. It reached us just before the birds did. Derek pulled the switch on the motorcycle's headlight, illuminating the road that stretched out ahead. I heard the engine hum, and as soon as the water droplets approached us, he turned the rain droplets into metallic darts. My mouth opened in surprise. I watched the darts slowly change their direction, and like magnets, they embedded themselves into the demon birds' bodies. There was a scream in the air that froze and died off, and instead of the rain, the birds fell onto the concrete and dissipated into dust like they were never there.

"That was great. How in the world did you do that?" I exclaimed.

"The perks of being a gatekeeper. Magic comes from a source of power, whether from the souls of the dead or living people. Both have to equally hate demons. I just draw on that power. And of course, the water is a natural energy transmitter."

I put my helmet back on and wrapped my arms around his waist. "I wish I was magical like you."

"You are. Otherwise, we would have never met," he stated.

I checked the two mirrors; the B&B stood still after the bird storm, but something didn't feel right. Suddenly the motorcycle got pulled away from the road and was thrown onto the nearby lawn. I fell hard, landing on the side of my back and my shoulder. It felt like I had just run into a stone wall. Derek stood over me with thunder electrifying behind him, his motorcycle a few feet from us and buzzing. Two paws appeared in my line of vision. They slowly approached the lawn but didn't step any closer. Even though the demon lacked a wing, it wasn't any less frightening. The fangs peering out of its mouth were uneven and blade-like, and they nestled under his upper lips, sticking out upward. His long and twitching tongue took the form of a snake. His eyes, black and soulless, were full of rage. His entire body was set alight with steam, as if he had dipped into lava from the Hell pond. He ferociously dug the ground underneath him to give a kick to his paws, trying to catch us both in his grip.

"Thunder will give us a momentary break. And as soon as it does, I want you to get on that motorcycle and keep driving. You hear me?" Derek said, helping me up.

"What about you?" I worried.

"I will be right behind you. You have to trust me," he whispered.

"I am not leaving you here," I protested, my lips turning pale.

"I *said* get on the bike, Rebecca," he repeated sternly.

I knew he really meant it this time. He began chanting. There were a few sparks of yellow racing in the air. They covered the demon, and I watched them send a shockwave through his shape. I didn't wait; I ran towards the motorcycle and lifted it from the lawn, hopped on it, and accelerated. It vibrated, the wheels hissed, and I started to think that I would wreck it, but the rain caught up with me. At once, a stream of water carried the motorcycle down the highway. It felt like I was on a surfboard in the open ocean.

In the distance, the sky was changing colors like fireworks. Derek's energy battled the demon from the Point, igniting the clouds. Then I heard a pop, and all the color faded away. My heart beat erratically, and cold sweat covered my forehead as I looked over my shoulder. With the speed of the motorcycle, the trees were nothing but a smudged photograph. Then there was a hum that pierced the air, and I saw Derek, scars on his face, riding alongside me, blood streaming off his lip. His motorcycle was a replica of the one I drove, but it appeared to be a ghost.

"The demon is gone. I sent him back to the other side for a while. I need you to keep your bike still so that I can merge, okay?" he said, and I just nodded, not letting him out of my sight.

His motorcycle went off the road into mine, and for a moment, I drove both of them. Two metallic shapes were joined together. Derek was holding on to my waist while I was leading.

"Now I know you have a shadow bike," I said, slowing down as we approached a thick line of fog.

"If one breaks or, let's say, a demon jumps it, I have an endless amount of shadow versions," he explained.

"Are you okay?" I asked.

He smiled, squeezing my waist warmly in his hands. "I'm fine."

"It'd be better if you drove," I confessed. "I feel lightheaded from the fall."

"Of course." He nodded and shifted his body to the front of the motorcycle.

* * *

"Derek, what are we going to do?" I whispered into his ear, holding him tight at the waist, feeling his every muscle suddenly tense up as I asked the question. The wind was working against us, and the speed of the motorcycle was almost imperceptible. The helmet I was wearing kept sliding uncomfortably back and forth on my head.

"We aren't going to do anything. You will go back home where it's safe. Now it's my problem— my burden— to carry, and I don't want you worrying about this. Do you understand?"

There was darkness in his eyes that I had never seen before, and it mingled in his irises, searching for a way to break through. I caught a rising wave of determination in his voice, swirling with desire— desire to end this once and for all.

I did understand— I just couldn't accept it. I wasn't about to trade his life for mine.

"Yes," I lied.

"Good, let's keep it this way," he said sternly. "If we are going to do this, you have to promise me something— no more secrets, no more hiding the truth, no more trips to the middle of nowhere. And please, don't say anything to Nicholas. We don't need him engaged in something that could possibly result in his death."

Oh, like he was going to live through this alone, I thought. Alone, fighting a thousand-year-old demon.

"What's the plan? Are you going to knock him down with your irresistible charm?"

I was just being sarcastic, but he looked at me as if I had said something inappropriate.

"I am going to trap him in this realm, make sure the diary is far out of his reach, and then send him back where he came from."

"Even if that means going with him?"

In response, I only heard silence.

"Derek, I am not going to let you do this," I said desperately.

"He took Shawn from you and made your life a living hell. This sacrifice is worth it, believe me."

"I didn't ask for this," I begged him.

"You didn't have to."

"That's the problem, Derek; this is my family heritage, my life, my decision. You don't get to decide what feels right. You don't get to be the hero."

The road suddenly opened up into a bridge, a wide hidden pathway in the middle of nowhere, and on all four sides was a thick blanket of fog preserving the bridge. There was nothing in front of us and nothing behind us; we were stuck inside another dimension. Derek got off his motorcycle, walked over into the fog, and vanished. I quickly followed him.

"I agree that there are bad parts of the spirit world, but there are also exciting parts. Parts you never knew existed. Let me show you. Give me your hands."

He grinned as I looked at him. I didn't feel any fear, just trust and desire to see what he saw, to feel what he felt— to know what he knew. As I reached over to Derek, he came closer, locked my hands inside of his, and told me to close my eyes.

He really was the gatekeeper. A magic wand. A coin you could flip and find a face on the other side. Seductively handsome, incredibly gifted, and so easily admired. As his touch vibrated through my every cell, I heard the fluttering of butterfly wings and the distant melody of church bells. Then, the whole bridge lit up as if it were a giant stage, and all around us, I saw the stars dazzle with brightness through the fog. Derek's face froze with excitement, waiting to be freed, and I realized why.

At last, I saw a wave of energy, like a tornado made of tiny diamonds, headed our way. It lifted my feet off the ground. Gravity didn't exist anymore— I just floated mid-air. The wave somehow cleansed my heart, and I felt nothing but belonging, joy, and love.

"Derek, are they— ?" I stopped. His mouth turned into a smile, and I couldn't help but smile in return.

"Yes, spirits."

"Why are they here?"

"Like a herd of muscled horses shifting the dust, aren't they?"

I just nodded in disbelief.

"They are racing to the mountain. The sun sets there in the west, and they want to see if they can reach the mountain faster than the sun itself; it's a little game they play. The bridge just happens to be their playground."

"I feel so light now," I said, releasing Derek's hands. My heart sang with the melody of a summer night somewhere in Paris, with warm wind caressing my skin and the scent of lavender drifting in the air.

"It's because wherever they find darkness, they take it with them. I wish there were more of them, actually."

"You have a name for them?" My curiosity refused to have limits.

Derek gently removed the locks of hair trapped under my dress and laid them in curls on my chest.

"They call themselves Spero. They're more like spirit-matter than faces of people," he said and ran his fingers through his dark walnut hair.

"How old are they, if you don't mind me asking?" I wondered, knocking the helmet against my leg.

"They don't have an age; no one knows when they were born or when they will die. They are like the wind; they rise, and they fall. What is left is only sensations."

I gazed across the colorful landscape of trees, and when the fog cleared, I saw Spero rising above the hills. Derek watched them disappear, and as the last of them were finally cloaked by the trees, he sighed contently.

"Spero just never cease to amaze me."

He walked over to the bridge and sank into the road, lying his back on the cold asphalt.

"What about the traffic?" I asked, and then I immediately felt embarrassed because no one was around.

"We aren't really here. The rules of gravity don't apply, nor does Newton's first law." A smile slid across Derek's face.

Every time Derek spoke, his voice had such a gentle timbre that I felt like he was teaching me the language of the wind. I slowly lay down next to him, and as we stared into the mingling blue and pearl-colored sky, it opened its gates to us even more, carrying our thoughts into the depths of its infinite existence.

"Apart from Spero, are there any other spiritual matters?" I asked.

He turned his head to the side to lock his gaze on mine, and, half-lying, half-sitting up, he fixed his leather jacket, which was crumbled like paper underneath him.

"Now, why would you want to know that?" he asked with a serious, dangerous tone.

I had to admit; it was hard to find the right words when all I could think about was how mysterious and beautiful he was. My thoughts were scattered… that was all there was to it.

I quickly found a loophole. "To prepare myself. It's dangerous out there— you told me so yourself."

Derek shook his head. "Curiosity will get you in trouble one day." Crossing his hands against his chest, he continued, "You want to know about Malum?"

I just nodded quietly, in case they heard me thinking about them.

"They are the shadows that you see playing amongst the trees when the sun shines through. But don't let their playfulness fool you. They are incredibly powerful. If bothered, they turn into a mist, sullen and dark, which, like rain, drains you dry. And by dry, I mean sucks the living soul out of you. All the good emotional parts, of course. Otherwise, what would be the point, right?"

"If bothered?" I asked, confused.

"They are peaceful, generally." He rubbed his velvety eyebrows with his fingers. "But if you put a mirror to them, to see their own reflection, whether natural or man-made glass, Malum

269

revolt. I guess I can see why: no one likes seeing their own, flawed selves up close. That's the whole reason why they're shadows."

I felt a sudden gust of wind on my back, and shivers rushed through my entire body. Derek sat up and put his arm around me.

I studied Derek's face for a moment and felt like it was a perfect time to free my heart from what I had hidden for so many months.

"You carried me off the ice, didn't you, Derek? That night my mother died?" I asked, listening to the wind whooshing. He kept staring into the distance, thinking.

"Yes," he admitted.

My heart leaped. "I have never forgiven her for leaving me. I know it's not right, and I know I have to let it go, but it's hard. Harder than I ever expected it to be. And it happened so suddenly..." I explained.

His emerald eyes were pinned on mine. "Death never knocks on doors to alarm you. It's lighting that strikes out of nowhere— a guest that shows up uninvited. A flood that takes everything with it. It doesn't care for age, social status, dreams, and desires; it doesn't care what war we fight. It drowns everything and everyone like a wave until nothing is left but pure blackness and tears. I have seen it on the fields. I have met it in my dreams. I have begged for mercy for my life and the life of people I love. It's always ugly. Your mother... She is gone, but it's not the bad parts that she should be remembered by, Rebecca. Find it in yourself to shed light on the good deeds, and maybe then the world won't seem so colorless. Maybe then you will find peace within yourself," Derek said.

Silence spoke to me. A shimmering blue butterfly sat on Derek's shoulder.

"I have seen her before," I said, studying its fragile insect legs and wing pattern.

He moved her from his shoulder to the palm of his hand.

"She is my eyes and ears; she is the river whisperer. She knows the language of the wind," Derek said, rubbing his fingers on the brim of her wing. I watched her lean closer to him. "She showed me the way when I thought I had lost you. And I can never lose you." His lips were coral and wet from the rain.

"Death is an agony only when you have something to love," I mumbled.

I whispered a wish to the butterfly, and she took off into the fog. As she vanished, I saw a blue mist ignite the fog, and it seemed that the sky fell to comfort us both.

TWENTY

BEFORE THE SUNRISE

We were sitting at the bank of the Potomac River with waves like hands clinging to the shore, stealing the sand and the shells into the water, lulling them into a false sense of security, and then throwing them against the rocks until they burst. If not for the stars, the night would have been dark above the water, and the mountain would have been nothing but a globe of ice hanging over us, a hawk looking into the darkness. The air was foggy yet somehow fresh, and the wind sent leaves quivering at the tops of the trees. Derek sat beside me, his face still and his expression full of mystery. I wondered what was on his mind— what magic was hidden away there.

"Before I met you, it was easier to just be myself, get accustomed to the reality of things, of setting order…" Derek's voice shook with the leaves. "Now, I just worry, and it has nothing to do with the ghosts and everything to do with you. Like you invaded my world and left me breathless… I still gasp for air, Rebecca. I don't think it will ever be enough."

His hand slowly reached to find a place below my ear, in the luxury of long curls of my hair. My heart beat fast, but I couldn't find the words. It was cold by the river, but my entire body was burning up as if I had a fever.

"You're like some mythical creature, Derek, and I…" I held my breath and then let it go, trying to calm the butterflies that had suddenly appeared in my stomach. "I'm just a girl from a world that cannot even be compared to yours. I look at you and see beautiful horizons, power some would only dream about. And here I am. I don't fit beside you; I only see you by mere chance, a gift that was given to me by some creepy old book. As much as I wish we did, we don't have forever."

"But isn't that the whole point? To make every moment count? To appreciate what we have now, and then think of it later?"

His revelation struck me. Later wouldn't matter if he wasn't in it. Why give it a thought if it would happen inevitably? If it was so out of our control? *Who knows? Maybe, just maybe, we can figure it out.*

He ran his hands through my hair, and I could almost feel the coldness of his lips— could almost feel the pressure of his strong body over mine, electricity and desire flowing between us like a wave. I reached out for him, flaming, ready to put my arms around his broad shoulders and unzip his leather jacket when he stood up and offered me his hand.

"I would like to think I am more romantic than that. I want you to never forget me," he declared. I waited. I couldn't understand if he was serious or just teasing me.

"Like it would be easy to forget you," I whispered.

He led me to the water. We both set our shoes by the roots of the trees and stepped into the stream. He brought me to the center; it was still shallow there, and he put his hand on the surface, as if he were testing the temperature of the water. At once, the stream brightened to the most azure color imaginable. We were stargazing, but through water that glowed from within. Fish circled by our feet and thought we were a part of their habitat. They looked translucent, filled with phosphors that shone in the dark water. Derek saw excitement rising in my eyes, and he grinned because what he offered was a fairy tale.

"Now, you need to come here," he commanded, but with gentleness in his voice. Like he had been waiting a long time for this.

I stepped closer to him, and he put one hand on my waist, the other on my blushing cheek, and locked me in a kiss— the most magical kiss ever. We just... combined the two worlds so easily. He was taking over me, and there was little I could do to withstand him. I hid inside of Derek's leather jacket right by his neck, breathed in the forest, and never wanted to let go.

"You just met Amnis, Becca," he said, still holding me in his arms. "Every time we see a change in the way the water flows, it is actually them smiling. All streams form faces, and the water travels in the direction of their contours. When we see strong splashes by the shore, it's them breathing, playfully striving to get our feet. They can also walk, and when they do, they demolish everything in their way." He was talking about them like he had just met them, and his voice projected adoration and delight, as if he had been made for this unreal life.

"They have a dark side to them, just like you." I gazed into Derek's green eyes while he studied the distant landscape. His heart started to race, and I noticed that he took his hand off my waist. "What is it, Derek? Is it something I said? I can't read your mind, so you better tell me," I insisted, trying to hide the worry.

"My dark side is a demon," he stated, not taking his eyes off the water. Just a moment ago, his eyes had been filled with brightness, and now there was nothing in them but blind emptiness.

"I know... I know..." I said gently. Then I brushed my fingers over Derek's face, hoping that the warmth of my body would bring him back from the dark place he waded into.

"You don't know." He turned his face away from me.

"Then tell me, please," I begged.

I had to know. I wanted to. After all, this demon had taken half of my life, not to mention all of Derek's life— or, at least, what I knew of it.

He breathed hard, and I could almost sense the pain that he exhaled. This dark creature of Hell had been running his life show for over a century; he deeply regretted ever crossing paths with it. Not that it was ever in his power not to.

"Fine," Derek said, breaking the silence. "Although we have to find a secluded place to talk. How about under the mountain? We could watch the sunrise..."

* * *

Darkness fell upon the town without warning. We had to pass through the woods in order to get to the top of the mountain, and if I didn't have Derek with me, it would have been the last place I would choose to disturb at night. The air was moist and heavy, and I thought I heard an animal rustling in the shadows of the oaks. At this time of day, those shadows looked like cloaked people.

Knowing what I knew of Derek, it would have been stupid of me to deny the possibility that the trees could move or talk. Owls were hooting loudly on the branches; squirrels froze like stone statues on the trees as we walked by. Derek moved slowly. He looked determined but still very much lost in his thoughts. I thought of putting my hand in his, but I didn't want to pressure him. To my surprise, he turned at once, as if he heard me thinking about him.

"Becca, are you all right up there? Come on, hold my hand."

And I did exactly as he said because it was the only thing that occupied my mind from thinking about the spooky forest.

When we finally found a trail to the mountain, I barely heard the crackling sound behind us. I turned to Derek, but it seemed like he wasn't bothered by its occurrence. It surely existed, though. I blamed the sound on my tiredness, but it still rose through my consciousness over and over again. In the corner of my eye, I saw streaks of light following my footsteps. The same lights I had seen before. This time they were brighter, even playful— magnetizing— as if someone had put on tiny lightbulb strings over the roots of the trees and broken branches.

"Derek, can spirits play with lights?" I asked, pretending to be simply curious.

"Sure they can. The realm of their possibilities is an open ocean."

"Is it a way to make you fear them?"

"No, they won't bother you that way unless I knew them during my lifetime, which is now hundreds of years ago. You have to understand that some spirits do this out of love, not hatred. They either want to talk, or they just want you to be their messenger. Why are you asking?" Derek asked, raising his dark velvety brows.

"Oh, no reason, I'm just interested," I lied.

Yet this spirit had been following me since I arrived at Harpers Ferry, and I needed to figure out who it was and why. As much as I wanted to believe it was just a way that spirits had been alerting me to their presence, I felt that it must be more than that. This spirit somehow knew me.

When we reached the waterfall, I felt a tingling in my legs, and not because I was afraid of heights. The scenery opened up into a beautiful landscape that one could only describe with a poem. The trees stood like flames, and the light lit up bronze rocks that surrounded the banks of the river from all sides. Willows hovered over the water, long branches gently covering the stones. Behind it was a cave, not visible from the first glance but very alluring. I could see why this was Derek's favorite place.

Derek led me to the mountain cave. Once inside, he locked me in his arms, put his head on my shoulder, arms around my waist, and hid his face in my long curly hair. His muscles tightened as he began his story, and I knew it would be hard for him to delve into the past.

"Did it hurt?" I asked carefully, still holding his hands in mine.

"Did what hurt?" Derek wondered.

"Dying."

He pierced me with his eyes. "Oh... that's one of the parts of my journey that I have no recollection of. All I know is that I lay in the open field with a thundering of cannons over my head. I had a strong taste of metal in my mouth. In the distance, through my blurred vision, I remember seeing three giant oaks, silky leaves waving with the wind. There was so much fog, and the sun was throwing shadows onto the fields, gilding the wildflowers."

It was still hard to believe. It wasn't every day that you met someone who walked straight out of the pages of history.

"It happened at Gettysburg," he clarified. The sun peeked out from the horizon, and Harpers Ferry began to slowly emerge from the night.

"Gettysburg? My God... I imagined you died during the war, but never at one of the most famous and bloodiest battles of all time." I was astonished. "Wait, but why is nobody else here? There were so many casualties... I've seen the panorama."

"As I lay there, dying under the oaks, George was also catching his last breath just a couple of feet away. Darkness invaded him when he was alive, I have told you before, and it stayed with him as he departed. I watched the demon float above him, sucking the soul out of him. He would have taken mine, too, for the hell ride. But Shawn and I escaped into the diary, and then the gate placed me as its keeper because I was the only one who knew the demon as closely as it knew itself."

"What do you mean the gate placed you? You sound like the gate is alive," I commented, not looking away from the waterfall, which now became even more noticeable.

"The gate breathes, and it thinks. It is a natural separator between the living and the dead. It keeps all the monsters you meet in the night at bay."

"It's pretty difficult for me to imagine a giant arc made of metal that can talk back."

"Oh, it's not made of metal. It is fringed with flowers from our side, and everything that's rotting from the other, like half-and-half," he said, and he laughed.

278

The gate terrified me. This metaphysical boundary became less and less clear the more we delved into the details.

"So, according to you, that demon is haunting me because he wants to take possession of my soul and get me on the gate's bad side?" I asked, the chilled mountain air hurting my airway.

He stared at me as if I had asked something ridiculous, but I knew I hadn't.

"Rebecca, you aren't evil. You are the complete opposite of that. The demon is after the diary; it needs to be in possession of it to gain control over the gate and be free. And the gate and I do not want that to happen. That is the reason why the diary has always been in the hands of a human."

"Shawn Grimwood, and eventually me." I nodded. It all started to make sense. "Why did it skip my father, then?"

"That is a mystery," was Derek's response, but even with the little I knew of him, I sensed he was hiding the truth from me. I decided not to go down that route.

My eyelids became heavy, and I realized that I hadn't slept all night. I took Derek's leather jacket and rolled it in a ball to put under my head. With the waterfall ringing in my ears, I closed my eyes.

"You say that you have a dark side, Derek, but I haven't seen it…" I mumbled. The sound of water was lulling me to sleep, and without hearing a response to my question, I drifted into a dream, abruptly but sweetly.

Derek whispered to the wind: "A soldier at war is no soldier in love. It's a sacrifice of life at the altar of the country we honored, an ever-lasting physical and mental massacre, for which we all had to pay too high of a price."

* * *

When I woke up, there was no moon or stars spread across the sky— just rain clattering against the pavement, and the sound of car tires ripping and racing into the storm. The headlights of a neighbor's car shone dimly onto the house across the street, and the sound of an impatient horn was lost inside of sudden thunderous rolls. Twisted in a ball, Charlie slept soundly at the end of the bed, his two front paws raised slightly above his body. The leather jacket hung crossways on the vanity, my only concrete reminder that last night wasn't a dream. *Derek must have brought me home*, I thought. I remembered the waterfall ringing in my ear and his subtle voice echoing inside of the rocky cave. The kiss. I would have been lying if I had told myself that fear didn't overcome my thoughts. It certainly did. I was afraid that he would vanish along with the world of ghosts. It was one of the scariest gifts I possessed— to see the dead— but that said, it was one of the most unbelievably wonderful experiences I'd ever had. And I had to keep it a secret.

I tucked myself under the feather-filled quilt and reached over to the nightstand for a glass of water, but a shadow projected itself onto the wall. It was a shape-shifting mass that stretched to the ceiling like a dark cloud of incense. In a matter of seconds, it took human form and headed in the direction of the bed. My heart skipped a beat. Charlie's back rose like an arc, and he began vigorously barking while I sat on the bed, horrified. The shadow laughed, and suddenly Derek was standing in front of me with some lilies of the valley in his hand.

"When I heard the bells of Saint Peter's church today, I thought of you and these flowers. They symbolize the bells in all their purity." He caressed the heads of the flowers. "I want you to always remember me when you hear the tinkling of the bells, Becca."

"I will if I don't die of a heart attack first! Do you have any idea what I've just been through? I thought you were a demon!" I said fiercely but accepted the flowers.

"Demons can't take shapes. Not as shadows. They are made of one matter; they are the lowest kind of creature. Though their Master is another story…" Derek admitted, his tone serious.

"Yeah, let me go get my guidebook on demons." I mimicked an attempt to get into the closet and pull out my trilogy series. "Next time, knocking would be nice. It's the polite thing to do, you know."

"And where would be the fun in that?" Derek teased. He carefully crawled onto the bed. "I must say, this is the comfiest bed I have ever been in."

"I don't believe you. There are plenty of down beds out there that are better," I said and pulled the covers even higher, so much so that Charlie fell onto the floor.

"During the Civil War, there were not many places you could put your head on. I saw officers sleep on pushed-together dining room chairs. There were also tents, but with all the cannon fire, there was hardly any sleep. You would be lucky to sleep through the night and not catch a bullet. So, yeah… Your bed is the comfiest." Derek said, continuing to toss and turn an oval brass pendant in his hand. His eyes brushed mine, and I, catching his gaze, sank deeper into the sheets.

He was right. Our generation couldn't even begin to imagine what they had gone through back then. Having a primary source lying next to you in bed was out of this world. Incredible.

"Can I see that?" More than anything, my curiosity was getting the best of me. Derek gently placed the relic into my hands. "Is that a pendant?"

"No, it's a very old watch. Looks like a pendant, sure. But if you unlock it, you will see different."

There was a frail, almost invisible piece on the metallic cover. My finger gave it a little pressure, and I heard a swift click. The watch transformed into two clocks from both sides. The bottom one resembled a fountain that appeared and disappeared, while the upper one had gold arrows and a tree of blooming flowers.

"It is not just a clock, is it?" I smiled, admiring the scent of fresh flowers. Our eyes met.

"One that counts life, right here." He pointed out the arrows. "And one that keeps track of death." As he touched the face of the clock, the fountain flowed with stronger power.

I glanced at Derek. "I understand why you would need one for life, but death? What good does that do for anyone?"

Derek shrugged. "In the world of the gate, death loses all its human qualities. Ghosts no longer fear death; they transform. In their mind, it's just a stage. They thrive in death. The clock simply keeps track of their age during the transformation."

"And then they take the train," I stated. "Just like Philip."

Thunder echoed somewhere in the distance, occasionally exhaling a prolonged electric beat that shook the windowsills.

Derek's diamond-like pupils were fixed on my lip gloss.

"And where do I find that train?"

"Well, that's the easy part. It's a ghost train. You get on at the Harpers Ferry train platform."

The epiphany came upon me like a vapor. "Wait, the ghosts that people see on the tracks at times…"

"Are all passengers on the train," Derek offered, finishing my sentence. "People might see them wander the tracks on some nights when activity spikes. That's why they report unexplained ghostly occurrences. They feel like they must have seen them, but they aren't sure."

I felt the air in the room getting heavier.

"But some ghosts do come back to the same locations," I noted, watching Derek stretch on the pillows. He placed his two arms under his neck to give it more support.

"Yes, they do, but that only happens when they forget the coins to pay for the ticket. The coins are tricky little things, and you have to grab them from your pocket before they disappear— either when you die or are in the process of dying. Phantom silver coins. A very symbolic way to show that life, just like those coins, runs out of time."

I lay my head on Derek's arm, bending my legs in the shape of a zigzag and nestling by his side as if I was listening to a fairy tale. "What does the train look like?"

Derek ran his fingers through his hair, pulling it upward in the form of a triangle, thinking. "More than anything, it resembles an early nineteenth-century steam train, if you have ever seen one. Remember that it is the fastest train out there. Being a train from another realm, it doesn't submit to time or speed constraints. Ghosts call it 'Hell on Wheels.' It's a velvet charcoal locomotive with a scarlet cowcatcher. The driving wheels burst into flame when the engine starts. The axles roll at the speed of lightning, leaving a dead wake of mist and silver spikes. The steam that comes out of the smokestack is nothing but the souls of the dead screaming in agony to fuel the locomotive. Mostly souls of murderers and rapists, or anyone else who committed an unforgivable sin during their lifetime. If you looked carefully, you would be able to make out their faces in the steam before it consumes them."

"'Hell on Wheels,' huh?" The mere existence of that train terrified me. "I would imagine a headless engineer driver in the cabin or an old merman with flowy white hair and a navy uniform."

"The train is a ghost matter, and therefore it has a mind of its own. There is no engineer for such a massive amount of energy. It's the law and the lawmaker," Derek explained and returned to browsing his book.

The rain ceased, and at once, Harpers Ferry's streets became alive with the scent of dampness. Derek was lying down on the bed, bouncing his feet up and down and turning page after page of the history book he pulled out of the closet. I was staring outside at the world, at people picking up branches of trees from the pavement after a windy storm, when suddenly I saw a hand coming through a wall. It was a long, rotten hand of something eerie. Its fingernails had mud caked underneath them, scratching the wooden floor. My legs became weak, and I tried not to make a single sound. I glanced at Derek. He had a finger pressed against his lips, signaling me to be silent.

His eyes commanded me to approach the bed, and so I did. As the creature pushed the wall apart and emerged fully into the bedroom, Derek and I peeked at it from under the bed box. We tried to hold our breath. The demon was about eight feet tall, with a fur stripe at the top of its head and veins so close to its paper-thin skin that I could vividly see its body's blood flow. It growled as he walked, but not louder than the ticking on the clock on the wall. Each movement was like that of a feline animal, and bones cracked at its spine. Its ears turned sideways and backward like locators. Behind its skeleton figure, there was a pair of black wings clipped at its shoulder blades. Before we knew it, the demon retreated to the closet door where I kept the diary.

This whole time, Derek hadn't moved; he had only whispered something in tongues on repeat. When he stopped, the bedroom froze. Like ballet figurines, we began our movements in slow motion. Derek was in the process of sliding out from under the mattress. I tried to contain my surprise, which was mixed with fear, and placed my two hands just under the edge of my nose. Old photographs on the walls trembled, and the clock's ticking became louder in my eardrums. Book pages rustled with the wind. A tornado of water, like a still block of cement, hung above us and the demon. It pulsated with power, which was intertwined with wires and electricity. Then it fell upon the demon, crushing it to the very ground. The whole room burst with light as if a stream had come down directly from Heaven, and all the darkness was gone. The water swiftly gathered from the floor, translucent now, and began rolling itself into a tornado. It soon took the shape of a head, torso, and limbs.

"It's about time, Carlyle," Derek said to the figure, shaking the dust off his jeans. Carlyle nodded, his form floating above the ground, and before I could say a word, he offered me his blue, fearless hand made of mist.

TWENTY-ONE

CARLYLE

Derek walked steadily around the perimeter of my tiny bedroom, taking a path from the window to the door and then back to the window as if it were mapped out for him. With his hands on his knees, Carlyle observed him meticulously from the loveseat, the water evaporating to steam above his head. Both he and Derek were lost in deep caves of thought.

"Master, we have let the butcher's filth come far too close to the relic. We have put the girl in danger of being fully discovered—not to mention that if the demons recover the diary, the gate is going to tremble. Beetlez is crawling beneath the earth as we speak. We would be fools to wait any longer." As Carlyle voiced his concerns, a mist of water came out of his mouth.

There was a brief silence in the room. Derek rolled his eyes, and Carlyle, catching a glimpse of him, continued: "His servants entered the realm of humans. You know what that means and how far they can take it. We have to make sure the second front is safe. It is our last chance. There might not be another."

"Don't be a pessimist, friend. We have found a way where there was none before. The gate remained closed for years until the arrival of the Gazer." Derek rubbed his five o'clock shadow and stared out the window into the street while the day turned into dusk. His skin glowed with freshness in the bright light of the room.

"Can one of you mythical creatures explain to me what is going on?" I said.

They both acted as if I wasn't in the room with them. "I'd rather leave you out of it," Derek quickly stated, his eyebrows, now raised, framing his beautiful sea-green eyes.

Derek's response made the blood in my veins boil in frustration. *I am in danger. I am threatened. I could die!* I deserved to know, but I bit my lip.

Carlyle, still watching Derek, decided to abandon the loveseat and head across the room to the closet, where I kept the diary. His body disintegrated into the air and then re-appeared again, water swirls bubbling inside him. As he shifted, the water droplets swiftly covered the carpet, leaving a noticeable trail. They almost looked like footprints, I thought. Then it struck me: I had seen them before! In the bathroom, when the water had burst onto the walls and no towel would stop it from spreading.

"Carlyle," I carefully addressed the water man. "If you leave a mess in my house, I expect you to clean it up, especially when you come uninvited and cause trouble." My cheeks flushed red. I wondered if I had made him angry; after all, he didn't have a face for me to use to even attempt to gauge his emotional state. He approached me slowly and floated like a statue over the carpet, ready to apologize.

"Rebecca, he was just following my commands." Derek came to his defense.

"I meant you no harm. That's a promise. The order was to keep you safe." Carlyle glanced at Derek, and after he received an approving nod, went back to searching the closet for the diary. Yet, for one reason or another, I felt like they were both keeping something from me.

"Derek, if I am going to die, I would like to know beforehand so that I can at least say my last goodbyes," I proclaimed. The image of my grandmother joyfully knitting a sweater appeared in my mind.

"Nobody is going to die. Not if I can help it."

"Then why are you both so secretive?" I asked. My hands ached from digging my nails into the fabric of the coverlet out of frustration.

"Because the less you know, the better. What do you expect me to reveal to you?" Derek still gazed into the streets. "With the demons crawling through the walls of your house, nobody in Harpers Ferry is safe anymore. If Beetlez takes possession of the diary and brings it to the butcher, we are all doomed. There will be no gate, no resting place, no peace for any person in your world or mine. We will dwell at the Gates of Hell, punishment upon us, and we will forever be in pain. Do you realize how pathetic and hopeless it sounds?" Derek released a deep sigh. "This is what is at stake. Generations of lives. This is bigger than any of us."

I didn't have anything to say to that. The thought alone brought in the darkness.

"What are we going to do?" I asked, my hands shaking. Seeing Derek bothered made me feel nervous. Something was out of balance.

Carlyle finally pulled the diary off the second shelf with a triumphant sigh, sending cards and blankets tumbling to the floor. He joyfully raised the book to his nose. "We fight. And we let the ghosts be on our side."

"That's right," Derek said with determination. "We are still one step ahead of the enemy. We can force them into checkmate. Think of it as if we are one move away from turning our pawn into a queen and owning the whole board."

The wind picked up, and the branches of trees were knocking on the roof of the house as if they were alive. "What is that we have that the butcher doesn't?"

"We have superiority. We have spirits. We have nature. When the gate was created, a magic pen came into existence with it; like an egg and a chicken, nobody can tell which was created first." Derek grabbed my beanie from the dressing table and slid it onto his head. "How do I look?" he asked, facing himself in the mirror.

"Ridiculous." I laughed, and so did the water man.

"What does the pen do?" My curiosity was getting the best of me yet again.

"It commands the gate," Carlyle answered instead of Derek. He rested his back on the pile of pillows at the headboard. "But the trick is that its commander has to be a shadow that belongs to both worlds."

"Not living nor dead. As if he is stuck in the purgatory between the two worlds," I added, now making sense of Carlyle's worlds. "So where can we find that shadow walker?"

"We don't find them. They find us," Derek cut me off. "A shadow walker is an entity of true sincerity and ultimate sacrifice, pure in heart, and has to willingly give up his life for good to rein over evil, thus closing the gate. It has to be a special kind of human, from a certain bloodline."

"And how many of those did you meet in your lifetime?" I asked, pulling the ribbon out of my hair. The knot had become heavy.

"Only one, and he made the gate."

I looked around the bedroom. I couldn't believe people like that existed in the world. "So we're doomed," I concluded.

"Not exactly. Carlyle will summon the army of ghosts. You and I will make sure the diary is at another location, unreachable to the butcher's filth, and then Carlyle and I will find and kill Beetlez and the other creatures the butcher has spying on us. He will be weakened, the gate will shut itself, and voila." Derek opened his arms almost triumphantly. "We will have won."

My heart lurched. "What if you're killed in the process?"

"Then I will have fulfilled my duty and met my supernatural fate. There is honor in death for people like me."

Derek met my eyes, and all I wanted was for him to take back his words. I practically begged him to. In the back of my mind, I searched for a solution but failed to find one. I felt desperation, like wind pushing me off a steep cliff.

"Master, the night is upon us. We must go fetch the spirits," Carlyle suddenly said.

"Go on, then. I will be right behind you," Derek said.

"Wait," I addressed Carlyle. "Let me give you something for good luck." I raced from the bed to the dressing table for a bag of crystals.

As I was digging through a pile of clothes, I thought I heard Derek whispering: "When I told you to watch the girl, I didn't expect you to be caught red-handed."

"Master, I couldn't help but have a little mischief. I needed to keep the boy away," Carlyle grimaced.

"And did you? Keep him away?" Derek asked, his voice raising an octave, revealing his interest.

"As long as I could," Carlyle said, looking away guiltily.

"They kissed," Derek concluded sourly, based on the silence and Carlyle's face.

"Master, he does not compare to you."

"I have been gone too long, Carlyle. The ghost business has taken its toll. I was a fool to think we could make it work." From where I was standing, I couldn't tell if it was anger or sadness that forced Derek to omit the word endings.

"Here," I came up behind them and, at once, silence fell upon them. "Keep the crystals safe. They trap good energy and keep the darkness at bay."

"Thank you." The water man stretched his hand out to mine as a sign of gratitude. His touch felt like the icy cold water of the ocean. Derek drew the curtain back, and Carlyle vanished out the open window, sending rain plummeting over the Harpers Ferry houses.

I was left with Derek, who stood just a couple of feet away from me. His sharp green eyes were piercing, mocking mine. I stared at the corners of his beautiful mouth and wondered what he was waiting for—what was inside of his mind. Then he started to move closer and stopped right before our bodies collided. I could feel his breath on my lips. I was afraid to move, to blink, to raise my eyelashes and look him in the eye one more time. He knew that— perhaps even before I knew it. He put his finger on the edge of my chin and brought my head forward, so close to his face that I could study the tiny pool of freckles on his nose. It was a precious moment, and it slipped away too fast. He pulled his hand away without attempting to kiss me. I spotted a difference in him. I reached towards his lips to lock them to mine, but he just stood there, not moving.

"If you don't want to kiss me, why stay at all?" I asked, frustrated.

"I wanted to see how far I could take this." Derek's voice was calm and steady. "Your affections aren't meant for one man, I presume? Or did I get it all wrong? Please, help me understand." His eyes were changing colors now.

"What is this all about?" I asked, putting a lock of my hair behind the ear.

I could feel his heart racing across my chest. We were standing so close. The light of the moon pierced his face, causing it to be darker.

"Derek," I said and attempted to stroke his rough beard, but he pulled away.

"Rebecca," he said and paused. "I might not have lived a long life on Earth, but I am pretty confident that a woman who loves a man stays faithful to him and doesn't go searching for happiness elsewhere."

"I wasn't searching for anything," I mumbled. "It just happened. He kissed me; I had no control over it, and you were gone. Gone, Derek, when you were supposed to be there for me."

"Don't make this about me. I have my duty to the gate. You know that better than anyone."

"Nick is my best friend. We quarreled, made up, broke up, got back together— every little thing between us happened years before I knew you existed. You might not understand him, but he loves me in his own way, and that kiss? It meant nothing. We are and always will be just friends."

"He didn't take it as nothing," Derek said, his tone serious.

"It doesn't matter what he took it as. What matters is what I feel towards him. I'm not going to apologize to you just to make you feel better. You can hate me all you want." I didn't notice how I had started swinging my arms, gesturing wildly with the palms of my hands.

Derek caught both of my hands and locked them inside of his. He brought them to his lips and released warm air in between our entangled fingers. My heart rate slowed down.

"Rebecca, I could never hate you. It upsets me that you two are so close. Any man would be upset. But I'm also here to remind you what it feels like to be in my arms. Forget about him for a moment."

"You're the one standing in front of me, reminding me about him. How can I forget?" I felt tears streaming down my cheeks.

"Forgive me," he said, flames of amber playing in his irises. "Would you still consider me to be your trustworthy companion who would lay his life down for your love?"

I wanted Derek; I knew I did. But the words— they wouldn't come out of my mouth.

He didn't act like he was surprised. Instead, he pressed his lips against mine. A sweet, electric wave ran from my mouth to my belly.

"Then tell me: what is it that you want, and *who* is it that you want, Rebecca?" he asked again.

"I want you." Relief. There, I'd said it. I did want him. "I want you," I said. It was easier this time, the words lying on the wind like frost on freshly emerged grass.

"I have to leave to help Carlyle, but I want you to remember that even though I am not with you, I am always going to be thinking about you, dreaming about you, and I will always come back for you. No matter where you are. It's not easy to love me, I know, but I promise you it will all be worth it in the end. In the end, when the butcher is gone, it will just be you and me," he said, and he kissed my forehead.

"Be careful, Derek," I said, but I realized I was talking to a man who had fought in the Civil War. A man who would never give up in a fight.

He left. There I was, in front of an open window, looking into the streets, just like Derek had. The only difference was that I was alone in the room, and tonight rain was my only companion.

* * *

I stormed into Nick's room, guilt eating away at my very soul.

"We need to talk," I proclaimed, lowering myself on the edge of the bed.

Nick was sitting on the bed, guitar resting on his lap. "Hell yeah, we do."

I walked into his room, but he didn't lift his head in my direction. I pulled my red scarf down from my neck. I could feel my cheeks flushing. My vocal cords trembled. Taking a deep breath and filling my lungs with air, I started:

"I love you so much, it hurts… You know that, but I can't be with you."

It was such a relief to say those words. As if the world had fallen to my feet and crumbled. Nick looked at me in the eyes this time. Sage green eyes; they reminded me of the sky right before the storm raided the sea.

He silently nodded his head. "Is it because of him? You think I don't know that you've been hiding him from me all this time? I'm not as stupid as you think." I noticed that he had all his pictures of Derek laid out on the table in front of him. He must have worked all night to develop them at the Historical Society.

"Nobody ever said you were stupid," I protested. "It's not about him, Nick, it's about me being truthful to myself—to my feelings towards you. I will always love you, just not like that."

"Spare me the guilt trip. You have no idea what truth is anymore. Just leave, Rebecca. Please, I beg you. You always find a way to make things worse, even when you don't try," Nick said, his voice estranged and cold.

"This is how you are going to treat me now? You act like we don't matter. You knew this was going to happen even before you brought it up in Gettysburg. Why can't you just grow up and handle this like an adult?"

The shadows on his face darkened. His lips carried his disappointment in me, and that was hurtful to see.

"I *am* an adult. You are the one who chases a love she can't obtain and lies to everyone. How are you going to be with a ghost?

Huh? Did you think of that?" He was clearly upset. "Love and danger. Seems like they always go together for you."

"You aren't being fair to me." I felt the air between us stiffen. My cheeks burned stronger.

"No, *you* aren't being fair. But go. Why are you still standing in the doorway? Go find him— your ghost from another world. Go run into the sunset together, for all I care. Leave me out of it," he said, squeezing the guitar in his hands a little tighter.

"You don't know him."

"I don't care who he is. You belong with me. He should be ashamed."

"I thought, as my friend, you would be happy for me," I said, and my hands meticulously began folding the red scarf on his bed. Nick's fingers were strumming the guitar strings. He acted as if I wasn't even there.

It felt like I was saying goodbye and like he wasn't hearing me, or like he was refusing to. I wasn't lying to him, though—not this time. I did love him, maybe even more than I did myself.

"Fine, I'll go," I said, holding back tears. "I'm sorry for hurting you. I never meant for any of this to happen. I wouldn't have come at all if I thought that my sincerity would drag you down with me. You mean the world to me. I ... I would give anything... Can't you..." I couldn't speak anymore. Tears were flowing down my cheeks, and I kept swallowing them with my words.

Nick stopped playing for a moment and stared at the distant landscape through the window. Even though I saw only his back, it felt like I was looking him straight in the eyes. The torment I had caused him was far beyond his capacity for forgiveness. I was sure that our hearts spoke in the silence of a dimly lit room. Together they ached from the sudden pain, sharing despairing beats. I longed to put my arms around him, feel the touch of his soft skin, but I had to let him go. Protect him from hurting even more because of the demons. I took a couple of steps closer to him, catching my tears with my scarf, and then I raced out of the door, not looking back. I was sure that he saw me in the reflection of his bedroom window: lost, sullen, and craving his touch. The scarf, lying in waves around my neck, fell to the floor, and I didn't bother picking it up. I left it with him, just like a piece of my soul.

Goodbye, Nick... I whispered to the wind, but in response, I only heard a violent hush. Then the flowerpots were knocked down from the windowsill.

TWENTY-TWO

THE PURPLE MOON

"It must be the night... You know, when the moon is full, and people's behavior is far worse than on any other day of the week," Derek spoke.

There was no need to hide behind John Brown's Fort anymore, I thought to myself. He had spotted me, as if he could sense me from afar. My heart was stalling, and my legs were trembling. My eyes were locked on his silhouette leaning over the railing. The Point was as still as the waters of the Potomac. I stepped out of the shadowy Harpers Ferry street. The night felt worn, and the wind fiercely tangled my hair.

"Did you know I would come?" I asked, breathlessly, while the light of the moon beautifully collapsed in shadows on his face.

"I am not a superhero, Rebecca— despite what you might think. That emotional world you carry doesn't come easily to me. Of course, I knew. You always come," Derek said, directing the waters the opposite way from each other at the confluence. Standing alone with him, looking the night in the eyes, my coat and shoes suddenly became two sizes bigger. I felt uncomfortable in my own skin.

"Then you know what I am about to say," I said and moved closer to the place where I had last seen the ghost lady.

Derek smiled genuinely. "Unfortunately, that, I wish I knew." After a moment of silence, he continued. "Go on. What else do you have to lose?" He did belong to the Civil War era; there was no doubt about it. He spoke gallantly and patiently.

"I have spoken to Nick, and I told him I can't be with him." Derek turned, his eyes shining with surprise. "But nor can I be with you. I need time, Derek, to think, to re-evaluate things, to understand what I want."

He suddenly became cold. "What does re-evaluate even mean? It's not that complicated."

"Oh yeah? What do you know about this, Mr. Soldier? Are you used to ladies falling at your feet?"

"At least I lived before. Sure, I had my own share of ladies. And none of them struggled to make a choice."

What a low blow, I thought. "You ask me to cut my best friend out of the equation. What kind of man are you?"

Now he was standing just a couple of feet away from me. "A man in love with a woman he doesn't want to share."

I felt as thin as the glass that was about to break under my feet. He was right. I was at fault for loving them both. At fault because I led them on and cared for no one but myself. It was hard to hear it, but I had to make things right. I just wasn't ready.

"Why don't I make it easier for you?" he said, climbing on top of the bridge. "It's convenient, you know, that men went to war. They almost always never returned, and there was a warm space in an empty bed and letters that got lost through carriers. The ladies, the ones who waited for soldiers to come home, displayed the true power of love. A grandiose gesture. Would you wait for me, Becca? Or would you wait for him? Because I sure as hell know that you're worth waiting for. And it just so happens that I have to fight the butcher. I'd rather go knowing that you are safe. That your world is safe. That I have done everything in my power to protect you."

"Derek..." I whispered, reaching out to his hands, but he pulled away.

"It's okay, Rebecca. It really is. You have one life to live, so don't you regret it."

"Please don't do this. I beg you. Derek, don't leave me!"

I lunged for him as he stood, poised to jump. The moment I ran forward, though, the shining vortex of light opened up and sucked him in, faster than I could reach him or call for him. My heart broke into a million pieces, and I felt pain where it had never hurt before, right by the ribcage, underneath all those layers of skin and muscles and bones— the place where my heart lay. At the Point, tonight, the moon was wicked, and the darkness swallowed me whole.

I returned to the house uneasily. Grandma opened the door when the bell rang and, catching a glimpse of me standing on the front steps in silence, immediately opened her arms to embrace me. I collapsed into her arms, tears warmly salting my lips.

"Come on..." she whispered.

I fell asleep in the living room, my head laying softly on her lap, the bright screen of Brazilian telenovelas on the TV fading behind me. She didn't ask what had brought this on, and I appreciated it, because the last thing I needed was to talk it over. I dreamed of Derek fighting the butcher; I also dreamed of him being killed. Every time I opened my eyes and realized the dream wasn't real, I took a deep breath. I knew he wouldn't come back no matter how long I called for him. I knew he was gone, but my heart didn't, and it hurt.

Nick wouldn't talk to me. The last time I called, the voice message box was full, and so I was unable to even hear him say: "Hello, this is Nick. You know what to do."

I had to get to the other side and destroy the butcher before he killed Derek. My pain needed to be directed somewhere, so it might as well be directed towards an unbeatable creature of the night.

Searching the Harpers Ferry library catalog wasn't an option. What exactly would I ask? How did one get on a magical train to the other side? What did you bring on a hunt for an ancient demon? There were plenty of answers in books— some astounding, some unbelievably disturbing, but none of them involved traveling through parallel worlds. *Although...* And the thought that popped in my head was the most obvious. The diary. That was the only book that came from the other side. But the real question was: how could I get it to talk to me?

The diary lay on the quilt in front of me, like an ordinary book from the Harpers Ferry library, except that it was illuminated by the pages within. I felt the cover with my fingers. The rustic leather protector was shedding into tiny pieces of parchment paper. I scooped up the dust and sent it careening to the floor. Then I picked up the diary and tried to shake it open, but it remained undisturbed. I pulled on the leather belt; it was locked in place and refused to shift. I tried whispering some childhood Russian tongue-twister, hoping that it would get the diary to open, but nothing happened, except that the pages started to glow brighter. I didn't have enough patience to deal with the book, so I threw it into the fireplace downstairs. At least that would end all the ghost adventures and vivid dreams I had been having. To my surprise, the diary didn't burn. It just smoked; nothing was charred.

I heard Grandma's voice coming from the kitchen. "Becca, what are you burning in there? It smells foul."

"Oh, nothing, just putting some more wood in the fire," I responded. God, if only she knew the position I had put myself into.

When the fire subsided, I reached my hand into the ashes and regained control of the diary, only to see a parchment piece of paper with black ink on it fall off the cover. I rolled the paper open like a map and saw one word: *Mr. Wolf.*

I guessed it was time to visit the old historian who lived at the end of town. There was only one problem with that, though—how would I keep my visit a secret from Nick? I was sure he would wonder what I was after. I didn't need him following me around.

I strolled up the stairs to get my coat, still rambling inside of my head when I saw a shadow crawling from the corner. It became wider and bigger, almost like a caricature. It flashed and disappeared into the bedroom. I was terrified, to say the least. I cracked the door open only to see a row of heads staring at me, as if Civil War townies were having a meeting in my bedroom. They were all waiting.

"Get out. Get out of here!" I heard a voice from the crowd.

I shut the door in desperation and pressed my face against the wood. An ungodly growling followed. I could barely hold on to the casing. Trying to burn the diary had been a bad idea, I told myself, hardly breathing. I had disturbed the ghosts and opened some kind of portal inside the house. I was not safe, and nobody who lived here was safe. I had to find Mr. Wolf, and I had to do it now. Otherwise, this town was going to be devoured by demons.

When the fog crawled onto the streets of Harpers Ferry, it was already dark, but I still saw the residue of it on the car lights traveling away from the town, passing under the mountain. The hood of my red anorak trembled on the wind, my galoshes sank into the wet leaves, and the water bubbled under my feet, streaming into drains as thunder rolled in waves above my head. My purple wool gloves shielded my skin from the cold.

Mr. Wolf's house had one single lightbulb coloring his kitchen cabinets. A bouquet of flowers adorned the middle of the lonely dining room table. The curtains were drawn, and I spotted his silhouette from the street, leaning over a writing desk. He was dipping his quill pen into the adjacent bottle of ink. The parchment paper spread to his legs and was lying under the desk in curls. He was transporting history into volumes and volumes of endless papers that would later be bound together into books. He rarely stopped; he believed there wasn't enough time to transcribe them all.

The majestic Harpers Ferry oak tree in front of the house had lost all its leaves and now stood there, silently. I rang the bell twice, but no one came to the door, so I knocked until the pain spread from my knuckles to my wrist. Mr. Wolf appeared on the doorstep; his glasses lowered on his nose— just like Grandma's— with a look of surprise on his face.

"Rebecca. Nice to see you. I wasn't expecting a guest in this unkind weather," he said, gesturing me in.

"It's an urgent matter, or else I wouldn't have bothered you so late," I responded.

His faux-fur slippers hurried into the kitchen. Pushing my galoshes into the corner and dropping the anorak onto the coat rack, I followed him inside. The living room smelled of cedarwood and bamboo. A candle from his desk threw shadows onto vintage recliners.

"For the love of God, please have a seat," Mr. Wolf said. He pushed his chair under the writing desk and picked up the quill pen after giving it a couple of swirls on the scribbling paper.

"Thank you." I perched on the charcoal-colored cushion on one of the loveseats. My hair was like a wet dog's, and it curled like the shape of icicles.

"So, what is the matter? Why would teenagers wander around at night searching for answers?" he asked.

"I have insomnia," I stated. "I came here because I want to know about the diary. And I would like to keep it between us. Can you promise me that?" Mr. Wolf's writing pace slowed; he was still sitting with his back turned to me.

"I can promise you that like I can promise you the appearance of the moon in the sky. Are you referring to your ancestor's diary?"

"You happen to know of it?" I felt instantaneous relief. I didn't have to sound crazy and try to explain how the damn book was haunting me.

"Of course. It has been in your family for a very long time."

"Then you know how to open it?" I asked eagerly. A tree branch hit the window with such force that my heart leaped.

"I don't think you want to open it. The evil you would release upon this world would be unbearable and destructive." His voice was serious. His white beard fell onto the desk, and at times it seemed to get tangled with the quill pen. Specks of ink covered it like dark snowflakes.

"Well, it's a little late for that." I giggled hysterically. A ball of nervousness was tearing me apart. "But there is a way to open it? If you happen to know, you have to tell me."

"It's all about the pen. It's how you talk to the other side. Is it in your possession?" The paper kept curling at Mr. Wolf's feet.

I didn't think it would come down to a simple utensil. "Not that I know of. I have no record of it, and it's not in my great-grandfather's boxes."

"Your ancestor was a Civil War General. Do you really think he would leave a pen that could possibly help destroy the world for everyone to find? He must have taken it with him."

"Where could he possibly have taken it?" I asked. Mr. Wolf didn't answer, and he didn't need to. The answer came to me quickly. "The cemetery. He put it with him into the casket." I paused. "Mr. Wolf..." I saw his head lean in the direction where I was sitting; he was listening. Thunder revved outside, and my voice got quieter. "Even if there is a pen, how do I get rid of the butcher?" I asked.

As soon as I mentioned Derek's enemy, Mr. Wolf stopped writing. He turned around and pierced me with his eyes, eyes full of darkness. Pupils white as the winter storm. In an inhuman voice, he whispered:

"Dead man walking."

"Excuse me?"

My right leg trembled and cramped. I stared at Mr. Wolf, shocked. There was a split second between a demon calling to me and an old historian writing his history volumes. Then he fell out of some whatever ritualistic coma he was in, and he mumbled, "It's best you get home before your grandmother starts looking for you."

"Yes, you are right. I better get going," I whispered in disbelief.

Harpers Ferry had changed drastically. Or was it me who had changed? Or perhaps it was the influence of the diary? Something dark lived in all of us in this town, and we had no perception, no recollection of it— not a single memory that we were possessed by that darkness at times. Whether it lived in our minds or was reflected in our actions, we were under its spell. Under attack.

* * *

With thunder rolling outside, Nicholas wandered to Mr. Wolf's house. Before knocking on the door, he spotted something in a puddle of water just underneath the historian's porch. When he picked up my purple glove out of the muddy water, he shook his head. He knew that it was only the beginning of the end.

TWENTY-THREE

WE NEED TO STOP MEETING LIKE THIS

They say that violets are the flowers of love. During the Civil War, Gettysburg was bursting with them— wildflowers that stained the very ground with blood. My great-grandmother, Mary, used to plant them on her husband's grave as a token of beauty and war. Of course, since then, the grounds had changed, and so had the cemetery. Instead of violets, there was just one deep patch of pale green moss resting upon my great-grandfather's stone. The letters inscribed on the stone were now sunken and hardly visible.

I lowered myself into the tree branches, put my back against the monument, and listened to the leaves whispering in the trees— to the squirrels throwing acorns to the ground and to the wind picking up in between the stones, raising dust and sand from the road. Was I really about to tarnish a Civil War general's resting place? I kicked my shovel with the edge of my galoshes until its handle rang against the ground. There was a pool of yellow leaves underneath me. I began gathering them with my hands when I suddenly noticed patinaed arrows. I swiftly removed all the leaves and found myself staring at an entire circle of arrows pointing directly to mausoleums across the street. *How odd*, I thought. *I've visited this cemetery multiple times before and yet have never spotted these arrows. It's like they've been freshly inserted into the ground.* I knew that they hadn't, though; I just hadn't been looking for them. I waded deeper into the cemetery, and each time I uncovered the ground from the branches, stones, and leaves, I saw the arrows. They were a map, a secret pathway, but to where?

Soon I realized that the arrows weren't all made of the same material. Someone had created two different pathways: patinaed and metallic. The whole thing looked like a labyrinth. I just had to follow the right road. I had spent too many long evenings with Grandma figuring out how to get the princess out of the castle.

The patinaed arrows led me to a mausoleum on the other side of the cemetery. A dark marble monument was covered with spiderwebs and moss. Light was playing through the mosaic glass in rays. I stepped closer to the door, and the chains rattled from my touch. Then they fell to the ground with the padlock ajar. It was too easy, I thought, but my curiosity kept leading the way.

Inside, dust floated in waves in the light, like frozen particles. Outside, the wind was picking up leaves, whistling in the corners of the mausoleum. The door remained open. There was a single coffin in the middle, the same marble plaque on top with an inscription: *Whoever Rests Here Shouldn't Be Disturbed.*

They always said that.

I had a lighter in my pocket, so I lit the candles and took a seat on a marble bench by the mosaic glass and a statue of a lady with a fountain that hadn't been working for centuries. Something was telling me to get into that coffin. I put my hands onto the marble and pushed, and the top of the coffin started to come off.

When I saw a face inside, sheltered by the velvet casing, I stepped away in shock, catching my breath. It was Derek's earthly body, perfectly preserved, with a pen shining in his hand. Recovering from my horror, I leaned forward to take a hold of it when I heard claws scratching the cement footsteps. I was standing with my back towards the mausoleum door when suddenly the light in front of me on the wall was replaced with darkness. I turned around and saw a giant vulture-like bird making its way through. Its neck was so long it didn't fit through the doorway. The eyes were scarlet with no life in them, and the head was covered with thin, rose-colored skin. Its beak reminded me of dinosaur bones I had seen in museums. The bird noticed me right away and began grunting and hissing in my face. My shaking hand reached over for the kaleidoscope.

I rotated the kaleidoscope, and the butterflies released with such force that I had to hold on to the coffin. They headed towards the bird. In a matter of seconds, I knew that the bird was hurt. A bloody puddle spread over the marble, but the creature that had appeared in the doorway of the mausoleum was still standing.

I had no more weapons. No defense.

I crawled into the coffin where Derek lay and searched frantically for anything sharp or anything that resembled a shield. Except for the body and the pen, there was nothing. I was desperately trying to push the top of the coffin back over Derek's body, sealing myself inside, when the bird began to shove its bloody beak at my feet. I cried out, and suddenly the bird backed off.

I wasn't the reason why. The fountain had suddenly released a gurgling sound and, like magic, blown the bird off its feet, sending it away from the mausoleum. The shape of a person formed out of the water.

"We need to stop meeting like this," Carlyle said.

He floated in front of me with his hands on his hips. What was he going to say? *Stay away from old coffins and magic pens? You don't belong to the world of ghosts?*

Carlyle walked in circles, water dripping all over the marble floor. The dead bird laid outside, its long black feathers caressed by the wind.

"Miss Rebecca, I don't appreciate your adventurous nature. You have put both of our lives in danger, and so with all due respect, miss, what is wrong with you? Master made it clear that you are not to worry about the world of shadows. You are to let him go."

"Do you even hear yourself, Carlyle? I am grateful you saved me from the demon-bird, but let's not pretend that I'm just going to sit around and let Derek die. That is just not going to happen. You expect me to sit at home with Grandma and be a Sentinel to the diary when the man I love is sacrificing himself for the good of the world? What's wrong with you? Isn't his life your concern too?" I voiced what had been a rock sitting on my chest for the last week. It felt good to finally say it.

The water inside of Carlyle's body began to swirl.

"Miss Rebecca, I would never jeopardize Master's life, and that is a promise. That is the whole point of my existence. But you must know, I have grown to fancy you, miss, and Master's word is stronger than Harpers Ferry's leaden rocks; he is in command. I will always look after you because what is a treasure to Master is a treasure to me," he said and took a seat on a marble bench close to the fountain, his head low.

He reminded me of one of those Greek sculptures in a museum: rock-solid, divinely influential, and amusing. The young god Adonis, with one significant difference— he was made of water.

"Why are you sullen, Carlyle?" I asked softly, sensing a change in his voice, taking a seat close to him on the bench. "I am responsible for the bird. My apologies. If I weren't here, you wouldn't be in this mess." My eyes fell into the white curtain of rain collapsing into the ground. "If love leads a woman, she will always think that the barriers in the world are nonexistent."

Carlyle lifted his head towards me, his arms melting like ice cream.

"It is not you, Miss Rebecca. Though, I wish you would have listened to Master." He sighed and then continued. "The army of ghosts that Master summoned failed to reach the desired numbers. Butcher's filth is overcrowding the other side of the gate. They overturned the Gardens of Doom with lava, burned the Rainbow Palace, and the ghosts... they are trembling with fear— hiding. They aren't ready to face the demons. Master is concerned. Without the Gazer, the battle will still take place, but it will be a lot harder to close the gate, if not impossible." Carlyle looked around the mausoleum. "What brought you to the tomb, miss? It's no place for a lady. These kinds of places are always crawling with filth."

With Carlyle's words so loud and so clear in my mind, I couldn't think of anything else. Impossible to close the gate... Why was there never a simpler solution? Why did the world need to crumble and fall, and why was it so hard for good to reign over evil? Maybe if it were easy, though, we wouldn't know the price of good and what it took to capture it.

"Miss?" Carlyle inquired one more time, forcing me out of my world of thoughts. "The tomb?"

"Oh, that... Shawn's gravesite led me here in search of a pen, but then this bird attacked me, and it's all kind of foggy in my memory now..."

Carlyle suddenly raced from the bench in the form of mist. "Have you seen the pen, Miss Rebecca?"

"Yes... I have it right here." I was surprised by his interest, and I slid my hand into the pocket of my ripped jeans. At once, I felt a burning sensation on my skin; my hands were pierced with lines of the red claw prints of the demon-bird, but the pocket was empty. "I'm sorry, Carlyle. It must have fallen out when I battled the demon. It must be in the coffin. Do you mind if I look? I need you to be my guard."

Carlyle nodded silently. "No worries, miss, I would not leave your side." I saw his silhouette by the fountain. He didn't lie— he was waiting. There was something on his mind, but I couldn't tell what.

With a slight tremor, perhaps dizziness from the fight, I poked my head into the coffin. The lid of the coffin was still peacefully lying on its side. If I moved one inch, it would fall and shatter on the marble floor. It was like breathing strong winter air, hurtful to the throat. It smelled of death inside, but nevertheless, my hand continued moving underneath the garments, around the folds of velvet, voyaging the corners, when I finally felt a metal edge piercing my skin.

"Ouch!" I jerked my hand away but forcefully removed the cause of my pain from the coffin. "Here it is!" I proclaimed to Carlyle.

His eyes squinted at the item I was holding, and it was only later that I understood why.

"Miss, is the pen really in your sight?" he asked.

"What does it look like to you, Carlyle? It's in my hand. Come on, look closer. Why are you standing so far away?" I asked and moved a couple of feet closer.

"No! Miss, stop! I believe you, though I cannot see it. If you approach me, you will be taking my life," he suddenly spoke from the darkness, and I saw the shape of water stretch on the wall by the fountain. It wasn't fear that overwhelmed him, but great concern.

"Carlyle, please tell me what's going on right now," I commanded.

"Press the invisible switch on the pen, miss, so that I can be in no danger."

I complied. "There. It's done."

Carlyle stepped out of the shadows with relief.

"Master never believed it to be true. Neither did I, until now. The pen is a powerful instrument. It commands the gate, and it belongs with the diary. Ghosts know about it as a myth, from stories that have been passed down through generations. It is not visible to the world of shadows. It brings torturous death to each and every man who tries to possess it, whether they know of its location or not. It has an aura— a translucent field that is a magnet. Unless you have a couple of feet in between you and the pen, it will suck you in and put an end to you. If you are able to see the pen, miss, it means that its ultimate desire was for you to find it. *You* are the long-awaited Gazer! You are the one hope that can save Master, along with the world of ghosts."

"I can't— I have no idea what I'm doing! I could just as easily destroy your world," I protested, cradling the pen in my arms.

"The pen doesn't fall into the hands of just anyone. You have to be of the bloodline. It means, miss, you have what it takes. Otherwise, the pen wouldn't have selected you." Carlyle drew circles of water on the marble floor into what resembled a family tree.

My eyes fell upon the shape of water, desperation lighting up in my eyes. "What do I do now?"

Carlyle shook his head in response. "Miss, the path of a Gazer is anything but easy. Your heart must be pure for the gate to accept you, and the gate makes no mistakes. Doubt in your heart will bring sorrow like you have never seen before. You will make sacrifices which, in turn, will lead to astounding rewards, but if you happen to fail, then hold on to your soul because they will try to take it away. Souls of the Gazers are a rarity— on the other side as well as here. In order to command the gate, you have to be as wise and as pure as the gate itself."

The reality of things was intimidating. "You mentioned that 'they' will take my soul away? Who do you mean, Carlyle?"

"Filth, miss— demonic filth. Or even the butcher himself. You are their prized possession. The minute they learn that you have the pen, it's over. That's why we must keep it a secret."

"But the pen will bring death to creatures who try to possess it... If I am to be in the aura of the pen, then am I safe?" I asked and felt a pinch under my ribcage. My heart was beating erratically.

"I wish it worked that way, miss. Unfortunately, the pen protects its own. It lets you in its aura because you are the Gazer, and you are able to utilize it against evil. It is in no way an instrument that will protect you from evil. You are still mortal."

The water inside of Carlyle changed colors: from sea-foam green to pearly white waves of eternity. Just like the ocean changing from sunrise to sundown. *Marvelous*, I thought.

It was a lot to take in, and I was afraid, to be honest. Not because I would doom my soul to Hell, no, but because of the pain my death would bring to my family and Nick. Being apart from Derek— not only in this life but also in the afterlife— was a choice I didn't want to be responsible for.

I placed my hand on top of Carlyle's and instantly felt the cold from the water. "We must not tell Derek."

Alarmed, he turned his head in my direction and looked me straight in the eye. "Master must know. It is your life, miss, that we are talking about."

"You know that he will try and stop me. I am the Gazer— you said so yourself. I have a duty now to fulfill, just like you do." I knew that referencing his devotion would make Carlyle agreeable.

"All right. But you must tell him when you arrive."

"When I arrive?" I was confused.

"To the other side. You must take the train, miss," Carlyle reminded me.

"Right. How does one take the train?" I asked, but I didn't need an answer. I already knew what I had to do.

TWENTY-FOUR

STORM

The road was wet and slippery, and the dusk slowly lowered its everlasting shadow onto the forest. I rolled the throttle until it clicked and felt the wind brush through my hair as the motorcycle gained speed and raced in the direction of the setting sun. My heart trembled inside my chest as if I had a million butterflies trapped inside me, waiting to be unleashed. My throat was dry, and I was gasping for air, but I was calm, steady, and concentrated inside. *Neither living nor dead*, I repeated to myself. I couldn't let Derek die, driven into the darkness and absorbed by the demon. The butcher didn't get to win this. Not after everything we had been through. And if I was the price to pay to save the two lives I cherished most— the town that I loved the most— then so be it. What was the life of one in exchange for the lives of many?

The spiciness of the air seemed familiar. The highway signs blinked in the distance, like the lights of the disco ball from an 80s homecoming. I glanced at the sky; the clouds gathered together, smoke hugging the trees in a shade of blue so dark that I couldn't spot a star. It was the time when dusk turned so swiftly to night that the change was unnoticeable. The motorcycle revved. The throttle trembled wildly. My hands— slippery from sweat or the drizzling rain— started to slide off the handles. I started to see scenery that made my heart thud hard. Electric waves of worry ran through my veins. *Wait, I've been here before...*

It was the road from the dream I'd seen multiple times— curvy, rocky, and snake-like, going under the mountain. The fear started to haunt me. A mountain, the dark forest, fog … The hills were silent, so gravely silent. The road morphed into a steep turn just below the mountain, and there was a deadly chill of autumn air that briefly compressed my lungs before the headlights of the ambulance glared in front of me. By that time, it was already too late. I felt a hard kick and flew off the motorcycle into the ditch, barely holding onto a broken branch, saving me from falling down the hill. The jacket I was wearing— Derek's jacket— was soaked in something very dark, and I quickly felt a pool of liquid saturating my back. There was a piece of glass cutting through my arm, probably from the ambulance windshield. The other driver was nowhere to be seen, and the sound of the sirens cut painfully through the air. Suddenly, it changed to the reverberation of a train whistle.

The ground trembled beneath me with the same ferocity of cars whizzing by on a highway. Invisible cars. Someone was having a conversation, so loud that the sound of his voice played inside of my mind like a broken record. At last, I was able to stand. The pain had drifted away, and a shiny metallic train appeared in front of me, hooting from the platform. I felt a jingle in my pocket, and then my hand revealed two silver coins, heavier than the usual artifacts, with two skeleton heads on the faces. I checked the leather jacket: the pen still rested over my heart, its feather tickling my collarbone.

The train was being prepared for departure and, stepping inside the wagon, I realized that Derek hadn't left out a single detail when he described the train. It resembled a train of death, eerie counters forming a face at the buffer-beam. Long fingernails scratched at the wheels, groping the tracks. Spiderwebs were used as curtains, flowing in the wind and forming a veil between two worlds: the living and the dead. Rows and rows of "ghostly" passengers lined the seats. Through the fog that wafted between the seats, I saw creatures, some with distorted faces and some with human features, that faded away and came back with a stronger presence. They were all looking out the windows at the Harpers Ferry bridge over the rivers. The backseat had already been occupied by a man with silver eyes, so I had to settle on a place close to a woman with red velvet hair and burns on her arms. She blinked twice at me, then floated above the seat in a yoga pose, her aura swirling pearl green and then crystal blue.

The wheels began rolling, but after a couple of turns, the train stopped. A mist of dark energy raced into the wagon, circling the man with silver eyes in the form of an ebony tornado. The next thing I knew, it captured the man and dragged him by his feet off the platform, leaving a trace of ashes on the ground. The red-haired woman mumbled in my ear:

"You can't trick the gate and still reserve a place on the train when you died a demon." A wave of laughter filled the air, but then her tone of voice became serious and low. "I died alone in my bed. Wanted to smoke a cigarette before the day ended, but I fell asleep and it set the whole house on fire. I know you're curious."

She patted my shoulder. I just nodded.

"How did you die?" she asked.

Great. What an icebreaker for a conversation.

"I hope I haven't yet," I said.

The redhead's eyes widened. "Oh honey, we all hoped that, but in the end, we landed on the train."

Of course, she was right. I had no way of knowing what was happening to my physical body. I just hoped there was enough time to close the gate and save Derek— enough time to stay alive.

We departed the station at midnight ghost time and headed into the forbidden territory of broken dreams. Natural landscapes descended into monster territory. The train passed a jungle of monkeys with human faces that were leaping up the branches, staring passengers in the face and chasing them if they showed any fear.

"They are big life admirers," the redhead said. "So narcissistic that they've been forced to pay attention to something other than themselves. If they ever learn, there will be a chance for them."

"That's what we do in the afterlife? Fix our life sins?" I asked, still curiously studying the monkey-people.

"That, and just enjoy the right way of living, when all the bad parts of us are gone. Like we were supposed to from the very beginning."

What is your name? I wondered.

The redhead offered me her miniature, manicured hand. She was older than Philip; she seemed to know more about the ghosts than he did. The gate must have put that knowledge into her head when she died. "Clara."

I did the same. "Becca."

"Oh, you are not here all the way, Miss Becca."

I glanced at my hand, and it was half translucent. My heart fell to my feet. When did I start turning into a ghost?

* * *

Nick followed me into the dense forest, his Mini Cooper's tires slashing the water puddles, taillights blinking red. He must have traced me to Mr. Wolf's house or seen me at the cemetery. But it didn't matter; what mattered that he was here.

Leaves sticking to his sneakers, glass breaking under his weight, he searched for me with a flashlight in his hand. Once he spotted me in the ditch, he carefully lifted my head to his lap, scooped my shoulders upward, and began lightly stroking my hair.

"Becca, don't you die on me! Wake up, please wake up!"

I remembered weakly reaching my hand towards his neck, my nails pulling on his necklace, breaking it at the clasp.

"Hold on to me, Beccs, you have to hold on."

Then, the smartphone screen shone into my face, and I saw 911 appear in bold black numbers. The ringing of a cellphone pierced the silence, but I didn't hear the voice on the other side of the line because, for me, the sky went blank.

* * *

Clara said that there would be crowding at the gate. She wasn't sure what was going on, but we were advised to stay inside. In a perfect world of ghosts, even I noticed a change. It was like the time before the storm begins. You know that thunder and rain are inevitable— it is what you expect.

"I think it's a day that I don't get to go to the other side," Clara whispered, tying her red hair into a knot.

As she finished her sentence, something bumped into the train and began knocking at the metal, shaking the whole wagon. Ghosts scattered in the middle of the row, and when I glanced at the window, I knew why. I breathed heavily onto the window, and it left a circle of condensation on the glass. I had to wipe it off with a sleeve of my sweatshirt. When I did, two scarlet eyes met mine, a red carpet of light streaming through the glass.

Don't move, I saw Clara mouthing. I listened. The creature scuffed its horns against the glass, which cut through the fabric of a gray cloak, and two bull legs began digging into the ground with a speed that sent rocks flying under its feet. I folded in my chair, sinking lower and lower into the cushions.

Someone had come up from behind me. I felt cold hands wrap around my shoulders from the back, as if an iced beverage was pressed against my skin. Then a face appeared in front of me— a familiar face.

"Becca, I cannot believe you right now! What are you doing here?" Derek, his face furious and terrified, pushed me onto the floor beneath the window.

The curtains touched our heads while the demon was floating above us from the other side of the train.

"I wanted to be with you. I couldn't let you go," I exclaimed, and he swiftly held his finger to my lips.

"Shh. You have to be quiet. It's the only way the demon will leave." Horror raced across his face as a realization rose at the back of his mind. "What did you do, Rebecca?" I felt his whisper, a warm trace of air, brush against my face.

"You told me once that the only way I could get to the other side was finding a balance between the living and the dead. So I did."

He pulled me tight into his arms and looked me straight into the eyes.

"You are a silly, little girl, Becca. Don't you understand? I can't bring you back! God, you had all this life ahead of you... your family..."

I untangled my hands from his and pushed him away. "You don't think I know that, Derek?"

"Then you better have a damn good reason why you're here," he demanded.

"You mean besides the fact that I'm in love with you?"

The look in his eyes suddenly changed.

"I also have something else." I unzipped the leather jacket, and the feather shone gold inside of the pocket. I had forgotten he couldn't see the pen.

"Derek, I know how to save us both. I have the pen," I whispered.

Derek's eyes widened, and then there was a wave of horror that ran across his face. "It's not possible."

"I'm the Gazer, and we are going to send the demons back to wherever the hell they came from!" I said, hope dancing in my eyes.

"I don't think you understand what that entails. You gave up your only chance of going back..."

"Why do you say that?" I asked, the pit inside my stomach widening.

"Because in order to use the pen, you have to have the diary, and the diary— being a physical part of your world— needed to be in your arms, before you…" His voice lowered. He placed his hands at the sides of his head. "Oh, God, Rebecca. What have you done?"

"It's okay, Derek…" I rubbed his hands, calming him down while panic rose in my chest. "We'll figure it out."

Suddenly my life flashed in front of my eyes. I momentarily lost consciousness and then returned. My legs began to fade.

"I don't have much time, Derek…"

He held his forehead close to mine, and we both closed our eyes. We had a connection no demon would want to mess with. Then his lips met mine, and the train wheels slowly progressed onto the tracks.

"We will see about that. Carlyle," Derek continued with a wave of determination, addressing the water man, "send some rain onto the filth. Tell them we are coming."

"Your wish is my command, Master," Carlyle said, and a mist of water came out of his mouth like a giant wave. It twisted in the air with the form of a snake and then burst from the wagon window, wiping out everything in its way.

* * *

We were standing in the middle of a round mosaic square, surrounded by ancient stone fountains with brass pipes. The gate glowed with neon lights behind us. The fog rolled in circles of white powder between the monuments, resting near our feet and making the ground seem detached from the sky. The golden, onion-shaped dome of a clock tower radiated through the heavy clouds. When the tower gonged midnight, shadows spread all over the mosaic square, and monsters began to rise from under the foam. They poked their heads out slowly from underneath the surface, hissing, growling, and howling to their dark Master. Their countless faces changed shapes, and among them, I recognized animal and bird forms of extraordinary complexity. The shadows mutated, and then the forest of demons turned into a pack of Bigfoots, taller than anything I had ever seen. It was petrifying to fight a darkness that didn't have a face.

I squeezed Derek's hands a little harder, and my eyes fell upon the shape of water. Carlyle wore his golden shield. The water inside of his body reminded me of the Florida beach where my father took me in the summers, glistening with yellow diamond specks. There were only three of us against the darkness: two princes and one fading ghost girl.

I heard a voice in the depths of my consciousness, though half of me had already diminished. *Just hold on a little longer, Rebecca... just hold on.* I knew I wouldn't survive to see the end of this battle. I wasn't sure any of us would without the ghosts.

I turned to glance at Derek. His face was remarkable: his forehead was directed at the crowds of demons; his lips, full and soft, were slightly open, and his eyes didn't twitch. They were as unmoving as the eyes of an eagle, focused on the enemy, except his were calm, like the surface of the sea before the upcoming storm. Behind them, I still saw the man I had fallen for, but I knew that the demons saw something different.

The gong echoed in the distance as if the mountain's peaks surrounded us. It reminded me of a chess game where white had their turn first. With my heart beating hard against my ribcage, I watched the demons make a move. Maroon bats the size of airplanes, with wings dripping in blood, raced towards the sky. They swirled into a hurricane of clouds and roared, setting fire to the ground with their mouths. I could hear their wings disturbing the air, sending waves of crushed wind to our feet. I barely held on; Derek had to put his arms around my waist, or else I would have turned into a balloon.

Then I heard a loud creaking, and all four fountains by our sides burst. The water streaming out of them formed a thick, pulsating wall, separating us from the demons. The fire swiftly subsided as Carlyle directed the water at the bats' mouths.

"Master," he whispered, "I'm ready when you are."

Derek nodded in response and raised his hands into the air. At once, the clouds parted. Thunder wailed above our heads, and lightning came down and struck the wall of water, electrifying it. As soon as the bloody bats reached the wall, they dropped dead like a deck of cards and laid motionless by the wall.

"Works every time," Derek noticed with triumph.

"How long will the wall hold?" I asked, fear crawling through my body.

"I'm afraid not long enough, miss," Carlyle responded.

I saw a pair of skeletons with gargoyle heads trying to break through the water to get to us, nails ripping apart its layers like it was cotton fabric. The wall stood strong and the demons attacking it died, but there were too many of them. In place of one dead came two alive, like they were multiplying. Soon the wall collapsed in heavy droplets, and the monsters gained access to the pathway to the gate.

I had already twisted the kaleidoscope handle. The metal butterflies thrust forward like a flowery perfume, forming a plume. If any creature of the night tried to come after me, the butterflies would let loose. Derek was chanting something in Latin beside me, and when his last words disappeared on the wind, I saw a mist heading our direction.

"Spero... the spirits racing to the sunset," I said underneath my breath.

They swirled the three of us into a tornado, diamond specks shattering the demons, blinding and disorienting them, and dragging them by their feet inside the tornado. They floated on the edge, heads wobbling out and necks broken.

I hardly saw anything through the mist because of its thickness, but in the distant landscape, I noticed something poking out from the fog in a couple of places.

"Derek." I hissed. "Look, there's something crawling in the fog."

Whatever it was, it vanished before Derek could look. Regardless, I kept looking into the fog searchingly when it raised a fraction, and a head appeared out of it.

"It's Beetlez!" I shouted, terrified.

As I spoke the demon's name, it rose from the four places I had spied him before. It turned out that all this time, he was lying in the fog, and when he stood up— his head taking the shapes of everyone I ever knew— he appeared to be ten feet tall. His teeth were like blades, and noticing Derek, he began to growl so hard that the ground trembled.

"Well, well, well, fancy meeting you here," Derek called to the demon.

"I will rip you and your little minion to shreds. The diary belongs with us, and so does the gate." Beetlez walked towards us.

"In your dreams, demon. Tell my brother to take back his filth. Oh, and have a nice ride back to Hell." Derek jumped out of the tornado.

Four-legged monsters were climbing the gate, crushing the skulls and rotten flesh that made up the other side with their paws.

"Derek, no!" I yelled, witnessing the impossible.

Concern was etched on Carlyle's face. We were both still floating in the tornado.

"Give up, gatekeeper! Your end is near! The domination has already begun," Beetlez hissed, and his laugh pierced the skies, more bats on their way.

Suddenly I saw a swift tangerine flash. Carlyle was knocked out of the Spero mist and fell, crashing heavily onto the ground. There was a shape of fire walking in his direction, melting the ground under its footsteps like wax, throwing fireballs at a breathless Carlyle. I commanded the butterflies, but they couldn't pierce the mist. I saw Derek turn to face the demon and make a quick glance at the place where Carlyle lay still. Now the three of us were separated, and all we could do was pray for a miracle.

I felt a tingling in my legs that changed to a painful cramp in my stomach, which was unusual. Since I arrived at the ghost train station, nothing had hurt, not even a slight headache. But now, I had an irregular heartbeat, and I was gasping for air. *Not now… Just a little bit more…* I managed to calm myself. *We are not finished yet.* And the feeling disappeared.

The Spero released me close to the gate, next to the Point, or the ghost resemblance of it. Carlyle was up and fighting. I saw a swirl of water drawn from the confluence, which fringed the sky like a rainbow. About one-hundred water men were walking out of the rivers, smashing demons left and right.

Derek and Beetlez were caught up in an uneven wave of power. The wide-open gate shone neon blue, and their fused silhouettes appeared right in front of the vortex. Demons cast shadows onto the square, and then Derek cast light and the sky changed its colors. It was as if I were standing underneath an oak tree in Harpers Ferry; the light glimmered through the branches, and the shadows played around me. This time, they played for death.

I had to do something. Anything. I took the pen from my pocket to see if there was an inscription on it to give me some sort of guidance. As soon as I did, the inevitable happened. Butcher's filth stopped fighting, their mouths open, and they all glared at me as if scandalized. Even Beetlez froze.

"Rebecca! What have you done?!" I heard Derek's voice calling my name, but I wasn't thinking, not anymore.

"Run!" Carlyle yelled from under the fire.

There was a split second where I didn't realize what was happening, but then I ran— and I ran hard. The demons from the entire square chased me. I stumbled and fell over a rock, and when I stood up, I saw the ghosts. Thousands and thousands of men were running towards me in Civil War uniforms— Confederate and

Union— all of them fighting for the same cause, their shining bayonets at hand. The rock I had tripped over turned out to be a cannon. Ghost cannons covered the square, separated by just a couple of yards. Men were pulling lanyards on command, gunpowder triggering the ball to erupt out of the machinery and fly four hundred yards. My ears popped. I saw smoke and heard the cannons roaring and demons wailing, slain by the gunfire. I remember Derek's face. Like he had walked out of that day from Gettysburg in 1863, he was clean-shaven— with a gray uniform and a beautiful smile— picking me off the mosaic tiles of the square. Fresh from the cover of a photo album.

"Rebecca! The 33rd and 5th Virginia regiments are here. We're saved! I need to get you out of here," he said, running his fingers through my hair.

I lifted my head slightly, about to embrace him, when that feeling I experienced inside of the Spero tornado returned. Instead of saying how much I loved him or how sorry I was to have taken the pen, I began coughing up blood. It spread like a red river on the mosaic tiles in front of my eyes.

"Der..." I tried to say when Beetlez's hand stretched out of the cannon smoke and grabbed Derek, dragging him away from me.

I think I lost consciousness and stopped breathing after that. My chest felt like it was on fire. I heard a woman's voice in the abyss of thoughts, saying, "Charge. Clear. Come back, Rebecca, come back."

I thought I heard Nick whispering something to me, his salty tears falling on my skin. Part of my soul was still flying through the forest on the ghost train, part of me was accepting house relics from my grandma when I had first arrived in Harpers Ferry, and the other parts were scattered all over Harpers Ferry's houses and alleys. There were lights around me in a dark room. They mingled and then formed a silhouette of a woman.

"Becca," I heard her voice. "Baby girl, you have to listen carefully."

"Mom?" I saw the light, but no face.

"You have to command the gate to close itself. Do you understand?"

"Yes, Mom. Where are you?" I asked, trying to find her in the darkness.

"Always with you. In your heart. Now go," she said, and she faded away.

I gained consciousness suddenly. Cannonballs were still flying over my head, exploding everyone and everything around them. My eyes caught Derek's shape. He had Beetlez trapped by the vortex, pushing his head towards the ground.

* * *

Nick was sitting at the hospital bed with the diary open in front of him. He held my hand in his, the beeping of the monitor ricocheting against the walls of the room.

"Damn book!" he exclaimed, wiping his tears with the sleeve of his shirt. "Give me an answer! I need her— you have no right to claim her!"

Suddenly the diary glowed with golden letters, and he knew what to do. He picked up the diary and placed it in my hands.

* * *

My weakness was love for them both, but my strength was my determination. I pulled the pen from my ripped pocket. The ghost diary laid on my chest, and I swiftly turned the pages, pressing my elbow against the paper so it wouldn't close, and started scribbling with golden ink: *I command you to close.*

The gate trembled, and suddenly the demons were dragged into the death carousel, passing through the vortex, their paws sticking out, holding on. Carlyle watched the chaos with his water friends from the Point while Derek, clutching Beetlez, was about to send him to Hell as he had promised. But my awakening disturbed him. The quick glance he sent me made him lose control of the demon. In seconds, Beetlez metamorphosed into Derek, and they battled. I couldn't distinguish who was who. The vortex sucked one of them in, leaving the other standing at the other side of the gate.

Then I lost consciousness, and the darkness consumed us both.

"Derek!" My voice shattered against the dark walls of the endless hospital hallways like glass beads on a marble floor. My heart was pumping blood, maybe a little too quickly. It was the fog... It got to my head.

Images shifted. Curtains closed as if I was watching a play, and they rolled into the dollhouse. It wasn't the dolls I was afraid of, but rather the demons crawling around through the walls. My eyes went wide, and the lights swiftly dimmed. Suddenly I was standing at the edge of a lake, mountains gliding in a carousel above me. It was like I had hit my head, like reality was a distorted watery illusion.

"Derek!" I cried out stronger, my voice receding like an echo, but it seemed that I was the only one listening. My chest was in flames. I breathed through a thousand garments. There was a train of lights streaming through a window onto the hospital bed— like lava from Heaven.

But what I couldn't see was Nick, standing behind the automatic hospital doors, blood soaked into the sleeves of his forever-tarnished shirt. His arms were hanging down, and he could hardly contain the desperation settled in his eyes. Tears fogged his line of vision, and he fell to the floor and sobbed.

While I lay there, surrounded by doctors and nurses— dying— they started CPR. Towels like scarlet-tinted cotton balls slid across the floor as medics kicked them away with their feet.

And I didn't feel anything; I didn't feel anything at all.

The End... for now.

Acknowledgments

This book would not be possible without GenZ Publishing and its wonderful team of editors, who spent countless hours transforming *Casting Shadows* into the novel it is today. I'd like to thank them for believing in Derek Cromwell and Rebecca Grimwood from the very first page and carrying their story into publication.

I'm grateful for my parents who inspired my love for books by reading out loud the *Wizard of Oz* and *Gone with the Wind*, by tirelessly searching the bookstores for a copy of *The Brothers Karamazov* when I expressed desire to read it. Thanks to my mother-in-law, Anne, her husband Ted, her sister Christie, and my aunt Violetta, who read the early copy of my manuscript and encouraged me to write even when I felt like giving up. To my brother and my uncle Ruslan—for dreaming, because without those dreams I wouldn't be where I am today. To Yurij Muraviev, Mikhail Chukhlantsau and Lida Daubert—I hope you are proud of me. To Jessica and Gregory Derr, for being my beta-readers. To Eriselda—for love, for criticism, for your true friendship. To my first editor, Brett Kinsey, whose dedication to the written word is simply astounding. To Cleveland Writers Group—for support and creativity. To Galina Muravieva—for being my brightest star in the dark.

And above all else: to Rich, without whom there would be no Harpers Ferry, and there will never be shadows because he is my sun.

About the Author

Dziyana Taylor is an Eastern European author who lives in Ohio with her husband and two felines, one of whom is named after a Civil War general. When she is not writing, you can find her travelling to Civil War battlefields and browsing Historical Society catalogs in search for new relics, artifacts and stories that serve as inspiration for her young adult novels. Connect with her via social media @grimwoodworld to learn more about *Casting Shadows* trilogy.